FOREST CREATURE

BOOK ONE
OF THE ANGEL OF DEATH TRILOGY

JACQUES VOORHEES

Obelisk Publishing
Denver, Colorado
www.obeliskpublishing.com

This book is a work of fiction. Any resemblances to actual persons, living or dead, events, or locales are purely coincidental.

Copyright © 2023 by Jacques Voorhees

ISBN: 978-1-7344041-2-8 Paperback
ISBN: 978-1-7344041-3-5 eBook

Cover art by
www.damonza.com

All rights reserved. All material in this book is the property of Jacques Voorhees, protected by copyright and other intellectual property laws. Reproduction, resale, and plagiarism, in whole or in part, without the prior written consent of the copyright holder is a violation of the copyright law.

PROLOGUE

Petrograd (St. Petersburg), Russia. March 8, 1917

HEARING THE SCREAMS and the guns firing, Helene knew they'd waited too long. The only way to save Princess Anastasia was to kidnap and smuggle her out of the palace. No matter which side won, the servant girl knew that if caught she—herself—would be executed.

Imported from France at eighteen, Helene was one of the Europeans brought in to help westernize the court. An indiscretion left her pregnant, but when the child died in labor it was only natural the palace staff made use of milk-filled breasts. Soon the newly born daughter of the tsar was feeding from them eagerly.

Years later, Ana was still in her care and Helene's love for the child could not be measured. But it was about to be tested. The young woman knew the rumors. The Leninists were planning a revolution and the Romanoff family was likely marked for death. Nicholas knew too, which was why the imperial court was moving outside Petrograd to one of the provincial estates where an army regiment could protect them.

But—tragically—the attack was tonight, and there would be no escape for the royal family. So Helene made the bravest decision of her life. She knew the palace as well as anyone, including where valuables were kept, often not well guarded. Five pounds of gold coins were in her pocket, plus a bag of gemstones—mostly diamonds. The coins were heavy but the jewels, far more valuable, weighed nothing.

Central Europe was at war but Finland was not. Dressed as commoners, they could reach Finlandski Railway Station—a gateway to freedom—and soon be outside Russia. When peace came, they could make their way to Paris where Helene had relatives. The plan was madness, but there was no other.

"Honey, wake up, it's me," she called softly in the darkness, touching the girl gently and trying to keep the fear hidden from her voice. Anastasia's eyes opened as she reached instinctively for the large ruby pendant around her neck—a gift from her father.

"What is it?" asked the sleepy child in French, the language she always spoke with Helene.

"We're going on an adventure. It's a game. But where we're going is a secret."

"I love secrets!" cried the princess, quickly falling asleep again in the servant girl's arms.

1

Montreux, Switzerland — Approximately 100 years later

The Japanese bokken sword slashed the air, moving into position at just the right angle to intercept the opposing weapon. The blades hit with such force it knocked one of them to the ground. Utilizing the momentum, the fighter executed a rapid spin for a follow-up strike, halting the curved surface just inches from the adversary's neck.

"Point!" called the instructor of the Shinkendo Japanese sword fighting class. "Three-zero makes it a win. We're running late so let's quit here. See you all next week."

The two combatants bowed ritually and began removing protective clothing. As the winner pulled off the heavy mask with its metal-grill face shield, long platinum-blonde hair cascaded out. Brushing it aside, Sophie Martine smiled up at her sparring partner, while her indigo-blue eyes glistened from a face with high cheekbones and delicate features. Her forehead was damp, and she wiped a sleeve across it carelessly.

"I don't know about you," she confessed, humbly, "but I'm *exhausted*. Someone may need to carry me to the train station."

"I can't believe you knocked my sword loose," exclaimed her male opponent, returning the smile. "How'd you do that?"

"Your hands were too close together on the hilt," she explained helpfully. "I knew you'd not have good leverage against a strong block."

"Ah, that makes sense," he agreed. "I'll have to watch that next time."

Back in street clothes, with no one to carry her to the station, Sophie walked slowly. It was the rare occasion when all three of her activities—ballet, Tae Kwon Do, and Shinkendo sword fighting—fell on the same day. It was already dark, and she'd probably not be able to move tomorrow from sore muscles. But for now, the goal was catching the final commuter train up to Les Avants.

She passed an alley and glimpsed an altercation going on. Curious, she walked closer but stayed hidden. She could hear voices.

"Hey, Camil, not so fast. Today's allowance day, right? So we came to take our share. You didn't forget about us, did you?"

Stealing a glance around the corner, Sophie recognized Camil from school, a boy one year behind her. Gangs were not common in this part of Switzerland. It seemed likely they were out-of-town ruffians preying on someone weaker. She liked Camil but felt sorry for him. Like her, he did not fit in well. Shy, introvertish, and a bookworm, he stayed mostly to himself—and attracted bullies. What was this about allowance money?

"Please," he said, his voice cracking. "It's for my school lunches. It's all I have!"

"School lunches?" said one of the mean kids. "Camil, you look like maybe you're gaining a few pounds. Best save the calories." There was laughter from the others. "We'll put the money to better use. Now hand it over. Otherwise, you know what happened last week."

"What happened last week?" asked Sophie, walking into plain view. "I remember Camil's face was battered up, and he said he'd fallen on some stairs. Did he fall on some stairs?"

"The fuck are you?" said one of them.

"Whoever you are, run home to mama," said another. "We're doing some private business here."

Since age five, Sophie's Tae Kwon Do instructor had impressed upon the class how martial arts should only be used defensively. Initiating violence was the one thing they must never do. On the other hand, Sun Tzu and *The Art of War*—the book she was reading for Foreign Lit—had stressed the importance of surprise. "If you're strong, appear weak."

"Hey, guys, let's not have any trouble. I have a train to catch, and Camil needs to get home as well. Hey, Camil, can you walk me to the station?"

The young boy tried to move toward her, but an outstretched leg tripped him, and he stumbled to the ground. At the same moment, a fist was launched at Sophie's abdomen. She parried it easily, moved instantly to fighting stance, and sent a powerful sidekick into her adversary's diaphragm. He collapsed, fighting for breath.

The other two rushed her. It was just like sparring practice, she thought, except they had no idea what they were doing. Her left hand blocked an arm as her right went automatically into a tight fist, wrist straight, arm back against her side. Then she unleashed the weapon directly at her attacker's nose. Not only was his forward motion stopped, but he fell to the ground, his face a mask of blood. Easily ducking another punch, she responded with a front kick to her third adversary's groin. He fell to the ground, cursing.

"Camil, let's get out of here," she cried.

The boy hesitated. "Now they're really going to kill me," he said, reluctant even to stand up.

Sophie realized that was possible. She'd humiliated them, and they'd take it out on Camil later.

She walked over to the closest one, still trying to catch his breath from a spasming diaphragm.

"Just to be clear," she said loudly. "If you ever bother Camil again, I will find you, and I will finish the job."

The one with the bruised testicles could at least talk. "*Finish* the job? The fuck you mean, *finish* the job? We're going to finish you and him together, *bitch!*"

Sophie didn't want to prolong their lesson with more violence. But perhaps she could scare them with threats. She thought about her Shinkendo fighting techniques and her kata practice with tanto daggers.

"What do I mean by finish the job? I mean in your case I'll slash your throat open with a single swipe of my knife. In his case…" She gestured to the one with a smashed nose. "I'll cut out his intestines with the same weapon. Then I'll take the dagger and pierce that other guy's eye, all the way to his brain. He'll die first. You other two will bleed out in ten minutes or less. That's what I mean by finish the job."

Sophie was shocked by her words. She'd never spoken this way to anyone. But there was something about the unfairness of the situation that had provoked and made her want to utterly terrify these adversaries. *"Appear strong, if you're actually weak,"* Sun Tzu had advised. But Sophie was not weak. She knew she could carry out her threats. She could kill them all so easily, even without a weapon.

She noticed her opponents were equally shocked, so she doubled down. "And you won't be able to get away, because I know where you're from."

"You're lying, bitch lady. Where do you think we're from?"

"Not one single place. If I told you the one I know about, you'd just avoid that spot."

She saw them try to reason this out, a look of confusion on their faces.

But their leader was street-smart enough to realize they were outmatched.

"OK, Christ, message received," he said finally. "We're outta here. C'mon, guys, let's get back to Geneva. Fuck this end of the lake."

Sophie took Camil's hand and pulled him to his feet. They walked towards the station.

"Are you OK?" she asked once they were alone.

"Yes, thank you. You're—Sophie, from school?"

"Yes, Sophie Martine."

"I, well, thank you. I don't know what to…" he paused as if there were too many emotions to communicate.

She smiled and touched him reassuringly on the arm. "It's OK. They were trying to rob you?"

"Yes. Same thing last week. When I wouldn't give them money, they beat me up."

"You said it was a fall down some stairs."

"They told me it would be worse if I blamed them."

Sophie thought he might cry. "I understand. You had no choice. You probably did the right thing."

"But how did you…? I mean…"

"I study Tae Kwon Do," she explained. "It's one of the martial arts."

"But I don't get it. Why did you help me? You don't even know me."

"They were stealing your money. How could I not help?"

"Most wouldn't. Last week no one did. But thank you."

They arrived at the station. "Hey, good night, Camil. Thanks for walking me here. See you at school, OK?"

"Sure," he said, smiling slightly.

Finally on the train, Sophie took a seat as it began moving and thought about the street fight. How would she explain it to her *sensei*? They were never supposed to use these skills outside of the dojo. She never had until tonight. And the rule was, if they did use their skills they had to confess at the next practice and explain what happened. The *sensei* would then deliver a stern lecture on how to avoid violence next time. She'd had to sit through several already when other students had "used their skills."

But it wasn't fair what they were doing to Camil. And she couldn't just ignore it and walk away. Why have these abilities if she couldn't use them? That's how she'd frame her defense to the instructor. But he'd find the argument unconvincing.

She'd not tell him about the threats. Not only would he be appalled, he'd insist on knowing if she meant them. She was reluctant to admit the truth. There was something terrifying inside her and it had only taken a case of injustice to let it out. The threats had not been a bluff. Far worse, she *wanted* to carry them out.

Needing something else to think about, she tried to concentrate on Swan Lake choreography but didn't have the mental energy. Instead, she pulled out *The Art of War* and read another chapter during the fifteen-minute trip up the mountain.

2

A DEAFENING SCREECH signaled the final curve, and sparks flashed as the electric train came to a stop at Les Avants, a geranium-covered village in French Switzerland. Stepping down to the platform, Sophie almost fell as her muscles tightened up. This was ridiculous. Why did she have to work so hard? Her classmates never did. She'd largely forgotten about the street fight and was now angry. The young girl was going to tell her parents, again, how much she hated what they were doing to her. And if Uncle Stefan was at the house, he'd be included in the fury.

Sophie tried to walk in a determined fashion toward the parking lot but slowed immediately. Her legs couldn't take it. God, she hated this life.

A Citroen DS5 pulled up. It was an expensive yet not ostentatious car. Her parents didn't like to stand out.

A window lowered. "Sophie, honey, get in! You must be exhausted. You had all three tonight!"

Her mother spoke Parisian French, without the Swiss accent, and made sure her daughter did as well. Yet when Sophie was alone with her father, the two spoke Russian. It was a weird family; not dysfunctional, just anything but normal. She hungered for normalcy.

"I hate what you're doing to me; I can't stand it!" Sophie declared, sliding effortlessly into Parisian French even though she spoke with the Swiss accent in school. She didn't like to stand out either.

"Oh honey, you say that every night."

"This time I mean it."

"You say that every night, too."

"I'm going to run away. Somewhere you'll never find me." This promise was delivered in the Swiss accent which infuriated her mother, who glanced at her in exasperation while backing out of the parking spot.

"Sophie, stop. You say *that* every night as well and it's become tedious. And please speak properly. I know it's awful when all three lessons fall on the same night, but we don't control that. At least you can sleep in tomorrow. It's the weekend."

The young girl threw her hands in the air. "Ah, the weekend, when my English tutor arrives, Dad schools me in geopolitics, and Stefan teaches me the wonders of free-market economics."

Her mom shifted into forward gear and accelerated rapidly onto the main road. "You said you find all that fascinating."

Sophie paused contemplatively. "OK, maybe. But do you realize I know more about what the rebels are trying to do in the Philippines than about choosing a dress for the Spring Dance which is in two weeks? And I know more about Bastiat's theories of economics than I know about how to meet boys, or go on a first date."

"Sophie!"

"And I read Shakespeare's *Romeo And Juliette* in English, but I can't relate because it involves, like, people falling in love and what would I know about that?"

"You're only sixteen," countered her mom. "You don't need to be falling in love."

Unabashed, Sophie continued her tirade. "And Corrine, that really nice girl at school I told you about, asked if I'd like to go hiking with them next weekend and I had to say no because I'll be at the Tae Kwon

Do tournament. I'll spend my seventeenth birthday in front of judges instead of having fun with my friends. Not like I have any."

"Oh, honey, I feel bad about that, I really do."

"I just want a normal life, Mom. I want to be like the other kids."

"But you're not like the other kids. You're very special, and your father and I want to make sure you're everything you can be."

"You've said that before, that I'm special. I don't get it. Why am I special? And what if I don't *want* to be special?"

"Some things can't be changed. But you're right. You should have friends and be able to do things with them. I'll make that a priority and find a way to schedule something."

"Mom, you don't *schedule* friends. You either have them or you don't."

"C'mon, Sophie. I'm trying to be supportive."

The young girl's stomach grumbled from hunger. It was almost nine p.m.

"What's for dinner?" She spoke proper French again, as a sign of surrender. Who had time for rebellion when they're starving?

Her mom raised her eyebrows. "Oh, now it's about dinner?"

"It's OK, I understand. You just want what's best for me, and in your twisted, foolish beliefs you think ballet, Tae Kwon Do, and Shinkendo sword fighting are what's best for me. Fine. Being a normal teenage girl—not so much, huh?"

"I don't approve of the sword fighting. That was Stefan's idea."

"Well, the sword fighting's the one thing I enjoy. I get to act out my fantasies of what I'd like to do to the ballet instructor."

"What a horribly awful thing to say!" exclaimed her mom, laughing. "OK, maybe that was funny. Please don't repeat it, though..."

Sophie looked out the window as the car climbed the narrow switchbacks up the side of the mountain. Across the valley she could see the *Dent du Jaman*, a spire of rock catching the light reflecting off Lake Geneva. Below that pinnacle was the village of Caux, hanging on a mountain hillside, now with its own lights twinkling. The funicular cable car was still operating, ferrying tourists and well-heeled locals up to the lodge at Sonloup, with its expensive restaurant and magnificent views over the lake and the French Alps beyond. It's beautiful, she thought. Why am I so unhappy living in this fairy-tale corner of the world?

"You know, they're really all the same thing," observed the young girl reflectively. "The ballet, Shinkendo, and Tae Kwon Do."

"The same thing?" protested her mom. "I can't imagine anything more opposite than sword fighting and ballet."

"They're almost identical. Don't you realize that?"

"I certainly do not! Sophie, this martial arts stuff was entirely your father's and uncle's idea. I want you to become a world-class ballerina. You're incredibly gifted. I'm worried they want to turn you into Rambo or something."

"Mom, it's the same muscles, the same balance, the same control over your body. A roundhouse back-kick, a pirouette, or a circular counter-parry with a sword—they're not that different."

"But Sophie, you were meant to be a dancer. The martial arts stuff takes time away from ballet practice. Nic worries for your safety, but you're already a third-degree black belt, for heaven's sakes. Obviously you can defend yourself—even without a sword."

"But what if I ever need to lead troops in combat, you know, like Joan of Arc? I've been reading about her on Wikipedia."

"What *war* are you planning to go off to? Is that why you're carrying that book?" Her mom glanced at it disapprovingly. "And another thing, Sophie, I'm not happy with all those violent games you're starting to play online, like 'Call of—something.'"

"Call of Duty."

"Right. I look over your shoulder and you're selecting weapons like RPGs, and shooting surface-to-air missiles at fighter jets, and stuff's blowing up. That can't be healthy."

"It helps me relax."

Her mother looked at her with a concerned expression. "And

what about that book? It's like you're planning a military campaign or something."

"No, *Art of War's* a classic I'm reading for Foreign Lit class. But what super-important ballet tournament am I planning to go off to?"

"You don't know?"

"Know what?"

"Madame Rollo said she has signed you up for *Dansa Milano* in April."

"What!"

"I thought she'd told you."

"All Madame Rollo tells me is that with my utter lack of dedication I should be training as a court jester."

"Madame Rollo is very strict."

"Dansa Milano? Did she really say that?"

"Yes. She told me last week. You have the Swiss competition coming up, but that's provincial. Milan is the world-class tournament. She says you're ready."

"Oh," said Sophie, too stunned to have a clever retort.

3

IN THE MARTINE household, Sunday dinners were to solve the world's problems. Her mom served cheese fondue with salad. Uncle Stefan, a businessman from Geneva who often visited on weekends, was already seated. Sophie was late to the table, needing extra time to finish homework.

"Well, Nic," said her mom, sitting down, "I know you've been looking forward to this for hours. What thorny international problem are you going to torture our poor daughter with tonight?"

Her dad glanced up sheepishly, but her mom's smile made clear she was kidding.

"Well, since you brought it up, Juli, the Columbian FARC rebels are making a comeback," he noted, opening the conversation as was tradition. "They're targeting local law enforcement and even national politicians."

"Are they?" asked Sophie, not sure she cared. At the other end of the table, her mom rolled her eyes.

"Yep. The Chief of Police in Medellin was massacred with all of his family on Tuesday, and every hardliner in the local and national government is now getting threats."

Sophie used tongs to dish salad onto her plate, pretending to be absorbed in the task.

"Well, what would you do if you were the Colombian president?" asked her dad.

It was a game they'd played since childhood. It not only kept her up to date on current events but gave her a chance to think strategically about making such decisions. She'd once asked her classmates if similar discussions were held around their dinner tables, and they'd looked at her as if she were crazy. That was when Sophie began to realize her family was a little—different.

Even so, she enjoyed it, once her mind engaged.

"What would I do? Well, what are the choices?" she asked, knowing her role.

"Three choices," explained Uncle Stefan, who sat opposite her. "Declare war and go all out to eradicate the drug lords. A lot of folks will die, including some of the politicians and their families. But the war could eventually be won. Or capitulate to them and let the drug lords conduct their trafficking with a wink and a nod from the government. Or status quo. Take half measures, a raid now and then just to show you're doing something but maintain a kind of uneasy détente. Which do you choose, Sophie?"

She thought of Sun Tzu and *The Art of War*, which she'd finished just before dinner. It was always about surprise—doing the one thing no one expected.

"Does everyone recognize those are the three choices?" she asked.

"Yes, it's pretty simple, not exactly three-dimensional chess," noted her dad. "The options are limited. Different regimes have tried various combinations of all of them."

"As long as the profits are there, I don't see how you can ever stamp out the drug trade," she noted contemplatively.

"You could certainly disrupt it."

"That would merely reduce supplies, meaning the price would

increase, meaning—ultimately—the profits would increase. Right, Stefan? Supply and demand—all that?"

She smiled at her uncle, knowing he saw everything through the lens of economics. In addition to running a chemical manufacturing business he taught the *dismal science* part-time at University of Geneva.

"Precisely," he agreed.

"I'd attack the profits themselves. Everything else is a symptom. The profits are the problem."

"You mean you'd increase their cost of doing business by seizing more drug shipments and so forth?" asked her dad. "That's choice one, a full-scale war."

"No, I'd not increase their cost of doing business. I'd lower it."

"What!" Her dad paused, his fork halfway to his mouth.

"I'd make poppy growing legal."

"You can't do that," he said, horrified.

"Why not?"

"Exports to America would soar. Sophie, this is what I keep telling you. You're very smart, but you don't think things through. If you legalized poppy growing, the U.S. would be furious."

"Isn't that *their* problem? It's not *their* politicians' families being threatened. Let the U.S. interdict shipments best they're able. Perhaps I'll share intelligence with them under the table, so they'll be more effective."

"But fully legalize? You'll make the problem worse."

"No, better. Full legalization will mean every farmer in the country can start growing poppies. The supply will flood the market. Profits will vanish. The drug lords won't have anything to fight over."

"But Sophie, you're playing with fire here. Something like that has never been tried."

"That alone would be a good reason to try it, don't you think? The current policies aren't working. But actually, it *has* been tried. Surely it hasn't always been illegal to grow poppies in Colombia. It's the attempt to outlaw the crop that's produced nothing but conflict and violence."

Sophie skewered one of the cubes of dried, coarse bread from the basket, dipped it into the pot of molten Gruyère cheese, twirled it around adeptly, and set it to cool on her plate.

"But you risk your own population becoming addicts under that plan," protested her father.

Sophie plopped the morsel of cheese-coated bread into her mouth, chewed contemplatively, and swallowed. She poured a glass of white wine from the half-carafe, always on the table at Martine dinners. In this her family was not unusual. Even young kids sipped wine moderately in French Switzerland, the heart of vineyard country.

"I don't think they'll become addicts. They weren't addicts before poppy growing became illegal."

"But the U.S. will tear you apart at the United Nations, and on the world stage. They'll impose trade sanctions against you. You'll become the *bête noire* of the Western Hemisphere."

"Fine," she said, starting again with a new cube of bread. "If I'm president of Colombia, I can endure all that. What I can't endure is having myself or my family murdered, or a civil war break out. Nor can I endure a parallel government of drug lords effectively running the country. Since I can't beat them, I'll let the market beat them, by flooding the supply."

Her father was speechless, but her uncle nodded his head contemplatively. Sophie saw him try to suppress a smile.

These dinner-time subjects were varied and dealt with current events globally. Yet the issue was always framed as what the head of the country should do. A tsunami in Thailand, with most of the foreign aid being siphoned off by corrupt officials. An outbreak of religious violence between Hindus and Sikhs in northwest India. A resurgence of the slave trade in sub-Saharan Africa with captives being marched in chains to waiting markets and local governments unwilling to stop it.

Her father always wanted to know what Sophie would do if she were in charge. She'd become adept at the game. It was fun and intellectually challenging. It had never occurred to her that it might be more than a game; that her father might be grooming her for some reason.

And despite whiny protests about all the ballet and martial arts practice, she found that rewarding too. During those sessions she'd rise up to an elevated plane of consciousness. When the ballet music began she'd lose touch with reality and be absorbed by the melody, almost unaware of what her body was doing. And in the violence of the Tae Kwon Do sparring and the flashing intricacies of the sword-fighting *katas*, she found her mind singularly focused and able to detach utterly from normal thought. It was a form of trance, and she seemed to be falling more deeply into it each time.

But Sophie also knew how rapidly she was diverging from her classmates, how even their overtures at friendship were now less common. No one disliked her. She'd managed to avoid a reputation of being cold or aloof. She was simply—never available. And when she was, and they'd go for a hike or spend the day shopping, or even the time they rented paddle boats and tried to chase the swans on Lake Geneva, her mind would be elsewhere. A question would be asked twice before she heard it. She'd miss a joke, and not know what the others were laughing about. Her own contributions were always so—unusual.

"I wonder if these swans were here when Hannibal marched his elephants up the Rhone valley?" she'd said once, eliciting only stares from her friends. "The swans must have been terrified."

"Elephants? Sophie, what are you talking about?"

Or when they'd tried to tour the *Chateau de Chillon* and arrived just after closing, Sophie had suggested they scale the walls with grappling hooks.

"Sophie, are you serious?" someone had asked.

"Of course not. We don't have any grappling hooks," she'd responded with an enigmatic smile, leaving them even more confused.

Impulsively she began trying to scale the walls, wedging herself into one of the corners and trying to pull her body upwards. Sophie had made it about fifteen feet when she'd slipped and fallen back to the ground, spraining her ankle slightly. Her ballet teacher had not been sympathetic. "You tried to climb the walls of Chillon? Sophie, Sophie, Sophie! Once again you act before you think. You could have been seriously hurt!"

Even during that most feminine of pursuits, shopping for cosmetics at the boutiques in Montreux, she seemed on a different level.

"Sophie, don't you want to try some of this eyeliner? It would look amazing on you."

"Sorry. I have to use so much stage makeup at the ballet events, offstage I try not to go near the stuff." She realized later that sounded condescending, but by then it was too late. There was never another cosmetics-shopping invitation.

She wanted to be sociable. She just didn't know how. Her father and uncle kept her brain filled with thorny questions of international politics. In the ballet and martial arts practice sessions and competitions, she'd ascend to an almost spiritual plane. Between the two, it was more than she could manage to concentrate even on schoolwork. And when a new book caught her fancy, like *The Art of War*, she'd be pulled into yet a different reality. Where did friends and a normal life fit in?

Now her mom was going to "schedule something" so she'd have time with friends.

She couldn't wait. Or was she dreading it? It broke her heart that she wasn't sure.

4

A WEEK LATER Sophie heard voices talking in the kitchen when they thought she was asleep.

"We can't pass this up," her father was saying. "An archaeology invitation like this comes along once in a lifetime. The government of the Central African Republic is inviting us to the newly discovered megaliths southwest of Bangui. They're similar to the ones at Bouar, which you know was what I did my dissertation on. This would be a first. No archeologist has been allowed into that area in twenty years because of the civil wars. They're over, fortunately. It's very peaceful these days."

"Central African...*what?* I don't even know where that is," protested her mother.

Another voice joined the conversation. It was her uncle Stefan.

"Central African Republic, which everyone calls C.A.R. or just *CAR*, is directly south of Chad," he explained.

"Great," said her mom. "Chad. Like that helps. Stefan, I know you've expanded your chemical sales into Africa. But you're probably the only person in fifty kilometers who could even find this Chad place on a map."

"Oh, *I* could find it," said her father. "It's just north of CAR!"

Julianne rolled her eyes. "I meant anyone other than you two, obviously."

Stefan had been tapping on his iPad and now pulled up a full-scale, color map of Africa.

"Right here," he said.

"OK," said her mom. "They certainly named it well. Central African Republic. It's right in the middle of Africa. But why do you need to bring Sophie and me?"

"It's just what she needs, honey. A break from all her studies. And the family could use some together time. With everyone running around, we never see each other anymore. And you could take a leave of absence from the clinic. Didn't you say they finally hired another nurse practitioner?"

"Yes. But four months? What will this do to Sophie's training?"

"That's my point. I think she needs a break."

"Nic, the Swiss ballet competition, *Prix de Lausanne*, is coming up. We can't let her miss that!"

"Yes!" said Sophie to herself, sensing a reprieve from the constant practice.

Her uncle joined in. "The Swiss competition is beneath her, Juli, you know that. Didn't you tell me her teacher said she was already one of the best in Europe?"

What! No one had ever told her that. Her coach had *never* given praise; only criticism. One of the best in *Europe*? Sophie smiled inwardly. Maybe all the practice had been worth it. She allowed herself a moment of private fantasy, imagining being on stage at the Mariinsky Theater in St. Petersburg; handed roses as the audience gave a standing ovation. After all, she spoke Russian as a first language because of her dad. Of course she should go to the Mariinsky, far more prestigious even than the Bolshoi.

"We don't need to leave before Lausanne," added her father. "She won't miss that."

Sophie's reprieve vanished.

"You're right, *Prix de Lausanne* is beneath her," said her mom. "Far more important is *Dansa Milano* on April 30th. Madame Rollo thinks she's ready. More than ready. She thinks she could place in the top ten."

Sophie put a hand over her mouth while sucking in a breath. *Top ten?*

Her dad considered the issue soberly. "OK, if we have to, we could postpone our departure until even then. If we arranged everything ahead of time, we could leave May 1st. That would be the day after the competition. We'd need to have everything packed."

"You'd whisk our daughter off the stage in Milan and fly her to the middle of Africa?"

"Look, if she does well in Milan, she'll deserve a vacation. If things don't go so well, we'll want to avoid burnout from disappointment. This would definitely break up thought patterns. Four months is all we'd be gone."

"That's an eternity in the world of ballet."

"It's not perfect, Juli. But she can bring her music. Her schoolwork. She can keep practicing her routines, even in the camp. It's not healthy for a young girl to come home every night saying she hates her parents. We know she's just being Sophie, but maybe there's something to it. Maybe she needs a break."

"Anyone would," observed her uncle. "She's gone nonstop for what, twelve years? And now she says she hates us every night. Let's not just laugh that off. I think it's her way of saying she needs a break."

"Fine, Stefan, you know the sword, knife, shinken…whatever-it's-called thing will suffer too, don't you?"

"She'll be going to Africa. Maybe a little sword-fighting skill could be useful," he joked.

"Well if that were true," said Juli, "we shouldn't be going at all."

"I'm kidding. These days, that part of Africa is very peaceful."

"Could you come with us, Stefan?" asked her mom.

"Not after that heart problem they diagnosed. Docs say I'm

probably out of the woods, but I doubt they'd want me to, well, go on vacation *into the wood*s, so to speak. I'm supposed to take it easy. No exotic trips and 'avoid excitement,' whatever that means."

"No scary movies?" suggested her mom.

Stefan grinned. "Something like that."

Her dad broke in. "Juli..."

His wife looked at him directly. "We moved to Switzerland for safety. For yours and for hers. Will we be safe in Africa?"

"Probably safer," said her father. "It's that much more distant from, well, you know."

Sophie, still hiding behind the corner, wondered: *Safer from what?*

"Look, when I married an older man I wasn't expecting camping to be on the agenda. And aren't you getting a bit old for field work? There's a thing called *retirement*, you know."

"What can I say; I have good genes, at least on my mom's side." Her dad grinned, and Sophie saw her parents exchange an odd glance.

"Nic, I'll think about it. That's all I'm agreeing to for now."

But her mom would give in. Africa. Wow. Back in her room, Sophie pulled up Google Maps and began studying Central African Republic. She zoomed in on the capital, Bangui, and switched over to satellite mode. The city was surrounded by wilderness, rivers, game preserves, and national parks. There was so much to learn, Sophie quickly forgot about the unnamed threat.

5

Two Months Later

Lying on the cot in her large tent, Sophie Martine stared at shadow-patterns as the overhanging tree limbs played havoc with the sun's rays. She'd just finished reading Sun Tzu's 2,500-year-old classic, *The Art of War*, for the second time and now had to do a book report, which would be easy. Despite being in the jungle she kept up with her studies and sent assignments by email back to her teacher in Montreux. As with judo, *The Art of War* was all about using deception to win: making your enemies think you were weak when you were strong, or strong when you were weak, or that you'd attack tomorrow when you were attacking today, or that you were on this hill, not that one. She loved the book and decided to read it a third time. It was a blueprint for winning battles and it came down to a single principle: make everything a surprise. Never do what your enemy expects. It seemed so obvious.

Outside her tent the temperature was climbing rapidly. She could hear a Land Rover departing the camp, or arriving, or maybe one of each. Things were busy at the newly discovered field of megaliths, as she understood they were called. Native diggers, shovels and other equipment, food and supplies, armed guards provided by the government—all of it meant lots of Land Rovers moving everything around.

Sophie couldn't decide if she loved it here or hated it.

On the "hate" side was the heat. After that was the problem of flies. She tried to learn the natives' way of just ignoring them, but how do you ignore a flying carnivore determined to take nibbles out of your flesh? They were consuming insect repellent in industrial quantities. Not surprisingly, the brand they used was made by Stefan's company back in Geneva—SCI, or Société des Chimiques Industrielles. He'd spent years extending his business interests throughout Africa, and now "SCI-Deet!" was the only brand sold in the whole country. It made her feel they weren't so far from civilization if her uncle's products were out here protecting them.

The camp was sixty kilometers southwest of Bangui, the capital, where the family had a reasonably modern apartment—with air conditioning. But that was only for weekends, and in truth, it was more interesting out here in the jungle.

Continuing the list was lack of modern amenities. They used field toilets, had cots to sleep on, and ate outdoors on large wooden tables. But that was part of the fun too. It was like a camping trip that never ended. The hardships were part of the experience, even if her mom wasn't thrilled with them.

On the "love" side of the equation, the fact that they had servants for everything made her feel like African royalty. No cleaning the dishes or setting the table for her. All that was done by native workers, as was cooking the food, serving it, everything.

She also adored the jungle and couldn't explore it enough. Her parents made sure there were never less than three armed guards accompanying her, because there was plenty of danger. This part of CAR bordered the country of Congo, just across the Ubangi River, and the whole area was technically a national park: the Dzanga Wildlife Reserve. It was a vast wilderness in which leopards, rhinos, cape buffalo, and even lions prowled, not counting hippos and crocodiles in the river, and more species of birds than could be counted.

Once a day she'd insist on a "forest walk" as it was called in camp. The dig was just to the east. She'd lead them in the opposite direction, to the west, deep into the jungle. And by the way, was it jungle or rainforest? She'd been Googling the difference. The area they were in was part of something called the Congo Rainforest which covered parts of six African countries including CAR. Jungle, most agreed, was a descriptive term, not a scientific one. Jungle sounded scary. Rainforest sounded more eco-friendly and noble.

Whatever it was, sometimes they could explore it in one of the Land Rovers, and those trips were like miniature safaris, or "game drives" as the natives called them.

The wildlife sightings were breathtaking. Elephants protecting their young. Cape buffalo milling about, staring at them with a bad attitude. Fish eagles soaring gracefully over the Ubangi River and frequently diving into it before flying aloft again with something silvery and squiggling in their beaks. It was mating season and the lions were often having sex. She thought that hilarious. The "king of the jungle" caught in a romantic embrace. She'd read on Wikipedia that lions often had sex for over an hour, and the ones they came upon seemed to each be going for a record.

They found a leopard, which Sophie named Raphael after a pet turtle she'd owned back in Switzerland. The leopard spent its days lounging on the same tree branch, often with an impala carcass for company, or at least for snacking.

Hyenas were everywhere: ugly, easily frightened animals that made a nasty laughing sound when they were nervous or angry, which was most of the time, she gathered. Warthogs snouted about, running squealing into the bush the moment they became aware of—anything.

Between the hikes and the Land Rover forays, she came to know the jungle well and felt on some level it knew her. She was just another forest creature, and most of the animals seemed happy to let her share it with them. Well, except for the cape buffalo, which hated everyone.

The weekends spent in Bangui were a welcome respite, a chance to take a shower, sleep in a real bed, and luxuriate in air conditioning. But mostly what they did was catch up on laundry, work on lists of supplies needed in camp, and shop at the colorful markets. Most importantly, they began a family tradition of always having dinner in town at a sidewalk café, when the heat of the day had ebbed.

Those meals were the one time she had her parents to herself: just the three of them. During the week, her mom used her medical skills to run an informal clinic for the workers and her dad was unapproachable with all the excavating. Everyone was exhausted by day's end. But weekend dinners in town allowed them to come together as a family—almost a normal one. Her dad would entertain with funny anecdotes from the week. Mom would reminisce about Paris, and how she so looked forward to showing it to her daughter when they returned to Europe. Sophie was now embarrassed she'd exhibited hate after school every day. These days she couldn't remember what she'd been so mad about. Her mom and dad were the warmest, most loving parents a girl could have. And the dinners in town—family time—were the best part of the week, moments she wished would never end.

But Monday morning they'd be picked up at six for the ninety-minute drive over dirt roads back to the dig, and everything would start again.

Her mom insisted on a routine even out in the bush, and that meant an hour and a half of ballet practice each morning and another ninety minutes of martial arts exercises in the afternoon. The proximity to real danger—or at least the appearance of it—had caused Julianne to fully support her daughter's self-defense training no less than the ballet.

She had everything needed, from ballet slippers, to an iPod and earbuds for music, to a steel katana blade and tanto dagger for sword fighting katas, to a Tae Kwon Do black-belt uniform. But she never wore the uniform. It was too hot. She dressed modestly, in a black, two-piece Adidas track suit.

Her blonde hair was kept in a braid or tied back in a bun. Sophie would have preferred it cropped short, but that wasn't allowed in ballet, and it wouldn't grow back before returning home. It was too much trouble to let it flow loosely and her mom used to complain the hairstyle was insufficiently feminine. But out here in the wilderness, surrounded by dozens of native workers, toning down femininity was encouraged.

With the dustiness of the dig, the lack of showers, and the utter inappropriateness of clothes beyond the working variety, Sophie appeared much more a small, adolescent boy, than an alluring young vixen.

"Back in Europe we're going to turn you into a real beauty," her mom promised. "With your face you could be a model in Paris or Milan. But for now, you're encouraged to stay as grubby and disheveled as you wish."

That suited Sophie just fine.

Well, so much for her brief after-lunch "siesta," as her dad called it. Now it was time for Shinkendo practice. Exiting the tent, Sophie glanced at the three medals her parents had hung from a pole near the door, to keep her inspired.

Swiss National Tae Kwon Do Open – 1st Place, overall. Sophie Martine

Prix de Lausanne – 1st Place. Sophie Martine

Dansa Milano – 2nd Place. Sophie Martine.

They did keep her inspired, and she thought again of her St. Petersburg dream. Mariinsky ballerinas were the best in the world, and she was determined to dance among them. A dirt floor with a mat thrown over it, inside a tent in a third-world country, music being played through earbuds, was an unusual route to the City of the Tsars. But it was only a detour. She was heading for Russia. And if anyone got in the way, well—she stifled a laugh—maybe that's what the sword fighting skills were for.

While she'd also brought a bokken practice sword, she preferred her real katana when not fighting an actual opponent. A gift from her father, the katana was custom made of high-carbon steel for Sophie's height and weight and was the most expensive thing she owned. It had been ordered with a matching tanto dagger that could be used for both stabbing and slashing strokes.

Today she'd practice her *dual-wielding* technique, using the katana and dagger together—one hand for each. It was a sophisticated and difficult style, but she'd been training on it for over a year.

Her Shinkendo practice area set up near the camp included homemade *tameshigiri* targets for slashing practice. She'd created these herself, using narrow banana-tree trunks two meters high, bound together with vines, and sunk halfway into the ground for rigidity.

Now, standing in the middle of her private *dojo*, she emptied her mind of everything but *the way of the sword*. The goal was not merely to demonstrate physical prowess, but to attain a higher and more disciplined mental state.

Moving with grace and speed, the young Shinkendo expert performed a leaping roundhouse spin, her dual blades shimmering in the sunlight. She unleashed a double slash, the sharp edge of her katana slicing the air with a resonating whoosh.

In a fluid motion, she re-sheathed her fighting sword, hand moving with practiced dexterity. Rolling onto her back, Sophie arched her body upwards, driving the tanto dagger fiercely into an imaginary opponent's chest cavity.

Springing back onto her feet, she propelled herself forward into a powerful somersault, displaying both agility and grace as she poised herself for the final strike. Lunging forward, she drove the tanto upward, cleanly penetrating the heart of her make-believe adversary.

The *tameshigiri* targets were next. With a primal battle cry, Sophie unleashed a flurry of slashes and cuts, her katana effortlessly cleaving through the wood, splintering it and toppling the makeshift structures to the ground.

She continued the kata, each movement flowing seamlessly into the next, and performed it with breathtaking speed and precision. As the last target fell, she resumed a ritual pose at the center of the field. Beads of sweat glistened on her brow, and her chest heaved with exertion. Her opponent had been destroyed not merely with blades, but equally with her focused mind and warrior's spirit.

The native workers who looked onto the open-air practice area were astonished. Presumably they'd never seen world-class martial arts fighting and were mesmerized when the young girl flashed around her blades in these intricate dance-like routines, or performed Tae Kwon Do katas.

Sophie knew it was another reason her mom encouraged the martial arts practice out in the open and didn't mind when the men watched curiously. The message was clear: This wisp of a child—armed with her blades or even without—is more deadly than a viper. Don't even think of messing with her.

By contrast, her mom insisted the ballet routines be performed inside the large tent, with the flaps down. Heat be damned. She didn't want anyone ogling her seventeen-year-old daughter as she performed evocative dance moves in a form-fitting black leotard and tights.

Mfuni Fango, one of the forest guides, drove up to the ring and called to her just as she was finishing Shinkendo practice.

"Sophie, if you're done, hop in. I just got back from the river and there were two giraffes down there. You have to see them!"

Giraffes? She'd never seen giraffes. That would be amazing.

"I need to return my stuff to the tent first, OK?"

"No time, who knows where they'll be by then. Toss your gear in the back. Hop in."

She did so, placing the sword, properly sheathed in its leather and wood scabbard, in the backseat. Her fighting knife was still in its own sheath, strapped to a leg, and she decided not to bother undoing it. In seconds they were flying away from camp, Mfuni honking impatiently whenever a worker, another "Landy," or an errant pig got in the way.

6

They never found the giraffes, but not for lack of trying, and were late returning to camp. Sophie knew she'd be in trouble. It was after five p.m. and, being Friday, the native workers had probably already left. Mfuni was their designated driver back to Bangui, so that wasn't a problem.

Half a kilometer short of camp, he stopped the Land Rover and turned off the engine.

"Hey, we're already late. Why are you stopping?" she asked.

"Something doesn't feel right."

A flood of adrenaline washed over Sophie because suddenly things didn't feel right to her, either. But what? There was no noise, and maybe that was part of it. Even if the native workers had left, her parents should be banging around, finishing up the work, hauling duffels to the parking lot. There was no sound of anything.

"Sophie, you stay here. Let me walk ahead." He took his rifle with him and cautiously jogged up the road.

She was too scared not to obey. But after fifteen minutes she couldn't stand it anymore. What was going on? Why wasn't Mfuni back yet?"

It was always a bad idea to get out of the Land Rover while still in the bush. In fact, that was one of the cardinal rules, unless it was a forest walk and she was surrounded by guards armed with high-powered rifles. A lion could be anywhere. For that matter, so could a baboon. And a baboon, she'd been told, could bite with three times the jaw strength of a lion. But for some reason, the jungle animals never attacked humans in a Land Rover—even a completely open one like this.

So she felt guilty stepping out. It was one of those times her dad would say she was being impetuous, not thinking things through. It *was* one of her faults—she often found her body moving faster than her mind. Well, if she *were* to think it through, what might she do differently? Not wait forever in the Land Rover, certainly. But a wiser person might… She grabbed the fighting sword and strapped it to her back. Sophie could now claim she was armed. A Japanese blade would not be as effective against a charging rhino as were the .458 Winchester Magnum rifles her guides carried. But having the two weapons might help win an argument about not being completely unprotected.

For some reason, she was looking forward to that argument, because it would mean everything was normal again. And things weren't feeling normal at all.

Rather than merely walk up the road, she decided to slip into the forest itself, where she'd be protected in case there was danger at the camp. She couldn't imagine what the danger might be. The country was totally at peace. The aggressive animals like lions and jackals never approached closely. What other dangers could there be?

But she stayed in the forest.

Several hundred yards from the Land Rover she saw a body lying in the center of the road. It was the first dead body she'd ever seen, but she knew intuitively what it was. And who it was. Mfune's red shirt was his trademark. She sucked in her breath, ready and needing to scream, but somehow she didn't. Letting her breath out slowly, she studied the body and noticed the rifle was missing. There had been no sound of a gunshot, so he must have been killed silently.

Sophie was already thinking tactically, not realizing she was doing so.

She'd now progressed from uneasy, to scared, to terrified. And she was most terrified for her parents. When she finally reached the camp, still hiding inside the jungle canopy, she knew she'd been right to be.

There were three unusual cars here: black Land Rovers, not the kind used at the dig. More than a dozen large native guys were patrolling about, holding rifles that looked more military, not like the hunting rifles used in camp. There was also a large white man with a blond crewcut, who perhaps was in charge. And then she saw her parents. Their hands were tied above them, to one of the horizontal poles holding up the tent where she practiced ballet.

Sophie began to whimper quietly in fear. A survival instinct was governing her—perhaps from all the martial arts practice where they were taught defensive as well as offensive moves. And the best defensive move, their instructor had pounded into them, was not being seen in the first place. And that meant not being heard. Sophie stayed silent and stayed hidden. And watched.

They knew there was a child in camp because the white guy began screaming questions at her parents in English.

"Where is she? Where is daughter!"

"She's not here," said her dad. "She's back in Bangui. She's not at the dig this week."

If her father was lying, that could only mean he was trying to protect her. But how could she protect them?

The white man punched her father in the stomach, as if knowing it was a lie.

Sophie again suppressed a scream, this time by physically forcing her hand over her mouth, just in time. But she couldn't stop the tears that flowed down her cheeks, even if she'd been aware of them.

"It's true! Our daughter's back in town, she's not here!" screamed her mother, crying in terror.

The man pulled his arm back and slapped her mom with full force across her face. She saw her father desperately pulling at the ropes that held him, consumed with pain and anger.

Sophie could race across the fifty-yard distance and remove the man's head with her katana before anyone could react. She was about to do so when she forced herself, again, to think calmly and plan. What about the dozen other men with guns? Killing one of them would accomplish nothing. And then they'd no doubt kill both her, and her parents.

She forced her fingers to let go of the sword hilt, where they'd automatically gone while preparing for an attack. That plan would not work. And she couldn't think of one that would.

The leader now turned and called out in the direction of the forest, as if suspecting someone was there hiding. "Little girl," he said. "Come back to your parents. If you come back, everyone will be safe. We just have some questions to ask. But if you stay hidden, I'm going to count to three and then shoot your father. And then I'm going to count to three and shoot your mother."

This time Sophie's whole body began trembling. Maybe he was right. Maybe she should reveal herself and everything would be safe again, and tonight they'd all go to their favorite café in Bangui and have a nice meal and drink red wine.

No. The body back in the road made it clear these were killers, and they'd not come to ask questions.

As if on cue, she saw the leader pull out a gun and point it at her father's head. "Little girl, I'm going to count to three before I shoot him. If you aren't here by then, I will pull the trigger, and it will be you who will have killed your father. 1…2…"

And then her mother screamed: "Sophie, run! Hide! Save yourself! If you love us, run! Don't let them catch you! Run!"

The man with the gun turned it away from her father and shot her mom in the head.

And then her father was screaming the same thing. "Run, Sophie! Run! Get out of here! Don't let them find you! Run!"

And then the man shot her father.

Sophie was beyond shock, beyond grief. She was paralyzed in horror. But while she stood, unable to move, somehow the last order each of her parents had screamed, finally registered. *"Run!"* It was the last thing they'd told her to do. She had to obey.

And with no conscious intervention, her body followed the command. With not even a second to look back, she turned, slipped farther into the forest, and took off like a gazelle.

Behind her she heard one of them call out "Remember, if we don't kill the daughter too, we don't get paid!"

Medieval samurai had devised simple yet effective scabbards to allow warriors—while carrying their weapons—to perform at maximum efficiency most any task, from riding a horse, to shooting arrows, to running through a forest. Sophie's katana did not bounce around or impede her now at all.

And with the "fight or flight" question resolved, her body's adrenaline rushed to her muscles and gave unusual stamina to the lithe girl who could practice martial arts for an hour without becoming winded.

Behind her were urgent cries and orders being given. The Land Rovers fired up, and they set off now to find her, no doubt certain she was nearby and could easily be captured.

What they did not know was the nature of the young girl they were chasing. Sophie was in peak physical condition. And, thanks to all the walks and game drives, she knew the forest. There were places to hide, trees to climb, hollow rotted-out logs to squeeze into if necessary. There was even a cave.

But her parents' last command had been imprinted on her soul, and she just ran. The hiking sneakers were ideal for this kind of mad dash through the jungle. But she had to be careful. This was no time to trip, fall down, or sprain an ankle. She knew this subliminally, even if her conscious mind was still in shock from what it had seen.

Not surprisingly, her mind turned away from that shock and focused solely on the urgent task at hand: running at high speed without making a mistake. It was better to give her mind something to concentrate on, so it could avoid the hell it had witnessed, let alone try to process any of it, let alone have time for grief.

Watching the ground closely, she jumped deftly over fallen logs, detoured as needed around trees, ducked under low-hanging boughs, and ignored the vines, weeds, and foliage that slapped against her face unavoidably and mercilessly.

Occasionally she'd risk glancing behind but could not tell if they were following. It was unlikely they could drive their Land Rovers this deep into the jungle itself. They'd have to stay mostly on the dirt roads. And she knew where those were and avoided them. She was fleeing west, into the deepest part of the jungle, and soon she was beyond the area anyone from camp had explored on foot. It was becoming less flat, and as she ran up small inclines and down into ravines she was sweating profusely, so much that she had to frequently wipe her eyes and forehead. But it didn't slow her down.

She remembered from studying the maps there was a small river somewhere ahead, which meant a river valley, and she must be approaching it. If she could somehow cross the river, maybe she'd be safe. But the sun was beginning to set, and she knew how quickly it became dark in Africa; especially in the jungle. Where was that river?

She pushed herself harder, running even faster, not least because the more physical exertion, the less room there was in her mind to remember what she'd seen. When she quit running it would come back and she couldn't let it come back. She *couldn't*. So she raced on, running even more swiftly, breathing more heavily, trying to stay alert with the fading light. The terrain was pitching down now at an increasing rate and her speed picked up dangerously.

Sophie turned once more, to glance behind, and ran full speed into a low-hanging tree limb.

The blow knocked her unconscious, but forward motion carried her several yards farther. It was just enough to reach a small cliff.

Sophie tumbled over the edge, hit the steep embankment ten feet below, and rolled—blades tumbling with her—another twenty yards and into the river itself. Forward movement stopped with her head still on the bank, just above waterline.

The last of the sun's rays disappeared, and the jungle turned black.

The unconscious, battered—yet still living—body of Sophie Martine lay motionless in the water.

7

Six thousand kilometers away, in St. Petersburg, Russia, a phone rang. It was late at night, but the man answering was awaiting the call. "Tell me you have good news."

"Sir, it's done."

"They're dead?"

"Yes, sir."

"*All* of them?"

There was only the slightest pause. "Yes sir, all of them."

"Enjoy your bonus," said the man in St. Petersburg, clicking off the phone. It was a dark room, but he was not alone.

"The Romanoff line has finally ended and it's time for a drink," he said to the other figure sitting in a chair in front of the desk. He poured from a nearby bottle placed there earlier for exactly this purpose.

"Congratulations, sir. To the last of the Romanoffs."

They clicked glasses and drank.

"And now, sir, if you'll allow me another toast?"

"Certainly."

"To the *newest* of the Romanoffs!"

Both men smiled.

8

Physical sensations returned slowly. Cold. That was her first conscious thought. Cold. There was room in her brain for that emotion, but the rest of her mind was gone.

She could stop the cold. That was her second conscious thought. She could pull away from the cold wetness.

She decided to do so; a third thought. There was nothing else. Her mind was empty but for those three concepts: cold, an ability to stop the cold, and a decision to do so.

The death-like form came to life, raised itself up tenuously, stumbled to its feet, and gazed about, confused.

The young ballerina was gone. In her place was a primitive, feral creature, with no memories of anything.

There was a knife on the ground. Her knife. She knew it was hers. She knew it was a knife. She knew it would cut flesh. She applied it to her own, the point pressed against her shoulder. She pressed farther and noticed pain.

Pain was an interesting sensation. A small trickle of blood flowed down her arm. It was red. Very red. She watched as her blood made the journey to her fingers and then fell to the ground.

It was interesting, but she didn't care about the pain or the blood. She didn't know what she cared about.

The stream at her feet flowed slowly, and the water was clear. Things were moving in the water.

She lay face down on a large, flat rock, and stared into the river. Fish. She could see fish in the water. Large fish. For over an hour she stared at the fish, watching how they moved, studying them, letting her empty mind fill with images of fish.

The small wound on her arm closed and the newly-risen sun dried the blood. She didn't notice. She was mesmerized by the fish.

Suddenly, without consciously willing it, the hand holding the knife stabbed into the water. The movement was so fast the weapon almost found its mark. She stared into the water for another hour, watching the fish. Then, even more swiftly, the knife attacked. Again it missed. Another hour went by.

She studied the fish, timed her attacks, and missed. She was not discouraged. She had no emotions at all, certainly not that one.

After three hours, the knife found its target. She withdrew the impaled fish from the stream and watched it intently, holding the pitiful, wriggling thing in front of her eyes. The fish took a long time to die completely.

Then she ate it, spitting out the parts she didn't like. She leaned down and drank deeply from the water.

The young girl sitting on the rock eating the raw fish and drinking from the river had no idea who she was, where she came from, or why she was alone in the jungle. Nor did she wonder about these things. There was not enough of her mind left to have such thoughts. There was enough to have become very good at killing fish with a knife. She killed three more, ate them, and then fell asleep again, on the rock, the last rays of the sun keeping her warm.

9

WHEN SHE AWOKE the next morning she remembered yesterday. She remembered about the fish and how to kill them. She killed and ate two more. She discovered that the knife fit into a sheath attached to her leg and she returned it there.

Refreshed with food, water, and rest—the concussion that had knocked her out beginning to heal—she left the riverbank. She'd only gone a few yards from the water when she discovered a sword in a scabbard. She knew what it was. It was a sword. She was curious how it came to be there.

She was not yet curious how she herself had come to be there.

She had no memory the sword was hers. But it was interesting, like the fish. She picked it up, unsheathed it, and was surprised when her body automatically moved into a type of fighting stance, holding the sword just so.

What did that mean? Setting down the scabbard, she gripped the sword again and found it contained almost special powers over her. As she held it, her body began to move. She began performing one of her many scripted sword fighting katas: high guard, rotate, roll backward, long point stance, circular parry, front roll, counter parry... She found the movements reassuring, calming, and pleasing. But she had no idea what they meant.

The sword gave her a purpose and something to do. Until then, she'd been too empty to know what to do—other than kill fish. But she could do this, and enjoyed it.

She practiced sword fighting dances for two hours, becoming more reassured and swifter by the minute. If some adversary had appeared, she'd have killed it easily. But no adversary did. She finally set down the sword, returned to the river, and made another meal of fish.

That afternoon she practiced further with the sword, ate more fish, and found the branch of a tree to sleep on that night.

10

On the third day she noticed a hyena watching her. She observed it, her mind still mostly empty but willing to be filled again with—anything. She was not afraid of the hyena.

She was not afraid because fear could only come from an aversion to pain or death. Most animals had this by nature, but the girl who awoke with no mind did not.

When she looked at the hyena, she thought of it as another type of fish and about how she would kill it. The thought process involved with such a concept was a sign of progress. She was analyzing the animal, observing how it moved, comparing it to how a fish moved.

It did not occur to her that she was in danger, nor would she have understood the concept.

After two hours of watching its prey, the hyena attacked, much as the girl expected it would: frontally and with great speed and force. She'd been visualizing this attack, preparing for it, knowing how she would respond; knowing how her body would move, knowing just what to do with the sword. She understood that it would be different than killing a fish. But not much different.

It was over quickly. The hyena, its severed head now six feet from its body, lay motionless while blood poured onto the ground. The hyena smelled bad, and Sophie ignored it. She killed two more fish and ate them, then practiced her katas diligently before falling asleep again.

The next day she killed a leopard. These animals of prey—while appearing to have overwhelming superiority over a small girl in the wilderness—were unprepared for the adversary they faced. Having evolved in a world where everything was predator or prey, they had no experience with something that was neither.

The girl with the empty mind had no capacity for anything other than studying animals and killing them with increasing efficiency. Sometimes she used her katana—she remembered its name—and sometimes her knife.

Given only one thing to focus on, a brain can become very good at it. When the leopard attacked in a classic leap, she merely collapsed backward and let the animal slice open its abdomen on her upraised knife. It was not dead when it landed. The leopard twisted and leaped in agonized contortions, entrails spilling out, screeching horribly before finally dying.

The girl thought it smelled bad too and went back to killing fish in the river. She liked eating the raw fish and drinking cool water from the stream.

11

Once, while staring into the water, analyzing the movements of fish, she was distracted by a flash of light coming from the sand at the bottom of the river. Curious, she walked into the water and began to swim toward the spot where she'd seen the flash. She did not wonder about knowing how to swim, any more than she wondered about knowing how to walk.

She performed a surface dive and retrieved the shiny thing from the bottom.

Back on the bank, she set the object in the sunlight. It was just a pretty rock. Her curiosity sated, she flung it back into the river. She didn't care about the shiny rock, but she had enjoyed the swim.

On impulse, she decided to cross to the other side of the river and back again. This gave her a new thing to do, a new purpose. She could watch the fish and eat them. She could practice with the sword. She could kill predators. And now she could swim in the river.

During one of these journeys, she saw a crocodile approaching and considered, tactically, how best to kill it. Timing the movement carefully, she dove deep into the river, and before the crocodile could react to this unexpected maneuver, she ricocheted off the bottom and shot upwards, plunging her knife into the reptile's abdomen and slicing upwards through its throat.

Other crocodiles appeared to take advantage of their wounded comrade and enjoy a meal at his expense. But they left the girl alone. They might be dumb but they weren't stupid.

Arriving on the far side, she decided to explore. The girl had no way of knowing that with the crossing of the Lobaye River she had entered the country of Congo. She noticed several more of the shiny rocks, here on the bank, and had fun tossing them back into the river. Entering the forest, she'd gone only a dozen yards when she came to a large hole somehow formed in limestone, about six feet across, filled with water, and fed by an underground spring. The water overflowed out of the hole and formed a tiny stream back to the main river. She could see to the bottom where dozens more of the shiny stones glistened off white sand.

She hopped in, surprised at how cold this water was, reached down, and grabbed one of the objects. It was much bigger than the ones she'd found earlier, and she decided to keep it. The girl swam back across the river and ate another fish for dinner.

12

She didn't always kill with her blades. Once she was caught off guard by a pack of African wild dogs. As the first leaped for her throat she broke its neck with a perfect Tae Kwon Do sidekick to the head. The second she grabbed by the skull as it lunged and poked out its eyes with her thumbs, a self-defense technique her hands remembered from a different lifetime, even if she didn't.

A third dog she grabbed by its front legs as it leapt at her. She whirled the dog at high speed and smashed it into a tree, cracking its spine. She'd never been taught that, but it worked. A girl with years of martial arts training could improvise. The final two animals ran off, terrified.

A diet of raw fish, water, and constant exercise from swimming, kata practice, or actual combat with wild animals turned the young girl—already highly fit—into a thing of steel. Lithe, agile, skilled, and empty of all ambition except a desire to destroy adversaries and occasionally eat them, the wild thing living by the river was like nothing the jungle had ever encountered.

And by now the girl did look more like a wild thing than a human. Her hair was irretrievably matted, she'd found that rolling her body in mud kept off the insects, and that brandishing palm fronds aggressively would confuse the animals trying to attack her. Also, palm fronds occasionally would give her cover when she sought to observe other life forms in the jungle, before attacking them.

Her tools were simple: a knife sheathed on her leg, a sword in its scabbard on her back, and palm fronds to confuse an attacker.

She still had no fear of pain or death—that part of her brain had not yet returned. But she did have a strong desire to win. She liked to outwit the fish by knowing precisely where to strike. She enjoyed killing the predators because doing so was an interesting challenge.

Animals in the jungle had their own pecking order and understood their status on a complex social ladder. At the top was the lion, which feared nothing but had its own emotions. A lion could feel hunger, sexual appetite, or anger. But it didn't know fear. Except perhaps from a more dominant lion.

As the girl walked through the jungle she was behaving like a lion: fearless, indomitable, and very willing to offer combat to anything that threatened her. The other forest creatures began avoiding her.

After a week she met a real lion.

The cat circled from a distance, watching. The girl began visualizing various ways of killing it.

The lion, to the extent its brain could accommodate such thoughts, was puzzled. The—thing—had the physical appearance of prey, but it was not running, as prey would do. Nor was it behaving as a lesser predator such as a hyena might do, waiting for the lion to kill something so it could feast on the scraps. No, this—thing—was appraising the lion itself, as if offering battle in defense of territory. It was behaving precisely as another male lion might behave.

This particular lion had recently eaten a gazelle, was not hungry, and could afford to be curious. The cat approached the thing, coming within a few feet of it, and then just stared. The thing stared back. Finally, the lion sat down.

So did the thing. Finding itself tired from the full meal, the lion finally lay down completely, still staring at the thing.

The thing lay down too, staring at the lion. The lion closed its eyes, not particularly concerned about the thing. The thing closed its eyes too, not particularly concerned about the lion.

After a short nap, the lion got up and walked away into the forest.

A day later, it returned with its pride. The other lions were also interested in this—thing.

The male lion again lay down, and after a while, so did his pride. Again, so did the thing.

They stayed together. The lions watched as the thing killed fish in the river and ate them. They watched as the thing once killed a hyena. The thing followed them occasionally when they hunted, but it never tried to eat the game they killed. One night the thing came over to the male lion, lay down next to it, and set its head on the lion's chest. They slept that way all night.

The two utterly different life forms had no way to communicate. Nor did they need to. Each was independent of the other, neither threatened by the other, in competition with it, nor in fear of it.

They stayed together because they were all a type of lion, and lions enjoyed each other's company. Another male lion would not have been welcome. But this—thing—was not a male lion. It just seemed to belong to their social order. And they accepted it. Perhaps, in their own way, they grew fond of it.

The girl gave the lions names. The fact that she could understand the concept of names was a sign that her brain was recovering. They were French names because that was the language she was now thinking in. The head of the pride, the male, was Emil. The three girls were Cecile, Annemarie, and Brigitte.

She became friendly with all of them, though which was the pet and which the master would be hard to say. She'd frequently fall asleep with her head on Emil. Once he stood up after a long nap to find the—thing—still on him.

The girl began to ride around on Emil's back. He didn't mind.

Once, perhaps forgetting the thing was still on him, Emil launched into a full-scale chase at a kudu. With the lion burdened, his prey was about to escape but at the last moment the thing leaped, a knife flashed, and the wounded kudu crashed to the ground. The lions ate the antelope. The thing ate fish from the river.

That night she again slept with her head nestled on Emil's body.

13

ONCE, JUST AS the sun was rising, the lions were puzzled to find the thing already awake and performing strange movements. It twirled around, rose up on its feet, moved its arms rapidly in a flowing motion, and—at one point—leapt almost horizontally through the air. The lions could make nothing of this. It didn't concern them, and one went back to sleep.

The girl with no mind did not understand it either or know what she was doing. There were sounds in her head—beautiful sounds. And they were controlling her. She could not stay still. She had to move, spin, and even leap. She wondered what the sounds were, what they meant, and why they enticed her to perform such strange motions.

14

"Aiiieiii!!" The scream pierced the jungle as the lash found its victim. The slaves were in iron chains, similar to those in use for hundreds of years.

This time the whip had fallen on the exposed back of a young female captive who was unable to keep up. Two nearby slaves helped, partially carrying her between them, because if she could not maintain their speed she would be killed and discarded at the side of the trail. The slaver wasn't satisfied and lashed out again with his whip.

Something exploded out of the trees, leapt onto the man's back, tore out his throat, and then disappeared into the jungle. It happened so fast, those still living had no idea what they'd just seen. It might have been human. But no human would do this. It must have been some animal. But no animal would do this either. A predator would stay and feed on its kill. And only a predator would make such a kill.

When the slave train reached the market at Nola, rumors spread of some kind of demon inhabiting the jungle; a forest creature that killed merely for pleasure. The fact that both the slavers, and their captives, had seen it made the rumor true. And in West Africa, even untrue rumors spread rapidly.

15

The girl, hiding once more in the trees, had no idea why she'd attacked. She'd observed the column of slaves, and their traffickers. She'd seen other, similar groups on this trail. It was perhaps the whip that had triggered her reaction. The whip was cruel. It was wrong. The part of her brain that noticed such things, and cared, was coming back. She couldn't abide cruelty.

So she attacked. She killed the one she believed evil, the concept itself a sign of a mind returning. Emil the lion watched her with only the mildest of interest. As before, he'd recently devoured an antelope and didn't need more flesh.

Within a week two more slave caravans came down the trail. The first she observed from a hill while riding on Emil. Both the slaves and their captors saw her. It was a woman with white skin and white hair, riding a lion, and holding a sword. Such a thing had never been seen in Africa.

A few minutes later she attacked, but without the lion. And this time she killed all the slavers before disappearing back into the jungle.

The captives were able to retrieve the keys from the bodies and release themselves. When they returned home the rumors exploded. The forest creature was in human form—white as a ghost—a woman who rode on the back of lions.

Soon—in these rumors—the lions themselves were white, and in one telling, their manes were perpetually ablaze. In another, it was the girl's hair that was aflame. Sometimes lightning bolts flew from her sword. In the superstitious minds of the West Africans, these rumors proved irresistible. News of the forest creature spread across the continent, from Nigeria to Kenya. From Congo to Sudan.

The killings continued and the slavers' losses mounted. Even with added security, one out of three caravans never reached its destination. Missing slavers—presumed dead—now totaled more than a hundred. Regional governors, who received kickbacks from the illicit trade, sent out armed patrols along the slave routes, but no trace of the forest creature could be found.

Back in the jungle, the girl had boldly—too boldly—attacked a slave caravan protected by more guards than usual. There were too many. Dead bodies now lay everywhere, with heads or limbs missing, or bleeding out from fatal knife thrusts. But she was exhausted. The final slaver pulled out his gun to finish off whatever rabid creature this was.

Summoning a last reserve of energy, the girl threw an unexpected roundhouse kick that knocked the man's weapon into the forest. Her sword was unavailable, being stuck tightly into the stomach of another slaver who was on the ground, writhing. She attacked her remaining foe with a knife, but tripped over an unseen root. The girl lost her balance and fell to the ground, face first—the knife coming loose from her hand.

The man grabbed the blade quickly and approached malevolently, a grin on his face; now determined to kill this monster of the jungle who had so terrified the slaving community.

It was only a filthy girl, a young white woman, who was now weaponless and on her back. It was time she died. He pulled back his hand, preparing to deliver a fatal thrust, when suddenly a lion leapt out of the forest and ripped off his arm.

Other lions appeared and began eating him alive. The slaver's screams ended quickly.

One of the lions approached the slaves themselves, huddled and in chains. The forest creature called to the lion, and it turned away. She directed it to the other two bodies, and it happily began feeding on those, leaving the slaves alone.

When the lions were satiated, they lay down for a nap, not caring about the other humans, still in chains, terrified out of their minds.

This time the girl did not flee back into the forest. She found the keys herself and released the slaves. And when she did, the eldest, a young man, used hand signals to urge her to come with them.

Yes, perhaps it was time for her to be with others like herself. She took a moment to cuddle with Emil and the girls, needing to say goodbye. They understood their pet had found a new home.

Emil yawned and went back to sleep, the bloodied bones of the now-eaten slavers scattered about him.

16

THE GIRL WITH the golden-white hair had rescued eight captives, and all of them wanted to touch her. She let them. They also wanted to communicate, and show their appreciation, but she did not speak their language. So they smiled, because smiles needed no translating. Signaling she was to follow, they began walking the opposite way down the forest path, presumably back to their original village. They chattered gaily.

Their leader, the oldest boy, was determined to introduce himself. He would touch his chest with both hands, and say one word, repeatedly: *Omylo. Omylo.*

She understood this was his name. *Omylo.* She said it a few times, pointing at him, and he nodded.

Then Omylo pointed at her with a questioning expression.

The forest creature stopped suddenly in the middle of the path. She knew he was asking for her name, and in that instant realized she had none. For the first time since waking up by the river, she began wondering about herself. Who was she? Why was she in the forest? Where had she come from? Why did she have no name?

She did not know. Omylo finally gave up questioning her, and they all began walking again.

It required a day and a half to reach the village, and twice on the journey, the forest creature used her sword. Once was a hyena attack, where the animal grabbed a young girl's leg in its jaw and tried to pull her into the jungle. The predator's head was quickly removed, and the others treated the victim's wounds with a poultice.

Another time they came upon a large snake, olive-brown in color and nearly three meters long. It was crossing the path and Omylo held up his hand, stopping everyone and urging them back. Apparently it was dangerous. The forest creature walked up to it carefully, sword ready. With astonishing speed, and no warning, the snake launched itself at her face. But the katana was faster, and the natives were soon roasting the meat over a hastily made fire. Omylo borrowed her knife and cut the snake into equal pieces which they ate silently. A nearby stream provided water. It was their first meal since the rescue but there was plenty of snake to go around.

When they arrived at the village in the jungle there were shrieks of joy and tears of relief. The girl from the jungle was touched again—not impolitely but with curiosity—and received smiles from everyone. Many of them bowed to her.

The girl smiled back. It made her happy, to smile. Emotions, like the ability to feel happiness, were returning.

Everyone talked excitedly, but in a language she could not understand. She did not know there were so many rumors about her, or that they were about to grow further. Now there were eyewitnesses who had seen her command an army of lions to devour her enemies. The forest creature was definitely some kind of spirit because its skin and hair were an unearthly white. They talked among themselves for hours, and it was not long before these first-hand accounts reached other villages.

The girl found herself interested in where she was now living, which was another sign her mind was healing. In the beginning, she'd been interested in nothing but fish.

The huts were circular and made of mud brick with steep roofs of palm fronds supported by wooden boughs. She counted the huts. There were twelve. She knew how to count.

The men wore mostly loin cloths—she knew that word—and the women were in colorful cottony skirts. They wore nothing above the waist. There was a stream nearby that made a pleasant sound as it gurgled its way through the jungle. In the center of all the huts was a large clearing and in the middle was a fire pit. Logs were set around it, and it seemed this was where they were to eat.

Food was brought, and the forest creature was given what seemed the place of honor, on the highest log. Perhaps the village chief normally sat there. She knew what a village chief was.

After living for weeks on fish and water, and part of a snake, the girl was eager for a broader diet. They gave her flattened bread, over which was smeared a black sauce which she discovered later was made from smashed insects. They also had mangoes. She knew that word.

That night they used hand signals to explain where she was to sleep. It was a hastily prepared bed on the floor of one of the huts, this one belonging to a man and woman who had no children and were eager to take her in—at least judging by their smiles and welcoming gestures.

She lay awake and listened to the jungle sounds, which she knew well. The chirping of crickets. The cawing of tropical birds. The leaves of the trees rustling in the wind. In the far distance, she heard a lion roar. She missed Emil and fell asleep thinking of him.

17

THE NEXT MORNING the villagers convened a meeting and were talking seriously about something, but the girl did not know what it was. Finally, Omylo, chosen as the spokesperson, came over and bowed politely. He reached out his hands to hold hers, and she responded, curious what this was about.

"Shari-ya," he said, carefully, looking at her intently. He dropped the hands and pointed to her again, carefully and intently. "Shari-ya." He pointed to himself. "Omylo." Then back to her. "Shari-ya."

They'd given her a name, she realized. That was probably a good idea since she didn't have one.

She touched her chest with both hands. "Shariya?" she asked questioningly.

He nodded eagerly. "Shari-ya. Shariya."

The forest creature liked the name, and everything became easier, now that they could call to her and refer to her. Next, they set about teaching her their language. It was very simple and based mostly around nouns and verbs relevant to jungle life. The girl who now had a name learned quickly. Bread. Paste. Basket. Fire. Hut. Tree. Snake. Girl. Boy. Adult. Child. Sometimes they would draw a picture of a noun, in the dirt, if there was not a sample nearby. Thus she learned lion, hyena, river, and many others.

Verbs came next. Child runs. Boy sits. Adult eats.

And adjectives. Hot bread. Cold water.

In two weeks she could express simple thoughts and communicate with the villagers.

The couple whose hut she shared were named Tololo and Oman. She learned the tasks that were performed as part of their everyday lives. They had plastic buckets with which to bring water from the stream. They gathered wood in the forest for their cooking fires. They had small gardens which needed tending, and a herd of goats which needed shepherding.

As her knowledge of the language increased, she discovered what her name meant. "Shari" was an angel, or spirit. "Ya" was death. They had named her the Angel of Death. Her hair and skin and blue eyes were clearly not of this Earth—no one in the village had ever seen such things. Her amazing fighting skills, a sword that moved impossibly fast, and the command of an army of lions that did her bidding, all were evidence of supernatural origins.

And of course, the "ya" part was from her ability to kill. She was an angel, sent by the heavens, to *kill* the slavers. And hyenas and snakes, too, if needed.

Sometimes the name was shortened. "Shari!" one of them would say and gesture her over. She liked the nickname even more.

Finally, with words she understood, they were able to ask where she was from. She explained that her memories began only weeks ago when she awoke by the river.

The villagers discussed this and found it added significantly to the theory that she was an angel sent down by the gods. Such a creature would likely not know how they came to be created and would awaken fully formed, with magical powers to perform a task. This was clearly what had happened in Shariya's case.

The girl herself doubted it but could produce no evidence to the contrary. She was willing to let them believe it, and maybe it *was* true. Who could say it was not?

Knowing the villagers were always short of meat, occasionally she'd wander into the forest alone, with her weapons, and hunt. The gazelles were too quick, and she wished Emil was with her. Between the two of them, they could bring down any gazelle. Once she was able to gift a small warthog to the village, and they were hugely grateful. Warthog was a delicacy. She delivered two more large snakes, a monkey which she killed with a whirling throw of her hunting knife, and—when she discovered a larger stream—a dozen fish.

What she did not know was that while living peacefully in the primitive tribal village, rumors of her existence were exploding across central Africa. Natives from the village journeyed to others, to nearby markets, and spread the tales.

It had been confirmed. Not only did the forest creature command an army of lions, they would attack humans and devour them on command. There were witnesses to this. Her identity was now known. She was the "Angel of Death," sent by gods to kill the slavers, and thousands had already died by her magic sword and lion army.

When she walked through the forest, an eerie white light emanated from her hair and body. Some held that her army of white lions, with blazing manes, actually had wings, and Shariya would soar across the sky during storms while riding them, the roars of her magical beasts indistinguishable from thunder.

18

One day, returning from a hunt that yielded nothing despite being gone almost a full day, she heard awful noises coming from the village. People were crying, even shrieking. She ran the final distance, hugely puzzled, and learned to her horror what had happened.

Slavers had come while she'd been gone. Nets had been thrown. Guns fired. And this time a full dozen had been seized. But that was not the worst news. Not at all. The woman whose hut she lived in, who had cared for her, was dead. Tololo had tried to fight the slavers, attacking with a spear, and one of them had shot her in the head. The rest had backed off, unable to overcome men with firearms.

She was shown the body. Oman was sobbing in grief, but Shari felt nothing.

Many emotions had returned. She could smile. She could sometimes laugh. She could enjoy the company of the villagers and the satisfaction of hunting food for them. She could even wonder about who she was and think critically on the question. But the death of someone close to her? She felt nothing. That part of her mind had not returned. She could not cry. She could not grieve. The concepts were meaningless. But another emotion had fully returned, and it flooded through her now: anger, and mostly at herself. She had stayed too long in this village. The slavers were growing confident again, and they were back in business. She needed to destroy them completely. They must be exterminated.

She turned away from the body and walked to the fire pit. This was where they'd normally be gathering for dinner, but no one was hungry. Twelve of the village's children had been stolen, and the chance of seeing them again was close to zero. Everyone was in tears. She found Nkole, the chief.

"Where will they take them?" she asked.

"To Nola. There is a slave market there, and it is protected by the local officials, who are corrupt."

"How far is Nola?"

"Two days from here. The slavers have almost a day's head start. The attack was this morning. But with slaves in chains, they will not go fast."

"Can someone guide me to Nola?"

He called to Omylo who hurried over.

"You will take Shariya to Nola. Maybe she can bring our children back."

"Yes," he replied. "I can bring others too. We can fight. We will take spears and knives."

"How many?" asked Shari.

Omylo looked to the chief.

"No more than six, total," he insisted. "We are so few now."

19

Departing at dawn, they were equipped with several days of lightweight food. Omylo and his friends each had a spear or assegai knife, that curved weapon so popular in central Africa. Just before leaving, the village chief brought Shari a gift.

"When you attack, you should wear this veil. It is more than a veil, it will cover your head and face. Try it on, please."

Shari took the black cloth and realized it was a full hood, with a thin lace mesh that would cover her face, but which she could see through easily.

"The women in the village made this for you last night."

"Why should I cover my face?"

"You are a death angel, sent by the gods. It is not right that mortals look upon you."

Shari thanked him, thinking she'd get rid of the thing as soon as possible but for now stuffed it in a pocket. They left the village with the cries of desperate parents still emanating from the huts. But she could sense hope. The Angel of Death was going to fight for them. She had done it before. Maybe she could do it again. Even in a place so impossibly far away as Nola.

As they jogged together on paths through the forest, the villagers wore only their loincloths, and Shari was still dressed in the clothes she'd been wearing on the riverbank. Her hiking sneakers had fallen apart weeks ago but—like the villagers—the soles of her feet were now hard leather and provided almost as much protection.

She still had no idea who she was or where she had come from, but she didn't think about it very much. She liked the simplicity of having a clear mission and using her skills for a purpose. Her past was an impenetrable dark void, but no longer was she adrift, without a goal. She was going to destroy the slavers permanently. Although she had no idea how to do that.

She knew nothing about the Nola slave market, nor did her band of tribesmen. No one had seen it.

Shari was desperate for real knowledge: about the slave market, who controlled it, whether it operated with the approval of the town leaders in Nolo itself, and, if so, who was being bribed to accommodate it.

Most of these concepts were simply too complex with her limited vocabulary. But Omylo had been to Nola itself, and she pried from him what information she could.

Was it bigger than their own village? Yes. How much bigger? Very much bigger. He tried to explain other things, but she didn't understand the words. She wanted to ask if there were cars and trucks and large buildings, and as these questions formed in her mind, she suddenly realized she knew what these things were. She knew about cities. She had images in her mind of bicycles and motor scooters and Land Rovers and swarms and swarms of people. So many people! She even had memories of people who looked like her. But it was all a distant, vague dream, nothing she could use to determine who she was or how she came to be here.

When she tried to clarify those visions, recall those dreams, she sensed something terrifying beneath the surface. Some horrible, awful thing her brain would not allow her to access. Even trying to think about the "before" time caused her to become nauseous. Once, she had fallen to her knees and vomited. So she left it alone. Whatever dreadful secret was behind that door, best it stayed there.

20

By the second morning after leaving the village they were on the outskirts of Nola, now following a dirt road that would lead to the town center. Whenever she heard a vehicle approach, as occasionally one did, she had them step a few yards into the jungle and disappear.

Their biggest challenge, Shari knew, was to find the slave market itself, but—just outside town—they came across a clearing in the jungle. She gestured to the others to stop and stay in the trees. She moved closer.

It was a grass-covered open space, several acres in size, roughly a square. The grass looked freshly mowed and exuded a heavy scent, made dense by the morning's humidity. The forest itself was quiet, and the day so far was clear. The sun had risen moments ago, but most of the area was still in shadow.

There was a wide parking area adjacent to the road and to Shari's left. On the opposite side of the square was a long, thin building, made of cinder blocks and with a metal roof. Near the roofline, there were holes in the concrete, each roughly a foot square, perhaps intended to provide light and air.

She could see only one door. A guard was sitting in a wooden chair beside it, possibly asleep.

In the clearing itself were multiple iron poles, about three meters high. From each hung a set of iron manacles, which could be raised or lowered as needed via pulley at the top. A slave affixed in such a position would be easy for a buyer to inspect.

There were two Land Rovers in the parking area. Suddenly another vehicle roared up. It was an army transport truck, the kind used for carrying troops. The truck pulled in beside the Land Rovers, honking its horn to signal arrival.

The guard jumped up quickly, and Shari noticed he was armed with a handgun.

She knew what a handgun was. Her mind was releasing information the moment it was required. When she saw the Land Rovers she knew what they were and what they were like inside. The troop transports were things she'd seen before and understood.

Two men climbed down from the truck's cab, and half a dozen others emerged from the Land Rovers.

As Shari watched, two more men came out of the small door in the building, and between them was a line of about thirty slaves. They were each shackled to a chain that held them together, and their legs were in chains as well, permitting only limited movement.

The men attached each end of the chain to metal posts, so the slaves were between them, available for inspection. Shari recognized several of those from her own village, which meant they'd arrived in time.

Security was minimal. No one feared slaves in chains. The single armed guard was deemed sufficient.

They were about to find out he wasn't.

Shariya's six *warriors* would only need to overcome ten unarmed men. She would kill the guard herself.

She outlined a plan. They were to stay hidden, moving in as close as possible without being seen. She would circle around to the other side of the brick building and approach the guard silently from behind.

On instinct, she retrieved the veiled hood she'd been given back at the village. There might be a tactical advantage in keeping her face hidden after all, she thought. Her hunting knife was in its scabbard tied to her right leg. The sword was on her back.

The moment the guard was killed, and no sooner, the warriors were to race across the field and kill or capture anyone not a slave. It was easy to know the difference. The slaves were in chains.

She explained it was essential to capture alive at least one of the slavers, for questioning, but she barely got her wish. When they saw her cut the guard's throat, it triggered a blood lust, and the tribal warriors raced across the short distance, screaming battle cries and brandishing spears and knives. The unarmed slavers, looking up in horror, died quickly.

"Stop!" Shari screamed as the last was about to be killed. The warrior with the assegai knife heard the command and then remembered the orders. He dropped the weapon sheepishly and grinned at Shari.

It took only minutes for slave shackles to be placed on the remaining slaver himself and removed from all those who'd been in bondage.

She ordered Omylo to ask the freed slaves to move the bodies out of sight and into the forest. She assigned two of the warriors to come with her and bring their captive. They entered the low, brick building, the slave prison, and the stench was sickening. Inside were individual cells with steel gratings and lockable doors. Straw lined the floors, and the smell of urine and feces was overwhelming. She noticed there was nothing more than a bucket in each cell, filled with human waste.

There were more manacles and chains affixed to the walls. A set of keys was hung on a spike opposite each cell door. Her prisoner was quickly secured in one of the cells, and the door locked. She told the warriors to guard him but kept the keys herself.

Shari returned to the clearing, desperate to be out of the awful slave quarters. She noted approvingly that the bodies had vanished.

The forest creature hadn't thought this far ahead. What was the next step? Return to the village? No. The slave trade must be utterly destroyed, not just a few slavers killed. Otherwise, they'd come back. But she couldn't do it alone.

Guessing most of the freed slaves would speak the villagers' language, she turned to them now.

"I am the Angel of Death. The men who rescued you are my army. It is the *Army of Death.*"

That name came to her suddenly, an inspiration. It sounded scary. Army of Death. Having an army with a scary name might yield a tactical advantage.

"You are now free. You may return to your own villages, your own homes. Or if you wish you may join my army. There may be other slave markets, and other slaves to free."

Shari noticed that about a third of the captives were young women, no doubt being trafficked for sexual purposes. Most of the others were young men in their prime, destined for fieldwork. She wasn't sure if she wanted young women as part of her army. On the other hand, it was unclear how they would survive the journey back to their homes—especially if she absconded with all the men. She'd worry about that later.

"If you join my Army of Death, you will obey my orders. The penalty for disobedience is to be dismissed and never allowed to return. Please consider your decision. I will be back shortly."

Once inside the hut, she asked the guards to wait outside. She wished to question the prisoner alone.

He didn't speak the tribal language she'd learned, but no doubt realized if they couldn't establish communication quickly, he'd likely be killed. He tried several alternatives.

And then she heard, *"Parlez vous francais?"*

Yes, of course she spoke French. That was the one language she did speak. She always thought in French but hadn't spoken it aloud since waking on the riverbank. Still, the words came easily.

"Yes, I speak French," Shari replied, subconsciously slipping into the Parisian accent because she remembered for some reason she'd get in trouble if she spoke it differently.

"Who—who *are* you?" asked the captive. "Why did you kill

my men? Do you know we pay good protection money to the local authorities! They will execute you for what you have done!"

"I am the Angel of Death," she said simply. "I cannot be killed for I am already dead."

Perhaps he would believe that. And then another inspiration came to her. "No mortal may look upon me and live. That is why I am covered. Anyone who sees my face melts instantly into a puddle of steaming tar. Would you like to see my face?" She reached for the veil, as if ready to remove it and destroy him with a glance.

The prisoner was visibly frightened. He began shivering and tried to cover his own face with manacled hands, head turning away. "No! Don't show me your face!" he screamed. "Let me live!"

"Very well. I will now ask you questions. If you do not answer my questions, I will remove my veil, you will see my face, and you will join me in the death world. If you give me dishonest answers, I will remove my veil. I will know if you are lying. Mortals cannot hide truths from me."

"Anything, I will answer anything! Please, just don't show me your face!"

Shari grinned beneath her hood, thrilled to discover the power it gave her, the mere threat to reveal her face. She also realized that once this rumor circulated, about how it was instant death to gaze upon her, far from anyone trying to discover her identity, or even forcibly remove her veil, they would now do anything to *not* see her face. That could be useful in many ways, she imagined.

"Very well. You know slavery is illegal in Central African Republic."

The words came to her lips easily. Before that instant she did not know what country she was in, or that there were countries. But suddenly, when she needed to, she did. It was a strange phenomenon, her mind releasing information on demand.

She knew what slavery was. She knew it was illegal though still practiced. She knew she was in a country called Central African Republic, or CAR, and that its capital was Bangui.

The moment she thought about most anything she found information easily accessed. She had only to consider a subject, and another door would open. Except, of course, the door she was not able to open. And didn't want to open. Now she asked questions of her prisoner as if she were an expert on African slavery, and how it functioned.

"If slavery is illegal, then obviously you were bribing local officials to permit the operation of this slave market, correct? A few moments ago you admitted it."

"Yes," said the prisoner, now cooperating fully but hesitant to look at her directly.

"Who do you pay?"

"We pay Monsier Argona, the provincial governor. He orders everyone to ignore us."

"Does this Monsier Argona have police, an army, people with guns?"

"Oh yes, all those things. The commander of the Provincial Guard reports to him, and the Guard is a kind of private army, although technically it's part of the national forces. There are also police, but they do not carry weapons and they are not very powerful. The Guard has the power."

"How many men in this Guard, and where are they located?"

She was already thinking tactically, not knowing each moment what question she would ask next, and the questions coming out almost automatically.

"In terms of numbers, maybe a thousand. And they're almost always stationed at the Provincial Guard base in Mintaka, the capital of Nyata Province. That's where Argona lives."

"And here locally, are there police, any authorities?"

"I think there is one policeman, maybe. If he suspects trouble, he phones someone in Mintaka and the Guard arrives."

"In trucks, large trucks?" Shari had a memory of seeing large trucks carrying troops back in Bangui. "Like that one?" She pointed to the army convoy vehicle by the Land Rovers.

"Yes, the trucks hold I believe about twenty men each, and usually they travel in groups of two. Forty men with modern weapons can handle most any problem in the whole country. No one else is allowed to own or possess weapons, except for the guardsmen."

"What about the man you had at the door? He was armed."

"He was an off-duty guardsman, who we hire when needed."

"If trucks were to come here, to Nola, from Mintaka, how would they arrive, on which road?"

"On this road, from that direction." He gestured to the left.

"How long would it take for them to arrive from Mintaka?"

"A little over an hour."

"Very well. I will return shortly."

Shari walked back to the open field to speak with Omylo, who had become a de facto officer.

"Shari," he said, "the slaves have all volunteered. They want to join your army."

"That would give us thirty plus our six, and about ten of the slaves are women."

"Yes."

"How can we feed and care for so many?"

"With an army that large, we can take any food we want."

"No. We are not a band of thieves. Have some of the men go back to the bodies and search them. They must have money. I don't mind robbing dead slavers."

They did have money, quite a bit. Over 10,000 CFA Francs, the national currency. But Shari didn't know how much that was.

After explaining her plan to Omylo, who embraced it immediately, she went back to her prisoner.

"First, how much would a kilo of wheat cost in CFA francs?" After he replied she did the arithmetic and knew she could feed her army for a month if necessary. She had the beginnings of a treasury.

"Second, I will allow you to live, at least for now, if you obey my orders."

"Of course I will!" he replied, clearly desperate to survive.

"Do you know where in the village the policeman is?"

"Yes, I know his house."

"Go there now. Take one of the Land Rovers. Arrive scared and breathless. Tell him there has been a slave revolt and only you escaped. In other words, the truth."

"If I tell him that, he will call Mintaka and the guard will be sent."

"When he is on the phone making the call, leave immediately and come back here. If you do not return, I will find you and kill you. No matter where you go in Africa, I will know where you are, and you will die. If you return and follow my orders, you will live."

"How do I know you will keep your word?"

"I am the Angel of Death, a spiritual creature. I am not physically capable of lying. If I tried to lie, I would myself dissolve into a puddle of steaming tar."

"Oh."

Shari released him, and he drove off in one of the Land Rovers. He was back in twenty minutes.

"I'm sure the trucks are already on the way," he reported. "I left as you ordered when the policeman was making the call."

Omylo and the slaves prepared what was needed, and at the expected time Shari could hear the trucks approaching from a distance. Large engines rumbling, gears grinding, occasionally the squeal of brakes. They would be intimidating, she thought, from their noise alone.

It was as simple as a trap could be. As the two army vehicles approached Nola, they encountered a barricade made of logs and cement blocks. The moment they stopped, two things happened. First, another barricade was placed behind them, by the efforts of a dozen men who swiftly pulled logs from out of the forest and onto the road. Second, and almost simultaneously, the trucks were attacked by an army of freed slaves rushing at them from two sides, and most now armed with a knife, a spear, or in some cases a large rock.

It happened so quickly, and was so unexpected, those in the trucks had no time to react, and it would have made no difference anyway. The guardsmen of Nyata Province were not experienced in combat. In their entire careers, they'd never had to fight anyone. They just showed up, in their impressive uniforms, with their trucks and their weapons, and any local disturbance ended quickly.

In this case, their weapons were not even loaded. The ammunition was in boxes in the second truck. And no one had thought to equip the guardsmen with knives. Defenseless, they were killed mercilessly by the slave army.

Except for one. Shari had assigned herself to the first truck, and to the two men in the front: the driver and a passenger who was likely an officer. She killed the driver and captured the other man, handing him off immediately to Omylo who—following orders—soon had him in irons and guarded.

Shari was not pleased with the massacre. Unlike the slavers, these guardsmen were not evil men—or no more evil than most men, she reasoned. Yet she'd seen no way to defeat military troops other than via this ruthless maneuver. And she had to defeat these troops if she was to topple the corrupt governor of the province who was enabling the slave trade.

At least there were no prisoners to deal with. And in future battles, she'd try to find ways to minimize the killing. The Angel of Death was surprised to discover she had a conscience and wondered where it had come from. She'd had nothing of the sort back in the jungle.

Shari had no military experience. But the steps needed came naturally. Perhaps in her past, she'd read books that had talked about battles, and the element of surprise. The name of one came to her suddenly: *The Art of War*. She remembered it was about tricking your enemy and always doing the unexpected.

She'd now won two "battles" and her casualties were zero. The element of surprise was the most important element in warfare, she realized. She couldn't imagine how you'd accomplish anything with an army if you didn't make everything a surprise. Otherwise, people would just kill each other until one side or the other surrendered. That sounded ridiculous.

She wondered how to keep the surprise going. And the answer was obvious. The captured officer spoke French, and—with only the mildest of inducements—agreed to work for his captors. Shari wasn't certain he bought into her divine nature, or the instant death even a glimpse of her face would cause. But it didn't matter. His own men were dead, and he understood he was being kept alive only so long as he cooperated.

So he cooperated.

Shari was pleased to discover the trucks themselves carried enough provisions to feed her army for up to a week. Better and better. At her direction, Omylo and his men removed the uniforms from the dead and hid the bodies in the forest. Some had cash on them, and her treasury expanded by that much. The log barriers also vanished, and Shari ordered that a quick meal be given to her "troops." It was difficult to believe it had only been two hours since the attack on the slave market had begun. This was their first chance to eat or drink anything.

With their morale high from being rescued, their victory in battle, and ample food and water, Shari's Army of Death was eager for whatever came next.

21

Just over an hour later, the two trucks had completed the return journey and were approaching their headquarters compound at Mintaka.

The officer whose life she'd spared was still cooperating, in this case by driving the lead vehicle with Shari in the passenger's seat. He would do the talking as needed when they arrived at the compound.

The ex-slaver drove the second truck, with Omylo beside him. The young man had been told to kill the slaver if he didn't follow the first truck precisely. And she'd translated the orders into French so the driver would know.

The slave army, now wearing the uniforms of those they'd conquered, was divided between the two trucks. None had ever ridden in a motorized vehicle, nor did they know how to use the rifles Shari had issued them. But they could hold them, which was all that mattered.

The sentry at the gate of the compound recognized the officer driving the first truck, saluted, and waved them through. Rather than park normally, the two trucks drove to a large cement and tin-roofed building on the far side of the base. They pulled up to the door, which was guarded by another sentry. Shariya, still wearing her veiled hood, climbed out of the truck and killed him swiftly and silently, with her knife. She had a conscience, but she also knew these provincial guards were protecting the slave trade. And capturing the armory was critical.

She arrayed half her Army of Death in front of the armory, holding their rifles visibly. They were told to allow no one in. She knew the guns were useless in their hands, but some still had their assegai knives as well, which weren't useless.

Before anyone on the base understood what was happening, the remaining guardsmen in the province had been neutralized, because now they could not access their weapons.

Unless a patrol was sent out, such as the one meant for Nola, all weapons were kept in locked boxes, inside the armory. Shari had learned this from the officer on the drive from Nola.

It had never occurred to anyone that the armory itself might be captured.

The guard officer-turned-traitor now led Shari and the remainder of the slave army to a small headquarters office that housed the unit's commanding officer, a colonel who reported directly to the Governor. He'd had a late breakfast and was taking a nap in a large reclining armchair.

He woke up quickly.

Shari informed him she was the Angel of Death and explained that her Army of Death had killed the men sent to Nola, confiscated their trucks, and had just captured the armory.

The Commanding Officer was given two choices. Join the Army of Death, with all his guardsmen, or be turned over to her lions who were already growing hungry.

Everyone had heard of Shariya's army of lions. It was not a difficult decision.

"My troops are yours, Shariya," he agreed eagerly. "And I am yours to command."

The officers of provincial troops in Africa had many qualities, but loyalty wasn't one of them. The moment any kind of coup or shifting of power occurred, they would always choose the side that was winning. And Shariya—with a rapidly growing army—was clearly winning. If the choice being offered was to join her, or die, few would choose the latter.

"Very well, Colonel," she said. "I will leave you in command of your men, and you'll retain your rank. You now report to me."

"Yes, Shariya," he replied. "What are your orders?"

"Please assemble your troops and explain that they have joined the Army of Death, led by the Angel of Death. Please let them know that I wear the veil to hide my face. Any mortal who sees it will immediately dissolve into a puddle of steaming tar."

"It's true," confirmed the guardsman whose life she'd spared, and who now wanted to prove his loyalty. "It happened by accident to three of our men in Nola. The wind briefly removed her veil and those who saw her face died screaming as they melted."

Shariya suspected such nonsense would only be believed in West Africa where everyone grew up listening to horrific tales of the occult and the consequences to those who angered the spirits. She doubted the colonel—no doubt an educated man—was buying it, but the more rumors the better.

When the assembled guardsmen were informed of their changed allegiance, little emotion was shown. They didn't care who they worked for. And far better to be part of Shariya's Army of Death than to be killed by it.

Her force was now over a thousand strong and consisted mostly of real soldiers.

"Colonel, please bring a dozen of your best men, with weapons, and take us to the governor's residence. Is it far?"

"No, Shariya. We can walk there. It is just outside the base."

Two sentries guarded the door to the mansion but, because they reported to the colonel, stepped aside on his orders.

Shari ordered the platoon to wait outside, while she and the officer walked in and found the governor in his study.

"What's all this?" demanded the governor of Nyata Province, looking up from his desk in surprise.

"I'm Shariya, the Angel of Death," she explained yet again. "I have destroyed the slavers in Nola. The platoon of provincial guards you sent down to stop me are all dead. Your entire guard unit here in Nyata, over a thousand men, has joined my Army of Death."

"We have," confirmed the Guard commander.

The governor leapt to his feet so fast his chair fell over backward.

"I, I didn't think you existed! I thought it was just a superstitious rumor."

"I exist, and I cannot be killed because I am already dead. I was sent by the gods from the land of the dead. And you should know that if you look upon my face you will die. That is why I stay veiled. For your protection."

"You have destroyed the slave market at Nola and conquered my entire provincial guard just *this morning?* You *must* be a supernatural force. Those guardsmen require half a day just to raise a tent!"

"You have two choices," she said, her story becoming more convincing with each telling. "You declare your loyalty to me, the Angel of Death, in which case you may continue as governor of this province and keep your home, and your income, and even your bribes. Slavery has ended, but in every other way, nothing will change."

"Except I will report to you."

"Yes, and you cede your army to me one hundred percent. It is now part of the Army of Death. I will personally guarantee the safety of your province, but the Army itself is under my command."

"And the other choice?"

"I will feed you alive to my lions, and whatever remains of your carcass, I will dump in a public latrine, where your spirit will be trapped for all eternity as your bones sink to the bottom of a pit of feces."

The governor stared at her in horror.

"My lions have not yet been fed today," she added. "Please make your choice."

"Your first offer is most generous, Shariya. I accept."

"A wise decision." Without invitation, she sat down in the chair opposite his desk and urged the governor to be seated as well.

He recovered his chair and joined her at the desk. The Colonel stood at ease behind Shariya.

"Tell me about the slave trade in this country," she ordered. "Is there one person who controls it, and do you know who it is?"

"In CAR there is very much one person who controls it. He is our country's President for Life, President Otangi."

"He controls the slave trade from his palace in Bangui?"

"Yes."

"Is he there now?"

"Probably. I was there yesterday meeting with him. The president had just returned from an international trip and was very busy. I understand he is going nowhere for at least two weeks."

"How far is Bangui from here, and how are the roads?"

"It is three hours by road. They are not so good, but the army trucks can handle them."

"Are you familiar with what military forces are in the area of Bangui, how many, where they are located, and so forth?"

"Certainly."

Sharia quizzed him for nearly thirty minutes and then announced her plans.

"We're going to Bangui to capture the president and stop the slave trade. Both of you will come with me. If either refuses to cooperate, I will remove my veil. And then slit your throat with my knife."

Again, she doubted they were buying the puddle of tar story, but there were already plenty of dead bodies in her wake. So she was either an occult who could kill with a glance, or she wasn't, in which case she'd kill with a blade.

"Of course I will cooperate," the governor assured her hastily.

"And I have already pledged my loyalty," confirmed the colonel.

She stood up and was just beginning to turn towards the door when she sensed movement as if the governor were reaching into a drawer. The gun was not even in firing position when her sword was out. She spun her body and had both hands on the hilt for maximum force when the blade reached the governor's neck. It passed through so swiftly that at first it seemed nothing had happened. Then the bureaucrat's head fell off its torso, dropped to the floor, and rolled slowly until coming to rest against a rubbish bin. It stopped there as if waiting for someone to put it in.

The colonel walked over to the severed head, reached down, grabbed it by the hair, and dropped it in.

"Congratulations, Colonel," she said. "You are now governor of this province. At least if we're successful in Bangui."

"We will be," he said grimly.

By noon the colonel had five hundred men loaded in trucks, fully armed. At Shari's request, he'd found someone else in the ranks who could speak Omylo's language and ordered his number two, a lieutenant colonel, to maintain order until he returned—and also to deliver the freed slaves back to their villages. Her slave army had given her a real one. The others could, and should, return home.

Shari spoke to Omylo.

"I will not be going back with you, my friend. I'm heading to the nation's capital to complete the job of stopping the slavers. It's going to take a real army, with guns, and that's what I now have, thanks to you and what you did. It's time to go home now. Your mission is complete."

"I understand, Shari. Thank you for rescuing our people."

"Omylo, you became a warrior today. You were victorious in battle—twice. Never forget your status as a warrior."

He smiled, beaming from the compliment.

"If I'm able, I will come visit. In the meantime, here, take the money." She handed him the cash they'd found on the slavers and the other guard troops. Please give some of it to Oman so he can rebuild his life and maybe find a new love. Tell him I'm sorry I wasn't there to protect Tololo. But I'm making sure there will never again be another slaver attack on the village. You keep the rest of the money and use it as you wish."

Shari knew it was a fortune for the young man. "Omylo, thank you for rescuing me from the jungle."

They embraced. Shari realized it was the first time she'd embraced anyone since waking up by the river.

22

The trucks moved as quickly as possible over the torn-up highway. Civil war had turned it into something resembling a jeep trail, and road repair was never a high priority in central Africa.

The colonel drove the lead truck, and Shari rode with him, still concealed behind her black lace.

Africa was accustomed to the slow rhythms of the rain forest, and the sedentary ebb and flow of sub-Saharan politics. A president-for-life might eventually lie, cheat and bribe his way to the top and, once there, use his power to destroy enemies. But it would take years. And if he were eventually to be replaced, that—also—would take years.

Blitzkrieg tactics were unknown in this part of the world, and Shari was going to gamble everything on them.

She'd started the day with six tribal warriors carrying assegai knives. Now she was in command of a thousand-man army, five hundred of whom were with her in the trucks, all equipped with modern weapons. But she was still covered in black, her outfit now including a pair of dark gloves she'd found in Mintaka and which on instinct she'd grabbed.

Shari felt the spirit of Sun Tzu guiding her. Yes, she remembered him fully now, and all of his wisdom.

As they entered Bangui, the Colonel steered the convoy directly to the headquarters of military power in the capital: the presidential guard barracks, less than a kilometer from the Palace. He and Shari had spent the three-hour drive considering tactics and had decided on a replay of how she'd neutered the Provincial Guard in Mintaka: by seizing the armory.

But this time as the truck convoy approached the barracks gate, rather than stop and ask permission to enter—which might easily not be granted without confirmation from higher authority—the lead truck picked up speed and hit the gate at forty kilometers an hour.

The chain-link barrier broke apart and was tossed aside like twigs as the trucks proceeded directly to the base armory. As ordered they parked in a semi-circle around the building's entrance, and the men under her command took position behind them, automatic weapons pointing outwards. There was now no force in the country that could break through this defensive perimeter and access the weapons.

Predictably, it was only minutes before the commanding officer of the base drove up in a Jeep with his own guards.

"What the hell is going on here!" he yelled.

"What is your name and title," Shari demanded.

"General Barasa, Commander of the Presidential Guard. And who the hell are you?"

"Leave your guns and your guards with the Jeep, and you may approach," Shari called out.

Soon he was standing beside her, inside the crescent of troops from Mintaka.

"You do not know who I am?" she asked, knowing it was an absurd question because of the veil.

"I have no idea who you are, or why these provincial troops have broken into the presidential guard compound. But there's going to be hell to pay."

"I am Shariya, the Angel of Death," she explained matter-of-factly.

The commanding officer froze, suddenly unsure.

"This morning I conquered Nyata Province, and the governor's head now lies in a rubbish bin by his desk. The colonel commanding Nyata's provincial troops has sworn loyalty to me. I am now going to capture President Otangi and end slavery in CAR. Do you wish to help me, or do you believe Otangi and the slave trade should be allowed to continue?"

The officer stared at her in silence, obviously calculating.

"Take your time," she encouraged. "It's an important decision."

"Your purpose is to stop slavery?"

"Yes, completely."

He turned away from her, looking at the compound now laced with shadow from the late-day sun. Then he turn back and regarded her closely.

"May we talk privately? There's an office just past those doors."

Shari gave orders to the Colonel and soon she was alone with the regiment's CO, sitting on opposite sides of a simple desk. The officer spoke first.

"Please, how do I address you?"

"Use my nickname, Shari."

"Very well." The officer paused, staring at something in the far distance. Finally, he spoke. "Shari, I once lived in a tribal village, many years ago, in northwest Kenya. My niece was stolen from us when she was twelve. We never saw her again but learned later she was killed trying to escape."

"Killed by slavers?"

"Yes."

"What is your full name, General, and who do you report to?"

"General Pili Barasa, at your service. And I report to Field Marshal Togoli who commands all military forces in CAR. However…"

"Yes, General?"

"If you are here to stop the slave trade…"

"Yes?"

"I will help you. There's never before been a force that had the power to do anything. But perhaps you are that force."

"Are you willing to report to me?"

"Yes. It's past time someone removed that corrupt slaver from the palace."

"Where is the Field Marshal?"

"Conveniently, on a safari vacation in Chinko Nature Reserve, many hours east of here."

"Are there any military units that could cause trouble for us, that we need to subdue?"

"Well, other than the presidential guard forces themselves, which I command, there are the forces stationed in each province. By far the most powerful is in Nyata Province, but apparently, they now report to *you*."

"Correct."

"The other provincial forces are not a threat if you control both the presidential guard and the Nyata regiment. With the field marshal on safari, I can contact each of them on my personal authority and say the palace has changed hands, and we have a new leader. I can ask them to bring the bulk of their men immediately to Bangui and invite them to swear allegiance. This will allow us to concentrate all the forces around the capital, in case there's trouble. "

"How long will that take?"

"Twenty-four hours, depending on road conditions. It is dry season, so the roads should be passable."

"General, if we can capture or kill the president, and if you can bring in the other provincial generals and obtain their loyalty, you will be promoted to ruler of all my forces in CAR."

"And what will you do with the field marshal?"

"Is he competent?"

"He is the nephew of the president," said Barasa with a neutral expression, as if that explained everything. Which it did, thought Shari.

"We will deal with him later. Where is President Otangi?"

"In his palace, as he almost always is at this hour. At least I assume so."

It was four p.m.

"We need to capture him. How would you suggest we proceed?"

"A platoon of my soldiers can overcome the palace guards. Especially if I lead it personally. May I have that honor?"

"Yes, but I'll go with you. How far is the palace from here, and how quickly can we begin?"

"Very close. Less than a kilometer. We'll arrive in convoy trucks, with flags flying. I'll address the guards at the gate, and they'll allow us to pass. Then, we'll just need to get past the palace guards inside. They may prove more formidable, but we'll fight them if needed."

"What kind of weapons do we have?"

"Automatic rifles of course. And rocket-propelled grenades if we need to breach the entrance."

"Very well. Choose your best men, and I will meet the convoy at the gate. I'll want someone to show me how to use an RPG. Can you do that?"

"Yes, of course."

Soon, a pair of convoy trucks were roaring through the streets of downtown Bangui, ceremonial CAR flags flying from the lead vehicle, driven by General Barasa. Shari was in the passenger seat. Each truck carried twenty armed soldiers who'd been told their commander had changed allegiances, and they would be assaulting the palace. Volunteers were requested and easily obtained. The corrupt, venal, and ineffectual president-for-life who lived there was not well-loved. Again, when it came to African coups, all that mattered was choosing the winning side.

And by now the rumor had spread. Shariya, the Angel of Death, the mystical creature who commanded an army of lions, was leading this rebellion. It was not difficult to know who would win.

In other respects, it was just another hot and dusty afternoon in Bangui. Military trucks carrying soldiers were a frequent sight. The palace came into view and Shariya realized she'd seen it before, in that life-behind-the-door. But she'd never been inside.

The trucks rolled to a stop at the gate, protected by a guardhouse. A sentry approached, but when he saw the general, saluted crisply.

"Open the gate, Sergeant, President Otangi is in danger, and we've been sent to protect him."

"Sir, I've received no such orders, I know nothing about this."

"We've just learned it ourselves. There's a renegade military unit from Nyata Province with a full battalion of rebels on its way to stage a coup. They'll be here within the hour. Now, who's going to stop them, you? Open the gate immediately or I'll inform the president that you're in league with the rebels!"

"Sir, sir, General, I know nothing about…Yes sir, 'er just a moment. Of course sir, I assure you I'm completely loyal to President Otangi!"

"Very well, prove your loyalty!"

"Sir, yes sir."

The sentry waved to the two others inside and the gate opened. The trucks rushed through, heading directly for the steps of the palace. Shari saw one of the guards make a phone call and knew the element of surprise was over for the day.

It was unfortunate, or perhaps deliberate, that the presidential grounds were so vast that the gate was several hundred meters from the palace entrance. Their trucks were not built for speed, even less for acceleration, and they consumed a precious sixty seconds covering the distance.

Just as they arrived, Shariya saw the double front door, a massive affair of steel that swung outward, close ominously. Worse, upstairs several windows opened. Rifles were now pointing at the lead truck.

No fools were these palace guards. They would not be intimidated into opening that door—meant for moments such as these.

The truck driven by Barasa pulled in front of the steps, arcing to the right before stopping, so the general himself could hop out and face the building.

The platoon climbed down swiftly from the trucks and formed up in soldierly rows behind their general. Shari slipped out the side door and climbed into the back, out of sight.

"What's the meaning of this, General?" called down a voice which spoke with authority from an open window on the top floor. "You have no authorization to enter the palace grounds without invitation."

"Mr. President, please excuse me. There was no time. We've just learned a renegade battalion from Nyata province is heading here to attempt a coup. These men were the only ones I could bring instantly to protect you. More are on the way."

"Very well, General. If this is true, you did the right thing. Please form your men up as you see fit in front of the palace entrance. Let no one pass."

Something roared past the general's head, missing it by inches. An explosion nearly knocked everyone off their feet as the metal doors exploded inwards violently.

Shari threw down the rocket-propelled grenade launcher and rushed through the doorway. General Barasa and his men followed through the smoke.

Automatic weapons fire erupted just inside, and Shariya ducked under a nearby staircase for protection.

Barasa's troops returned fire, and soon there were the screams and shrieks Shariya was used to when living things were killed or wounded. After the initial volley, it seemed everyone needed to reload simultaneously. On impulse, she raced up the stairway and found a soldier fumbling with a magazine. She sliced his throat and hurled his body off the balcony, to make a statement.

Encouraged, her men followed up the stairs. There were wounded everywhere, broken glass, bullet holes in the walls, smoke permeating the scene. Five more times Shariya met resistance and killed rapidly with her knife or sword. She understood that these African soldiers—probably never before in a real battle—would not conserve ammunition. Once they pulled back on the triggers they'd not let up until a magazine was empty.

Which meant when a particular gun quit firing, she could advance, and did—with astonishing speed and agility. Her soldiers watched as she performed what to them seemed an intricate dance of death, pivoting rapidly, using her arms, her legs, her blades like some supernatural being—which they already knew her to be.

The artistry of a world-class Shinkendo expert, whose skill had been honed by weeks of violence in the jungle, was something no one in the world had ever seen; certainly no one in Bangui.

She came to a large oak door and guessed this would be the president's last redoubt. Setting down her sword, she flew across the open space and leaped into the air in a classic Tae Kwon Do flying sidekick, worthy of any third-degree black belt in Korea. Although she weighed just over a hundred pounds, her outstretched foot hit the obstacle with such force it smashed the lock easily and the twin doors exploded inwards.

Shariya rolled swiftly as she made contact with the floor, continuing her forward motion, and escaping the shotgun blast that roared out from the weapon held by the man in a suit and tie standing in front of her. She was on him in an instant, and he died with a knife in his throat.

Suddenly everything was quiet.

Catching her breath, allowing the killing fever to flow out of her, she looked around the room calmly.

In a far corner, behind a desk, was another man. He, also, was in a suit, his hands on the desk, palms down, looking at her calmly. There seemed no threat. When General Barasa rushed in moments later, with half a dozen soldiers, she held up her hand, stopping further violence.

Shariya glanced again at the mysterious man in the corner, surprised anyone could sit calmly in the midst of a battle. Or perhaps he was bright enough to realize that sitting still was the only way to survive it. She'd worry about him later.

"Is the palace secure?" she asked, turning to the general.

"Yes, although we have some mopping up to do."

As if to confirm, intermittent rifle fire could be heard in the courtyard.

She gestured to the man with his throat cut, dead on the floor. "Is that President Otangi?"

"Yes. I thought you wanted him alive."

"He had a shotgun."

"It's better this way."

"I wonder how many slaves died or were sold into misery, from the trade he enabled."

"Thousands, I would think. What are my orders, Shariya?"

"Your orders are to do whatever you think necessary to secure the rest of the country, as we discussed. The moment you've obtained signed declarations of loyalty from the other provincial generals and have captured or killed the field marshal, you take his place. You will be in overall command of CAR's military and report directly to me."

"Yes, Shariya."

"Try to keep everything that has happened confidential. There has been a change at the palace. That's all anyone needs to know, and most don't even need to know that. Please give your own orders, and report back to me by—" she checked a clock on the wall, suddenly remembering how to tell time, "—let's say, seven p.m. Leave these troops here, reporting to me in your absence. Also, have someone remove the bodies from the palace, starting with that one. Give care to the wounded. There's to be no more killing, if possible."

"Yes, Shariya. And congratulations. You are the new leader of our nation." He left the room swiftly.

She stared after him, trying to process that concept. She wasn't sure she wanted to be the leader of a nation, least of all this one.

She'd tried to rescue a dozen slaves this morning and had inadvertently taken over the whole country. How had that happened?

Then, unbidden, came the memory of Tololo stretched out on the floor of the hut with a bullet hole in her forehead, eyes staring lifelessly, while Oman sobbed beside her. She could still feel no grief. She could not cry, let alone sob. She did not know how. But she could stop the slavers who had done this thing. That was her guiding principle and she clung to it.

She had no others.

23

When the soldiers and the body of the former president were gone, Shari walked over to the doors with the broken locks and closed them best she could. Then she turned to the quiet man in the corner, who it seemed had not so much as blinked.

He was slender and graying slightly at the temples. African, but dressed as a Westerner in an expensive suit and tie—surprised she understood such concepts. But everything was coming back to her now. Except for the important things.

The man looked at her with curiosity, remaining motionless. If he was afraid, he did not betray it.

Shari sat down across from him at the desk, studying the man closely. His eyes were now downcast, as if to confirm he was no threat.

"I hope we didn't disturb you," she said finally.

He looked up and responded in perfect French, smiling. "Not at all. I'm here for a job interview."

"What position were you applying for?"

"Chief of Staff to the president. If hired, it would have been a position of considerable power, essentially second to the president himself. I brought my résumé," he said, smiling even more broadly.

Shariya laughed out loud. Perhaps it was the after-effects of the fighting, but she used laughter now to avoid trembling in shock—as she thought she might do otherwise. Despite her training, this was her first full-scale battle.

"Do you have a name?"

"Eduardo Danjuma, at your service," he said, dipping his head respectfully.

"Where are you from, Mr. Danjuma? And please move your hands. Make yourself comfortable."

"Thank you." He leaned back in his chair, arms now comfortably at his side. "And I hope you'll call me Eduardo. I was born in Lagos, Nigeria. My father is a prominent businessman, connected with the petroleum industry. But I was raised in Barcelona, where he was stationed for fifteen years. In Spain, my parents gave me the name Eduardo, so I'd fit in better at school."

Sharia knew where Nigeria was, and also Barcelona, Spain. She didn't dwell on the fact that she knew these things.

"So you speak…?"

"English, which is the official language of Nigeria; Spanish, obviously; French which I learned in Paris; Arabic, which I studied in school; plus half a dozen African tribal tongues from Nigeria and central Africa."

"I'll look at your full résumé later. Could you summarize it for me? Just a few sentences please."

"Of course. I was sent to a private academy in Paris for my middle school years. I graduated Oxford ten years ago. I joined my father's firm to learn the business world after graduation, but then he was able—through connections—to secure for me a position in government."

"What position?"

"I was appointed Nigeria's ambassador to the United Nations, after my father made a generous donation to the president's re-election campaign."

Shari knew what the United Nations was.

"Were you qualified for such a high position?"

"I studied international relations at Oxford, with a second in languages. Most of what they do at the UN is talk and, given all the languages I speak, I am very qualified to…talk," he said, grinning again.

Shari stood and began pacing, still adrenalized from the fighting. Yet she continued the dialogue.

"And what prompted you to apply for a position as President Otangi's chief of staff?" Shari was gathering information, but was not quite sure why.

"I'd learned all I could in New York. My father was grooming me for high office in Nigeria, perhaps one day even president. But there are no high-level openings at the moment. We decided I needed experience running a country, not just representing it diplomatically, and I should seek an appropriate position in any African nation that could use me, you know, to build up the résumé."

"And President Otangi could use you?"

"It seems all the senior government jobs here—as with most African countries—have gone to the relatives of the president, which means not much gets accomplished. President Otangi was frustrated and wanted someone as his number two who could get things done, crack the whip, that kind of thing. Our Nigerian president made the introductions, and this was my first interview for the job. Seems I arrived at an interesting time."

Shari stopped pacing, sat down, and looked at him closely.

"I believe you watched the entire battle without moving a muscle."

"I suspected it was the only way to stay alive."

"Quite likely. But I doubt many people could have pulled it off, or even understood the necessity."

"I'm fairly good at appraising situations quickly."

"How old are you, Eduardo?"

"I turned forty-eight last week."

"Do you know who I am?"

"I know who you might be."

Shari stood up and resumed pacing. The ceilings were very high, and the architecture of the palace was European. Tall, stately windows afforded a view over a deck, and beyond that, the Ubangi River. She knew its name.

"Tell me who you think I might be."

"The rumors are all over central Africa. They say there's a mysterious presence in female form inhabiting the deepest parts of the jungle, who kills violently and who cannot be killed. They call her the Angel of Death, or Shari-Ya in the Ningala tongue. It seems she commands an army of lions who kill on her command and devour her enemies."

"They also say that any mortal who sees her face will dissolve into a puddle of steaming tar and die screaming," noted Shari.

"Do they? I hadn't heard that rumor."

"I made it up this morning."

Shari was recklessly allowing this man into her confidence, for reasons she didn't fully understand. She was operating purely on instinct and suspected Eduardo Danjuma could be an ally.

"So you're her."

"And that's why my face is covered. I'd hate to see you dissolve."

The man grinned. "As would I. So if you are this Death Angel, my first question is what do I call you? How are you to be addressed?"

"You can address me as Shariya, formally. But I hope you'll use my nickname, Shari. I've grown to like it."

"Shari by itself would be 'angel' in Ningala."

"What girl doesn't wish to be thought of that way? The 'death' part is not so attractive."

"May I speak openly?"

"Please."

"I mean no disrespect, but I am not some voodoo-practicing illiterate from the rainforest. I do not believe you're an avenging angel of death sent from the gods. I don't believe I'll collapse into steaming tar if I see your face. I don't believe you control an army of lions who will devour your enemies on command."

"What *do* you believe?"

"I'm not sure. I'm not familiar with any country in the history of Africa being conquered by an unknown girl from the jungle, as seems to have just happened. May I ask, how long did it take you?"

"I started this morning."

"You conquered an entire country in one day!"

She glanced again at the clock. "It's been about ten hours. I wasn't trying to take over the whole country, really."

"What *were* you trying to do?"

"You've heard the rumors about the Angel of Death disrupting slave caravans? She kills the slavers and sets the slaves free."

"Yes, those stories have reached even Lagos."

"There's a slave market at Nola. There were a dozen slaves I needed to rescue."

"Alone?"

"Not exactly."

Shari summarized the day's events and sat down again.

Eduardo looked astonished. Without asking permission he stood up and began pacing, hands moving through the air to emphasize his points.

"So you used the element of surprise to overcome a slave market when you only had half a dozen tribal warriors. Then you tricked the local constabulary into calling in army units from the provincial capital. A military detachment was sent down, which you captured with your newly formed slave army. You then used those trucks to move your growing forces to Mintaka, where you captured the military base and convinced the commanding officer to join you. The local governor tried to shoot you and you beheaded him. You then grabbed five hundred troops from the provincial guard, transported them to Bangui, and pulled off exactly the same stunt—convincing the Presidential Guard commander here in the capital to join your coup attempt. With his help, you attacked the palace and killed the president in combat as I just saw. Do I have that right?

"Yes."

"Despite myself, I'm beginning to believe you must be some kind of divine angel. How were you able to do all this?"

"I once read a book, *The Art of War*, by Sun Tzu."

"Yes, it's all about ways to deceive your enemies."

"So at each point I just asked myself what would Sun Tzu do and the answer was obvious."

"So how did a girl from the jungles of central Africa learn how to speak Parisian French and read books like *The Art of War*?"

Shariya realized Eduardo had not seen her skin, and just assumed she was a native woman, chastely covered in Muslim attire.

Glancing at the door, she reassured herself it was still closed and then, with a quick motion, removed her hood completely.

"I don't think I'm from the jungle," she confessed.

24

Eduardo approached her cautiously and held out his hand.

"Go ahead, touch me if you want. I'm real. Not a specter. Your hand will not pass through my body."

Eduardo extended his arm farther, letting his fingers touch her head lightly. He held a few strands of the platinum-blonde hair in his fingers and then placed his palm on her forehead. He withdrew respectfully.

"Perhaps there's still a bit of superstitious African in me," he confessed. "You do seem like an angel, some kind of divine being. But you're right, my hand does not pass through your body. You're real."

"Very glad that's settled."

"So where *are* you from? Are you French?"

"Eduardo, listen carefully. My first memories are of waking up on a riverbank in the jungle roughly a month ago. My mind was gone. It was blank. There was nothing in it. I was wearing clothes; the same ones I'm wearing now."

Shari glanced down at her outfit, noticing for the first time it was a filthy ragged mess.

All I had was a sheathed sword and a hunting knife. That's it. I also have unusual skills. I'm good at killing. I have no idea how I became so. Maybe the sword and knife are clues to who I once was; perhaps some kind of mercenary or—"

"Or what?"

"Or maybe I really *am* an avenging angel of death. That's what the tribe believed that finally brought me in from the wilderness. Before then I was simply a forest creature. I lived with lions. I was part of the pride. I rode one of the males, whom I called Emil. I helped him hunt."

"You lived with lions, and you rode them—like horses?"

"Just Emil, the male. I doubt the others, the females, would have allowed it."

"So that's where the *army of lions* rumor came from."

"Yes, but there's more to it. When I began attacking the slave caravans, during one of the attacks I slipped and fell and was about to be killed. Emil must have sensed I was in danger. He ripped the slaver's arm off, and then the other lions arrived and ate the slavers. The slaves themselves, still in chains, saw it all, and no doubt told others."

"But I don't understand what you were trying to do in the first place. Why did you, a 'forest creature' as you say, attack the slave caravans?"

"When I saw them and saw their mistreatment of the slaves, something in me snapped. Before that point I had no emotion, no goals, no hopes or fears, no thoughts about anything. I just survived and lived day to day, hour to hour, killing and eating anything I wished. But suddenly I had a goal, a purpose; a reason to exist."

"Killing slavers and setting free their captives."

"Yes, and that's been going on now for weeks, which is where the rumors came from. I had no idea they'd reached Nigeria."

"Few there believe them, but those connected to the slave trade know *something* is happening. They may not believe the angel of death story about a divine being arising out of the jungle, but they know someone or some *thing* is stopping the slave caravans."

"Yes, that particular route I'm sure has been seriously disrupted. Also, each day more of my mind comes back. I found I knew so much, beyond simply being able to kill with a knife or sword—or my bare hands. It's especially been coming back in the last twenty-four hours—coming out of the jungle, entering Nolo, speaking with people outside the tribal village. I think my mind has completely returned, except for what's behind that most important door: Where I came from. I can only believe something terrible must have happened. That's why my mind won't let me see it."

"You're obviously an amnesiac," nodded Eduardo. "Something must have triggered it, some traumatic event."

"When I try to force it, when I try to think about my past, I become nauseous. It's like my whole body is conspiring to keep the door to those memories closed. Maybe it needs to stay closed, for my own sanity," continued Shari. "Especially now that I have a purpose."

25

"So, you've taken over an entire country. What happens next?" asked Eduardo.

"I need to eliminate the slavers. Now I've apparently conquered one of the countries most complicit in the trade. It's a good start. But I need to finish the job."

"To eliminate slavery in Africa you'd need to do more than seize control of one country. You'd have to conquer Africa itself."

"Well I can't do *that*."

"No."

"So what *can* I do?"

"You might consolidate gains, make sure your victory here is complete, organize everything, and use your power to make sure slavery is absolutely eradicated from CAR or..."

"Or what?"

"Well, I'm not trained in military coups although I've certainly studied them as a concept. I'm just wondering..."

"Yes?"

"Could you keep the formula going? You now have an entire nation behind you and control a military that I believe has about five thousand soldiers in uniform, total. That's only a small army. But it's your army. And the epicenter of the slave trade is South Sudan."

"Tell me about it."

"Well, South Sudan is one of the poorest, most ill-educated, most corrupt countries on the planet. They spend most of their time starving and have no way to defend themselves. Slave traders swoop in from Sudan to the north, and Kenya to the south. They raid any area of population that is weakly defended, which is almost all of it, and take their captives north down the Nile to waiting markets in Egypt, or through Kenya to Arabian slave traders they meet on the coast.

"Conquering CAR will disrupt the slavers hugely, but nothing compared to what would happen if you could do the same thing in South Sudan."

"Do you think it's possible?"

Well, everything you've done has been based on surprise, and keeping your momentum going. If you started your crusade this morning, it would take time for the world to even learn something's amiss here. No offense, but most won't care. Use the world's indifference to buy time. Central and sub-Saharan Africa, despite the wars of the last decade, are pretty calm now. No one's forces are on high alert. Military spending has been cut back."

"Go on."

"If you sent your army against South Sudan, you could probably capture the capital, and the key military threats, before anyone realized it."

"OK, let's say we did that, what might we do next?"

"I'd cross that bridge later."

"No. I want to have a larger vision than merely taking over two backward countries. Think more broadly."

There was a large map of Africa on one side of the palatially sized room and they walked over to it. Eduardo picked up a pointer stick.

"Well, if you could seize control of South Sudan, here, and somehow keep the element of surprise going, maybe you could do the same in Chad—another hotbed of sub-Saharan slavery. Then you'd have three countries under your belt. I think then you stop and declare yourself the Central African Empire. That was CAR's name for a while when an insane dictator seized control and tried to play Genghis Khan."

"Interesting."

"You could resurrect the name itself, apply it to all three countries, and proclaim the whole thing a slave-free zone. You could justify the conquering as a geopolitical necessity to stop the slave trade. UN groups would approve. And the international community, when they found out what had happened, would probably shrug and say at least you won't make anything worse. I could help with that, at the United Nations, and with the ambassadors."

"And what would all this accomplish?"

"You'd have disrupted if not eliminated probably eighty percent of the slave trade in Africa. You'd have achieved something far more significant than merely killing a few slavers occasionally on one trade route. And you'd be making a strong statement to the world that slavery would no longer be tolerated in Africa."

"OK, I like that plan. Will you be part of it?"

"In what capacity?"

"Look, we just met, but I need someone with your skills. If you want the job of Chief of Staff to the head of the Central African Republic—soon to be empire, perhaps—consider yourself hired."

"If I say no?"

"Then you're free to walk out of here and make your way back to Lagos—provided only that you swear utter secrecy about everything you've learned."

"Helping you build a small empire sounds more interesting than listening to gab fests at the UN or serving as second-in-command to a corrupt African politician. Actually, it sounds like a very interesting challenge."

"And it would look far better on your résumé," she said, smiling.

"Yes. I hadn't expected to sign up for a war, though. I know nothing of battle."

"I'll worry about the battles. You run everything else, including figuring out where we're going to get some food for a meal tonight. The cooks must still be around or at least can be summoned back. I think we should discuss these plans with our new Field Marshal, Barasa, who will join us for dinner."

"Would he report to me, or to you?"

"The military must report to me," said Shari, slipping increasingly into the persona of Sun Tzu. "Let's divide it up that way. I'll lead the military. Everything non-military, you're in charge. I'll always have the right to overrule you, but unless I do, the decisions are yours."

"Not to be crude, but can I ask how much the position pays?"

"Ask yourself. You're in charge of the treasury, and the tax collection, everything. You're in charge of how much you'll pay yourself. But keep it reasonable for now. Let's at least pretend we're not corrupt African bureaucrats and are truly trying to make a difference. I'm sure we'll be able to make you comfortable when things stabilize. Will that work?"

Eduardo looked into her eyes, considering, and she returned his gaze steadily, without guile.

"I accept your offer, young and soon-to-be Empress Shariya. Now please excuse me. I need to organize a new management structure for the country, beginning with the kitchen staff."

After he left, and she was finally alone, Shari walked onto the balcony which overlooked the broad Ubangi River and watched the sunset. She'd awakened this morning on a jungle path with the goal of rescuing a dozen slaves.

Now she was leading a nation.

Her mind had returned. All of it, except for the part behind the door. She was completely alive, perhaps more so than she'd ever been. Her head was churning with the geopolitical implications of taking over an African country, perhaps more than one, and how she might expand her slave-free zone outwards. She was thinking of battle tactics, economic policies, political systems. She had strong opinions about all of it, but no idea where those opinions, those ideas, had come from.

A fish eagle soared gracefully over the water, dove into it, and flew aloft again with something silvery and squiggling in its beak. The last rays of the sun scintillated off its wings.

She'd experienced this scene before. But from what time and place, she had no idea. And maybe it no longer mattered. Maybe that door should be shut permanently. A new door had opened for her today, a very large one.

She would walk through it and build herself a new world.

And maybe, someday, learn to cry again.

26

EDUARDO MOVED EFFORTLESSLY into his role as Chief of Staff and quickly had the Presidential Palace running smoothly. Shari had her own suite, including a large master bedroom, a casual living area, and the expansive office with conference table where food could be served and meetings held.

They'd also agreed that—for now—she'd continue wearing the veil outside those three interconnected rooms, her "private zone." And access to the private zone, by anyone else, was forbidden.

"I'll help with whatever cleaning, changing sheets, and so forth, are needed," offered Eduardo. "But we can't let even the servants—especially the servants—know who you are. If they know, all Africa will know. And there's too much value in keeping your identity hidden."

They'd brought General Barasa in on Shari's secret, as he would always be part of their strategic planning. The military leader agreed about the veil.

"The rumor that it's instant death to see your face is probably worth more than three divisions of troops," he explained. "It paints you as an invincible, supernatural creature. And in battle…"

"Yes," interrupted Shari while they sat at the conference table. "If an army thinks it will win, it wins, and vice versa."

"And having a conquering Angel of Death on our team will make a big difference," noted Barasa. "Let's not give that up."

"We should expand on the rumors, where possible," suggested Eduardo.

"The rumors are already ridiculous," Shari noted. "I'm told my lions now howl at the moon, after a kill."

"That's certainly what half of Nigeria believes," agreed Eduardo.

"Lions don't howl at the moon," she protested. "It's nonsense."

"I suppose you're going to tell me next they don't have wings, and their manes aren't even aflame?"

Sophie studied Eduardo closely, and then stood up and paced, thinking deeply. Finally, she stopped.

"*Most* don't have wings," she explained. "But the ones who do, their manes burst into flame when they howl at the moon."

"Now you're getting it." Eduardo grinned.

"The bulk of the lion army—all five thousand of them—stay on the ground, where they can more easily devour my enemies."

"Yes, exactly."

"The white lions with the wings and the combustible manes and so forth, I brought with me from the spiritual world. When Africa is freed of slavery and corruption, we shall return there."

"It would be entirely reasonable for you to do that, yes," agreed Eduardo.

"I think we need a flag," suggested the general.

"Winged lions are all the rage in European heraldry," noted her Chief of Staff.

"Ours will have wings *and* flaming manes. I bet there aren't any of those in European heraldry," Shari mused.

"Not that I recall," said Eduardo. "I'll organize it."

"Fine. But I need to get something off my chest."

The young girl stood, walked to the tall windows, and looked out at the river. She stared at its slow waters for a long time. Abruptly she turned back and faced her two allies.

"Can I speak openly."

"Of course," urged Eduardo, as the general nodded.

"Preserving an image of supernatural power, yeah, I get that. Militarily, it's brilliant. But might there be a racial element here?"

"What do you mean?" asked her prime minister.

"I'm white, and everyone in this country is black. Are you sure you're not wanting me to wear the veil to hide my skin color? Is there a whiff of white colonial oppression we're trying to cover up? Is that part of why I need to stay hidden?"

The two men exchanged a glance.

"Look, Shari…" Eduardo began.

"I insist on honesty." The Angel of Death took her seat again.

"I don't give a crap about anyone's skin color," interjected the general impatiently. "I just want slavery stamped out."

"Noted," agreed Shari. "But it's not just what the two of you believe. Eduardo, you were going to say—?"

"There are parts of Africa where race is important. In South Africa, you can cut the racial tension with a knife. Coastal countries, with lots of interaction with Europeans and a history of colonialism and oppression, yeah, skin color's a big deal. But in the interior…"

Barasa interrupted. "Shari, you said it yourself. Everyone here is black. CAR gained independence from France in 1960 and it's been ruled by Africans ever since. Few alive today would even remember the colonial period—let alone harbor resentment against it. Outside Bangui, many have never *seen* a white person. To them, if they saw your white skin and blonde hair, they'd not consider you an enemy. They'd more likely think you were a creature from Mars. Except they've never heard of Mars, either."

Eduardo now stood up and began pacing. Shari let him gather his thoughts.

"All that said, the skin color thing could still be an issue," he finally concluded.

"You think it's a problem?" asked Barasa, eyebrows raised.

"Probably not here, for the reasons you said. But when the world starts looking at us, as they will, the idea of a young white girl running an African country might be problematic."

"Exactly," agreed Shari. "That's what's concerning me."

"I think," continued her chief of staff, "there's an easy solution. The rumors have already spread that the Angel of Death is a supernatural creature and that it's instant death for a mere mortal to see her face."

"An African Medusa," Shari observed, marveling again at how much she knew of the world while knowing so little of herself.

"Precisely. But the danger is not just seeing your face. It's seeing any part of your skin. That's why it's not just your face that must be veiled, but all parts of you."

"So, gloves on my hands even?"

"Yes, and stockings on your feet," urged Eduardo. "There are many Islamic women in this part of Africa, and most of them are covered in various ways. Being covered completely is not that unusual."

"So they'll never learn I'm white."

"I like it," agreed Barasa.

"Only those who believe in the occult will buy the 'instant death to see her skin' part," mused the chief of staff. "But others will recognize it as merely a clever way to maintain power. Africa has a long history of sovereigns claiming some form of divinity."

"Like the ancient pharaohs of Egypt," suggested Shari.

"More recently than that," noted Barasa. "In Sudan, in the late 19th century, they had the Mahdi, a divine figure who defeated the British at Khartoum."

Shari thought about it. "I don't mind being supernatural, but I draw the line at divinity. Let's not turn this whole thing into a religious movement."

"Good idea," agreed Eduardo. "The Medusa model is better. You're a supernatural being. You can't be killed because you're already dead. And anyone who sees your face, or even your skin, joins you in the death world."

"Works for me," said the young girl. "And as long as no one can see any part of my skin at all, the racial issue won't even come up. Those who don't buy the supernatural part will just assume I'm African, because why wouldn't I be?"

"Well," noted Eduardo, "let's not forget that early rumors had not only the lions white but the Angel of Death white also."

"But that was a ridiculous exaggeration," Shari mused. "Like the wings and the flaming sword."

"Yes," he agreed. "No one who matters will believe the lions were white, and the rumors of white skin color will fall in the same basket. Those who don't buy the supernatural stuff will assume you're just some opportunistic local girl who's good at fighting."

"Like Joan of Arc," suggested Shari, eyes focused on the river. She hesitated after mentioning that name, but didn't know why. The feeling passed and the overall plan was accepted.

After the palace staff consulted with local Islamic women, numerous outfits were quickly designed and sewn.

For official meetings, public appearances, or when just walking around palace grounds or the city, the Angel of Death now had several elegant black *abaya* gowns, some with intricate gold filigree designs in the cloth. The abayas were paired with matching *boshiyas*, the full Islamic head-covering that was sheer enough to even cover the eyes. Matching elbow-length black gloves and equally long black stockings ensured no white skin would be seen.

Knowing a different kind of outfit would be needed for battle or where more flexibility of movement was desired, she also had a body-length, turtleneck unitard. Conveniently, the flowing abaya and boshiya could fit easily over the slimmer outfit, if she needed to quickly convert from one to the other.

Shari wasn't willing to hide inside all-black clothing forever but for now it was no great hardship. The boshiya fabric was so fine she often forgot it was there.

Modeling the outfit for Eduardo, in front of a wall-length mirror in the conference room, she began laughing.

"I can't decide if I'm Zorro or Phantom of the Opera," she grinned, knowing her facial expression was invisible.

"Or in that black unitard, a ninja speed skater from Hell," said Eduardo, laughing.

Shari reached back and pulled out her sword. "Well, I do have a ninja blade!"

On impulse, the Angel of Death began performing kata-like dances with the dangerous weapon. *High guard—rotate—lunge—parry—half-kneel—thrust.*

The katana, which she was controlling perfectly, passed close to Eduardo's neck. He pulled back in fright, caught his leg on a chair, and fell backward to the floor with a cry of alarm.

Shari stopped the play-acting, sheathed the weapon, and pulled her chief of staff off the ground with an outstretched arm.

"Sorry, Eduardo, but I'm an expert with this stuff. How I became so I have no clue, but you were not in danger."

He collected himself and then stared at her contemplatively. "So the Central African Republic now has its own supernatural female ninja warrior. What will the world think of her?"

Shari pulled off her head covering and laughed. "You're going to tell me I have to use my powers for good, not evil, right?"

"Best if you did," nodded the UN diplomat, returning her smile.

27

Two days after the Battle of Bangui, they were up early and meeting in the large presidential conference room. Eduardo had found someone to repair the door, which was now properly closed and locked. There were hard-boiled eggs, croissants, and slices of papaya on the table, along with a large thermos of coffee.

General Barasa had embraced Eduardo's plan to take over their two neighbors—South Sudan and Chad—and create a "slave-free" empire. Now they had to figure out how to do it.

CAR had a large enough army to make a successful attack on each country's capital, as long as they could keep the element of surprise going. But they couldn't.

"Juba, the capital of South Sudan, which is where I used to live, by the way, is twenty-six hours from here by road," explained the General. "Nine hours from the border. And Djamena in Chad is sixteen hours, ten from the border. We could attack one or the other by surprise. But then we'd have to race to the other."

"And lose the element of surprise," agreed Eduardo. "It would simply take too long, and we probably have only a couple of days before what's happened becomes known."

"Yes," agreed Barasa. "And then everyone's forces will go on high alert."

"We attacked the presidential palace here with only two transport trucks and about forty troops," said Shari. "I don't think the key to winning these battles is the size of your army. As you just said, it's the element of surprise."

Both agreed.

"So let's look at this differently. The goal isn't to fight a war, let alone two of them. The goal is to stage more coups. One in Juba, one in Djamena. What's the right number of trucks needed for a stealth approach?"

"It's true we only had two trucks here in Bangui," noted Barasa. "But that was the bare minimum, as you saw. I'd say four trucks, a total of eighty troops, would be enough to capture any presidential palace in Central Africa—at least if it's done by surprise—yet not be so many as to suggest a military invasion."

"Which means," she continued, "our army is vastly larger than it needs to be for a couple more coups. General, you could pick your best men and lead them against South Sudan. You know the capital already. I'll take four more trucks and make a surprise attack on the presidential palace in Djamena."

"Here in Bangui," said the general, "our troop transports were less than a kilometer from the palace. And no one thought to question us. How do we maneuver CAR forces—even small ones—secretly through enemy territory, so they're in position to attack the presidential palace in each city?"

"Have either of you heard of a false-flag operation?" asked Shari, tapping her Sun Tzu strategic thinking again.

"Remind us," suggested Eduardo diplomatically.

"It's a *ruse-de-guerre*, a trick of war. Our trucks are safe enough inside this country, but once they cross the border, they'll be vulnerable to a more superior force, or anyone who sees them and can alert the capital. And they'll have let's say ten hours of exposure in each country."

"Yes, that will be the dangerous part," confirmed the general.

"But we could make it less dangerous by showing false flags. Can we disguise our trucks as South Sudan forces, and Chad forces, respectively? Could we paint those insignias on them?"

"Why not?" agreed Barasa.

"I have a better idea," suggested Eduardo. "United Nations colors. Make your troops look like UN peacekeeping forces. No one in central Africa, or most anywhere, will go up against a UN military mission, because they know it would bring down the wrath of the whole world."

"Are there any in Chad or South Sudan?" asked Shari.

"There have been in the past and there may even be some now, but it doesn't really matter," the former UN diplomat continued. "Everyone recognizes UN colors—black letters on white. Impersonating UN forces would outrage the United Nations itself, but that's only in the future when they hear about what happened. And *if* they hear about what happened. They probably won't, and if rumors ever drift up to New York, we'll deny it, and mumble something about the fog of war, and people being confused. And by then we'll be in control—at least if all this works."

"And if it doesn't work, the UN will be the least of our problems," noted Shari.

"True," agreed Eduardo, stroking his chin contemplatively.

"Let's schedule these attacks around four in the morning," suggested the general. "Everyone will be asleep. Four UN troop transports won't look too alarming. I can storm the palace in Juba with hand-picked troops. We might even be able to do it silently, with minimal if any gunfire."

"And I'll do the same in Djamena," said Shari. "Can you pick the best men for me, as well?"

"Yes, plus I'll include Captain Ilya, one of my top officers. He grew up in Djamena and can be your guide. He'll command the men, and report to you. But once we take the palace and let's say capture each country's president, what happens then?"

"My understanding of African coups," said Eduardo, "is that the key is gaining the loyalty of whoever commands the military. Typically you capture or kill the local strongman president-for-life, and with him out of the way, the military leaders have to make a decision. If they think you're on the winning side, they declare for you and then you *are* on the winning side."

"We'll have to ad lib this," said Shari. "But I think that's the general script. Use false UN colors to get the troops across the country and up to the palace for an early morning surprise attack. Try to make the attack as quiet as possible. Kill or capture the president. Force either him or whoever's most senior to summon the military commander for an emergency meeting. Say it's an emergency meeting with UN staff. That way the UN trucks will not be a surprise and will in fact give credibility."

"Yes, but then what do we say when that person arrives?" asked Barasa.

"The truth. Say the Angel of Death is leading a slave revolt and has already captured Bangui and CAR. She's creating a slave-free zone, a new empire, to eradicate the slave trade in central Africa. She invites South Sudan to join her empire, and she invites whoever you're speaking to—the military commander—to be the next president of South Sudan, reporting to her. And say that Chad has already fallen. I'll tell those in Djamena that South Sudan has already fallen."

"Not 'fallen,'" protested Eduardo. "I think you mean, 'enthusiastically joined the new empire.'"

"Yes, that's what I meant to say." Shari smiled.

"One more refinement," suggested Barasa. "Take a far more powerful force, say fifty trucks, two such forces, and have them waiting at the border with South Sudan and Chad, respectively. As soon as each palace is captured, and the military commander turned, send those forces across the border, to provide 'logistical support.' That will help convince anyone who still needs convincing and make the coup irreversible."

"Good idea," agreed Shari.

28

They spent the rest of the day assembling strike teams, painting eight trucks with United Nations colors, explaining plans to the troops, and equipping them with weapons, ammunition, and other supplies.

Eduardo would stay in Bangui and continue his rapid consolidation of control over the country. The general issued Shari and Eduardo satellite phones so they could all stay in communication, regardless of location.

The second and much larger wave of troops would be sent out ten hours later. Barasa left a senior officer in charge to organize all that with instructions to report to Eduardo until the operation was over.

The four UN-painted trucks heading to Juba, with Barasa leading them, were ready to depart by one in the morning, and with an estimated time of arrival outside the palace at four a.m. the following day. Shari's team would leave twelve hours later.

The trucks had their engines running when Shari rushed up, carrying a jar of white paint. She walked over to the passenger's side of the lead truck and spoke to the general.

"What was the name of your niece, the one the slavers took," she asked.

"Katinka," he said. "Why?"

"Her name is going on your front bumper, and on all the trucks in the convoy. She will spiritually be leading us."

And the fearsome Angel of Death knelt down and painted KATINKA on the front of the truck.

"Thank you, Shari," said the General, his voice breaking. Then he saluted her crisply, while urgently gesturing to his driver to begin. She knew he was hiding tears.

Workers began painting that name on all the trucks. But when it was time to paint the one she'd be riding in, heading to Chad—Shari took the paintbrush back and instead wrote OMYLO. The woman killed by the slavers back in the village would have her own vengeance.

29

When Shari's caravan departed Bangui it was ten in the morning and she found herself retracing much of the route that had originally brought her to the capital. But at the intersection with the Mintaka road, they continued north on CAR's National 24. She noticed the scenery was changing rapidly. They were leaving the jungle behind, and the landscape was opening up. This was the edge of the Sahel, the dry, flat plain which continued up to the Sahara desert itself.

The trees here were shorter and farther apart. The four trucks had to space out to avoid each other's reddish plumes of dust. There was less wildlife here, compared to the rainforest. They passed a herd of ostriches, who didn't seem to mind the dry conditions. Meerkats poked their heads above ground in curiosity as the caravan passed. Most interesting were the termite mounds, tall pinnacles of dried mud rising up from the plain, some over four meters tall.

A few kilometers shy of the border, Shari ordered a rest and full meal. It was four p.m., and no one could predict what the next ten hours would bring. The first challenge would be crossing the border, and she knew Captain Ilya had his story prepared. They'd been practicing for hours, for every combination of what might await them.

Shari also used this break to have her troops hide their weapons completely. The trucks contained vast storage boxes, and she made sure every weapon was out of sight. In Bangui, she'd had them load a dozen shovels and pickaxes, and the troops held these now, quite visibly. They were a team of road workers, sent by the UN to help repair some of Africa's worst highways. They'd been fixing roads in Bangui but were now ordered to Djamena.

The cover story worked. Nothing looked less threatening than a four-truck, UN road-repair crew, carrying shovels and pickaxes.

"Are they expecting you?" the senior border guard asked Ilya, the driver of the lead truck.

"They were expecting us two days ago," he replied. "But we were delayed with a bridge falling apart, near Bossangoa. Now we're trying to make up for lost time. The president himself has asked for us urgently, because of all the potholes on the roads leading to the palace."

"Then you'd best hurry," said the border guard, waving them all through and dispensing with normal immigration procedures.

Shari's convoy arrived on the outskirts of Chad's capital at two in the morning They found a deserted parking lot to park the trucks, stretch, use up time, and replace their shovels with automatic weapons. Remembering the effectiveness of RPGs on locked doors and gates, Shari had one man in each vehicle so equipped. They were to ignore any other fighting and use these weapons only if the team was stopped by a barrier they couldn't overcome.

Shari had a handgun but knew she was most effective in combat with a sword and knife. She had these properly sheathed and ready for instant use. The Angel of Death was—as always—covered in black.

Ilya was masterful at guiding them through back roads and serpentine streets on the way to the palace. It was his idea they should be seen by as few as possible, so the convoy approached from an unusual direction.

The four trucks pulled to a stop at the palace's main gate, precisely at four in the morning, and the sleepy guard approached them with a flashlight.

"What's all this?" he asked, not especially interested.

"President Watana is concerned about security," replied Ilya. "And he's asked our peacekeeping force to help guard the palace. We were ordered to come as quickly as possible."

"Well, I'm not surprised. We had another platoon of palace guards arrive just thirty minutes ago, and I guess it's the same worries about security. There's rumor of a coup in Bangui, so everyone's tightening up. Their trucks are parked over there near the entrance, but I guess you could park behind them."

He opened the gate and waved them through.

"A platoon of guards just arrived," said Shari, concerned. "We didn't plan for that."

"Do we continue?" asked Ilya. "It's going to be harder."

"We have no choice; we can't turn around now. But drive slowly."

Shari looked closely at the approach to the Palace. It had extremely broad steps flowing outward in a semi-circle from the main door. There were two trucks pulled up in front, with plenty of space between them and on either side. There were no physical barriers other than the steps and the vastly large door. African potentates loved these monstrous doors.

She used her mobile phone to speed dial a conference with the senior officer in each of the other trucks.

"Change of plans. We're going in hot. Go between or around those trucks and park at the base of the stairs. We'll ram the door with the lead truck and then I want everyone to storm the palace. I will lead."

She briefed the troops in back and then turned to Ilya.

"I was really hoping to avoid this. We're about to kill innocent soldiers."

"Who support a regime that is enabling the slave trade," Captain Ilya reminded her.

Shariya sighed.

"Very well. Full speed. Ram the door."

"Hold on!" she yelled to the soldiers in back.

Two hundred yards from the entrance, Shari's truck aimed for the space between the two parked vehicles. It accelerated slowly but reached seventy kilometers an hour just as the front wheels hit the steps. The ungainly vehicle shot upwards, crashed into the heavy wood doors, and kept going. The truck came to a stop in the middle of a large central atrium, with presidential guards surrounding them. It was the worst possible situation.

But she was with hand-picked troops, and they'd rehearsed this possibility. The canvas sides on the truck vanished and AK-47s began firing into the defending troops, who hadn't had time to even move their rifles into position.

Shari was out of the truck instantly, katana in one hand, tanto dagger in the other.

She engaged the nearest soldier. Before he could fire his weapon the Angel of Death pierced him in the heart. She spun around and removed the head of another who was trying to cock the slide on his rifle.

Now it was chaotic hand-to-hand combat, and Shariya unleashed all her weapons.

A Tae Kwon Do sidekick crushed the kneecap of one attacker, sending him reeling backward in pain. A swipe of her knife cut another's face in half. A second head was flung off its shoulders as she pivoted again with the katana. Her knife plunged into a man's abdomen and he fell to his knees, moaning.

Now more soldiers had entered the melee, no doubt the remainder of the presidential guard converging from elsewhere in the palace. Then her own troops from the other trucks burst into the atrium.

Automatic weapons fire filled the room, and she knew they could lose this fight. If they did, she would be captured and executed. They all would be—those still alive.

And then she remembered Katinka who was leading them spiritually. This was a fight against slavery itself, and the regimes that enabled it. It invigorated her, and she knew now she did not care if she died. She had a purpose, and she would not give it up. Her katana slashed through the air, and three more of the enemy collapsed, headless.

There was a brief pause in the firing and the young warrior took advantage of it.

"I am Shariya, the Angel of Death," she cried in a voice so powerful it surprised even her. "I cannot be killed for I am already dead. Put down your weapons and my Death Army will let you live!"

No one moved, and the silence became complete. It was as if a magic incantation, a staying spell, had been cast. Both sides paused, regarding this all-black figure standing there on the stairs, brandishing a sword larger than anyone had ever seen, and with dead bodies around her. It was the spirit creature from the jungle they'd heard about. She was real and far deadlier than any had imagined.

One second. Several seconds. And the tide turned.

"I want to live!" cried one, and he dropped his weapon and went down on his knees, bowing before her.

Another did the same. Then a third. "I will not fight the Angel of Death," he cried.

And then, as one, they all dropped to their knees and cast aside their weapons in surrender.

"Any of you who wish may join the Army of Death," she cried. "If you stand up, it means you have joined my Army, and I am your new commander."

Again, there were only the slightest of pauses before one stood up. Another. And then everyone was standing.

"You have chosen wisely," she said. "Your orders are to take me to the president's chambers and help me capture him."

"I will guide you, Death Angel," said one. "Follow me."

She did, and her newly expanded army stayed close behind. Those few guards left defending the president's suite realized the hopelessness of the situation and instantly dropped their weapons. She nodded to the guide, now under her command. "Take any of these men you wish and bring the president here. He does not need to fear death unless he opposes me."

Soon the terrified president of Chad was standing in front of the horrific, all-in-black, Angel of Death, the rumors of whom had been expanding for weeks. He went to his knees in front of her, even though she'd not asked it of him.

Shari preferred him on his knees. It was a nice visual to the surrounding troops and would no doubt trigger rumors of her growing power.

"Where is the commander of all military forces in Chad?" she asked. "How quickly can he be here?"

"He's in the barracks rallying more troops, but can be here in five minutes if I call him," said the president, keeping his eyes fixed on the floor but his voice loud enough to be heard by everyone.

"Do so, and tell him to come alone."

Soon Chad's senior military commander, astonished by what had happened, was escorted through the battle chaos and up to where Shariya waited, surrounded by her army. Guards forced him to his knees in front of the veiled woman.

"I am the Angel of Death," she said. "I've already liberated the Central African Republic, South Sudan, and now Chad. I am building an empire and eradicating slavery. Your president will be expelled but will not be harmed. If you declare yourself under my command, I will make you the new President of Chad. If you do not, I will remove your head with this sword." She held it up menacingly and was thrilled when light glinted off the blade, making it seem almost alive. "Please make your decision."

He looked up solemnly. "I swear my allegiance to you, Shariya, the Angel of Death. I, and my troops, are yours to command."

Her mobile phone rang.

"Um, please excuse me a moment, everyone," she said, a bit sheepishly, sheathing her weapons and answering the phone.

"Yes?"

"It's me," said Barasa. "It went just as we hoped here in Juba. We didn't have to fire a shot, not a single casualty. The president has been captured and the Military Commander has sworn loyalty to you. How's it going on your end? Just as easy?"

"I'll tell you another time, but Chad has joined the Central African Empire. Busy here, talk later." She clicked off the phone and looked around at the fifty or so soldiers watching and listening, perhaps curious at hearing the name *Central African Empire.*

"The Central African Empire is also known as the Empire of *Death*," she said loudly and menacingly, needing to re-establish a degree of fear after the awkward phone call. They all dropped to their knees again, bowing in terror.

Shari smiled, knowing they could not see her face. Note to file. Next time, turn off your damn cell phone before the battle. She kept them kneeling for several more seconds.

"As you have all sworn loyalty, you have nothing to fear. Please rise."

They did so, and her empire was born.

30

Shari and Eduardo were back in the conference room. The debris from a recently consumed breakfast littered the expansive table, including the remains of mangos, eggs in their shells, croissants, and empty coffee cups. The girl from the jungle, now an empress, paced in front of the floor-to-ceiling map of the continent, eying it curiously.

Finally, she turned to Eduardo, who was still sitting at the table. "OK, what's next?" she asked.

Eduardo refilled his cup and added both milk and sugar. With painstaking attention to detail, he mixed the contents endlessly with a wooden stick, giving the matter—or at least his beverage—careful thought.

Shari became exasperated and threw up her hands. "Eduardo, whatever momentum we've gained is rapidly dissipating while the world awaits the preparation of your coffee."

He set down the stick and took a careful drink of the hot liquid before smiling slightly.

"I think they *should* wait."

"Explain."

"Usually an African coup is followed by a high-profile speech, press releases, etc. and soon the world knows that country "x" has changed hands. But I see no reason to go public just yet."

"Why not?" asked the empress. "I'm not disagreeing, just wanting to understand."

"Better if we consolidate our gains first," he cautioned. "We need to knit these three countries together, organize the militaries into a single unit, make sure the bureaucracies are running smoothly, and so forth. We don't need the whole world staring at us under a microscope while we work this out."

"But can we stay in stealth mode? Won't someone notice something?"

"No offense, but you've *conquered* three of the most backward, unimportant, and isolated nations on Earth," explained the seasoned diplomat. "The outside world isn't going to notice, let alone care. But the embassies and consulates are a problem. They interact constantly with their governments, and we can't keep this a secret from them. They'll report back to their superiors."

"And the solution would be—?"

"Kick them all out."

Charter aircraft were arranged swiftly and in less than twenty-four hours, messengers were sent to every embassy and consulate in Chad, CAR, and South Sudan, politely but forcefully insisting that the ambassador and all foreign staff leave immediately.

Eduardo composed the letters himself.

Dear Ambassadors, Consuls, and Representatives,

We respectfully ask you and your staff to immediately leave [South Sudan]. We are expelling all diplomatic staff from our country, but we hasten to assure you this is not from disrespect or antagonism. We are making administrative changes to our political structure, and possibly some amendments to our constitution, and because of this it is not possible to rule out the potential for upheaval in the coming weeks. In short, we may not be able to guarantee your safety.

We expect things will return to normal very soon, and you may be assured that at such time we will eagerly welcome you back to [South Sudan]. In your absence, we will take full responsibility for the safeguarding of your diplomatic compound, including all official and personal items you leave behind, so that when you return you will find nothing amiss. The messenger who delivers this letter will be honored to escort you immediately to the airport, where a chartered plane is ready to deliver all diplomatic personnel to Lagos, from where you can easily return to your home countries.

Best Regards,

The Foreign Office

Fortunately, there were very few embassies or even consulates in these "unimportant" third-world countries. Typically, other nations sub-contracted with the few that did exist, to handle any consular issues that might arise. For example, if a Swedish national were traveling in South Sudan and was arrested, Sweden would contract with the Swiss consulate to handle the communications. Everyone trusted the Swiss, which is why they had one of the most extensive networks of consulates around the world. But in places like South Sudan, even they rarely had much to do.

So it was not difficult to remove from all three countries the foreign diplomatic staff within twenty-four hours.

"Don't let's pretend," said Eduardo, "that this won't be noticed. Three identical letters, arriving simultaneously? But it will take time to work itself up the communication ladder, for people to begin wondering what's up in central Africa, and for some degree of attention to come our way. It won't happen quickly, because—as I've said before—no one really cares about these places. Memos will get written, they'll arrive at inboxes, the recipients will read them, compose other memos to higher-ups, and some task will be assigned to some other office to look into this more closely, subject to other priorities, which will mean we probably have a week or two, at least, before serious investigation begins."

True to prediction, in far-off capitals as the diplomats returned home, debriefings occurred, low-priority memos were circulated, more senior bureaucrats eventually read them, and appropriate reports were created for the file.

It seemed likely some president-for-life was seeking to tweak the constitution to make sure his wife would succeed him, or tax rates could be higher, or some other privilege granted and was needing to make it all happen without anyone looking too closely, which was why the diplomats had been expelled, and by the way, who the hell cared what happened in Weird-o-stan. Yeah, it was strange the same thing occurred in all three countries simultaneously, but—why are we even talking about this?

~

Shariya and Eduardo were back in the meeting room, staring at the large map of Africa on the wall.

"By conquering CAR, South Sudan, and Chad, I realize we've disrupted maybe eighty percent of the slave trade, correct?" she asked.

"I would guess so, yes."

"And I understand we need to take a moment to catch our breath and make sure these countries are all now working properly, and things are under control, and so forth, right?"

"Yes, exactly."

"But then what?"

"Well, then we'll be in charge of a combined nation that in terms of land area is now the largest in Africa. As discussed, we rename it Central African Empire, as it once was, and you can be its empress."

"My only goal here was to eliminate the slave trade. I don't need to be an empress."

"Once you firmly control this territory you'll be able to encourage anti-slavery measures in surrounding regions. That can be your theme. You'll call the attention of the world to the need to eradicate slavery. You can be a spokesperson. Or send in your own military to areas where it's practiced. The title empress will be very useful for generating publicity."

"Remind me again, what is *your* goal, Eduardo?"

He grinned sheepishly while spreading out his hands in an encompassing gesture. "I'm just trying to build up my résumé so I can one day be president of Nigeria."

"You told me northern Nigeria is now almost completely Muslim and the Islamists, Boko Haram in particular, are enslaving non-Muslim women at increasing rates."

"Yes, that's true."

"Chad shares a border with Nigeria, which means our little empire now does."

"What are you getting at, Shari?"

"You also told me that slavers are increasingly penetrating into Kenya from Somalia, feeding the Arabic slave trade and sending Kenyan tribal girls off to Oman."

"Ever it was so, although when the British ran things it was less."

"Was it?"

"Yes. As these African nations have regained independence much of the worst practices from the old days have returned."

"We need to stop it," declared Shari.

"You're not suggesting we try to take over Nigeria or Kenya, certainly, just because we share borders with them?"

"We're not strong enough, are we?"

"Not even close. Nigeria is the most populated country in Africa, and Lagos is Africa's largest city. The country has vast oil resources and a correspondingly large army. Kenya has significant wealth from the tourist trade and is also far stronger than the countries you conquered. And by the way, you 'conquered' them with perfectly executed coups, not with traditional warfare. Those tactics won't work against a country like Nigeria. Your trucks would be stopped at the border. And if you launched a full military attack, you'd lose."

"Very well. I'm sure you're right. We'll consolidate the three countries as you suggest. And decide what our next step is after we've sorted it all out."

"I believe that's wise, Shari."

After dinner, properly covered in veils, she left the palace clandestinely and went out into the African night.

She enjoyed the vibrancy of the city after the sun went down and the temperatures became bearable. Walking through the streets, she realized people were noticing. They knew the *Angel of Death* was living in the presidential palace, and that this was her. She was the only one covered head to toe, with not a trace of skin showing.

And everyone knew the reason: Any sight of her physical body meant death.

A young girl, maybe six or seven, raced up to the veiled woman, despite her parents trying to stop her.

"Are you the Shari-ya?" she asked breathlessly. The little girl spoke French in the patois common to central Africa.

"Yes, I am," Shari responded, touched by the girl's eagerness.

"Are you stopping the slavers?" asked the young child.

"Yes, that is my mission. That is why I was sent to Earth."

"Where are you going now?" asked the girl innocently.

Shari thought about her conversation with Eduardo.

"As soon as possible I am going to Nigeria," she mused, and walked away into the night.

She did not see the little girl hurry back to her parents and speak to them. Nor did she see the parents talking eagerly to others on the street. Nor did she realize the direction she was walking was west—towards Nigeria.

31

Shari was inside the regimental compound in Bangui, and General Pili Barasa had just finished giving her a tour, accompanied by a formal troop inspection. Now they were in his private office. She'd earlier offered him the title of Field Marshal, as promised, but he'd declined politely. "This isn't Napoleon's army," he observed. "Make me a two-star general. That's a large enough promotion. And there aren't any other two-stars, which means I'm in full command."

She'd been impressed with his modesty and practicality and was needing to learn more about the man.

"General, clearly you've had an education. Tell me about yourself."

He shrugged. "It's not a long story. I was raised in a small town in Kenya without a lot of career opportunities so I joined the army. It was a good fit and I earned promotion. There was an Officers Training Program which I qualified for, and through that I earned a degree from Kenyatta University, in military history, along with a promotion to Lieutenant."

"How did you end up in Juba? You said you once lived there."

"The Kenyan army had officer exchange programs with several countries, and for two years I was stationed in Juba. Five years ago, as CAR was expanding its military and seeking experienced officers, a deal was made with the Kenyan Army and others. As part of that, I was honorably discharged and rehired by CAR. Earlier this year I was promoted to general and given command of the presidential guard."

"I'm confused," said Shari. "Why would they give a foreigner a position of such trust and responsibility?"

"I think the president worried that his local officers might stage a coup. He needed someone neutral. A foreigner would not try to replace him."

"You seem quite young to be a general," she probed.

"Forty-three—if you're asking my age—*is* quite young. Third-world militaries are often generous with rank," he explained, grinning, "to make up for poor pay."

"Wife, children, family?"

"Hard to maintain in the military. I was married briefly but she left me before there were any kids. Ran off with a rich Egyptian. Probably a good decision for everyone."

He tried to make a joke of it but Shari noticed he wasn't smiling, eyes downcast.

"But there was a niece."

"Yes, my brother married early and had a large family. As I explained, one of his daughters, Katinka, was kidnapped by slavers. It happened when she was on a field trip to South Sudan."

"I understand. Well, shall we talk business?"

"Of course."

Shari stood up from her chair at the desk, and began pacing in the small, windowless room.

"You don't know me well, General, but you've seen what I can do. My primary mission is to eradicate the slave trade."

"And because of that I will be your most loyal follower."

She glanced at him and nodded. "Thank you. I now control three countries. To truly eradicate slavery, I must control more. I don't know where all this is going. I can't see the future clearly."

"Whatever the future, I'll do anything you ask."

"Will you take on an additional position?"
The general raised his eyebrows, questioningly.
"Minister of Defense. You have the résumé for it."
"Will Katinka be leading us spiritually?"
"Always."
"Then you know my answer."

32

Admiral Lord James Winterset, head of MI6, the British Secret Intelligence Service, paused in the document he was reading and looked up as the door opened. His secretary made the announcement.

"My lord, agent Tai Emerson to see you."

Winterset nodded, and MI6's newest recruit walked in. Having completed tradecraft school two weeks ago, he was only a few days on the job and presumably ready for his first assignment. It was Emerson's CV that Winterset had been studying.

Taimeer Emerson, né Rabbani, had been a homeless waif on the streets of Cairo when MI6's station chief had noticed him hanging outside HQ, offering to do errands, guard vehicles, or deliver messages for the Europeans entering or exiting the building. His endearing smile, good looks, and quick intelligence caught the station chief's eye. He tested the young orphan with half a dozen non-critical tasks, and the results were impressive.

The twelve-year-old was not only street smart and clever, he had somehow managed to learn English and seemed eager for any challenge. Soon "Tai" had become a de facto errand boy for the station chief, who employed him informally to gather information. Often a *fiver* handed to the kid would return more useful intelligence than an MI6 agent could gain in a month.

They became close, and when the station chief's tour of duty ended, he legally adopted the young man whose surname thus changed to Emerson. MI6 sponsored him into Cairo University on a full scholarship, where Tai's bright mind and voracious appetite for learning earned him a BA degree in Finance by age nineteen. His adoptive father—again with the support of the Secret Service—arranged a fast-track Master's program in languages at Oxford, after which MI6 recruited the man as a full-time agent.

Winterset scanned the CV further. Top marks at university. Native language Arabic. Fluent in French and Farsi. Near perfect English. He had a gift for mastering accents. Gushing reports from MI6 instructors at the School. Smart as hell, everyone agreed, and equally charismatic and personable. Sociable and gregarious, as well as gay, he made friends easily. Irreverent sense of humor. He was tall, lanky, and with a light-brown skin color that made him hard to place, ethnically.

Winterset needed someone to go to Africa, someone who could speak French and Arabic, and—hopefully—make friends.

Or at least become close with the right people. On paper Emerson was perfect. Time to find out if MI6's considerable investment in the lad would pay off.

The two shook hands and Emerson was invited to sit in the chair facing the director's expansive desk.

"Nervous?" asked Winterset.

"Mortally terrified, my lord," Tai responded instantly and with a charming smile. The director could see how he'd make friends easily. Able to handle himself in a stressful situation, self-deprecating, a good sense of humor, and honest to a fault. Better and better.

"We have a situation in Africa…"

"Yes, my lord?"

"Look, you can drop that 'my lord' business. Here at the agency my director title takes precedence. 'Director' or just 'sir' is how I'm mostly addressed around here. Only Maggie, out front, insists on the formal title."

"Yes, sir," responded Tai, respectfully. "But, like Maggie, I may slip up occasionally." He grinned. "Now what's up in Africa?"

"I've just come from the Foreign Office. Damndest thing they've ever seen. A week ago our entire consular staff in three central African countries was expelled, as were every nation's diplomats. It was all done politely. No animosity. It was just out of the blue and with identical expulsion letters in each case. Here, take a look."

The Director handed over one of the letters and Tai read it quickly. "Which countries?"

"Central African Republic, South Sudan, and Chad."

"They share common borders," mused Emerson. "In parts of South Sudan and in northern Chad they speak Arabic. Otherwise, French would be the common language."

Winterset, who'd needed to consult a map, was impressed. "The Foreign Secretary needs us to find out what's up."

"It's obvious," said Emerson. "There's been some kind of coup. Or more likely three coups. Somehow all three countries are now controlled by a single ruler. That's the only explanation for identical letters. It would also explain why they want the diplomats out. They're trying to be hush-hush about it. Perhaps to consolidate gains. They don't need the world's attention on them right now."

"Yes, my thoughts exactly," agreed the MI6 chief. "But why identical letters? That clearly telegraphs there's a single ruler in control. Seems a stupid mistake. They could have varied the letters, and made it look like merely a coincidence the expulsions were happening in three countries at once. Are we dealing with idiots?"

Tai stared out the window, obviously thinking deeply. Finally he turned back. "It was not a stupid mistake. I think we're dealing with very shrewd people. They probably knew that pretending it was a coincidence wouldn't work, at least not with anyone who mattered.

So they didn't try. Most likely, they probably hoped it would *look* like a stupid mistake, so people would start underestimating them."

"Hmmm," mused Winterset. "Well, then, let's not underestimate them."

"What orders do you have for me, sir?"

"Get down there. Start in Bangui which is more central so it might be their headquarters. Find out what's going on. If you have an opportunity to make contact with anyone on the inside, do so. There's arguably no place on the planet less important to British interests, but still…"

"We need to know what's happening," Emerson said, completing the sentence.

"Precisely."

"And my identity?"

"You're a young adventurer. Just a backpacker taking time off after university. Wandering around the continent. Q's section will fix you up with supplies, as a cover. He'll also provide an encrypted satellite phone. Mobile coverage isn't all it could be, in those areas."

"And I'm to simply report in when I find something?"

"Yes. You leave tomorrow. You're booked London to Khartoum. From there you'll have to find your own way to Bangui, as it's not clear which airlines are still flying in, if any. Report back in one week. And there's another thing."

"Yes, sir?"

"If someone, or some group, has managed to seize all three of these countries and keep it under the radar, it suggests we're dealing with someone of unusual competence. If you're able, try to get close to the center of power. I authorize you to even disclose your identity as a British intelligence agent if you wish. It's hardly surprising we'd try to learn what's going on. Try to establish friendly relations. Unless it's an Islamic terror cell, or a proxy of China playing for mineral rights, I see no reason we have to be adversarial with them. Again, not a lot of

British interests at stake in that part of the world, but one can't have too many friends."

"Or too few enemies," Emerson noted.

"Precisely."

33

The "couple of weeks" Eduardo and Shari hoped they might have were not granted. Astonishingly, word had somehow spread to Nigeria not only that the Angel of Death was building an empire in central Africa but that Nigeria was her next target. She was expected to arrive any day, overthrow the president, and put an end to slavery and corruption.

Nigeria was now in flames. Pro-Shariya riots were everywhere. In the North, silent vigils were being held in the center of every village. In the populous south, spontaneous parades of liberation were spilling over. In the capital of Abuja, permanent demonstrators were encamped outside the presidential palace and their numbers were swelling.

In Lagos, the largest city in Africa, public employees were striking, and even oil shipments had stalled.

Politics as usual was one thing, with endless and never fulfilled promises from the candidates. But a divine *angel* sent with terrifying powers to rid the country of all that was evil? This was something to give everyone hope. Confirmed rumors of her capabilities had trickled in weeks ago. This was the spirit creature who commanded an army of lions, who could kill a man with merely a glance, who had already toppled half the countries in Africa and was now going to liberate Nigeria.

The rumors grew at astonishing speed and to incredible heights. Most everyone believed this was the most wonderful and remarkable thing that had ever happened on the continent. The country came to a standstill, while all awaited the arrival of the supernatural being.

"Great, *now* what do we do?" asked Shari, watching the news coverage on television.

"I think..." began Eduardo.

"Yes?"

"I think the advice I gave earlier is no longer correct."

"You claimed we weren't strong enough militarily to take on Nigeria or Kenya."

"But now it doesn't require a military solution."

"How so?"

"Nigeria is paralyzed merely on the rumor that you might be coming."

"How do we use that?"

"I know the president. I'll call him."

"And say?"

"The truth. That I work for you, that you've already conquered three countries, and that you're now planning to take over Nigeria. I'll suggest, very politely, that he and his family leave immediately for Switzerland with whatever wealth he can take with him."

"Will that work?"

"Of course. At this point he's barricaded inside the presidential palace terrified of being burned alive by the protestors who now nearly control the city. I'll offer him safe passage to Switzerland. In a few days, you can add Nigeria to your empire."

"And end their part in the slave trade?"

"Yes."

"Very well. We'll do that, and then..."

Eduardo's phone rang. It was from a secretary, and he put it on speaker.

"Excuse me, sir, but a young man has approached the palace gate.

He told the guards he's a British secret agent sent down here to look like a backpacker, but his real mission is to make contact with Shariya if possible and try to be her friend, and he'd rather skip the—the bullshit—that's how he put it, sir, and just be her friend."

Shari and Eduardo looked at each other disbelievingly, and then Shari broke into laughter.

"I think I really want to be this guy's friend!" she decided. "He sounds hilarious."

"A not-so-secret, secret agent," agreed Eduardo, smiling.

Soon MI6 operative Tai Emerson was sitting with the two of them. Shari had donned her veil, and Eduardo was relaxed, as always.

"I'm Shariya," she said in French. "Who are you, exactly?"

"I'm from British Intelligence," he replied. Shari noticed his French was Parisian. "My mission is to look like a backpacker and try to learn what's happening in this country. By the way, what do you think of my disguise? Cool backpack, huh? Are you convinced?"

Shari laughed. "It's perfect," she agreed.

"So, I've been hearing the rumors. If you don't kill me immediately or feed me to your lions or turn me into toxic tar with a glance, do you think we could be—you know—friends?"

"Is a name too much to ask? You know, *between friends?*" Shari couldn't quit smiling.

He stood up and endeavored to bow low, and formally.

"British MI6 Secret Agent Tai Emerson, originally from Cairo, now fully at your service. And please don't forget the secret part. If you disclose my identity, I'll have to kill you or something." He grinned.

"I'm utterly terrified," she announced, laughing. "Well, friend, please sit back down."

Tai glanced around the room. "I guess I've been living in England too long. Can I ask when a cup of fucking tea might be served?"

This time even Eduardo laughed.

34

Nigerian President Muboro formally abdicated, and a close friend of Eduardo was chosen to form a new government loyal to Shariya. Muboro and his closest relatives flew off to Geneva in a private jet, well in possession of the Swiss bank accounts that would allow them to live comfortably for the rest of their lives. It was generally agreed that if they'd waited another twenty-four hours, they'd not have had lives at all.

Shariya now controlled the wealthiest and most populated country in Africa. And there was no longer any reason to remain in stealth mode, nor the ability to do so. Eduardo composed the press release himself.

> *NEW EMPIRE PROCLAIMED IN CENTRAL AFRICA*
>
> *Imperial Headquarters, Bangui, [Date] – The government press office announced today that the countries known as Central African Republic, South Sudan, Chad, and Nigeria are now merged, and the name of the combined entity is the Central African Empire. The individual countries remain as political subdivisions.*

The newly formed Central African Empire is under the control of the Empress Shariya, known to many as the Angel of Death. Linguistically, "Shari-ya" comes from a tribal tongue in which 'ya' means 'death' and 'Shari' means angel. A few weeks ago the empress launched a tribal war against the slave caravans of central Africa, and because slavery was implicitly supported by the rulers of these countries, the rulers were overthrown and the countries themselves seized.

Eduardo Danjuma, previously Nigeria's Ambassador to the United Nations, has been named Prime Minister of the Empire, reporting directly to the empress.

The ongoing strategic goal of the Empire is the eradication of slavery from Africa, and equally the eradication of corruption in government.

"One thing we wish to make clear," noted Danjuma, "is that despite the reference to our empress as the Angel of Death, which suggests a spiritual element, the Empire has no religious agenda. It is not affiliated with any religion and believes strongly in the free exercise of religion in the territories it controls."

"It must also be made explicit," he continued, "that the Empire is not aligned with any other nation, or pact, or international community. It serves only its own people. For this reason and others, the Empire is not seeking to be recognized by the international community and is not seeking membership in the United Nations. The General Assembly seats formerly held by the four countries which currently make up the Empire are hereby abandoned.

"While it is not the intention of the Empire to stay disengaged from the world community indefinitely, the Empire at the moment is focused only on Africa.

"We do hope that our goals of eradicating slavery, eliminating corruption, and bringing prosperity to the people of Africa will be supported by the international community." [END]

It was headline news globally, but only for one news cycle. A day later, the creation of the Central African Empire had been pushed off the front page by the lead-up to the World Cup championship in Buenos Aires.

Several days later a rumor began in Nairobi, and spread rapidly, that Kenya was Shariya's next takeover target. The East African country was not as corrupt as some, but its people had plenty of grievances. Sensing a new hope, they also turned out in the streets, and the riots took hold and grew rapidly.

Worried about merely staying alive, the Kenyan ruling family accepted the offer of complete abdication in return for safe passage to Western Europe. They left, firmly in control of lucrative bank accounts.

This time, the Empire's command of the news cycle was absolute. A few central and west African countries that no one cared about, merging into one and calling itself an empire, elicited yawns globally. But now anyone looking at a map could see what had happened. The newly born *empire* suddenly stretched across Africa, from the Atlantic coast to the Indian Ocean, cutting the continent in half. And if it could grow so quickly, absorbing five countries in less than two weeks, how much larger might it become?

The world was desperate to find out what was happening but the Central African Empire had closed its doors. Visas were required, and none were granted. Back in London, the head of MI6 paced nervously, desperate for his newly minted agent to report back.

35

IN THE SEVERAL days since Shari had met Tai she'd become impressed. Not only was he funny, irreverent, and even cheeky, but he possessed a quick intelligence and an almost encyclopedic knowledge of the world.

She'd insisted he move into the presidential palace and act as advisor. But today was their first meeting in that capacity.

Eduardo was in Nairobi sorting out Kenya so she met with Tai alone.

"Have you reported back to London since arriving in Bangui?" she asked, as they sat on an L-shaped settee in the conference room, the large map of Africa taking up much of one wall.

"No. I was told to report back in one week at the latest, by encrypted satellite phone. So I thought I'd use the full week, as I'd have that much more to report."

"When you do, I expect they'll be surprised you've managed to become an adviser to Empress Shariya herself." The hidden figure spoke loftily, referring to herself in third person.

"It will look smashing on my résumé." Tai grinned.

Shari stayed serious. "What do you intend to say about everything going on here?"

"I won't lie. But I can also invoke confidentiality like a reporter with an unnamed source. I can truthfully say that you've allowed me into your inner circle, and I can't abuse that trust. Hence, I will be guarded in what I communicate."

"Very good. We'll come back to that in a moment. Eduardo and I have come to the conclusion you are very clever, very intelligent, and potentially very useful to the empire. I've already designated you informally as an advisor. If it's not in conflict with your MI6 role, I'd like to formalize that with the title 'Chief Advisor on Strategic Affairs.' That should look good on your résumé as well, and that title will cover anything important. If it's not important I don't want you wasting time on it."

"Your Chief Advisor on Strategic Affairs stands ready to advise, my lady." He stood and bowed graciously.

The empress rolled her eyes, even though hidden behind the veil. "'My *lady*,' please. Let's stick with Shari."

"If that is my lady's command, I shall obey—Shari."

She smiled again, knowing he still couldn't see her face.

"Here are the rules. You may communicate to London anything you wish, as long as it's truthful, of course. If there is anything I do not wish you to communicate, I will specifically flag that. If it's not flagged, you're a free agent."

"That's reasonable. What's flagged?"

"This."

And Shari, for the first time in his presence, whisked off her head covering.

Tai stood transfixed but was speechless only for a moment.

"So," he began, "my only question is: How many gallons of hair coloring and skin dye, not to mention contact lenses, did it take to transform a native African tribal girl into a platinum blonde with blue eyes and white skin?"

"Very funny."

"Well, I can't wait to hear *this* story!"

"You'd expect me to say 'it's a long one,' but it's not. It's very short.

And everything I'm now going to tell you is flagged. You're not to communicate any of it."

Shari reviewed her brief history, the only one she knew, starting from when she awoke on the riverbank with her mind gone.

"So you're an amnesiac. Fascinating."

"And every time I try to force myself to think about it, I become physically nauseous and sometimes vomit. There's something horrible in my past, but it's behind a door that won't open. And I don't want it to. Maybe someday I'll try harder. But for now, I'm Empress Shariya, the Angel of Death. Perhaps I *was* set down in the middle of Africa by supernatural forces and charged with a mission, as so many believe. So if you're willing to take orders from me…?"

Tai nodded.

"That's the most important one. I don't want you to question where I came from, try to investigate it, or learn anything. Whatever's back there, on the other side of the door, we leave it alone. Understood?"

"Yes, totally."

"When you communicate with MI6, you are to say I'm a village girl from the jungles of CAR, who developed a hatred for the slavers, and who led a revolt against them. Everything flowed from there. And that is one hundred percent true."

"They will of course assume you're African."

"Yes, they will probably not ask if I'm actually white with blonde hair and blue eyes. So you'll not have to lie. Nor will they ask if I'm an amnesiac, so that part can stay private, too."

"But they'll ask me to describe you, what kind of person you are, age, education, things like that."

"I don't know my exact age, nor my education. But I speak French, and somehow have a knowledge of the world, an understanding of geopolitics, economics, stuff like that. Although I have no idea where it came from. I also seem to be a gifted martial artist. I must have had training somewhere. Oh, and one more thing. I've not mentioned it to anyone else."

"What?"

"Sometimes when I'm alone, in the forest, here in the palace, anywhere, sometimes I'll hear music in my head, and I'll start to dance to the music."

"That doesn't sound too unusual."

"I don't mean dance casually. I mean *dance*, as a ballerina. I find myself sometimes doing spins, pirouettes they're called, and rising up on my toes with my arms extended. I think that was a part of my prior life."

"And somehow this expert martial artist, this ballerina, this perfect French-speaking European with white skin, awoke beside a river in the middle of Africa with her mind gone."

"Yes. Precisely."

"I would very much like to know what's on the other side of that door."

"When I'm ready to handle it, so would I. That time is not now."

"So what do I tell MI6 about your level of education, your worldly knowledge, and so forth?"

"Don't bring it up. You can say this truthfully. Before she started her slave revolt she was living in a small tribal village in Africa. You don't know her age because she hasn't told you and you've not been so impolite as to ask. But she's a ferocious warrior and quite young. Certainly under thirty."

"Way under. My guess is you're a teenager."

"Just say 'certainly under thirty.'"

"Very well."

"Say I speak enough French for you to be able to communicate. French is one of the national languages in CAR so it's not impossible even a villager might know a few words of it."

"Yes, that's plausible."

"And as for everything else, say I'm clever enough to have surrounded myself with competent people. And they're handling the rise of the empire. And you can be utterly honest about Eduardo. He has all the skills necessary to pull off this empire-building. I'm primarily the rallying point, the inspirational figure who makes it possible."

"Yes, who ties it all together."

"So, I think you should report back today even though it hasn't been a full week yet. You can also be truthful about how you fast-tracked yourself into my inner circle, how you arrived at the presidential palace, how we were intrigued with your frontal and honest approach, and so forth. Will they have a problem with that?"

"They should be pleased."

"Will they allow you to remain here and serve as an advisor?"

"I'm certain of it. It's a coup for them. Suddenly the whole world is taking your empire seriously, and only the Brits have managed to establish a connection and insert an agent as your confidante. I have just one question."

"Yes?"

"What, exactly, am I supposed to advise you on?"

"Just this. Eduardo is a quintessential diplomat and manager, doing a brilliant job bringing other countries into our empire and making sure everything runs smoothly. But we're missing one thing."

"Which is?"

"A strategic vision. My strategic vision has nearly run its course. I wanted to eradicate slavery. With Nigeria and Kenya and the others under our control, we've wiped out ninety percent of it. We might try to push that to ninety-five percent but at some point we'll see diminishing returns. So this is your job: Over the next few weeks or months, try to develop a strategic vision for what the Central African Empire should do next. What are we trying to accomplish?"

"Well that's perhaps the easiest task anyone's been handed," noted Tai.

"How so?"

"Because I've already completed it. It's obvious what the Central African Empire should now do."

"What?"

"Take over the rest of Africa."

"Don't be ridiculous, Tai. That's not possible."

"It's not only not ridiculous, it's not only possible, I believe it's inevitable. And with the help of the British, you're going to do it. Also, then we can abandon that horrid Central African Empire name."

"In favor of what?"

"Duh. The Empire of Africa. Much more impressive."

"This whole conversation is insane."

"Africa—more than any other continent—suffers from misrule, despair, poverty, and economic insanity. Someone needs to take over the whole place—much as the British almost did in the nineteenth century—and sort it out. But this time it can be done by Africans. Eduardo, Barasa, myself, and others you'll bring in. You can be the spark who set it off, but it's now time for Africans themselves to rise up and manage their continent properly. It may have taken a supernatural avenging angel to wake everyone up. But now Africa *is* awake. Consider the riots in Nigeria and Kenya. Africa is ready to rise on the world stage—and control its own destiny at last."

"I just wanted to stop slavery. I don't need a huge empire."

"No, *you* don't. But Africa does. Africa needs the spark you gave us. We'll be forever grateful for that spark. But also in a way you do need this."

"Why?"

"You told me yourself. You're an amnesiac. You're a blank slate. You have no past. What's your future? What's your goal, your mission? You have none. As I understand it, you were essentially 'born' roughly eight weeks ago on the banks of a river."

"Yes, I was."

"Then other than the conquest of Africa, you have nothing on the agenda, do you?"

"I suppose not."

"Most importantly…"

"Yes?"

"Well, if I help the Angel of Death conquer Africa, screw the résumé. Just imagine the book deal!"

"Book deal!" she yelled at him. "Try *this* book deal," and she started tossing throw-pillows at his head. He threw one back, and they both laughed.

Shari was thrilled to find she could still kid around and have fun. Wasn't that what a young girl *should* be doing?

Tai's satellite phone rang.

36

They looked at each other and then Tai stood up and walked over to his pack.

"Agent Emerson here, encryption filter on."

"On here as well," said Winterset. "I gave you a week, but I couldn't wait any longer."

"I understand, my lord. I mean, Director."

"Can you talk?"

"Yes, no problem."

"Did you manage to make it to Bangui? Have you had any contact with anyone in the new government, the 'imperial court,' I guess they're calling it. Do you have even one clue about what the hell is going on down there?"

"Well, sir…"

"Just so you know, this has suddenly turned into an extreme priority for the world, and very much for MI6. I should never have sent our least experienced agent but there was no way to know how fast things would move."

"Actually, sir…"

"Anyway, I'll be grateful for whatever you can tell us. Even the smallest insight about what's happening and who's behind it all could be useful."

"Sir, I hope I've not exceeded my authority, but you are right now speaking to the empire's Chief Advisor for Strategic Affairs. I report to the empress directly. I am charged with helping her develop a strategic plan for the empire which is already well advanced, and by the way she's standing here with me right now, in the main conference room of the Imperial Palace."

"Rubbish. Tai, I know everyone enjoys your humor, but I'm not in the mood for it. I need to know if you've made any progress at all. Any progress. Please be serious."

"I've never been more serious, sir. And you should know that I've recommended to the empress that her strategic plan should be to take over the rest of Africa. She's dubious, but we were just discussing it when you called."

There was silence.

"You've made contact with Shariya *herself?*"

"More than contact, sir. I'm now one of her chief advisors, and I'm living at the palace. I think this can be quite beneficial to our interests. As I said, I've recommended she keep the momentum going and continue her conquests. You saw how quickly Nigeria and Kenya fell? This is like the Arab Spring but on steroids. I think she could run the table."

"You mean to say that one of my agents is actually on the inside, helping *direct* all this?"

"Indeed, sir. And of course I still report to you in my capacity as an MI6 agent, so if you have instruction for me on the advice I should give her, well, as I said, she's standing right here."

More silence.

"OK, Tai, I'm beginning to get the picture. Sorry to be slow on the uptake. It seems you've exceeded our expectations by several orders of magnitude."

"Just keeping the British end up, sir. Nothing too challenging for an Oxford man, as we say."

"It's utterly remarkable. I'm still trying to catch my bearings. Did you say that the empress is with you right now, in the room, hearing your end of the conversation?"

"She is, sir. Could I relay a message from you?"

"Let me think. Well, I suppose just this. Please tell her that the government of the United Kingdom is very interested in the developments in central Africa and that we're very grateful she's seen fit to bring one of our team into her inner circle, and, and…And how the hell did you manage all this, Tai? You've only been there a few days. How did you even *meet* her?"

"I walked up to the front gate of the Palace and announced I was a British secret agent sent down to look like a backpacker, but my real goal was to try to make contact with the new government."

"And that *worked*?"

"Like a charm, sir. Perhaps in our business we tend to forget that sometimes honesty is the best policy."

"Would never have occurred to me to just walk up to the bloody front gate. Damned cheeky of you, Emerson."

"Sir, if you'd like, I could ask the empress to leave the room so that you and I may speak privately."

"Would that look rude?"

"I don't know, let's find out."

Tai switched to French and asked Shari if she'd mind granting him some privacy.

"Take as much time as you need," she said, smiling, and left—closing the door discreetly.

"Now, sir, we're completely alone. Shari, I mean the empress, has left."

"You call her *Shari*?"

"Yes, she's not enamored with fancy titles and ceremony. A month ago she was living in a primitive tribal village in the jungle."

"Tai, tell me about her. Tell me everything. The call's being recorded. This is priceless. No other government has any intelligence on her at all."

Tai reviewed everything, stepping around the land mines as they'd agreed.

"So that's about it, sir. Her prime minister, Eduardo Danjuma, is utterly brilliant. He favors all the things we favor: free trade, free markets, rolling back the bureaucracy, everything. I really think this is quite favorable to our interests, as I said. If Shari can keep these nearly blood-free revolutions going, I think she should."

"Perhaps we could help her."

"I said as much, Director. She doesn't seem to need help at the moment, but perhaps Britain could be sort of an advocate for the empire on the world stage. Say good things about it. Use its influence to subtly promote her brand, that kind of thing."

"Yes, and perhaps more, but no need to get ahead of ourselves. So, you're authorized to stay there and do whatever you think best, to advance our interests. And you can keep reporting back to us—wait a minute. Is the empress OK with having a British spy in her court, reporting to an outside government?"

"We discussed it, sir. She gave me free rein to report anything I wish, as long as I'm truthful. She said anything she doesn't want me to report, she'll flag."

"Has she flagged anything?"

"Yes, sir, she has."

This time there was a longer pause.

"Is it anything I should be concerned about?"

"Not in the least, but even if it were, I'd not disclose it. I have to maintain a position of trust. I hope you'll agree that's most important to our long-term interests."

"Now you'll have me scratching my head over what you're not allowed to communicate."

"Don't worry, sir, you'd never guess. And I can assure you it's not a concern. You'd find it interesting, but not especially important."

"Very well, Tai. We'll leave it at that. Please report in anytime you think we need to know something, and I'll call you with any specific questions or issues we have regarding the empire."

"Yes, Director."

"One more thing. I'm damned impressed. This violates protocol but I'm promoting you to Senior Agent, with a corresponding increase in salary. We'll make sure the funds go into your bank account, directly, while you're out of the country."

"Thank you, sir. It's been an exceptionally good week for my résumé."

"Keep up the good work, and it will be an exceptionally good year."

37

SHARI WAS HOLDING an executive council meeting with both her Prime Minister and Senior Advisor for Strategic Affairs. It had been one week since Kenya fell, and the three of them were running the empire almost as equals.

As was becoming routine, they were in the large presidential office suite with its vast conference table. Large windows and a balcony provided an elegant view of the Ubangi River to the south. On the north wall was a floor-to-ceiling map of Africa—a continent which was changing faster than any printed chart could record.

It was convenient to combine breakfast with their frequent strategy meetings, and the used dishes had been pushed away. With Shari unveiled, servants were forbidden to enter. The empress sat at one end of the table, and the two advisers occupied the seats next to her on either side.

Eduardo was now standing, gesturing to the map with his hands.

"With the conquest of Nigeria and Kenya, you've cut Africa in half. Your empire runs from the Atlantic coast to the Indian Ocean."

"What's next?" asked Shari.

"We have some policy decisions to make within the lands we've already conquered," explained Eduardo soberly.

"Such as?" pressed the empress.

"Well, what are the laws? We probably need consistency. Most importantly, what are the tax rates? The tariffs and so forth? We've proven we can conquer. But can we govern?"

"Well, let's do the obvious stuff first," she responded.

"And in your mind what would that be?" asked Tai.

"Tariffs on imports. Are there any?"

"Yes," noted Eduardo. "Quite a few. It varies between countries and I can provide a list."

"No tariffs. The entire empire is a free trade zone, and the empire is also a free port."

"A free port? Do you mean like Hong Kong?" asked Eduardo.

"Exactly. No tariffs on anything."

"Tariffs protect special interests," he mused. "Eliminate them and you'll make enemies."

"Anyone who protests, invite them to the palace and I will grant them an audience. Start a rumor that the Angel of Death deals mercilessly with protestors, and those invited to the Palace never return. Mention something about lions."

"Done." Eduardo returned to his seat and began taking notes on a laptop.

"As for tax rates," queried the young empress, "what are we talking about? Income taxes. Sales taxes? Do we have any VATs?"

"No VATs in these countries," explained Eduardo. "There are sales taxes of between five and ten percent but almost no one pays them because so much business is done in cash and under the table."

"Income taxes?"

"Yes, they exist on private incomes and on corporate profits, although right now they vary between the countries. Of course there is vast cheating going on," explained the Prime Minister. "Income is hidden. Profits are funneled offshore. Large amounts go to bribe the bureaucrats responsible for collecting the taxes."

"Then how do these countries generate enough revenue to support their bureaucracies?" asked Shari.

"Very little comes from taxation, for the reasons said. The bureaucracies are largely self-sustaining because the regulators don't regulate, they just accept bribes to look the other way. The real revenue to the governments comes from lease agreements with mining and petroleum interests. And there's a lot of foreign aid floating about that funds social programs like schools, hospitals, and such. Some of that money actually finds its way to those things."

"So we don't have to worry about safety nets as they have in Europe? No welfare state, right?"

"Almost none in Africa. The welfare comes from the NGOs, the non-governmental organizations like Unicef and Doctors without Borders. Oxfam, that kind of thing."

"And the rules and regulations exist," noted the empress, "just as a front to allow the bureaucrats to force bribes. It sounds like the entire bureaucracy is basically a protection racket." Shari stood up and began pacing in frustration.

"Very much so," agreed Eduardo. "Licensing agreements generate the revenue to fund the modest armed forces and a national police, and of course to make sure the president lives in style."

"What if we eliminated the entire bureaucracy?" asked the young girl who'd once thought creatively about destroying the drug lords in Columbia. "It seems to be doing nothing but serving as a net drag on the economy. Couldn't we dump most of the business regulations which aren't being enforced anyway?"

"It would be a huge shot in the arm to the economy," acknowledged Eduardo. "But you'd have thousands of starving bureaucrats. You can't feed *all* of them to your lions."

Tai, who'd been sitting contemplatively, jumped in. "Could I make a suggestion?"

"Please," said the empress.

"I read a novel once, by Gary Jennings. It imagined a 13th-century Chinese empire funded entirely by lottery."

"Lottery?"

"Yes, imagine a vast, empire-wide national lottery. Lotteries are highly profitable for those who run them. In the novel, the emperor was frustrated at his inability to receive tax revenue. Everyone was cheating. So they tried a different approach. They eliminated all taxes. They weren't generating that much net tax revenue anyway, after deducting the costs of trying to enforce the tax code. Much like here.

"So they implemented a national lottery, with prizes daily, weekly, monthly, annually. Rather than everyone using tricks to not pay taxes, the opposite incentives were in play. Everyone found money somehow, by borrowing, stealing, whatever, and gambled it away on the lottery. The empire was suddenly awash in revenue. They'd used the human psychology of greed in their favor, by harnessing it."

"So it worked in a novel," observed Shari skeptically. "Has anyone ever tried to do it in real life?"

"There are lotteries in various countries, of course," said Tai. "But what's envisioned here is to simply replace the tax code with gambling. Suddenly everyone has tons of extra money, and no one's bribing bureaucrats or hiring clever accountants to hide revenue. There's suddenly much more productive money left in the economy. Much of that finds its way into the national lottery."

"But what about our unemployed bureaucrats? Eduardo's right. We can't feed all of them to my lions."

"They'd be trained to run the lottery itself. Send them out to all the towns and villages, with instructions to push lottery tickets on everyone."

"What do you think, Eduardo?"

The prime minister stared at Tai silently for a moment before rendering a verdict.

"Craziest idea I've ever heard, but for some reason I like it.

Informal gambling is very popular in Africa. We could leverage that, but organize it all into a continent-wide Imperial Lottery."

"Surely we could still cut the size of government," protested Shari. "I don't like encouraging gambling—which isn't a very productive activity—just to keep an army of useless politicians and bureaucrats afloat."

"We can gently but steadily cut the size of government via attrition, observed Eduardo. "As people retire, or leave their jobs, or die, we just don't replace them. We eliminate those positions, or move people around as needed. Obviously, I'm still hiring quality staff for empirical headquarters, but on the national levels, the workforce can shrink. Overall, a huge reduction."

"It would take time to do all this, set it up, train the bureaucrats to run the lottery, and so forth," noted Shari. "How do we cover expenses in the meantime?"

"The treasuries from Kenya and Nigeria were mostly looted by the ex-presidents, which is one reason they surrendered so quickly," acknowledged the prime minister. "But the real wealth is from ongoing licensing fees paid by petroleum and mining companies. We could use that as collateral and borrow what we need to make the transition."

"Do you have the staff to make all this happen, Eduardo? There are a lot of moving parts here."

"Shari, I've trained for this job my whole life. When we only had the three poor countries I was worried. But with Nigeria and Kenya we've got resources. I'm going full speed hiring Deputy Ministers and Assistant Deputy Ministers. I'm grabbing the smartest and the most competent from all five countries.

"So just give the word," he continued, "and I'll make it happen. Zero tariffs. Free port status. Removing almost all the worthless business regulations. Retraining the bureaucrats as lottery ticket salespeople. All of it."

"The word's given," said Shari, on her feet again, pacing this time with excitement. "What's that phrase? Make it so?"

Eduardo smiled.

The phone rang and the prime minister put it on speaker.

"Sir, there's an urgent call for you from the President of Congo."

The empress exchanged a meaningful glance with her prime minister.

"We're done here, go!" she said, and he rushed from the room.

She turned back to Tai, who she noticed was staring at her.

"Shari, I hope this isn't rude, but what's that little pendant around your neck?"

"Oh, this? It's just a pretty rock I found near the riverbank where I first regained consciousness. For some reason I kept it. There were many of these on the far bank the several times I crossed the river. When I began living in the tribal village, one of the women fashioned a cradle of yarn around it, so I could wear it on my neck."

"I've never seen it before."

"Well, I don't usually have it on."

"You don't suppose it's a diamond?"

"No, it's not a diamond. Diamonds are sparkly and shiny. See how this is very dull and opaque. It's probably quartz or something."

"Shari, diamonds are sparkly and shiny only when they're cut, when they've been faceted. Most rough diamonds look like this. Do you mind if I borrow it? There are jewelers in town who could identify it. You say there were many of these by the river?"

The two of them locked eyes.

Silently, Shari removed the pendant and handed it to Tai.

38

The empire's Chief Advisor for Strategic Affairs had just left the palace, heading for downtown Bangui, when Eduardo rushed back in.

The breakfast dishes were still at the other end of the conference table, and the empress was on the balcony, enjoying the river view. When she heard the door open and saw Eduardo, she returned to her seat, and gestured for him to be seated as well.

"Sorry, I'm too excited to sit," he said, grinning.

"Tell me."

"Congratulations, Shari, your empire just expanded again."

"Congo?"

"Yep, Congo!" He slapped it on the map for dramatic emphasis.

"OK, stand if you must, but tell me everything."

As he paced in front of the giant map, Eduardo recapped the conversation.

"President Omase's hold on power is weak and he knows it. He's terrified that if you turn your eyes on his country not only would it erupt in riots and violence but he and his family would probably be massacred with machetes in a matter of hours. That's how high the level of discontent is."

"So…?"

"So he's being proactive, and we cut a deal. Tomorrow morning at ten a.m. he's going to declare for the Empress Shariya and announce that Congo is now part of the empire, via press conference from the presidential palace in Kinshasa. We'll issue our own press release here in Bangui, confirming it."

"Wow. Congo. That's huge!"

"Thank God we now have a corporate jet at our disposal, compliments of the Nigerian government. With your permission I'll fly to Kinshasa today to organize things, and then instruct our pilot to fly the president and his family to anywhere in Europe he wishes, immediately after the press conference in the morning."

"He doesn't want to stay around?"

"Not at all. I explored that with him. But he opted for the same deal I offered the Nigerian leader."

"I can't believe how fast this is happening," said Shari. "Tai called it the Arab Spring on steroids."

"Good description."

"So, what will it do for us strategically to have Congo?"

"Well, until recently there were two Congos. Republic of Congo and Democratic Republic of Congo. No one could keep them straight, and nine months ago they finally merged, so you now gain the whole thing. In terms of visual impact on the map it's huge. But look which countries are now surrounded by the empire."

"Cameroon, Gabon, and Equatorial Guinea," said Shari, studying the map and reading off their names.

"I'll call up the president of each and ask when they'd like to have our private jet fly them to Europe."

"Isn't that presumptuous?"

"The map makes their decision inescapable. You could swallow them militarily without raising a sweat. Worse, if you declare them targets, the local populations will erupt. They can't afford the risk. That's why Congo was proactive and contacted *us*. And these other countries are far weaker."

Shari stared at the large map, appraisingly. "Maybe not every ruler needs to be sent to Europe. If they just declare for the empire and accept our control over them, isn't that sufficient?"

"In some cases, yes. It will depend on the popularity of the country's leader. We'll consider it case by case."

"This is amazing, Eduardo. If we can add those other three, it will mean the empire's grown to nine countries—in less than a month! I'm beginning to think Tai might be right. That we could take over Africa itself. All of it. Am I dreaming?"

Eduardo sat down and looked at her seriously.

"*All of it* might be dreaming. The toughest nuts would be the Arabic countries of the Sahara—from Morocco to Egypt, and of course Sudan. Egypt and Sudan have the most powerful militaries in Africa and the Arab populations are the least likely to revolt on cue. Also, South Africa would be very difficult. It's not a third-world country although it's starting to turn back into one now that they're forcibly ejecting from government anyone with actual experience. I really can't predict South Africa. But let's not get ahead of ourselves."

"Eduardo, I can't merely watch all this happening from the comfort of my palace. I'm seeing it on television, the angry crowds, the protests, and the burning down of buildings. All of it. But I need to get closer. I need to understand how these people are feeling."

"You want to join one of these mobs, be a part of it?"

"Yes, and talk to the people. But incognito. I'll dress as a conservative Muslim woman, with my abaya and so forth. Let's do this after you sort out Congo. You come with me, pretending to be my husband. And not in a business suit. Wear Islamic dress appropriate for whatever country we visit. Which one should we visit?"

He stared at the map contemplatively.

"Cameroon," he said. "Protests have already started in Yaoundé. When it's learned that Congo is now part of the empire, and those three countries surrounded, Cameroon will erupt first."

39

Eduardo had left for Kinshasa by the time Tai returned with the mystery stone.

The empress had again donned her veil and had helped the servants move dishes to the kitchen. She was determined not to act like spoiled and pampered nobility. By now everyone was used to what an unusual empress they had on their hands.

"Shari, we need to meet in the most private location possible," whispered Tai.

"Well, if we need that much privacy, let's go to the gazebo in the courtyard. We'll be in full view, but no one will be able to approach closer than fifty yards without being spotted."

She posted sentries just to make sure.

Tai's eyes were sparkling as he spoke to her quietly. "It's a diamond."

"Really?"

"I went to the most reputable jeweler in Bangui and he had all the needed gemological equipment. It's definitely a diamond. And it's what's called a type 2A diamond, extremely rare, and with a particular chemistry. He polished a window into the rough surface so he could see inside. He could find no flaw, and said the color is likely a D."

"What's that?"

"The very best. And it's almost sixty carats."

"So it's valuable?"

"Sixty carats of rough, he told me, will polish down to about thirty carats of finished stone, and maybe a few smaller ones. A thirty-carat D-flawless is worth…"

"How much?"

"Around five million dollars."

Shari gasped, her mind recalling the rocks she'd seen along the riverbank, not to mention the little spring-fed, limestone hole where this one had come from.

Tai looked at her closely. "You said there were many of these back on the riverbank?"

"Yes, on the far side from where I was living. It was the inside bank of a broad curve of the river."

"That would make sense. Water slows on the inside curve of a river, and that's why the stones were deposited there. But they must have come from upstream. Alluvial diamonds are carried downstream from some kind of mother lode, like gold."

"I suppose so."

"Shari, can we get back there? Can you remember where that spot in the river was?"

She let her mind return to the place where her current life had begun. It was just over a day's hike from the tribal village that had taken her in. She could find the village because it appeared on large scale maps of the area. The paths were clear and she knew she could retrace her steps if she started at the village. The villagers themselves, the ones who fetched her out of the jungle, would remember where they'd found her as well. Wait a minute—the river.

"Tai, pull up Google Earth."

Soon they had the general area displayed on a laptop screen. Shari fiddled with the mouse, zooming in on what had to be the spot.

"It would be roughly here, Tai. Here's the river, and here's the curve. The stones were on the far side of it. I swam across and found them there. I'm sure I could locate it again. My God, it was just months ago I was living there, alone, with lions."

"Don't start with the lions."

"I'm not kidding. For a couple weeks, I was living with lions. Sleeping with them at night. Hunting with them. One of them saved me during an attack on the slavers by eating the one who was about to kill me. Then the rest of the pride arrived and devoured the other slavers. That's where the rumors came from."

"You actually commanded an army of lions in the jungle? I thought that was like the steaming tar."

"Not an army. Just four of them. Emil and the girls."

"You *named* them?"

"Look, it's not important. What's important is that we get back to that spot. And then to the other side of the river."

"And there's the problem," noted Tai.

"What?"

"You cross that river, Shari, you're in the Congo. Those diamonds are outside the empire."

"Hardly. While you were frivolously visiting jewelry stores, Congo joined us."

"*What?*"

"That was the phone call that pulled Eduardo from our meeting."

"Then you own these diamond fields?"

"Tomorrow I will."

40

As Eduardo predicted, with the Congo announcement two days ago Yaoundé—Cameroon's capital—was in a fever of revolt. Those determined to overthrow the president and join with the Central African Empire were now gathering each night with signs, placards, and in some cases clubs and bats. Many carried burning torches.

Tonight the protests had started in Charles Atangana Park, which centered around a statue of the prominent Cameroon hero.

National guardsmen were there as a show of force, but they tended to huddle together on the opposite side of the street, suggesting a government in retreat, isolated, and avoiding confrontation.

Eduardo and Shari took a taxi from the airport and blended into the crowd effortlessly. Cameroon was twenty percent Muslim and couples in full Islamic dress were common.

Exiting the air-conditioned cab at Atangana Park, Shari noticed the humidity. Bangui was far drier, being inland and sub-Saharan. But in other respects Yaoundé was nearly indistinguishable from her own capital. Except it was on the edge of revolution. The crowds milling about were angry and seemingly eager for violence.

Eduardo eyed them with concern. "Shari, there could be security issues here. This may not be such a good idea."

"It's an excellent idea," the empress declared, increasingly confident when trusting her instincts. "I need to understand what's happening across Africa, and right now it's happening *here*. Just stay close. Hold hands if it feels right. I'll cling to your arm occasionally and we'll look like a married couple. But I'm going to ask them questions."

One young man, at the top of steps leading to the statue, was using a bullhorn to incite the crowd. French was the official language, and he spoke it with a predictable tribal accent.

"*President Magombe! WE are talking to YOU!*"

[Applause]

"*President Magombe, YOU are not wanted!*"

[Applause]

"*President Magombe, YOU are not needed.*"

[Applause]

"*President Magombe, YOU must go!*"

Applause and some whistles and cheering.

"*One, Two, Three, Four, Shariya is wanted more!*"

The crowd joined him vocally, knowing this chant.

"*Five, Six, Seven, Eight, Leave the country—don't be late!*"

Scattered applause.

Shari climbed up the steps herself, approached the speaker, and said in a loud voice, "May I ask a question?"

"Who is this?" he asked loudly and rhetorically. "Who is this Islamic woman who would question our move to freedom?"

"I do not question your move to freedom," the veiled figure reassured quickly. "And I am indeed a worthless woman of no account. Please, may I respectfully ask a question?"

"You may!" the young man decided, seeming to enjoy this new development.

Shari, now only a few feet from the man with the bullhorn, spoke to him in a voice loud enough to be carried to the crowd. "Why do you wish to overthrow President Magombe, and why do you wish to join Shariya's empire?"

The protestors, sensing an adversary, erupted in hostile cries of anger.

"Please," she added quickly. "I am not from Cameroon. We are from a different country. I am trying to understand what is happening here. It is a serious question."

"Very well, Madame from a different country with a serious question," the protest leader shouted through his bullhorn. He was speaking to everyone in the park. "We will tell you. For years, the people of Cameroon have been ruled by one corrupt president after another. Each has promised us prosperity. Each has stolen from the people to enrich themselves."

The veiled woman gestured to the crowd and spoke so all could hear. "How do you know it will be any better if you join with the Central African Empire?"

Another young man rushed up the steps and asked for the electric megaphone—ceded willingly.

"Shariya, the empress, is not another president-for-life," he called out passionately, distorting the acoustics with his loud anger. "She is a divine being. She is sent by God to rescue Africa from corrupt politicians."

The audience applauded in agreement.

"Do you really believe she is divine?" asked Shari, trying unsuccessfully to match his volume but still loud enough to be heard by most nearby. "Can you trust her? Maybe she is just another corrupt African politician."

The crowd erupted in fury, voices crying out in indignation.

"Shariya is divine!"

"Shariya is pure and not corrupt!"

"Shariya cannot be killed for she is already dead!"

"Shariya will save us from corruption. How dare you question the Angel of Death?"

They began moving towards her menacingly, and the empress

realized she'd gone too far. Challenging their desperately-held beliefs was dangerous.

"We have to get out of here, *now!*" whispered Eduardo urgently, placing a hand on her arm, seeking to pull her away. But she shrugged him off.

Ignoring Eduardo, the veiled form moved *towards* the bullhorn and reached out for it. Everyone had expected her to flee. Needing an outlet for their anger, the crowd was ready to give chase and rip the heretic to shreds. Now she was demanding the bullhorn? It was so unexpected the man gave it to her. The veiled woman raised up an arm to the crowd and moved it in a sweeping motion across all those in the park. Then she spoke.

"I am Shariya."

The crowd went silent, astonished. She continued swiftly. "This man with me is Eduardo Danjuma, the Prime Minister of the Central African Empire. I wanted to come among you and hear for myself. And I have heard. Now we are done talking, and protesting, and waving torches angrily. Tonight we are going to march to the presidential palace and demand abdication. Who will follow me? And who will stay here in this park, playing with stupid megaphones?"

She tossed the device on the ground contemptuously but whispered urgently to its owner.

"Point out the way."

"Up that street," he said with a gesture, now in awe, as was everyone. "The Palace is only a few hundred meters from here. I can guide you, Empress," he added, apparently not doubting her claim.

"I need a torch," she said, matter-of-factly, anticipating the visuals required to lead the mob.

One of the short blazing poles with kerosene-soaked cotton was handed to her without question. She grabbed it firmly, walked down the steps, and set off at a fast pace towards the home of Cameroon's leader.

Everyone followed, and the crowd seemed to double with each

block. This was the spark they'd been waiting for, and had needed only a leader determined to do more than shout slogans. The empress soon realized the flaming torch was both heavy and unwieldy.

"Take this!" she ordered the man who'd owned the now-forgotten megaphone. "Walk beside me, just slightly back. "You!" she called to another nearby, also holding a torch. "Walk on this side."

The mysterious veiled woman—astonishing claim aside—had transformed into the group's leader through force of will. She was being escorted by torch-bearers, and followed unquestioningly by a mob now in the hundreds.

Approaching the palace they met a line of armed guards, twenty rifles at the ready across their chests.

Shari held up her hand, signaling a stop.

"Go back!" yelled the sergeant, commanding from the middle of the line. "We don't want to hurt you."

"Your president must leave," announced the empress loudly, speaking through her black veil. "You protect him at your peril."

"We are ordered to fire if necessary, and we will," replied the officer, but an uncertain voice betrayed the words.

"Wait here," Shari whispered to her escorts, and walked forward alone.

She stopped within ten meters of the sergeant. "Do you know who I am?" she asked in a confident voice.

He hesitated, disbelieving. "No, it's—it's not possible. You cannot be—*her!*"

"I am Shariya, the Angel of Death," the veiled form replied matter-of-factly. "I wear full hijab for *your* protection. You understand the danger of seeing my face?"

The man was uncertain but knew his duty. "Company! Aim!"

Twenty rifles were raised and pointed directly at the woman in black. She did not move even slightly.

"If we shoot you now, you will not be able to lower your veil," said the sergeant, with a surprising reserve of bravery.

It was an interesting argument, and Shari decided to engage with it. She reached up swiftly and grabbed the top of her boshiya.

Several of the guards gasped and prepared to turn away if necessary.

"As you see I am holding my veil. If you shoot me, my hand will fall and my face will be exposed. It won't matter if you turn away or close your eyes. It will be too late."

The officer pondered the claim, uncertain.

"I speak to all of you," she cried, more loudly this time. "You are risking your lives to protect a corrupt and evil man in the palace behind you. Why are you doing this?" she asked rhetorically. "Why do you risk your own death?"

And then, still holding the veil with one hand, the empress reached behind to a concealed scabbard and brought forth her katana. Its blade reflected back the streetlights and torches, shimmered in the dusk, and seemed to come alive. All had heard of Shariya's lion army, and the blazing sword which led it.

"You know I cannot be killed," she called to the line of sentries. "But all of you can be."

It was too much for one of the guards, who cried out—his young voice breaking. "What—what do you want us to do, sir?"

"Tomas! Be quiet!" shouted the officer. The sun had set, and a light evening breeze wafted across the wide boulevard where the future of Cameroon was being decided. Palm trees swayed impatiently, adding drama to the scene. The flames of the oil torches hissed and sparkled. All cars in the area had stopped, and quiet permeated the night.

"*Tomas,*" called Shari, in a commanding yet maternal tone that was not unkind. "I want you to lay down your weapon, and then run—as fast as you can—away from here. It's not too late to save your life."

The guard looked at the captain, looked at the glistening sword, and made his decision. The rifle was thrown to the ground in disgust, and he ran off at full speed into the night. Other rifles followed, and soon the police sergeant stood alone in the street facing Shariya.

"What is your name, Sergeant?" she asked in a soft, encouraging voice, defusing the situation further by removing her hand from the veil and lowering her sword.

"I...my name is Sergeant Michel Vanuta."

"Are you married?" she inquired, as if they were now having merely a social conversation, while the mob waited, curious to see what would happen.

"Yes, I am married."

"Do you have any children?"

"I have two girls. Seven and five."

"Do you love your wife, the mother of these precious children?"

"Of course I do."

"Would you do anything for her?"

"Certainly."

"If she were here with us right now, what do you think she would ask you to do?"

The policeman stared at the black form and then, glancing briefly over his shoulder at the palace he was supposed to be guarding, laid his rifle carefully on the ground.

"I think you should join us, Sergeant."

He walked up to the veiled woman, kept his eyes downcast, and knelt in front of her.

The mob—everyone who'd witnessed the astounding scene—broke into applause.

"You have joined the Army of Death," announced the empress. "It was a wise choice. Please pick up your rifle and take your place behind me."

He did so.

Shari heard Eduardo greet him personally, and there was another scattering of applause. She sheathed the sword.

When they arrived at the palace gate there was already a white flag of surrender hanging from it. The remaining guards had witnessed everything and knew when it was time to change sides.

"Make it happen, Eduardo," she said to him quietly. "I'll stay here with the protestors."

She turned to the policeman. "Sergeant Vanuta, please take your rifle and accompany Eduardo as escort."

"Yes, Empress."

Shari's chief diplomat, and her newest recruit, walked up the steps and entered the mansion. Men with guns stood aside, letting them pass.

Shari turned to the one who'd originally brought the bullhorn. "Who are you?"

"I'm Jon Okana, a professor at Cameroon University."

"Subject?"

"Political science."

Shari looked at him closely, wondering if she was thinking things through properly.

"I'm looking for a new president who will take orders from me," she said, impetuously. "To avoid anarchy I need to choose quickly. Would you like to be considered, at least in an interim capacity?"

"I ... is that possible? You don't even know me."

"So I'll need to learn quickly." Shari placed a hand on his shoulder. "The Empire is based on personal liberty and free markets. Do you believe in that, or are you a socialist?" She withdrew her hand, as if suddenly unsure of her choice.

The mob was now milling about, conversations breaking out spontaneously in the midst of what all knew was an historic moment.

The professor handed his torch to another and spoke honestly. "I used to lean left. Today I'm a pragmatist. Whatever you're doing in Bangui is working. It should happen here. That is my goal."

"Can you resist corruption, unlike the others you spoke of?"

"I believe so. I believe so, yes, Empress."

"My lions enjoy a diet of corrupt politicians. That fact should motivate you."

The man smiled uncertainly, unsure if she was kidding.

"If I lead Cameroon, your lions will starve here," he said finally.

"Very well. I'll give you the position temporarily at least. Bow down before me right now, publicly. Head touching the ground so all can see. Quick!"

He did so.

"Here is your new president!" proclaimed Shari loudly to the crowd. "Cameroon is now a part of my empire. And you have a new president. Let us applaud him!"

She led the clapping and suddenly it became infectious. There was wild cheering and celebration which—with upraised arm gestures—she encouraged to continue.

The empress whispered urgently to the man kneeling at her feet.

"If you ever mention price controls, I will kill you personally. I just want to be clear about that."

"I am yours to command, Empress," he said, forehead pressed against the pavement.

"Any talk of minimum wages, increased taxes, or trade barriers, and I'll rip your throat out."

"You won't need to, Empress. Please, command me."

"Say even a word about public employee unions and you won't die quickly, you'll die slowly."

Shari was making these threats knowing she'd never carry them out. She'd be happy to discuss any area of governance with these national leaders—and certainly not kill them for bringing up a subject. But he didn't know that, and she wanted Cameroon firmly on a free-market path right from the beginning. Shari made a mental note to follow up later and make it clear she'd been kidding—after the correct policies were in place.

"Your most loyal subject bows before you, Empress. Give me a command. I beg it of you."

"Stand up," she ordered.

He obeyed, to further accolades.

"Take my hand, raise it high, and we will walk into the palace together."

They did so and the cheering increased.

※

Before midnight, Shari, Eduardo, and the deposed President Magombe with his immediate family, were in the private jet for the short flight to Bangui. Shari spoke not at all, and simply gazed out the window, watching the moon cast its light on the clouds below. Eduardo and Cameroon's former leader sat across from each other and talked continuously in soft voices, addressing details of the hand-off.

After dropping off the empress and prime minister, and refueling, the plane continued on to Geneva, Switzerland, where private bank accounts awaited.

Back in their own palace, the empress and her prime minister shared a drink on the balcony.

"Satisfied?" he asked. "Did our little visit quench your thirst to see what's happening up close and personal?"

"It can't be stopped, can it?" she asked, looking up at him. "We're all caught in this. I could no more stop it than could have President Magombe."

"Now you understand. Africa will no longer tolerate corrupt leadership. It sees an alternative. It sees you."

"On one level, that terrifies me," she confessed.

"And on another?"

"Well, perhaps I finally have a purpose, a reason to exist. That's what was missing when I woke up on the riverbank. Why am I here? Why am I alive? What am I supposed to do?"

"And now you know?"

"Tai was right. This isn't just about slavery anymore. Apparently, I'm supposed to take over the whole continent. Or at least try to. God help us…"

41

Shari was having breakfast alone on her private balcony, enjoying the river view.

"May I join you?" asked Eduardo, announcing his presence.

"Of course." She turned to him, smiling.

"Shari, I have a present. I think you're going to love it."

"Tell me!" The young girl's eyes were bright with anticipation.

"No, finish your breakfast and come with me to the airport."

"I'm finished now. Let's go." She stood up quickly and led the way, ignoring the remainder of her papaya.

Thirty minutes later they were standing in a hangar looking at a very strange aircraft.

"What is it?" asked the empress.

"It's an Apache attack helicopter. I'm told it's the most sophisticated and deadly assault helicopter in the world."

"Where did it come from?" she asked, moving towards it in wonder.

"From Nairobi. Before joining our empire, Kenya received a military aid package from the United States and three of these attack helicopters were included. The U.S. wanted Kenya to oppose the terrorists in Somalia and this was the first of the Apaches. The training of one pilot was included."

"I see," said Shari, her eyes not leaving the formidable machine. There was respect in her gaze—a warrior sizing up a worthy opponent, or in this case a new ally.

"But after Kenya declared for us, the political situation changed and the United States canceled the remaining two helicopters. So Kenya just has this one, plus the pilot."

"Why is it here?" Shari's hand reached out, fingers tracing the sleek lines of the Apache's fuselage.

Eduardo smiled. "It's tribute. The president we installed in Nairobi insisted on making a statement of loyalty, and asked the one pilot in Africa who knows how to fly this thing to deliver it to you, personally, as a gift. The president said he has no idea what he would do with it anyway."

Shari's eyes sparkled with a mixture of curiosity and excitement. "I love it," she said, stepping deftly onto a wing stub. Climbing into the cockpit, she ran her hands over the controls, vowing to somehow master them. In her mind, this was not a machine, but an extension of her own body in the same way Shinkendo swords were an extension of her arms.

"What can it do?" she asked.

The prime minister consulted his notes. "This one's been modified, and has twin miniguns—whatever those are—that can each fire six thousand rounds a minute of something called .308 caliber ammunition. And it can hold up to six Hellfire air-to-ground missiles that can take out tanks, buildings, even small ships. It can fly up to one hundred and forty-two knots and has a range of two hundred and fifty-seven nautical miles. It's set up for a crew of two, a pilot and gunner, but supports single-pilot operation."

Climbing out again, she ran her hand along the barrel of a minigun, visualizing its destructive power. No, to truly master this weapon, she must incorporate martial arts discipline. Strike with purpose. Move with grace. And always anticipate the opponent's next move. Her training had emphasized a defensive mindset—to never be the aggressor. But this attack helicopter was a weapon of conquest. Sun Tzu, at least, would approve.

"Where's the pilot?" she asked.

"Right there." Eduardo waved to a man on the far side of the hanger and gestured him over.

"He speaks English, Shari."

The man from Kenya knelt on one knee in front of her.

"Are you the pilot of this helicopter?" she asked in English. "What's your name?"

"Yes, Empress. My name is Captain Tawa Mumbi, now detached from the Kenyan Army, at your service."

"Please stand up, Captain."

"Yes, Empress." He rose but kept his head bowed before the woman covered in black hijab.

"Captain Tawa, you may look at me. You are ordered to do so. How long will it take to teach me to fly this helicopter?"

"You want to learn to fly the Apache?"

"Yes, I want to know everything you know. How long?"

"Well, how much time could you spend each day?"

"Every waking moment," she said. "This is the only thing I want to spend time on until I can fly it myself."

"Then, well, perhaps a couple of weeks."

"Is there any reason we can't begin right now, this morning?"

"None, Empress."

"What does the helicopter need? Special fuel? Mechanics? Spare parts?"

"It uses military jet fuel, which you have at this airport. Yes, mechanics and spare parts will be needed to keep it operational."

"Eduardo, can you work with Captain Tawa to acquire whatever's necessary?"

"Of course. So you're pleased with this gift?"

"It's the most beautiful thing I've ever seen in my life."

"OK, then Tai and I will consider you on vacation for the next two weeks. We'll make the decisions and bother you only if there's something the two of us can't agree on."

"You're ordered to agree on everything. At least until I've learned how to fly this thing."

42

The Apache helicopter was a thousand feet in the air when the instructor initiated a simulated engine failure. Shari executed the autorotation procedure and transitioned rapidly into a controlled descent towards a clearing in the forest which she selected instantly, in accordance with her training.

"Remember to maintain airspeed and descent rate," admonished the instructor, and Shari adjusted accordingly. Nearing the ground, the empress tapped the right side of her brain and performed the flare and touch-down as elegantly as if she were on a ballet stage.

"Very nice," said Captain Tawa from the back seat. "Well, that completes the basics. It's been two weeks, today, since you started. Mastering this engine-out procedure was your final test. You've qualified already on the weapons systems."

"We're at the end of the training?" Shari asked, excited.

"You're only a VFR pilot but I can train you to fly instruments if you want. That's an advanced skill. We'd need another two weeks for that."

"Yes, I want IFR training, but let's do that more leisurely. I need to get back to my real job. Wait, I haven't flown solo at all. You've always been with me. Maybe I need to practice flying solo."

"Oh yes, good point! As you know, I'm not a certified instructor. I've just been teaching you everything that was taught to me. I've been signing your logbook as 'acting instructor' but I'm not sure that's legally meaningful."

"I don't think it needs to be legally meaningful," she replied. "As long as you think I've learned what's necessary."

They were speaking through the aircraft's intercom system, using headphones with integrated mics, with the Apache still on the ground in the clearing, blades spinning.

"You have definitely learned the basics," agreed the pilot. "You learned far more quickly than I did. Anyway, it's your helicopter, and your country, so I suppose you decide what's legal."

"Yes," Shari turned around and smiled from the front seat, knowing of course he couldn't see her face. She'd kept it masked during flight training. "If you think I'm qualified to fly the helicopter, then I hereby legally declare I am!"

"Great. Let's return to base. I'll sign your logbook showing your flight test is complete and you are now fully qualified in the Apache."

"And then I can fly it myself?"

"Of course, Shari. It is your aircraft. I only hope you will continue to employ me. How else can I be useful?"

"Are you worried about employment?"

"Very much so."

"Don't be. It's my helicopter, but I place you in charge of it, full time. Perhaps at some point we'll be able to add to the fleet, and you can train me further when we have more time. I'll have Eduardo work out details."

Thirty minutes later, refueled and her instructor dropped off at the base, Shari was back in the air, now experiencing a sense of unbridled freedom. The newly-minted pilot could have practiced more emergency procedures, but for her first solo she had something else in mind.

Flying west from the airfield she stayed close to the treetops—dangerously low—but was thrilled by the sense of motion. The Ubangi

River entered a canyon downstream of Bangui, and she dipped into it, flying only a few yards above the water itself and well below the canyon rim.

She flung off her mask and enjoyed additional freedom and visibility. On the right bank was a pod of hippos eyeing the strange and noisy contraption with annoyance. One opened its vast maw and roared at her.

She could circle back around, level off directly in front of the herd, and blast them into small pieces of hippo fat with her .308 caliber miniguns that could fire 6,000 rounds a minute. It would be worthwhile training, the sober part of her mind noted. But she could never kill such beautiful living things just for practice.

Enjoying her new toy she did circle back, again leveled off close to the surface, faced the very disturbed hippos, aimed high, and pulled triggers on both mini-guns. Behind the river animals, trees were cut in half and began toppling over.

The hippos freaked and disappeared underwater. The young pilot laughed.

Shari and her helicopter continued down the river. She'd brought coordinates from Google Earth and entered them manually into her flight computer. Instantly the helicopter was directed on a new course and in thirty minutes arrived at its destination.

This was her birthplace—the small river where life had begun several months ago. She let herself remember those first few moments, including how fascinated she was with fish.

Shari set the Apache down on the far bank, in the country of Congo which was now part of her empire.

Leaving the aircraft's rotor spinning in idle, she jumped out and made her way into the forest. The empress found the spring-fed limestone hole easily. The diamonds were still there. Dozens of them. She lay down and began scooping them into her daypack.

An hour later, back under her veil, she returned the helicopter to the Bangui airfield where Captain Tawa met her on the tarmac.

"You were gone longer than I expected. Where'd you go?" he asked, leaning into the cockpit and studying the panel.

"Oh, nowhere really. I just flew up and down the river and had fun scaring some hippos with the miniguns."

He laughed and then glanced at the Apache's wheels. "And where did this red dirt come from, if I can ask?"

"You notice everything, don't you? I also practiced a few landings on a flat area near the river."

"Well, according to the tachometer, this flight puts us over the maximum for another maintenance. I'll taxi it to the hangar."

Shari tossed him the keys, retrieved her backpack—now considerably heavier—and began walking off the field. She heard the Apache's rotors winding up and soon felt the hurricane-like force of wind off its blades. She was just reaching for her boshiya hood when the garment flew off completely, coming to rest against a nearby fence. She ran several yards and retrieved it quickly. Once properly covered she looked around for witnesses. Other than cars, the parking lot seemed empty. The Apache was taxiing away from her.

She made a mental note to secure the garment better in the future, at least at the airport.

43

IT WAS EMPRESS Shariya's daily breakfast meeting with Eduardo. Their policy was to review developments from the last twenty-four hours and make quick decisions on which ones required action by the empire.

A teachers' strike in Nairobi. A sexual abuse lawsuit against a government minister in Kinshasa. A train derailment near Lagos. Rarely did the Imperial Court need to intervene. But a month earlier a corrupt politician seized from Unicef a shipment of medical supplies destined for a plague-ravaged village, which he tried to sell on the black market. Without the vital medicine, scores died. The politician had been arrested by Shariya's forces and publicly executed. Eduardo made sure the event was covered extensively in African media to send a message. Medical supplies were no longer being hijacked.

Despite rarely needing intervention, it was useful for the empress to be aware of such news. Eduardo had assembled a staff tasked solely with gathering intelligence from around the empire and condensing it into a daily briefing.

Eduardo delivered the information personally, dressed as always in a conservative suit and tie. Shari wore an embroidered, purple abaya gown, and nothing above the neck.

They sat on her balcony overlooking the river. Eduardo himself had brought in the tray containing fried eggs, mangos, and a basket of croissants. At this hour, Shari was mostly interested in the coffee.

"So, how's our empire doing this morning?" she began.

"The problem isn't our empire, it's the other one."

"Ah, expansionist Iran. You've mentioned them before. Look, I'm just waking up," she said, gazing out at the mist on the river. "Remind me the background again?"

"Well, it starts with the Shia/Sunni split. You've got Shia Iran and much of the rest of the Middle East is Sunni. The two sects hate each other."

The empress yawned sleepily. "Remind me again why."

"It doesn't matter. But think of it like Protestants and Catholics in the sixteenth century if you remember your reformation history. In this case it's about who should have been the successor to Muhammed."

"Oh, that's right. A thousand-year-old succession dispute. Go ahead."

"Well, Iran is the primary Shia state, and Saudi Arabia is the primary Sunni state. So they're natural enemies. Iran has been causing no end of trouble in the Middle East, and they're the primary exporters of terrorism. Since the Americans pulled out of Iraq—which is majority Shia—Iran has turned that country into a client state. Lebanon is already in their pocket. The Shia Houthis are now firmly in control of Yemen, and they're backed heavily by Iran. With the Americans out of Afghanistan, Iran is poised to dominate that country as well, which they can easily do as Afghanistan's weak and disorganized, and Iran is right on their border."

Shari nibbled on a croissant and said nothing, enjoying the river view.

Her prime minister continued. "Anyway, with effective control of Iraq, the Iranians are already stationing military assets there, claiming they're necessary for defense. But they have their eye on Saudi Arabia. If they can conquer it militarily, that will be game over for the Middle

East. Other countries will fall in line as satellites, as so many have done with our own empire."

The empress looked at him, concerned. "How much of the Middle East would they control?"

"Everything east of Egypt, maybe up to the border with Pakistan."

"So that's the background. What's the new problem?"

"They just issued a press release that they're changing the country's name back to Persia."

Shari smiled, glad today's problem was not serious. "Merely a name change? Do we care?"

"You've heard of the Persian empire?"

"Of course."

"It ruled much of western Asia from sixth century BC to the twentieth. At its peak, the borders stretched from the Balkans to India."

"OK."

"Today's Iran is far smaller. The much-reduced Persia changed its name to Iran in 1935 because that word more accurately reflected how the locals once called themselves, or something. It was like Rhodesia changing its name back to Zimbabwe."

"Got it. So now they're changing back to Persia. Why?"

"There can be only one reason. They're about to resurrect the empire and they want to get the branding right. The world will remember Persia as an empire. Iran sounds like a single country."

"Ah, so changing their name signals intent to resurrect imperial status. Does it threaten us?"

"Not at the moment. The capital, Tehran, is a long way even from Cairo. If they're about to embark on a strategy of Middle East conquest, they'll have their hands full."

"So we ignore this new Persia?"

"For now, yes. Our goal is to complete the conquest of Africa or at least try to. Let's say we do that. But let's say their empire grows as fast as ours. At some point, we'll come face-to-face with the Persians. There could be a détente."

"Or they could become our greatest enemy."

"Yes. The goal here is to be aware of the Persians, but not be distracted by them. And that's all there is to this morning's briefing."

"Can you hand me the marmalade?" asked Shari, pretending to have dismissed Persia.

In fact the empress was thinking deeply about her rival empire.

44

The sleek, single-engine helicopter, chartered by De Beers and carrying two of their geologists plus Tai and Shari, landed gently on the Congolese side of the Lobaye River. The passengers stepped out.

The moist, heavy air and the scent of rainforest was rich and alluring. With the helicopter's engine silent they could hear water gurgling over rocks and around fallen trees. From somewhere in the deep foliage, a loud bird cawed impatiently. Insect noises were continuous.

"So, this is where it began for you," noted Tai, watching Shari as she walked over to the water's edge. The geologists were already scurrying around, examining the soil. Soon they disappeared upstream, the pilot following them.

"I was born here," exclaimed the empress as if stating a fact. "Right over there. On that flat rock, see it? That's where I used to lie down and study fish."

Suddenly the Angel of Death stiffened and sucked in her breath. A gigantic male lion emerged out of the forest. Shari stared at it. Then, before Tai could stop her, she stepped out of her shoes, ripped off her hijab clothing, and dove into the river. In moments she emerged on the far bank wearing only her black unitard.

Tai watched as the male lion approached the girl. She stood there, unafraid, as the jungle beast came up to her, sniffed, and then let itself be cuddled. Three other lions—females—appeared and seemed mildly interested as well. Shari cuddled with each of them. Then she flung herself atop the male lion and held onto its mane. The lion didn't mind. He sauntered around a bit, and a couple of times took off in a run as if he were enjoying the game as much as she was.

Finally the empress climbed off, cuddled again with the animals, and returned across the river. Tai helped her back into the gown, noticing the lions had already vanished.

"That looked like a family reunion," he said.

"Yes. They're the only family I have. I love them."

"They're *not* your only family, Shari."

They exchanged a meaningful glance.

"You're right. You, Eduardo, and the others are also my family. And those back in the village were another family. But this was my first."

The geologists returned and wanted to fly upriver, low and slow. The helicopter lifted off and stayed just above treetop.

The De Beers agents had them touch down again at several spots, on either side of the river, so they could take more measurements, examine the soil, and study landforms. Eventually they spotted it: an anomalous protrusion of gray rock above the forest canopy, itself covered in fine moss and shrub. Although slightly rounded, the pilot was able to set the helicopter directly on top of the geologic formation, over a hundred feet high.

The scientists jumped out and began attacking the bare sections with spiked hammers and chisels. Soon the verdict was delivered. "It's a kimberlite pipe," one of them explained. "This is where the diamonds downstream came from."

Ranging instruments were used to gauge its size.

"It's larger than the one at Kimberley, South Africa," their spokesman declared. "Maybe fifty percent larger. And the alluvial diamonds it's sending downstream are proof of its richness."

"What happens next?" Tai asked, as the woman in black stayed silent.

"With your permission, we'll take these two diamonds we found along the stream back to London, along with the soil samples, and of course all the measurements and photography."

Shari nodded.

A week later a representative of De Beers arrived at the Imperial Palace in Bangui.

"We have a proposal, Empress," said the mining company agent when they were seated around the conference table. They'd been drinking espresso coffees and speaking casually but now it was time for business.

The man from London, whose business card said Director of Acquisitions, had brought with him a company solicitor to handle the contracts. They both wore dark pinstripe suits, white shirts, and school ties. With Shari were Eduardo, also dressed conservatively, Tai dressed casually, and a solicitor of their own pulled in from Kinshasa—an expert in raw-materials licensing agreements.

"Please continue," said the empress, nodding her veiled head.

The solicitors had met earlier and the document itself, along with its basic terms, was acceptable to both parties. All that remained was to fill in the numbers.

"As you know," explained the De Beers officer, "we propose mining the kimberlite pipe as a joint venture. We'll mine the diamonds and sell them. You'll receive fifty percent of the sales price on every rough stone. Plus there's a signing bonus."

"Yes," noted Shari. "So we've been told, but in what amount?"

"If you sign the agreement today, we are prepared to offer a signing bonus of—" he paused for effect. "Of twenty-five billion dollars, U.S."

The empress stared at him, too shocked to speak.

"However, I'm authorized to go to thirty billion, if necessary," he said, perhaps misinterpreting the silence.

"We might accept as low as forty billion," said Eduardo, realizing Shari was speechless.

"I'd need to clear it, but we might manage thirty-five," said the De Beers agent. "However I absolutely can't go higher."

"Thirty-seven will be acceptable," said Shari, now fully recovered. "If you can wire the funds by noon tomorrow."

"Done," said the official, apparently the need to clear with management already forgotten. "And the funds are ready to be wired now. Into your London account."

Shari nodded to Eduardo, who reached for the papers and, after the agreed number was written in, signed them. The De Beers agent did the same, both initialing the $37 billion handwritten entry.

"Is anyone interested in a glass of champagne?" asked Shari. "As soon as the wire is confirmed, the cork will come off."

The De Beers agent smiled and picked up his cell phone.

45

SHARI'S EYES OPENED reluctantly as she lay in bed. Her normally sharp mind hesitated to engage, preferring a drowsy emptiness while enjoying the intriguing sounds of the rain forest outside the window. She let her toes curl and stretch, sensuously appreciating the Egyptian cotton sheets that somehow stayed cool even while keeping her warm. She could stay here for hours, just slithering around in the pleasing fabric while listening to birds.

Then she remembered. This was the day they were to decide what to do with the thirty-seven billion dollars. With that thought all sleep vanished and she rose quickly from bed. What *does* one do with $37 billion? she asked herself rhetorically while showering. Thank God for clever advisors.

The empress, now wearing a pink silk gown, ate her light breakfast quickly on the balcony, enjoying the morning view of soft mist coating the surface of the Ubangi river. No fish eagles at work this morning, in this fog, she thought. I wonder what *they* would do with $37 billion?

The meeting in the conference room began at 8 a.m. sharp. Eduardo had no patience for "African time," as it was called. He not only dressed like a London banker, but managed the Empire's business like one. Meetings started on schedule. He sat upright in his chair, an expensive leather briefcase on one side, a legal pad in front of him. He was fiddling with a Montblanc pen, conscientiously making notes, and studying earlier ones.

Tai, the only other advisor in today's session, respected punctuality but followed a different dress code. Perennially in jeans and a black t-shirt, he still looked like someone hoping to pass for a backpacker. He slouched irreverently and played with his smart phone. "I don't do *paper*," he'd once said, as if referring to a vile substance wholly beneath him.

Shari, as was custom sat at the head of the table in her abaya gown, but with its matching boshiya mask set conveniently on a nearby chair. She'd grown used to wearing the hijab coverings, and when necessary could don the mask in seconds.

"Shall we begin?" asked the prime minister, checking his watch, as if ready to call to order a meeting of the U.N. security council.

Shari was amused by the ceremony and enjoyed playing along with it.

"Yes, I believe it's time," she declared, matching his solemnity.

"Thirty-seven billion bucks!" said Tai. "To hell with coffee. Maybe we should bring in some mimosas and caviar."

"The purpose of this meeting is to decide how best to use the funds," admonished Eduardo.

"You mean, how much is left over, after the champagne?" needled their Strategic Advisor.

Shari enjoyed Tai's sense of humor but was ready to be serious. "Eduardo, maybe this means we won't have to borrow any money at all as we transition to a lottery-based revenue system."

"We won't," agreed her prime minister.

"How much will you require for that purpose—for the transition?" asked Tai, finally engaging.

"We've done projections. As little as five billion will get us to positive cash flow under the lottery, if our assumptions hold."

The empress asked the obvious question. "So what do we do with the rest?"

The conference room was silent.

"How much do either of you know about cryptocurrencies?" asked Tai, finally.

"A little, but not much," answered Eduardo.

"Nothing," said Shari. "Please educate us."

Tai gave them a quick explanation of the concept, which took several minutes. Then he came to the point.

"The two big advantages are, first, that crypto-currencies such as bitcoin can't be inflated by fiat, as all other currencies can be and are; and second, they have a payment system built in. So you can transact business instantly, without a third party like a credit card company or bank having to be involved. You just need a mobile phone. And these days everyone has a mobile phone, even in Africa, correct?"

"Yes," said Shari. "The tribal village I was in had two mobile phones. I can't imagine how they paid for them. I guess from selling goats or something."

"What if tickets for the Imperial Lottery could only be purchased with, let's say, bitcoin?" asked Tai. "Simultaneously you'd declare bitcoin the national currency of the Empire."

"Go on," urged Shari.

"After such an announcement, that a large nation—a growing empire—was going to embrace bitcoin as its official currency, the price would soar. It might increase by a factor of ten and continue up from there."

"And how do we benefit from that?" asked the prime minister.

"Before the announcement, take the thirty-two billion that Eduardo won't need and use it to slowly acquire bitcoin. When the announcement happens, your thirty-two billion, if it goes up by a factor of ten, will now be worth three hundred and twenty billion."

"Couldn't it fall just as fast?" observed Eduardo.

"It's a risk but unlikely if we make good on using it as our national currency. Also by embracing bitcoin as the empire's payment system, you won't need a central bank, you won't have to worry about storing cash or safeguarding it or making payments. Everything will be simple."

"It would give us a state-of-the-art, twenty-first-century medium of exchange," agreed Eduardo.

"And the adoption rate would be quite high," continued Tai. "Because without bitcoin, you won't be able to play the Imperial Lottery. Everyone will set up an account and run it from their cell phone. Once they have that, they'll start using bitcoin for other transactions as well."

Shari stood up and began pacing, never able to sit still while thinking deeply. "I guess what we're talking about," she mused, "is an African empire which has eliminated all taxes, all trade restrictions, all tariffs, and all the nonsense bureaucracy that goes along with it; and which has also embraced the most modern and efficient monetary system imaginable."

"Yes," agreed Tai. "That's exactly what we're talking about."

"Foreign investment will pour in," predicted Eduardo. "Multinationals will locate headquarters here. But how do we pay for building the infrastructure to handle it all? Modern airports and such?"

"We shouldn't have to pay anything," observed Shari. "Let private industry build everything. They can build airports and charge airlines to use them, just as governments do. Private companies can build roads and charge tolls to use them. All services can be provided by the free market," she said, wondering again where these concepts came from. All she knew was that she cared about these concepts deeply. And understood them. And could defend them intellectually. Someone—on the other side of that door— had taught her all this.

"It could work," agreed Eduardo. "So the only things the government has to provide would be, let's see, maybe education…"

"Not education," interrupted Tai. "If everyone has a mobile phone, then everyone can access YouTube. You can learn anything on YouTube, from how to read and write, to quantum mechanics. Formal, onsite education is mostly obsolete in the twenty-first century. If someone wants to pay for private school or whatever, fine. Let 'em. But anyone that just wants to get an education, even a specialized education, can do it for free, online. The government might formalize a suggested curriculum. You know, first grade should watch *these* videos. Second grade should watch *those*. And so on up to secondary school, trade school, and even university level. We'd include links."

"Some training would require hands-on work, like chemistry labs or auto-repair garages."

"Sure, some would," Tai continued. "Let brands offer those up at low cost or even free, in return for publicity. Think: 'Pennzoil Training Centers For Mechanics.'"

"Dupont National Chemistry Laboratories," suggested Eduardo, smiling.

Tai raised two thumbs up.

"We could create a University of Africa," said Eduardo, warming to the concept. "A virtual university. Education would be delivered via a collection of YouTube videos, in many languages, even tribal languages. We could include a regimen of testing that could also be delivered remotely, using current technologies, which would allow us to grant degrees or certificates of completion or whatever we call them. There are many online schools and universities these days which work like that. "

"And the University of Africa could, itself, be charged with administering the same services for K through 12," added Tai.

"Perfect," said Shari. "I think the only thing the government has to provide is a system of laws based on property rights, and whatever military and police forces we need."

"If you take this philosophy further," added Tai, "the courts won't cost either, because court fees will be assessed against any party that loses. That's how the system works in the UK, for example."

"So we really just need a military, a police force, and enough revenue to pay for our own government expenses," said the empress contemplatively.

"And the revenue from the lottery will more than pay for all that," said Eduardo.

"We're going to turn Africa into a free-market utopia," concluded Shari. "We'll not only embrace the forces of capitalism, we'll turn them loose."

There was a knock on the door.

Shari quickly donned her head covering and a messenger entered. "Sorry to interrupt, but it's the Prime Minister of Tanzania on the phone. He's asking to speak immediately to someone in authority."

Shari glanced at her own prime minister and nodded.

46

"Dr. Roberto Anzio is here to see you, Shariya," announced the receptionist after the finance meeting had adjourned.

She had to remember. Oh yes, the psychiatrist from South Africa that Eduardo suggested be hired as her personal physician.

"I'll meet him on the balcony."

Eduardo had earlier explained his thinking about bringing one of the world's top amnesia experts on board, and she recalled the conversation.

"An Italian name, from South Africa?" Shari had asked.

Eduardo consulted his notes. "Family in the jewelry business from Vicenza since the 1700s, but many Italians immigrated to Kimberley when the diamond fields opened up in the late 19th century. He descends from a branch of the family that did that. Great-grandfather fought for the Boers against the English. Undergraduate degree from University of South Africa. Medical studies at University of Bologna, with an internship at Johns Hopkins in the States. Served a stint as Minister of Health for South Africa. Now runs an elite private practice, with offices in Cape Town, 'Joburg,' and Durban. Fluent in English, Italian, and Afrikaans."

She met him in full hijab covering. After exchanging greetings

Shari poured both of them sparkling water, on ice. She noticed he was tall but with the swarthy coloring of southern Europe. Perhaps in his mid-fifties, he was graying slightly, had short-cropped hair, and his glasses gave him the appearance of an academic. He wore a full suit, navy, with white shirt and a red tie: classic interview attire. The Angel of Death also noticed a gold Rolex watch and a wedding ring. Shari moved directly to business.

"Dr. Anzio, I understand you're one of the most experienced psychiatrists in the world when it comes to treating amnesiacs."

He bowed his head, graciously.

"You've been told I suffer occasional memory lapses that might be a mild form of amnesia?"

"Yes, Empress."

"Has Eduardo reviewed with you our employment offer?"

"He has, Empress."

"Are you willing to accept the position, for a minimum of twelve months I believe is the offer, and move here to Bangui with your family?"

"Your offer was most generous and would be difficult to refuse. I can take a leave of absence from my private firm. Our kids have left home, and my wife says she'd enjoy new horizons. Yes, if you wish to employ me full time, on those terms, I think we could work something out."

"You hereby accept? Employment starts today."

"I do."

"Very well. Now that you're a member of the team, please call me Shari. I'll be honest with you. I do not 'suffer occasional memory lapses.' I'm a complete amnesiac."

Shari reviewed her short history.

"You have no memories—at all—before waking up on the riverbank in the jungle?"

"None. And when I even think about what came before, when I try to open that door and force my mind to think about it…"

"You become nauseous and sometimes even vomit?"

"Yes, there's something horrible there, something I can't face."

"Do you want to face it?" The psychiatrist was already probing, presumably as he would with any new patient.

"I'm not sure. I may not be that brave. Do you think the door will ever open?"

"We'll do full diagnostics later, a psychiatric exam and so forth. Lots of tests. I hesitate to comment, before—"

"Yes of course, but please answer the most important question. In a case like this does the memory ever return?"

He took a moment to compose his thoughts, staring judiciously at the ceiling. Then he faced her.

"I can say this. Having now met you, it's obvious you're the opposite of a catatonic invalid needing to be hospitalized—which amnesiacs often are. Also, I've been reading about how you built your empire in just a few months. It's quite remarkable."

"Is that relevant?"

"Very much so. You're obviously a very talented and knowledgeable human being who likely is performing at peak capacity. Something is pushing you forward, almost like your mind is on mental steroids."

"And what does that tell you?"

"That you're healing. Your mind is processing whatever horrible thing it saw I think in this case by motivating you towards great achievements. It's like your subconscious wants you to create a new world, a new history, a new person—we might say a new life—before it allows you to see the one you lost."

Shari considered this. "Then when and if I do see it I'll have the support structures around me to handle it. I won't be empty any longer."

"Yes. I believe on some level your amnesia was itself a subliminal, but powerful, motivating force behind everything you've accomplished."

"So what happens now? How do I get my memory back? How do I open that door without becoming physically ill?"

"Studies suggest the memories are likely to come back all at once. You'll encounter something that will trigger a memory from the other side of that door, and once it does, the door opens completely—the entire wall comes down. We call it a triggering event."

"Sounds traumatic."

"Yes. But if your mind has healed sufficiently you can recover from it."

"Does it always happen that way?"

"No, but it's the most common. In some cases, the memory returns slowly. A piece here. A detail there. Or…"

"Or what?"

"The third possibility is that the memories never come back."

"I see." Shari considered it all. "Doctor, can you excuse me a moment?"

She stood up and leaned against the rail, looking out at the river. Did she even want those horrible memories—whatever they were—to come back? How could it be anything but awful? But curiosity was building as her empire grew. She needed to know how it all started. How did she end up alone, in the jungle?

Shari sat down again, across from the doctor. "May we change the subject a bit?"

"Certainly," agreed the doctor.

"Our government has checked on you, your reputation, the papers you've written, and also your time as Minister of Education in South Africa. Very impressive."

"Thank you, Shari," he responded, nodding humbly.

"I don't think serving as my personal physician is a full-time job. I think you'll be bored."

"Well—"

"Our empire is growing rapidly. Perhaps too rapidly. We can't hire people fast enough for the positions available."

"What are you suggesting?"

"Would you consider also serving as Minister of Health in our government? Your résumé is a perfect fit."

"Shari, you just met me."

"I trust my instincts. I'd like having you on board at a high level. No further pay increase I'm afraid. As you noted the employment offer's already lavish. But I think you'd find it an interesting challenge. You'd not be bored."

Now it was Anzio's turn to stand up and pace, obviously thinking deeply.

"Oh, there's one more thing, Doctor. Since you're already my personal physician, here's something important you should know."

Shari removed her boshiya.

Anzio stared at her, speechless at first. "You're white!" he finally exclaimed.

"I'm white. And I have no idea where I'm from. Probably not Africa."

"Well," he said, smiling, "I guess you're right. I'm not going to be bored."

47

Lord Winterset studied the satellite images sent over from the Defense Ministry, along with a military assessment—papers scattered over his desk.

He'd been on a call with the First Sea Lord, commander-in-chief of the Royal Navy.

After a few moments of deliberation the MI6 chief pressed a button on his desk.

"Maggie, please get Tai on the phone. Encrypted, as always."

"Yes, my lord."

In a few moments Winterset was talking to his most accomplished agent, presumably somewhere in the Central African Empire.

"How are things going, Emerson? Been a while since we talked."

"Swimmingly, my lord. By the way, now that we have an empire on our hands I find myself eager to use your lordship title myself. Practice, you know."

The naval officer rolled his eyes.

"Anyway," continued the agent, "Ever since we picked up Nigeria, Kenya, and Congo, we're getting nearly one country a day bowing to the inevitable and volunteering to join us."

"Where do things stand with Somalia?"

"Not part of the empire yet, sir. Those heavily Muslim countries will be tougher nuts to crack."

"Tai, are you alone; anyone around who might hear you?"

"Completely alone, sir. I'm in my own office at the Bangui palace. It's swept twice a day. Thanks for the tools to do so, by the way. Very kind of you."

"Tai, I doubt anyone at your end is aware of this, but we've just received disturbing imagery from the Gulf of Oman."

"What's up, sir?"

"There's a fleet of about fifty small-to-medium-sized warships and troop transports heading towards the Somalian coast. It's most of the Iranian navy, or I should say the Persian navy as they're calling themselves these days."

"An invasion force."

"Seems to be. Well, obviously it is."

"They hope to take Somalia before we do, and contest our dominance in Africa."

"No doubt. Once the Persians get a beachhead on your continent, they'll try to push their own empire into North Africa. Somalia's a perfect spot from which to launch it."

There was a pause on the line, and Winterset knew his cleverest agent was thinking deeply.

"You know, these Persians aren't exactly bumbling fools, are they?" observed Tai, finally.

"Not at all," agreed the MI6 chief.

"This is a very astute chess move; one that we have no way to counter."

"Agreed."

"How much time do we have?"

"At current course and speed, they'll arrive off the port of Xaafuun by sunrise, day after tomorrow."

"We're not in a position to oppose them," confessed Tai. "The closest naval vessels we control are in Kenya, and that navy's almost non-existent."

"Yes, that's my understanding."

The conversation paused, briefly.

"If memory serves," began Tai, "I believe your lordship once said Britain could perhaps help Shariya if it became necessary."

"That time has arrived. She very much needs our help."

"What do you propose, exactly?"

"Tai, please listen very carefully. Don't even write this down, it's too confidential."

"Understood."

"Our own navy is modest these days, but it's set up for light, expeditionary missions. After I saw what Shariya was accomplishing, I met with the prime minister herself, and the First Sea Lord. They agreed the tumult in Africa could incentivize a foreign actor to grab some of the continent, likely via a sea invasion. The Persians were an obvious threat, but there were others I won't mention."

"I'm listening."

"So over the last few weeks, we've moved naval assets into the northwestern Indian Ocean and the eastern Mediterranean."

"Interesting."

"We have no desire to trigger an open clash between Britain and the Persians. No one's in the mood for a shooting war right now, especially in that part of the world."

"I understand completely, sir."

"But we do have three submarines on station. I have good news and bad."

"Go ahead."

"The bad news is that the prime minister absolutely refuses to use ships of the Royal Navy to sink neutral vessels on the high seas."

"That's regrettable. And the good news?"

"She might be willing to lease three submarines, temporarily, to the Shariyan Empire."

"Is that what they're calling us now? Shariyan Empire does rather roll off the tongue."

"Yes, it is what they're calling you. Central African Empire is tedious."

"Shariyan Empire. Well, I rather like it," mused Tai. "Anyway, you'd lease us three submarines in return for what?"

"One British pound, per year, per submarine."

"On behalf of the Central African Empire, I hereby accept the offer."

"Agent Emerson, I'm asking you formally, do you have the authority, as an officer of that country, to handle all this yourself? I'd like to keep the parties who are aware of it as small as possible. Best if you could answer in the affirmative."

"Affirmative, sir. Yes, I absolutely have such authority."

Winterset doubted he did, but for legal reasons, if it ever came out, he'd received the answer needed.

"And a moment ago I heard you say you accept the proposal. Therefore, if you don't mind, I'd like to patch in the senior commander of those submarines which have been designated a task force under his command. His boat is currently at antenna depth, awaiting the call."

In less than a minute, a third voice joined the conversation.

"Gentlemen," said the MI6 director, "I'd like to keep this very short. We have Captain Daynsford on one end, and a representative of the Shariyan Empire, formally known as the Central African Empire, on the other. I won't mention his name. Captain, do I understand you're commanding the task force of three Royal Navy submarines in the Indian Ocean?"

"Yes, Admiral."

"And do I understand you're aware of the fleet of warships heading for Somalia?"

"Affirmative."

"Does your task force have the ability to stop them?"

"Yes, sir. Would you like to know how?"

"No, I wouldn't. Captain Daynsford, the prime minister has just worked out an arrangement where your task force is being leased temporarily to the Central African Empire. I believe you've received a communication about this from the Admiralty, correct?"

"Affirmative, sir."

"Consistent with your Admiralty orders, I've been asked to inform you that as of this moment, your boats, officers, and crew are all hereby transferred to the Central African Empire. Please note that in ship's log as soon as we're off the phone. The man on the other end of the line, whose name you don't need, is your contact. For the duration of this lease arrangement, which is likely to be very short, you will take orders from him, again consistent with your own orders from the Admiralty. My office will serve as a communication hub anytime either of you wishes to contact the other."

"I understand, sir."

"So, Mr. Official of the Empire," said Winterset, "please tell Captain Daynsford what your orders are for him."

"Captain Daynsford," said Tai, "you are ordered to stop the Persian fleet."

"Aye aye, sir."

"Are those orders clear, Captain?" asked Winterset.

"Perfectly clear, sir."

"When you judge the Persian fleet has been stopped, the lease agreement will automatically end, and you'll contact your previous commanding officer for further orders. Understood?"

"Yes, sir."

"This call is now over."

48

THE PERSIAN AMBASSADOR, a short man with black hair and a thin mustache, was speaking to representatives of all member nations at a hastily convened meeting of the UN's general assembly.

"It's an outrage!" he screamed into the microphone, specks of moisture flying off his lips. "More than an outrage! It is an unprovoked act of war, of aggression! Yesterday fifty-six ships of the Persian Navy, which were performing innocent exercises at sea in the Indian Ocean, were sunk! All fifty-six ships were sunk! Thousands of lives were lost. We believe they were sunk by torpedoes. And we are almost certain it was done by the Americans. We have referred to America more than once as the Great Satan. It seems the Great Satan has committed an unforgivable act of war against the peaceful Persian empire. We demand compensation. We demand redress. We demand an apology. We demand—"

The U.S. ambassador stood up and grabbed a microphone, rudely interrupting the Persian ambassador and not even waiting for recognition by the Chair.

"I protest these lies!" he shouted. "We had nothing to do with this, Mr. Ambassador. The American Navy had no ships anywhere near this area. We urge you to stop your slanderous attacks on the United States, or *we* will be the ones demanding redress."

The Persian ambassador paused, only slightly abashed. "You deny your crime, to the entire world?"

"Mr. Ambassador, if you have any evidence this was done by the United States, please present it immediately. If you don't, then you are slandering America, and the American people, inexcusably."

"Our entire fleet was destroyed by torpedoes! It could only have been done by a navy possessed of submarines."

The U.S. Ambassador was ready for this line of argument and responded quickly. "There are many navies which have submarines. Even North Korea has submarines. So do India, Pakistan, Australia, Thailand, Britain, France, China, Russia, Germany, the Philippines…"

"Don't insult my intelligence, Mr. Ambassador," the Persian screamed into the microphone. "Why would the Philippines attack Persia?"

"A better question is why would Persia attack Africa? And please don't insult the intelligence of anyone in this chamber by pretending you were not attacking Africa. No one in this room, for one second, buys that nonsense about peaceful exercises in the Indian Ocean. Peaceful exercises with troop transports steaming at full speed towards the coast of Somalia? Knowing you would seek to blame America, we made sure satellite imagery of your fleet's activities was delivered to every ambassador seated here. You were sending an invasion force against Africa. Don't even think of pretending you weren't."

"Aha, then you admit you were tracking us!"

"We track everyone. That's what our satellites are for. And obviously someone didn't wish your little invasion to be successful. But it was not the United States. You have our word of honor on that. It was probably this African Empire itself which stopped your invasion force."

"Don't be ridiculous. The so-called Central African Empire has almost no navy whatsoever and certainly no submarines."

"Well, it seems likely they do. Because someone stopped you. And they had the best motive of all."

A new voice joined the conversation, from the other side of the assembly. "Mr. President, if I may add a note?"

"The chair recognizes the ambassador from the United Kingdom."

"I suspect we'll never know which nation, or perhaps even an extra-national mercenary force, sank the Persian invasion fleet. But I think we all understand that Persia was unlawfully seeking to invade another country. And somehow, by someone, was stopped in doing so. I understand why the Persians are upset. But it would seem they have only themselves to blame. Mr. Ambassador, if you don't wish to have your entire navy sunk, perhaps you shouldn't send it to invade other countries."

Spontaneous applause broke out in support of the British ambassador's comments.

The Persian ambassador, seeing which way the wind was blowing, gathered up his papers and furiously walked out of the chamber, noisily slamming the door behind him.

49

At their breakfast meeting the next day, which now often included Tai, Shari was livid.

"Tai, did you realize the Persian Empire was on the verge of invading Africa! Did you *know* about this?"

"Yes."

The prime minister looked at him closely. "You knew about this and didn't bother to mention it?"

"Eduardo, I don't come running to you for help with every little problem. You're a busy person. You too, Shari."

"Who sank the invasion force? Goddammit, Tai, I want the truth," insisted the empress.

"I did."

"*What?*"

"You wanted the truth. Careful what you wish for."

The empress stood up and began pacing. "And how did *you* sink the invasion force?" she finally asked.

"With submarines. Three of them, to be precise. They carry forty torpedoes apiece, I checked. Fifty-six ships? No problem. We're not talking battleships or carriers. I'm sure one torpedo per ship was enough."

Shari resumed pacing back and forth, trying to understand.

"But we don't *have* any submarines."

"The Central African Empire had precisely three submarines, two days ago, when it needed them."

"How did we acquire three submarines?" asked Eduardo.

"I leased them from the British."

"For how much money?" asked the prime minister.

"One British pound per submarine."

"And you ordered them to sink the Persian fleet?" continued Eduardo.

"I didn't order them to sink it. I ordered them to stop it."

"They sank it," noted Shari.

"Which seems to have stopped it," observed Tai.

"Well, those are fifty-six ships we'll never have to worry about again," mused Eduardo approvingly. "And which Persia won't easily or quickly be able to replace. It seems almost their entire navy is now gone—not just the ships themselves, but also the people who know how to run them and the troops they were transporting to invade us."

Shari finally sat back down and stared at Tai, trying to decide if she was furious or ecstatic.

"Well, it seems our friends the British did us quite the favor," she concluded. "How do we pay them back, Tai? Not with three pounds sterling."

"If my boss were here, I think I'd know what he'd say."

"Which is?"

"Keep doing what you're doing. Britain hopes you'll continue building your empire. If another naval force comes against you, I rather suspect it might be sunk as well."

Shari smiled. "Tai, let them know I'm grateful. I mean, these speeches at the United Nations. It's all a bit above me. But please, just let them know I'm grateful. And that I owe them a big favor. A very big favor. Can you do that?"

"Of course, Shari. But Lord Winterset takes favors very seriously. Are you sure you want to make clear you owe him one?"

"I do owe him one. A huge one."

Tai hesitated. "Very well. I'll communicate accordingly. But some day he'll ask for a favor in return. Probably a huge one."

"And I'll grant it," she said at once, eager to do so and puzzled that Tai was being so solemn.

50

With the Persian threat neutralized at least temporarily, and its navy sunk permanently, Eduardo was able to expand the Central African Empire much as expected.

Gabon and Equatorial Guinea saw their presidents leave for Europe a week after Cameroon's did.

The empire's prime minister acquired three more countries by offering their leaders a chance to stay on if they declared for Shariya, which brought in Angola, Zambia, and Tanzania.

"Why is it so easy, Eduardo?" Shari asked at their breakfast meeting. "The visit to Yaoundé was educational, I got it, but now things are going even faster. This empire is falling into our laps. How is this possible?"

"May I provide a history lesson?"

"Please."

"I'd enjoy one too," added Tai.

It was only the three of them. General Barasa was on a multi-country tour, seeking to bind their far-flung military assets into a unified force, taking stock of supplies and equipment, judging troop readiness, and working out command and control structures. Anzio often skipped the meetings as he had his hands full setting up a national health system based on free markets.

The prime minister stood by the map, holding the pointer.

"For most of the last several thousand years, Africa—at least sub-Saharan Africa—has been little more than a stone-age culture. Europeans began arriving in the interior around the seventeenth century but had very little impact on the continent until they built empires in the 1800s. By the mid-twentieth century, most of Africa had been divided up between European powers, mostly the French, Belgians, and British, plus Germans and Italians. In a way, that was good, because it brought Africa out of the Stone Age and introduced concepts like railroads which revolutionized the continent."

"Go on," Shari urged.

"But then the age of nationalist revolts began, which coincided with the Europeans deciding Africa was more trouble than it was worth, and being happy to bow out. Kind of a 'You're fired/No I quit' deal. Since then, most African governments have been run by one dysfunctional president-for-life after another. Everything is based on corruption, which is a kind of de facto feudalism. You pay a bribe to the official you need to please. He pays a bribe to maintain his position. That one does the same, and on upwards to the president, who rakes in the dough. In medieval Europe, the serf delivers grain to the local squire, who pays it upwards to the local baron or whatever, and then up to the king. It's really all the same thing. And the Africans themselves have always accepted it as how the world works. It's the only system they know."

"Yes, I understand," Shari agreed.

"Then another revolution happened, really just in the last twenty years or so: mobile phones and the Internet. Suddenly Africans are learning what developed countries look like. They're watching TV shows from America and movies from Hollywood. They contrast the lifestyles they see in these films with their own situation. From primitive camel herders in southern Morocco to destitute shanty-dwellers in the slums of Cape Town, they are increasingly realizing how sorry is their lot.

"Combine that with social media where flash mobs can form like locust hordes, and Africa is a tinderbox."

"Continue."

"Against that background, an Angel of Death arrives who is determined to bring *death* to everything wrong with Africa. She destroys the slavers, in some cases by feeding them to lions, in others by revealing her face and causing them to melt. Rumor spreads of her being an avenging angel with a sword, a spiritual being who cannot be defeated in battle.

"Suddenly Africa sees her as a way out of its destitution and despair. And every corrupt leader is terrified, because an Angel of Death is something new—arguably more powerful than a religious prophet. Shari, do you realize we're receiving inquiries every day asking how you're to be worshipped?"

Tai looked up, concerned. "Worshipped?"

"I don't want to be *worshipped*," objected the empress. "We covered that before. I'm just trying to stop slavery and corruption."

"I'm not sure it's your choice. You're increasingly seen as divine."

"Can't I just be supernatural? That's more modest. Maybe we took the army of lions thing too far."

"I don't think so," said Eduardo. "Africa is vast and diverse, and perhaps nothing less than a quasi-religious movement would have the power to conquer it."

"This is nuts," said Tai.

"Look, I wasn't going to tell you this, but I think you should know. In Uganda, when the pro-Shariya riots began, the president turned his national guard units loose and massacred over two hundred protestors."

"My God."

"Twenty-four hours later, his palace was burned to the ground, with the president and all his family inside. Some said the rioters were responsible. Others said it was a divine act of vengeance by Shariya, the Death Angel. Most believe it was Shariya. Some have already dispensed with the 'angel' part of it and are calling you the Goddess of Death."

"The *Goddess* of Death. Lovely."

"So that's one more rumor spreading across Africa," continued the prime minister. "You command fire and can burn a tyrant's palace to the ground merely by raising your hand, even if hundreds of kilometers away."

"That does sound like something a Goddess of Death would do," observed Shari, rolling her eyes.

"It's what they believe. Which means, again, everyone thinks you're unstoppable; an irresistible force. And when people believe something's an irresistible force, they don't try to resist it."

"Hmmm," she mused.

"Perhaps no one else could have lit the fire. But the way you arrived, from nowhere, with these rumors about commanding lions, and enemies dying when they see your face, and a shimmering, heavenly white glow about you…well, it all feeds into many Africans' fear of the occult, and anger that the world their mobile phones show them is not *their* world."

"I see."

"These African rulers are at heart cowards. They're venal, corrupt cowards. And incompetent, to boot. And they know they are. That's why they're fleeing. They're running for their lives. Whether they believe you're an avenging angel or not, they know the people believe it. So they know you'll win."

"Eduardo, we touched on this before," confessed Shari. "Even though almost no one knows I'm white, *I* know. And I can't help but feel guilty that a European—I assume that's what I am—is once again conquering Africa. It just seems so…neo-colonial."

Tai laughed. "Don't flatter yourself, Shariya-the-would-be-white-overlord. Eduardo's doing most of the conquering. He's the chess grandmaster. You're just the supernatural figurehead who rides lions around the sky at night baying at the moon."

"Well, there is that," she agreed, with a smile.

"Anyway, look who's running your actual government. Eduardo is Nigerian. Your defense minister is Kenyan. Anzio, your health and education minister—even though he's technically white—his family's been in Africa for generations. I'm North African."

"So you're saying this time it's Africans conquering Africa?"

"Precisely. The Angel of Death is merely our—"

"Mascot?" she volunteered, eyebrows raised.

"I was going to say *spiritual inspiration.*"

"Shari, depending on how large your empire becomes," suggested Eduardo, "at some point, you lose the mask, and we all can laugh at the silly rumors—about seeing your face and so forth—and of course deny them publicly. By then they'll have served their purpose. And as Tai says, with mostly Africans in charge of Africa, no one can claim this is 'Black Exploitation version 2.0' or anything."

Tai agreed. "This is 'Africa-finally-gets-its-act-together-and-eliminates-slavery-for-good version 1.0."

"And if a young white girl is part of the team, no one will care," concluded Shari.

"Yeah," said Tai, smiling. "Because every team needs a mascot!"

She gave him the evil eye, and this time they all laughed.

Jacques Voorhees

51

HER CONQUESTS EXPANDED much as Eduardo predicted. The small West African countries were easiest. They had limited resources, small armies, and no ability to stand against a fast-growing empire. Often they would surrender even before being asked. But if asked—with a strategically placed phone call—they quickly acceded. South of Congo it was different. Many of these nations were large and resource-rich, with the wealth to maintain more than trivial armies.

Not wanting her momentum stopped, on several occasions Shari flew clandestinely into targeted capitals, allied herself with rebel groups, and led pitched battles against government forces. Tai and Eduardo were appalled at the risk, but General Barasa—who often accompanied her—was supportive.

Today, the four ministers were meeting alone, as the empress was in her room recovering from knife and bullet wounds.

Eduardo sat at the head of the vast conference table, Tai at his right, the general on his left, and Anzio—who'd personally stitched up Shari's injuries, none of which were serious—seated further down. They were discussing the Angel of Death's now-frequent trips to areas of conflict.

"To be blunt, General," began Eduardo, "I'm not happy about it. The danger is real. She could have been killed in that skirmish."

"I'm not happy about it either," agreed Anzio. "We're lucky I did a stint in the emergency room back at Johannesburg General, during residency. I'm pretty good at stitching people back together. But sometimes I feel I'm more Shari's Emergency Medical Technician than her psychiatrist. And one of these days, we could be dealing with something beyond my skill set. Or anyone's."

Barasa pulled his chair back slightly and looked at each of them in turn. "Shari's appearance on the battlefield, sword in hand, calmly proclaiming to her opponents that she cannot be killed for she is already dead, has an uncanny effect."

"Oh, none of us doubt *that*," said Tai, grinning.

"The rebel forces believe her magic protects *them* as well, and the enemy troops are terrified. They know her reputation and that she's never been defeated in battle."

"Does she really use her sword?" asked Anzio. "I've seen her wounds, but I have a hard time visualizing her as a combat soldier."

"She's terrifying in combat," confirmed the general. "None of us know where these skills came from, but on the battlefield—with her katana—Shari's a force of nature."

"I'm not doubting you, General," the psychiatrist explained. "It's just hard to visualize, to process."

"I've personally seen her kill scores of men," continued Barasa. "To me, she's a warrior first, everything else second."

"Astonishing," said the doctor.

"The problem," continued the general, "is that she's reckless. She's so intent on surprising her enemies that even her allies can't keep up and properly cover her. That's what happened yesterday. We were about to lose the skirmish, and when Shari realized what was happening she just launched herself into the melee, without regard for her personal safety. She was wounded almost immediately, but simply kept fighting. Those nearby took that as proof of her immortality, and that's when they all fled. They believe the rumors that she can't be killed."

"But she *can* be killed," contradicted Eduardo, raising his hands for emphasis. "We can't afford to lose her. She shouldn't be leading these charges."

"Yeah," observed Barasa. "Try telling her that. Anyway, the skirmishes rarely last long. It's as if the ruler needs to at least test what he's up against and doesn't mind losing a few dozen troops in the process."

"Tough luck for them," noted Tai.

"Indeed," continued the general. "Shari told me privately she hates this kind of killing, knowing it's the leaders who are at fault, not the men. But I explained there's no choice."

"Ever it was so," agreed Tai. "At least in the Middle Ages, kings used to lead their own troops into battle. But these days presidents-for-life find that inconvenient."

"There's another reason she chooses to lead personally," offered Barasa. "She fears long, drawn-out engagements with vast numbers of killed and wounded. With her help, victory is quick."

"I think," concluded Tai, "the best way to protect her is to complete our conquests as quickly as possible. We're not going to pull her off the battlefield against her will."

Eduardo was staring at the large wall map of Africa. "Unfortunately," he said ominously, "our biggest confrontations lie ahead."

52

The model of an Imperial Lottery, no taxes, free markets, and limited bureaucracy was working. Tai had suggested a federalist system for the lottery so that not only did it fund the Imperial Court and military expenses, each participating country also received a hefty cut for its own government, in direct proportion to lottery sales in that country. Also, he made sure every time there was a lottery drawing there would be at least one winner in each country and more winners in direct proportion to that country's lottery sales. This ensured the lottery wasn't inadvertently moving wealth from, say, Cameroon to Kenya.

Billions in prizes were being handed out, heavily publicized and with each winner feted on billboards, national television and with parades in the national capitals. But billions more were flooding into Shariya's treasury. And all those bureaucrats who were previously contributing nothing to society were now useful lottery-ticket salespeople.

The math was inescapable. A government could better generate revenue from lottery sales in a rapidly growing economy than from a vast and expensive bureaucracy that spent its time enticing bribes from a moribund or even failing private sector.

Once the model was provably working, as it now was, African

countries began joining the Empire less out of fear and increasingly out of greed.

After the tiny nations bordering the Gulf of Guinea were absorbed, all movement in that direction stopped. The plan was to leave the Arab countries for last. So Mauritania, Mali, Niger, Sudan, and everything north was ignored.

Next, the empire began growing in the South. Namibia, Botswana, Zimbabwe, and Mozambique were invited to join and eagerly did. Uganda, Rwanda, Burundi, and Malawi were also willing, but it was not possible to integrate so many, so quickly.

It was the first time in history that nations were lining up asking to be conquered by an expansionist empire but were told to wait in line. Meanwhile South Africa was left alone.

Eduardo next turned his attention to Ethiopia, and as soon as its president was on a plane to Paris, the smaller and now isolated nations of Eritrea, Djibouti, and Somalia declared for Shariya.

Several days later, a press release was issued from Bangui proclaiming that the Central African Empire would henceforth be known as the Empire of Africa. The implication of that name—suggesting an inevitable takeover of the entire continent—was not lost on anyone, certainly not on the Saharan countries which were eyeing the Empire's expansion with alarm.

Jacques Voorhees

53

The United Nations ambassador from Algeria spoke for many when he went to the podium. He was a tall, thin man, whose expensive clothes were not tailored well and hung from him like shrouds. Thinning gray hair, and even thinner spectacles, made him an odd choice as an orator. But he did his best.

"It is beyond my comprehension, and beyond the comprehension of my fellow delegates in this assembly, how the one body established to maintain world order can allow the expansion of this so-called Empire of Africa to remain unopposed," he said, attempting to be forceful. "This mystery woman who calls herself the Angel of Death is engaged in toppling peaceful countries that were once members of this very assembly, but which have been overcome by the cancer of Shariya. She seems to think she's a latter-day Alexander the Great."

He paused and looked at the audience, many of whom appeared distracted, writing notes, texting, checking the clock. He continued gamely even so.

"And this supernatural nonsense about how she can't be killed because she is already dead? Does anyone believe that? This is the twenty-first century, not the Age of Witchcraft!"

That at least brought a few chuckles, although he wasn't trying to be funny.

"Most importantly," he continued, "the days of conquest by the sword should be over in the twenty-first century. How can we sit here and watch the rape and looting of an entire continent and just ignore it? As we speak, nations are falling, and her murderous armies are roaming at will over what has become already the second-largest empire in history."

Finally he gave his overheated rhetoric full rein.

"We must act! We must stop the genocide, the enslavement of populations, the terror, and the violence! We must pass a resolution calling for the Empire's expansion to immediately cease, and if she tries to push farther, to oppose her with the full military strength that a coalition of the willing can summon from this body!"

The British ambassador asked for the microphone.

"I have several problems with what the honorable ambassador from Algeria just said," he began. "First, there doesn't seem to be any rape and looting going on. Unlike previous expansionist empires, Empress Shariya seems to be improving the lives of those in the lands she conquers. Second, her armies don't seem to be murderous, let alone genocidal. The empire is expanding rapidly—I'll grant the ambassador that—but not so much 'by the sword.' We see it more as a growing commonwealth of states joining together for mutual benefit—much as did the European Union—rather than any kind of military conquest. It's happening mostly peacefully. Or put another way, this Angel of Death doesn't seem to be very interested in death.

"And finally, as for 'toppling peaceful countries,' well, they seem to become more peaceful and more prosperous after being 'toppled.' Pro-Shariya parades are now happening regularly and spontaneously throughout her empire.

"In short, as we look around at the world's problems, the one place that doesn't seem to be causing any is Africa. And it used to be responsible for most of them.

"If this assembly were to take any action, I would propose that it pass a resolution praising the Empire of Africa for having improved the lives of so many in what was formerly referred to as the Dark Continent."

The Ambassador paused, as some modest applause broke out.

"Now, if we did wish to worry about something," he continued, "I would suggest we give attention to that other expansionist empire, Persia, which in many ways is engaged in precisely the kind of deplorable behavior the honorable ambassador from Algeria was just talking about. Perhaps a resolution condemning Persia for its recent actions in…"

The room erupted in shouts, applause, and angry demands for time at the podium from other ambassadors. The president of the General Assembly pounded his gavel for silence and insisted on a thirty-minute break so everyone could calm down.

But the mood of most delegates was clear. Sharia's growing empire was viewed favorably by the international community.

54

They were in the conference room for another update meeting, Shari at the head of the table, her advisors seated around it. Dr. Anzio, head of a combined Health and Education Ministry, was now fully part of the team.

"The courses being made available by the University of Africa are already having an effect," the doctor explained. "Reading comprehension scores—at least in those areas where it's tracked—are up twenty-two percent. Even better, our free program of inoculations…"

Shari interrupted. "You mean the ones where we retrained the tax collectors to be vaccinators and sent them back out in the field to provide health care rather than collect taxes?"

"Yes, that program. I have the statistics here."

"I'll look at them later," interrupted the empress. "What's important is that it's working."

Anzio nodded.

"Tai, how's the economy doing?" The MI6 agent's expanded title was now Minister of Strategic and Economic Affairs.

"We're enjoying a sustained boom," he responded eagerly. "A big challenge is collecting the necessary statistics across the empire, but we're building the infrastructure for that."

"Is there one primary thing causing it?"

"What's causing it is the explosion in small business activity. Once we swept away the useless regulations and unenforceable tax burdens, the economy just took off. I think it was always ready to."

"Good. How can we keep the momentum going?"

"We're already doing it," explained Tai, "by encouraging more business startups. 'Er, Doctor, would you like to fill in this part?"

"Sure. My ministry's working closely with Tai's to provide a syllabus for young entrepreneurs. The thrust of it is to create a culture where working for *yourself* becomes the goal."

Tai interrupted. "I've got a whole TV production crew going around documenting success stories and interviewing entrepreneurs who are bootstrapping themselves up from poverty. Mainly it's service businesses. You know, bicycle repair, simple construction, food delivery, stuff like that. We have them tell the stories in their own words, explain how they got started, how it's going, and so forth. We create the videos and Roberto's department then builds them into its curriculum for how to start one's own business. They can be delivered with closed captioning so most any language in Africa is supported."

"And you have plenty of case studies?"

Prime Minister Eduardo interrupted. "We have too many, Shari. The problem is how to choose. The whole empire is booming with economic growth thanks to your reforms. But if I could change the subject—there's another agenda item, a question Roberto has raised."

Shari reached out and poured herself another glass of guava juice. She'd become addicted to guavas back in the village. "Sure. What's your question, Doctor?"

Anzio shifted uncomfortably. "Well, I hesitate to bring this up. Perhaps it's a trivial issue, but as it touches on human psychology, I thought…" He let his voice trail off.

Shari grinned. "OK, now I'm curious. Keep going."

"Well, it's about the name of your army. You know, 'Army of Death.' Now that you've become a force to be reckoned with, on the world stage, is that the right messaging? Wouldn't a kinder, gentler name signal that you are a benign movement, rather than a barbarous, despotic one? Something like Army of Peace, or even Army of Prosperity."

General Barasa was first to respond. "I'd like to note for the record," he said, laughing, "that I don't have an opinion. Even though I'm the head of the Army, this is above my pay grade."

Shari stood up and walked over to the windows, staring out, trying to remember why she'd chosen that name in the first place. Finally, she turned back to the others, reminiscing.

"It was that first day, when I came out of the jungle and re-entered civilization. I was the Angel of Death. My army should be the Army of Death. Plus, it sounded intimidating. I really haven't thought about it since."

She joined them again at the table. "Tai, what do you think?"

Her strategic advisor raised his eyebrows. "Angel of Death. Army of Death. There's a nice cadence to it; a symmetry if you will. And changing a brand message is always tricky—especially in the middle of a campaign. I understand the doctor's point. But this may fall under the 'if it ain't broke don't fix it' rule." He turned to the man across the table. "Eduardo, you're the diplomat. Do you think it's a problem?"

The debonaire Prime Minister glanced briefly at each of them, marshalling his thoughts. "I think it might be a problem if we were *behaving* like an army of death. In fact, as the British ambassador noted recently at the U.N., we're pretty darn peaceful."

"Let's not change it for now," Shari decided. "Let our actions speak louder than our slogans."

The others, including Dr. Anzio, nodded in agreement.

The intercom buzzed, and Eduardo pressed a button.

"I'm sorry to bother you, Prime Minister, but we have a situation here at the front gate. And it might require the empress's attention herself."

"What's happening?"

"Well, we have a visitor who says he knows the empress and hopes to see her. Said he's a personal friend. His name is…Ohnyro or something. From a village whose name I can't pronounce. Does anyone know an Ohnyro?"

They all glanced at each other, confused. Then Shari smiled and leaned towards the phone. "You don't mean *Omylo* do you? Is *Omylo* at the front gate?"

"Yes! That's it. Sorry I wasn't pronouncing it correctly. And he also has a very young woman with him. Will you see them?"

"Yes, I will see them. Please have someone escort them to my office."

"Gentlemen, let's adjourn. Omylo is the young man who rescued me from the jungle. I owe him everything."

The others exited quickly.

Shari couldn't wait, donned her veil, and rushed down the stairs to greet him personally. Yes, it was Omylo, from the tribal village. Several dozen lifetimes ago. She'd nearly forgotten, and felt guilty.

He looked at her veiled form, confused.

"Shariya?" asked the young man who'd given her that name. "Is that you?" He was speaking Ningala, and the empress still remembered it.

"Yes, Omylo," she replied, out of practice with the tribal tongue. The girl with him looked familiar. "Please come…" She wanted to say, "Please come upstairs to my office," but Ningala had no word for *stairs*, or *office*.

"Please follow me," she said, gesturing. Soon they were alone, and Shari removed her veil. It was the Ningala-speaking villagers who'd given her the original one.

"Your hair, it sparkles and is so beautiful," observed the young man.

Shari laughed. "Yes, when you knew me, it was a filthy, twisted mess." The empress paused, trying to remember the words. "Omylo, it's so good to see you," she gushed. "How did you find me? How did you get here?" She glanced at his companion. "And who is this young woman? I feel I know her."

"I am Anka," said the girl in heavily accented French. "I am Omylo's younger sister. Do you remember me from the village?"

"Oh yes, now I do." Shari replied in French. "I'm sorry, but I don't think I ever learned your name. But yes, I remember. How did you learn French?"

"I learned, too," said Omylo, speaking the same language slowly, pausing as needed to recall a word. "The driver who returned us to our village, after you left, explained that you spoke French. Since we hoped to visit someday, we've been studying it while working in Nolo. The money you gave me, do you remember? It let Anka and me move into town. Anka is a housekeeper in Nolo, and I do odd jobs—whatever someone needs. Working in Nolo, we were able to learn French."

"Also," said Anka, "the new program of free education helped us learn to read and write."

"Oh, that is so good to hear!" exclaimed Shari. "So the YouTube education system from University of Africa is working?"

"Yes," agreed Omylo. "It also taught my sister search skills on the Internet. She spends all her spare time now on her mobile phone, learning things."

"But how did you know I was in Bangui, at the palace?"

"We've been reading the newspapers. We've been watching you build your empire."

"And how did you even travel here?"

"There's bus service from Nolo. We saved our money so we could come visit."

"Do you have any money left?"

"Not much," admitted Anka. "But now that we speak French, we can do jobs here to earn enough to go back home."

"Are you hungry? When did you last eat?"

"Yesterday," said Omylo. "Maybe the day before."

Shari reached for the intercom and ordered food. "If Eduardo is free, could you ask him to bring the cart himself and to join me here?" She switched off the intercom.

"Well, now you must tell me everything. Did Oman find a new wife?"

"Yes," said Omylo with excitement. "And this one's already pregnant. If it's a girl, they're going to name her Shari."

The Angel of Death smiled. "I'm glad they didn't forget me," she said, enjoying the memories of her second family. "But maybe the two of you should stay in Bangui. Do you need to go back?"

The young man glanced quickly at his sister. "No, we'd be happy to stay and work in Bangui. It's the biggest city we've ever seen. Everything's so exciting."

Eduardo arrived and Shari urged Omylo and Anka to enjoy the food while she talked to him privately.

"Shari, what are you doing?" asked the prime minister as they moved to the far side of the room and spoke in soft voices. "Why aren't you wearing a veil?"

"Because they know me already. They're from the tribal village, remember?"

"Oh, yes, of course. The head covering would be silly."

"Exactly. Look, Eduardo, they're both learning French and they're new at it, but they're also looking for work. Could we find jobs for them here, in the palace?"

"I insist. It will make things easier to have two others who can come into your private quarters. We can make the girl your house servant so you don't have to keep making your own bed and so forth. And I'll have the boy work directly for me—as a personal assistant. I can't have enough of those. Where do you want them to live? There's no room at the palace, unfortunately…"

"Find someplace nearby. Easy walking distance. Have them live together. Maybe a two-bedroom apartment or cottage."

"Yes, Shari. I could also arrange private tutoring lessons in French."

"Wonderful idea. And please keep an eye on them. Pay them well. Make sure they don't have any difficulties. I'd probably still be living with lions today if it weren't for Omylo."

55

Shari was performing ballet moves, barefoot, in her spacious conference room. Chairs were pulled to one side and classical music played over wireless headphones. She'd been a ballerina, obviously, in addition to whatever else was in her past. Those "strange movements" practiced in the forest and which she didn't understand were fully formed now. Enjoying the music, she ran through routines her body remembered. Arabesque. Petit sauté. Elevé. Pas de cheval. She'd just finished a grand jeté when her eye caught movement near the door.

Fumbling with the controls she silenced the music. It was Eduardo and Tai, surprisingly early for their morning get-together.

"I'm impressed," said Tai sincerely. "You look quite good. Very professional."

"Thanks, I think maybe I *was* a professional. Or in training or something."

Tai raised his eyebrows. "We could pursue your identity using ballet as a possible clue."

"Don't even think about it," Shari said instantly. "All that's behind the door. Remember your promise."

"Sure, OK."

"Shari, we've got a problem," announced Eduardo. "That's why I've moved up our meeting. It's serious."

They took accustomed places around the conference table and the empress waited for the bad news.

Eduardo began. "Shari, remember you told me what happened with your veil one day during helicopter flight training?"

"You mean when the rotors blew off my boshiya?"

"Yes. I know it was only for a moment, and you were able to recover quickly, and the pilot never saw you."

"Someone else did?"

"Someone with a camera. Look."

He tossed a copy of London's Daily Mirror onto the desk, open to page six.

It was a picture of Shari looking directly at a camera with the helicopter behind her. She was completely exposed above the shoulders.

"Is this Empress Shariya?" asked the caption. The article went on to note the photo had been sent from someone in the Central African Republic, at the Bangui airport, several weeks earlier.

There was little evidence provided, except to note it was highly unusual for a young, blue-eyed, blonde woman to wear Islamic dress in central Africa—or even for someone like that to *be* in Central Africa. And here this mystery woman was, in the capital city of the Empire of Africa, with her hijab covering blown off by a helicopter's rotor wash.

Shari continued reading.

"Everyone's been told, and believes, that the Angel of Death is a native African girl from a tribal village in the jungle. Yet no one has been able to explain how she's grown her empire at such breathtaking speed—in only a matter of months. Is it possible she isn't African at all, but rather a very young, blonde, blue-eyed beauty as was captured here at Bangui's airport recently, when her head covering was accidentally blown off? Of course that would make the mystery greater, not less."

"Thank God it wasn't on the front page," said Shari.

"It doesn't matter," noted Eduardo. "It's already trending on social media. Most won't believe it, but—"

"This is dangerous, isn't it?" asked Shari.

"Yes. People will begin asking questions, forcing us to comment, or appear like we're hiding something if we don't. At the very least it will put us on the defensive and blow any hope of you remaining incognito. If you were to appear in public unmasked, anywhere, people would remember this face. Whatever we do, this photograph will increasingly go viral."

"What *can* we do?" she asked. "It's already out there. We can't stop it!"

"Let's not try to stop it," suggested Tai. "Let's accelerate it. Let's make this photo of Shariya go totally viral. Let's promote Shariya photos ourselves, drown the world in them."

"You can't be serious!" protested Eduardo. "That would make it worse."

"What do you mean, Tai?" asked Shari. "Why should we promote Shariya pictures ourselves?"

"When you can't beat something, the next best choice is to make it look ridiculous. This true photo of Shari is already out there. Let's flood the Internet with other photos just like it, but with different faces. Let's do photoshopped versions with movie stars, with politicians, with fashion models. We'll make it the most over-saturated meme on Twitter and Instagram: fake Shariya photos at the Bangui airport in front of a helicopter."

"You mean, we'll drown the world in replicas?" asked Eduardo, beginning to smile.

"Yes, but we need to make sure this one, the original, looks like one of the fakes. Let me think a moment. We can't turn Shari into a politician or an actress. But we *can* turn her into a fashion model."

"A fashion model!" She laughed. "Tai, what are you talking about? I'm no fashion model."

"But you could be."

"Tai!"

"I think I understand," said Eduardo. "If we could arrange a photo shoot, come up with some great shots, somehow get them printed, then this helicopter shot…"

"Will look as fake as all the others," she said, completing the sentence. "But how do we get the pictures taken? How do we get them published?"

"A friend of mine from Oxford, well, more than friends actually, is now one of the top fashion photographers in Paris. He'll do this favor for me, I'm sure."

"It doesn't need to be a favor. We'll pay him," added Eduardo.

"Even better."

"But how can we guarantee some newspaper or magazine will print them and make our empress a supermodel?" asked the prime minister.

"One bridge at a time. I'll ask Francois for help with that once we get to Paris."

56

It was Shari's first time in a modern, Western city—at least that she could remember. Perhaps she'd been in such places before but regardless it was delightful to hear French spoken as she did.

Tai arranged everything and accompanied Shari in one of their corporate jets. She was fully veiled during the trip but the moment they exited the airport in a taxi the veil came off and the Empress of Africa transitioned to Western clothing. This was strange, to be out in public without her veil. But the goal now was *not* to be hidden. She was a fashion model, on her way to a shoot. Anyone was welcome to look at her, and if they took photos, even better.

She'd tried to dress the part and—with Tai's advice—was now in crisp jeans, a soft-pink cashmere V-neck sweater, black ballet flats, pearl-stud earrings, and—given it was early fall—a short-length, tan trench coat. Watching other young women on the sidewalk, she felt appropriately attired.

Arriving at the studio, a completely renovated top floor of an ancient building off the Champs-Élysées, Shari was fascinated with everything. It was all so modern, so elegant, so *très chic*. She noticed that the receptionist, with short-cut auburn hair and heavily made-up, was very attractive. Perhaps that was a job requirement.

They were ushered into a conference room. On the walls were dozens of photographs of glamorous faces and framed magazine covers. Intense, directional spot lighting illuminated the room unevenly, creating patterns of shadow and brightness and transforming the space into almost a three-dimensional work of art. A seating area was to one side, and opposing sofas were in shimmering white leather surrounding a glass coffee table discreetly graced with fashion magazines.

They took their seats.

"Monsieur Matthieu will be with you shortly," said the pretty receptionist in French, smiling. "May I bring you cappuccinos?"

"That would be lovely," acknowledged Tai.

The coffees had just arrived when the photographer joined them.

"Tai!"

"Francois!"

The two hugged and it looked to Shari, who'd been warned, like they were indeed more than friends. Unable to control it, jealousy washed over her. But she knew Tai was gay.

"Francois, allow me to present my very good friend, *Danielle Crecy*."

They'd chosen that name because it sounded French and very fashion-modelish. And because they had no idea what Shari's real name was.

"*Vous parlez Francais, mademoiselle?*" he asked.

"*Oui, bien sur,*" she replied, both of them speaking with Parisian accents.

The photographer checked his Audemars Piguet watch. "Forgive me, friends, no time for social courtesies, as we're very pressed for time today."

"Understood," said Tai. "Let's jump right in."

"Mademoiselle, if you don't mind, may I examine your face?" asked Francois.

The would-be model smiled. "I don't believe I've ever been asked that question."

"In this business, it's almost the only one we ask."

"What do I do?"

He took the Empress of Africa gently by the arm and guided her to an area with even more intense, high-wattage, spot lighting.

"I must move your head around a bit. Please relax your muscles."

He touched gently with both hands, shifting her head in and out of the light, tipping it slightly, rotating it, checking shadows and accents. "*Incroyable!*" he gushed. "*Mon ami*, where did you find this angel?"

Shari suppressed a grin at the choice of words.

"Is she as stunning as she looks?" asked Tai. "You're the pro."

"She's one of those women who almost make me wish I were straight," he confessed.

Tai laughed. "Tell me about it. So, can you give us the photographs we need?"

"I cannot make her one of the most beautiful women in the world, because she already is that," he noted soberly. "But I can record the fact that she is. I can make the world gasp."

"How do we circulate the photographs? How do we show her as a fashion model? Remember, as we discussed by phone, that's part of the goal."

Shari knew Tai had outlined the plan, although not the reason for it, and asked that his friend probe no further. The photographer made clear that discretion was included in the rates.

"I'm owed a few favors in this town," Francois noted, smiling at Tai.

"No, who would guess?"

"Givenchy has a new collection coming out. We'll use Mademoiselle Crécy as a preview model."

"Preview model?" she asked.

"The haute couture houses typically settle on a single face to represent their brand or a new line," the photographer explained. "But that would be difficult to arrange and would take too long."

"Speed is everything," confirmed Shari.

"A preview model is just one that is used temporarily, to get initial reaction. I have ladies I use for that purpose when the client just needs quick shots. Givenchy sent over some designs yesterday for previewing, and they'll look amazing on you, Mademoiselle. I'll tell the editor of *Vogue-Paris* he's got right of first refusal to publish them. Once that happens, trust me, they'll go viral."

"Remember the photograph against the helicopter," said Tai. "We need you to imitate that one as well. Perfectly."

"Everything I do, I do perfectly. Especially when a client pays my outrageous prices," said Francois, with a laugh. "We'll use a green screen for the helicopter shot. My friends, an apology, I have another shoot that begins in a few minutes. Tai, *mon cher*, please come back tomorrow at ten."

"Mademoiselle…"

"Yes, Francois?"

"Don't worry about what to wear. Come in jeans, as you are, or anything comfortable. And zero makeup please. We'll have you shower and wash your hair on-site. We must have total control and we start from the beginning, with shampoo and conditioner that is camera-friendly. You wouldn't believe the difference it makes. Our technicians will spend a couple of hours prepping you. They'll handle the shampooing, the makeup, the hair, the clothes, everything. I must ask, do you care if they are men or women? They may see you in *dishabille*—it's the nature of our business. But if it makes you uncomfortable…"

"It doesn't matter," she said, meaning it, and vastly enjoying this journey into another world. Although it was strange to go from one where she was covered head-to-toe, to being perhaps naked in front of strangers.

After a visit to the Louvre, Shari and Tai had dinner that night at a sidewalk café overlooking the Seine river, and afterwards walked around a bit on the cobbled streets of the Left Bank. The Empress of Africa peered curiously into some of the charming bookstores and enjoyed the aroma of fresh-baked pastries wafting from a patisserie.

A week later, hauntingly beautiful images of *Danielle Crécy*, the latest supermodel to hit Europe, were featured in the online edition of *Vogue-Paris*. Meanwhile dozens of pictures of politicians, movie stars, and fashion models—deepfakes of the famous helicopter shot from

Bangui—were now appearing everywhere. A week after that, a new meme arrived. The face of the President of the United States being compared to an angry chimpanzee was now breaking the Internet, and the helicopter picture was forgotten. Even the *Daily Mirror* lost interest, realizing they'd been the victim of a hoax.

Back in her palace, Tai sat with Shari on the private balcony.

"Francois tells me all Paris is in an uproar," he began, teasingly.

"Over what?"

"He's talking about the haute couture houses. Everyone's seeking contact information for Mademoiselle Crécy's agent. Your face stunned the fashion world. You could have your pick of over a dozen long-term contracts, according to Francois."

"Hmmm... The *Angel of Death* re-branded a fashion model. Quite the career change."

"You could probably launch your own fragrance line."

"*Eau de Mort?*"

They both laughed.

"Seriously, what is Francois telling them?"

"Only that you were a friend of a friend, in town for a few days, and he used you for the Givenchy shoot on a lark. He's made clear you've already left town and are not interested in being a professional model. He says the fashion world is crushed, but believes *House of Givenchy* will survive."

Shari smiled.

The sun was low, and the fish eagles were putting on a show, diving into the water, finding their dinner.

"It's such a different world," she said. "I mean Europe compared to Africa. I was glad to see Paris."

"You're worried about which world you belong to, right?"

Shari paused, considering. "I'm worried that at this point I may not belong to either."

57

Shari, Eduardo, Tai, and the Defense Minister were in the conference room studying the map—seeking a plan that would win them the continent.

Eduardo summed up the tactical situation.

"Shari, there are fifty-one countries in Africa. Of these, and not counting South Africa, all but nine have joined our empire. Of the nine, only two matter: Sudan and Egypt. Here's the bad news. They've entered a mutual defense pact. Those countries have the two largest military forces on the continent. Together they'll be invincible."

"And remind me who are the other holdouts?"

"Mauritania, Niger, Western Sahara, Morocco, Algeria, Libya, and Tunisia," he counted off, eyes marching across the continent's Mediterranean coast. Plus South Africa, obviously. All of them will wait to see what happens with Egypt and Sudan."

"So, we first need to defeat those two?"

"Yes."

"Let's play devil's advocate. Remind me again why we need to conquer these Arab countries at all. Why not stop with what we have?"

Eduardo, as always dressed like a banker, stood up and walked over to the map. His hand gestured towards the entire continent.

"Shari, intended or not, you're building a large empire and it's happened at lightning speed. But you're like a car careening without brakes down a hill. You need to find a way to reach a soft landing. If you bring all of Africa together, then you've reached a natural stopping point—where the car can come to a rest. But if you stop before the job's completed, then you show weakness and damage your reputation of inevitability."

The others listened closely, respecting the prime minister's grasp of the political situation.

"Once you've 'conquered' all of Africa," he continued, "you both *can* stop, and *should* stop, and everyone will expect you to stop. Your inevitability won't be questioned because Africa is as large as your empire needs to be. In fact, it would be silly for the Empire of Africa to be anywhere else.

"But if you pause in that conquest, if you show that you can be defeated—or at least your empire-building stalled—then you signal vulnerability. Your enemies will push back, using the stalemate as proof of your weakness. Those already pledged will consider recanting their loyalty. Egypt and Sudan will grow stronger and build up their militaries further. Local warlords will sense an opportunity and start rebellions."

"Sounds likely." Shari stood up and walked out on the deck and stared at the river. She understood the problem but could see no solution. Finally, she returned to the group. "I never asked for this empire."

"No," agreed Eduardo. "But I told you that to defeat slavery you'd need to conquer the whole continent. I didn't realize how prescient those words would be. But now if you *don't* conquer Africa, voluntarily or militarily, absolutely all of it, Africa will turn around and conquer *you*. Imagine you're in a locked room containing several dozen poisonous snakes. You need to get those snakes safely contained in cages. And you need to get all of them in cages. Leaving even a few loose, even one loose, means you'll soon be dead. You need to conquer Africa completely, Shari. Otherwise, you're in a dangerous room with snakes slithering around."

Forest Creature

The empress, now pacing in front of the map, threw up her hands in frustration. "I'm happy to kill *snakes*. But I'm not thrilled about killing people. Sub-Saharan Africa fell into our lap, with minimal loss of life. But now we're talking about what can only be called a war of aggression—against countries that don't want to be absorbed. How do we justify this morally? Someone at the UN compared me to Alexander the Great, and they didn't mean it as a compliment. At some point, we need to ask ourselves, are we still the good guys?"

There was silence around the room, and none were willing to meet her eyes. Finally Tai responded. "I see only one way out of this dilemma," he observed. "I think Eduardo's correct, that you have no choice but to keep going. But you're correct too. We don't want to morph into the bad guys, just because we need to expand the empire to its natural boundaries."

"You said there was a solution, Tai. What is it?"

"Find a way to take over the remaining countries, but without warfare; with minimum loss of life."

"Well, that's helpful," the empress said, sarcastically, and immediately regretted the tone. She knew it was a sign of growing stress, and tried to soften the remark.

"Look, Tai. At this point I don't know how to defeat these countries even *with* warfare. We've never conquered any nation with a set-piece military battle, you all know that."

"You're wondering if you can truly win an on-the-field military battle against Egypt/Sudan?" asked Eduardo.

"What do *you* think, General?" she asked, nodding in his direction.

Her staunchest ally shifted uncomfortably in his chair. "I see no way to do it," confessed Barasa. "The logistics alone—of collecting and bringing into battle the national forces of all the empire's countries—would be a nightmare. You have incompatibility of language, diverse levels of training, completely different weapons systems, plus the fact that they're scattered over millions of square kilometers. Look at the map. Egypt/Sudan are nicely contained in a strategically defensible corner of the continent. Their combined armies are easily brought together into a concentrated force. And all they have to defend is the western and southern border of Sudan. They all speak the same language and their level of training is very high.

"Worse, if we tried to invade militarily, they'd see us coming and be able to bring their own forces to bear. It would likely be a massacre. Between them they have over five thousand tanks, not to mention jet aircraft. In our entire empire, we have no more than two thousand tanks, only half of which could be brought to bear in a reasonable time. The rest are spread over Africa, and it would take months to collect them. The combined air power of the countries we control is equally pathetic. They would be wiped out by the Egyptian Air Force which has trained scores of fighter pilots for opposing Israel, should that ever again be needed."

"So, are you suggesting, as Defense Minister, that it's a battle we can't win?"

"I'm afraid so."

Shari was silent, staring at the map. Then she began pacing back and forth. Finally she stopped and looked at her prime minister. "But Eduardo, your point is that we *must* finish our conquest of Africa. We can't afford to stall, and I think that's probably good advice. Here's a hypothetical: What if we *could* defeat Egypt and Sudan? What happens to the chessboard?"

"It would be like capturing your opponent's queen near the end of the game. It would end the game," explained Eduardo, and the general nodded.

"How so, exactly?"

"If you somehow did the impossible and defeated Egypt and Sudan militarily, the rest of the Arab countries would sue for peace and declare themselves for your empire. Because if you could defeat Egypt and Sudan together, you could defeat any of the others, easily."

"And South Africa?"

"They might be the very last, but if they saw the rest of the continent in your hands, they'd fold."

"So, we have to defeat Egypt and Sudan militarily, yet we can't defeat Egypt and Sudan militarily. And even if we could, we have no moral basis to do so. Do I have this right, gentlemen?"

"Correct, Shari," said Eduardo, and the others nodded.

"Let's adjourn for now. Obviously I need to give this some thought. All of us do."

They stood up and left the room, while the empress sat down again and stared at the map in frustration.

58

When Shari finally returned to her suite she was not surprised to notice—while she'd been in the meeting—that Anka had used the time to change sheets and clean up everything. She was a clever girl, very smart, a hard worker, and her French got better each day.

If she had a fault it was her addiction to learning. She spent all spare time on a mobile device watching YouTube videos and researching things on Google.

And here she was sprawled on the couch, clicking away.

"Hi, Anka," said Shari.

The girl jumped up; eyes downcast sheepishly. "Sorry. I got distracted and was trying to find the answer to something."

"What were you trying to find the answer to?"

"Those fish eagles you see from the balcony, I was curious what kind of fish they find in the river."

"And did you learn?"

"Yes! They feed on elephant-fish, bagrids, and carp."

"Wow, I guess you can find anything on Google these days," said the empress, smiling supportively.

"Anything! I love it. Let me search for something for you, Shari. What information do you need? It will be good practice for me."

FOREST CREATURE

Shari looked out over the river and said quietly. "Search for a way my empire can defeat Sudan."

"Is that your next country?" asked Anka, excited.

"Sudan and Egypt have joined forces, and they have the largest army in Africa. They can't be toppled by a coup. And we can't defeat them militarily."

"So how will you defeat them?"

"I don't know. It can't be with a large battle. We need to find a way to trick them. We need some kind of special knowledge that will let us trick them, or trick the President of Sudan into surrendering."

"What's his name?"

"Samir Abbas. Here, let me write it down for you." Shari jotted down the spelling on a notepad and handed it to Anka.

"I will make this my top priority. May I begin at once?" asked Anka.

Shari smiled, knowing Google would not give Anka the key to defeating Sudan. But she enjoyed the girl's enthusiasm.

"At once, Anka!"

Three days later Shari was sitting in the conference room alone, staring again at the large map on the wall. There was a knock on the door and Anka walked in.

"Shari, I've completed my assignment," she announced proudly.

"Sorry, *what* assignment?" The Angel of Death looked up quizzically.

"You said you needed special information that would help you defeat Sudan."

Shari laughed. "Oh, Anka. I wasn't serious. I'm not expecting— Wait, did you say you *completed* the assignment?"

"Yes, Shari. I have the information you need."

59

The Empress of Africa reconvened her advisors. Eduardo, Tai, and General Barasa were once again sitting around the conference table. As always, the prime minister was dressed for business, Tai was in his signature jeans and t-shirt, and General Barasa wore camo attire, gold stars showing his rank.

Shari had donned a frivolous purple abaya gown, with silver embroidery, and was in an upbeat mood.

"I'd like to re-open the question of Egypt and Sudan," she began.

"I've gathered more information, and it's not encouraging," said the general. "Their combined army has over five thousand tanks, as we discussed, and they're concentrating all of them as a single force, near Khartoum."

"They're preparing for an attack by the Empire of Africa?" asked Shari, her eyes lively and curious. "Don't they realize we're too weak to attack them in a tank battle? We only have, how many tanks did you say?"

"About a thousand we can deploy. I've been trying to bring them together from nearby countries, and we've assembled that many so far in Juba. Given time, I could add more from other parts of the empire."

"Yet even with such a small force, Egypt and Sudan think we'll invade?"

"Yes, that's the most likely reason they're building up forces in Khartoum."

"Shari, here's how it looks to them," said Eduardo. "Everyone knows the Empire of Africa sees its destiny as uniting all of Africa. We've achieved so much, so quickly, that it's expected we'll be overconfident. It's expected that the primitive, Mahdi-like figure, this Angel of Death, will prove vastly unsophisticated trying to command actual military units in an open battle, and this will prove her undoing. General, isn't that what you'd think if you were Egypt/Sudan?"

"That's precisely what I'd think," agreed Barasa, nodding soberly.

"Me too," said Tai, chair back from the table, legs outstretched.

"Then, gentlemen, let's give them the war they want," said the empress with a glint in her eye. "Let's fall right into the trap they've set. I'm a primitive ruler from the jungle, after all. It's just the kind of thing I'd do—fall into such a trap." She was smiling, but the others weren't.

"What orders do you have for me, Shari," asked Barasa, formally.

"Bring the generals together. Tell them we're going to invade Egypt/Sudan and have them organize an invasion plan. We want this all very public. We're certain of victory and don't need to conceal our movements. We're arrogantly ignoring the need for secrecy. Quite the opposite, we'll proudly announce a declaration of war against Egypt/Sudan."

"Where will we attack?"

"Where they'll expect us to; the nearest capital. We'll go against Khartoum, the very spot they've concentrated forces. They'll oppose us with a combined army of tanks, planes, all that stuff, under the direct command of Abbas, the field marshal and President of Sudan. He'll insist on having full operational control of the combined military and Egypt will happily give it to him, quite pleased their neighbor to the south will do the fighting for them."

"Yes, from what we know about the situation that's exactly what will happen," agreed the prime minister.

"We'll invade from South Sudan which has a border less than four hundred kilometers from Khartoum. The battle can be right here, at Rabat." She noted a spot on the map with her pointer.

"We'll go against it with whatever forces we can throw together on the grounds that our army is divinely supported, and the Angel of Death can't be defeated. Even by tanks."

"We can do all that, Shari, but how do we *win?*" asked Barasa. "As we've discussed, we can never defeat the combined Sudanese and Egyptian forces in open battle. I will do anything you order, and happily die for you, but I will also tell you when a plan won't work. I'd be disloyal if I didn't."

"Of course. Eduardo, what do *you* think of my plan?"

"You're proposing that we take our entire Army of Death, which possesses no more than a thousand available tanks and almost no experienced tank commanders, and send it onto the open plain in front of Khartoum, challenging battle?"

"Yes."

"And we know Sudan, with their Egyptian allies, will be opposing us with three divisions, including over five thousand tanks, not to mention air superiority which they probably won't even need to use. I'm sorry, I'm not understanding your plan. This is what they will *expect*. As the general said, how can we win?"

"But, Eduardo, aren't you forgetting that we have momentum on our side? Everyone knows that the Angel of Death can't be beaten, that she is divinely sponsored. This will have a devastating effect on their troops. They will be terrified to face us in battle."

"Shari, with respect," said Eduardo, "you've been operating in sub-Saharan Africa, where the occult, voodoo, and spirituality play a far greater role. Now that we're facing modern armies, we can't rely on superstition as we did before. They will consider you a trumped-up tribal leader who is too sure of herself and over-confident. They will look forward to teaching you that a *lion-riding angel* is no match for five thousand tanks."

"But General Barasa, you will conduct this attack as I've outlined, if I order it, correct?"

"Absolutely, Shari. It will mean my death, but the day you painted Katinka's name on my truck, I knew I would happily die for you."

"Thank you, General. I appreciate the loyalty. And you, Tai? You've not said much. Do you think I'm crazy?"

"You've read the Art of War, and you're not crazy. Not in a thousand lifetimes would Sun Tzu expect to win such a battle. Nor would you."

"All that really matters," she said, "is what my enemies think. Will they believe I'll be overconfident and expect to win?"

"Then—then this isn't really your plan?" said Barasa, brightening instantly.

"Of course it's my plan. General, you are hereby ordered to execute as we have discussed. You will take the Army of Death and launch it against Khartoum. You will meet the opposing forces here on the plain, south of the city."

"It's a suicide mission, Shari."

"What will the enemy do when they see you there?"

"Obviously, they'll immediately attack with their tank forces. Are my orders to stand and fight to the last man?"

"You are indeed ordered to stand and fight, but not *quite* to the last man," said the empress, grinning.

"For how long, then?"

"I'm thinking maybe five minutes. No, let's call it two."

"*What!*" Barasa sat up suddenly.

"I want you to fight for two minutes and then turn around and get the hell out of there."

"I don't understand," said the general, eyebrows coming together.

"They will pursue you, correct?"

"Of course."

"Can you outrun them?"

"Well, we can try to race back to the border. But they could use their superiority in tank numbers to flank us and try to encircle. Or even pursue us across the border. Or use their air force for that matter. Why not? Their goal will be to utterly destroy the Army of Death."

"Let me be very clear on one thing, General."

"Yes, Shari?"

"When the Sudanese forces surrender, there is to be no killing. They are to be invited to join the Army of Death, and when they do, you'll treat them with dignity. Make sure every one of your men knows this."

There was stunned silence.

"When the Sudanese forces *surrender* to us? What are you talking about?" exclaimed Eduardo, normal decorum forgotten.

"Anka, my housekeeper, the one who's addicted to Google, was able to find out something very interesting about the Sudanese president," she explained. "It seems that Samir Abbas has an inordinate fear of being burned alive. He saw his brother die that way in a car accident, screaming, and it left him with a deep phobia for that kind of death."

"How does that help us," asked Tai, no less confused than the others.

"Where do you think he will be during this battle?"

"Back in his palace," said Eduardo. "He still calls himself field marshal of the Sudanese forces and wears an army uniform everywhere, but the truth is, as president, he prefers the comforts of home to the open field."

"Exactly. So, when you, General, challenge the Sudanese Army on the plain in front of Khartoum, I think you know where I will be."

The room was silent, as everyone considered the plan.

Finally, Tai spoke for all of them. "It seems the spirit of Sun Tzu is with us after all," he said with a grin.

60

Shari sat on a wooden bench in a dusty field tent near the border with Sudan, and watched the news reports from CNN. She was dressed in a black, long-sleeve unitard. A version of her boshiya mask, this one able to be secured more tightly around her head, plus black socks and gloves, completed the job of rendering her invisible—or at least opaque. She listened to the news, pleased her strategic moves were being taken at face value and being judged foolish.

"Steve Ogden here, reporting in from the Meheiriba Plain just south of Khartoum. Shariya's so-called 'Army of Death' invaded the Sudanese territory from South Sudan as expected this morning, just after midnight, with almost a thousand tanks, several hundred pieces of lightly armored mobile cavalry units, plus troop transports.

"Yet we're told this may be one of the shortest battles in history because opposing them are the combined forces of Egypt and Sudan, which include over five thousand tanks and a similar imbalance in lightly armored equipment and transports. The battle is expected to begin sometime in the next few hours, and there's no way Shariya's army can win such an unequal contest."

The CNN anchor in New York interrupted with a question. "Steve, as we know, Shariya and her forces have never been defeated in battle, but it seems they're about to be. How do you explain this ill-advised move on her part?"

"Well, the African Empire's forces have never, until now, engaged in traditional combat. Much of what Shariya's achieved has been through coups, and with frightened national leaders acceding to her empire-building inevitability, largely because of discontent among their own people. This is her first actual set-piece battle, and it appears she thinks she can win purely on reputation. Back to you, Jim."

"With us here," continued the anchor, "is former Army General Walter Hammond from the Institute of War to give us his insight. General Hammond, thanks so much for joining us."

"My pleasure," said the retired officer, his gray hair and civilian clothing not disguising an erect military posture and serious countenance.

"So, what's your analysis of all this?" prodded the interviewer.

"Well, I would second what your reporter on the scene said. Shariya has been incredibly lucky up to now. We still don't know much about her, only that she's a tribal girl from a village in Central African Republic who began leading a band of natives who used surprise attacks on poorly defended assets to 'conquer' several countries essentially by coup, before anyone really knew what was happening.

"She threw in a host of spiritual nonsense about being an Angel of Death and commanding an army of lions, and the whole thing spread like wildfire among the people of sub-Saharan Africa. The uprisings it triggered allowed her to build an empire on the cheap, so to speak, and what's clearly happened is she's become overconfident.

"Or maybe she believes her own propaganda," the expert continued, rolling his eyes, "of being an avenging angel against injustice and has God on her side or something. Maybe she hears voices, for all we know. This will be the first time she's had to engage with a modern, reasonably well-trained army, where surprise *isn't* a factor."

"But how good are the Sudanese and Egyptians? Didn't Israel defeat the Egyptians easily?" asked the CNN anchor.

"It's true the Israelis defeated the Egyptians in 1967, but (a) the Egyptian and Sudanese militaries learned the lessons from that and are today a far superior military force than they were then, and (b) let's just say the primitive regions of Africa which constitute most of Shariya's empire are militarily not in Israel's league by a long shot."

"So, you're saying we're about to see a major defeat for the empress."

"Obviously. She's gambled her entire army, throwing all her tanks from this part of Africa into this one battle, but she'll be opposed by numbers almost five times greater and with far higher levels of training and competence. Remember, everything we know about Shariya is that she's simply a primitive village girl who enjoyed a run of good luck. She's clearly no military genius because this is one of the stupidest chess moves anyone could make."

61

THE ANGEL OF Death switched off the broadcast and eyed the Apache helicopter being readied by the ground crew a hundred meters from the tent. She once again considered its weaponry: twin M134 Miniguns that could fire 6,000 rounds per minute, each, and half a dozen air-to-ground missiles. Plus, she thought, a pilot armed with a sword and a knife. And a bulletproof vest. And a backup force that would be sent in automatically if Plan A failed. That was the one concession she made to her planning team, who didn't like this solo mission at all. So there was a Plan B, but if they needed Plan B it meant she was probably dead. Best not to think about that. Plan A was their best option. And the Angel of Death knew she was most effective working alone.

The empress climbed in, adjusted her scabbard, and set the small backpack with its vital contents on the empty co-pilot's seat. Safety belt on. Door closed.

The ground crew chief made a spinning motion, and she engaged the starter motor. The four blades began to move ever so slowly. It took nearly five minutes of pre-flight preparations before the rotors were at operational speed and the Apache ready to fly.

The crew chief made a thumbs-up motion and backed away. Shari lifted the helicopter off the ground, gained altitude, and headed north as the sun neared its zenith.

The Apache crossed into Sudanese airspace safely below radar coverage and stayed there, 100 feet above the ground. At maximum cruise speed she'd reach her destination in roughly ninety minutes.

The empress steered the helicopter on an elliptical course towards Khartoum, using pre-programmed GPS waypoints to avoid being seen by Sudanese forces defending the capital. Upon entering the city she dropped even lower, flying along the streets beneath rooftop level. An occasional clothesline would present an obstruction, but she could easily soar above it and drop down again below radar. One appeared too late to avoid and the Apache's fuselage snapped the wire and sent clothes flying chaotically. Her target was the palace itself—which she'd been studying from schematics and photographs, both inside and out.

The building was protected by a small company of guards although according to reports half had been sent to join the soon-to-be victorious Sudanese army. No one wished to miss that spectacle.

Shari's Apache helicopter arrived at the palace like a giant, conquering insect from hell. It hovered twenty-five feet above the ground, propellers slicing the air furiously, generating a vast dust storm and an astonishing amount of noise.

A helicopter gunship was one of the most devastating weapons of war to use against ground troops and fortified positions. Her Apache could easily kill every guard and demolish the palace itself, but that wasn't Shari's goal.

Using rudder pedals to swing the craft back and forth, she unleashed twin miniguns and poured 12,000 rounds a minute into the palace grounds, doing what she could to minimize casualties. Even formerly-disciplined guards dove for cover.

These troops had likely never experienced actual battle, shielding the president instead from cameras wielded by tourists, the occasional protest march, or perhaps a pizza delivery boy on a bicycle who'd lost his way.

Having terrified those nominally protecting Sudan's president and field marshal, she turned the helicopter towards the building itself.

A vast central atrium was protected by a wall of glass, and Shari fired two missiles into it which exploded on contact, spraying lethal shards like shrapnel in all directions.

The wall collapsed, leaving a gaping hole and beyond, a vast, empty space. Shari flew her gunship directly inside the atrium of the palace and noticed there was no one left standing. Using the rudder pedals again, and hovering now only ten feet in the air, she rotated a full 360 degrees, occasionally firing bursts from the miniguns at nothing in particular, just to keep everyone terrified.

A special forces team inside the palace itself rushed into the atrium with AK-47s and began firing at the Apache. Shari spun the helicopter instantly and miniguns ripped apart her attackers with several dozen heavy caliber bullets apiece, causing the bodies to explode and sending fountains of blood onto the walls.

She waited several more seconds but there was not a second team—at least not one willing to show itself.

The Angel of Death pivoted the helicopter again so it was facing outwards and set the autopilot to maintain hover just above ground level. Seeing no one left in opposition, she unbuckled the seatbelt, grabbed her supplies, and jumped to the ground.

The aircraft's rotors were generating a hurricane-force windstorm, and palace furnishings were soaring around the room. Chairs were crashing into walls. Carpets were whipping back and forth. Tables were overturning. Wall hangings and other decorations rearranged themselves violently.

Shari held the pack in front of her eyes for protection and raced up a flight of stairs. From the second-floor landing she looked down on the helicopter. No one would suspect it was now flying itself and the guns were unmanned. She ducked through a doorway and down a hall, having memorized the layout.

The palace wasn't empty. As an occasional door would open, and officials or servants peered out or stepped into the hall, Shari would yell at them in English: "Back inside or die!"

Most chose the former and rapidly closed the door behind them. But some were combat soldiers determined to protect the president. These she killed.

The Angel of Death was so fast with her sword and knife that blades were coming in contact with flesh before most of her opponents could even bring their own weapons to bear. Two heads were removed, five hearts pierced, and three throats slashed as she made her way to the president's quarters.

But it came at a cost. Her left arm was bleeding from a bullet she'd not been quick enough to avoid. Another bullet had grazed her temple. Annoyingly, head wounds always bled profusely, and she was now having to wipe away blood that was dripping over one eye, using her right arm. She knew from experience that neither injury was life-threatening, and hopefully she'd be able to field-dress them soon. But—now covered in blood—she must look like some kind of enraged zombie.

62

Rounding the final corner, automatic weapons began firing and bullets shredded the wall above her head. She jumped back just in time and tossed a grenade down the hall. When it exploded the young martial-artist moved forward again, passing three guards now dead on the floor.

This was the president's suite. The guards must have been his last defense.

Considering options, she decided an explosive entry was best. From ten meters down the corridor she ran at sprint speed and launched herself at the door in a flying sidekick, much as she'd done in the attack on Bangui. The door exploded inwards.

Landing deftly, she rolled forward and was instantly back on her feet. A final special forces guard was still inside protecting the president, but as he'd been behind the door when it crashed inwards, he'd gone down with it.

As the soldier awkwardly tried to stand, Shari's knife flashed and he died instantly.

President Abbas was now alone, standing in the middle of the room. He pulled out a revolver but before it was in firing position Shari spun, flinging her knife into his hand and piercing it. The field marshal screamed and dropped the weapon.

Forest Creature

A round-house back-kick landed in his stomach, and Sudan's president fell to the floor moaning.

Before he could recover, Shari grabbed from her pack a two-liter plastic bottle containing gasoline, opened it, and emptied the contents over the man's head. He gasped, sputtered, and tried to rise to his feet as the highly flammable liquid soaked quickly into his hair and clothing.

Backing away from the man who by now had risen to his knees, Shari took from her pocket a Bic lighter, clicked open a flame, and began moving towards him slowly, her arm outstretched.

"You're soaked in gasoline," said Shari. "This lighter will keep moving towards you until you order your army to surrender."

Sudan's president, one hand covered with blood and the other steadying him against the floor, stared at the black form in horror. "Are you—are you the Angel of..."

"Yes."

"You're here to kill me?" he asked, clearly terrified.

"I'm here to burn you alive—unless you surrender."

"Unless I *surrender?*"

"If you surrender now, you will be my prisoner. You will not be ill-treated, but you will never rule Sudan again. If you don't surrender you'll soon be a pile of burnt ash."

"But my army is going to conquer yours today! Shariyan forces are already in retreat and will be destroyed. You have no army!"

"I have a Bic lighter."

She continued moving it slowly towards him.

He stared at it in panic.

"And right now," she added, "my Bic lighter is more powerful than all your tanks."

"No! No, you wouldn't!"

"President Abbas, to be honest, I don't know at what distance the fumes from the gasoline will ignite, but it smells pretty strong in here already. Once the gasoline catches fire, even I won't be able to save you."

That was a lie. She'd practiced this maneuver multiple times, wearing protective clothing, and knew precisely how much distance was left.

"I surrender!"

"Order your field commander. Now!"

"I will! Move the lighter back!"

She withdrew it slightly but kept the flame burning.

He reached for his cell phone with his good hand, from inside a pocket. Still trembling in fear, he managed to push a rapid-dial key and his commander answered immediately.

"Put it on speaker," ordered Shari, and he did so.

"Mr. President! Good news. The Army of Death is in full retreat, and they will not escape us," said the excited voice on the other end.

"You are ordered to surrender immediately to the Army of Death," growled Abbas urgently.

"Excuse me, Mr. President, what did you say?"

"You are ordered to surrender. Right now, this minute."

"But, but sir, we're winning!"

"Fool! You have already lost! Shariya's real forces have captured the city. What you're facing was nothing but a diversion. Surrender now. That's an order!"

"You want me to surrender to a *retreating army!*"

"That's not their main force. The whole thing was a trick. Khartoum has been taken while you were playing games in the desert! Surrender this moment or I will shoot you myself when we next meet!"

"Yes. Yes, sir. If those are your orders. I will comply."

"Very well, see to it!"

He hung up the phone and Shari closed the lighter. She tossed him a pair of handcuffs.

"Lock your wounded hand to that metal railing." She gestured to a spiral staircase that led to his personal chambers.

He did so, grimacing in pain. The empress called General Barasa by satellite phone.

"It's arranged," she said. "They've been ordered to surrender."

"Apparently so. They've stopped their pursuit."

"You can turn around now and accept their flag. Remember, treat them with respect. Invite them to join *our* army. Anyone who joins maintains their rank and receives a signing bonus. Anyone who refuses will be granted safe passage home, so long as they give up their military titles and equipment. Pass the word."

"Most will join, and the rest will comply," said the general. "Brilliantly done, Shari. Congratulations!"

"Save the celebrations. I want most of your forces to stay with the surrendered army. Send three tanks and ten troop transports into the city and have them join up with me to secure the palace. Let them know I'm in the president's office and he's in handcuffs. But not everyone will have gotten word about the surrender, so order them to enter cautiously, weapons drawn. There are corpses everywhere. You stay put and manage things there. Again, treat it like a celebration. Suggest to their commander that he's going to go far with the Empire of Africa. You're ordered to make him your new BFF."

"I will do so with pleasure."

She raced back to the atrium where the Apache was still hovering. With fuel reserves it could keep flying for another half hour. But as she watched, the final survivors of the palace guard, two dozen she estimated, were moving towards it stealthily, guns out, approaching cautiously. Perhaps they realized it was a paper tiger, now pilotless. Or they thought they could sneak into the atrium undetected and overcome it. If so, they would rush upstairs and try to protect their president, who they would not know had already surrendered.

She might kill half of them, but two dozen troops equipped with automatic weapons would overcome her. They'd release Abbas and he, in turn, might find a way to communicate with his field commander and reverse the surrender. A wiser Angel of Death, she thought, would take back her promise of humane treatment and simply kill the Sudanese leader—thereby making it impossible to reverse the surrender. But that wouldn't stop these special forces who would still kill her if they could.

Shari waited until the men were fully inside the atrium. She watched as their leader discovered the helicopter was empty. He just had time to call to the others and gesture for them to race up the stairs to the presidential suite. Shari slipped a hand into her pocket and pulled out a remote transmitter. Hating herself, but having no choice, she pressed a button.

Her beloved Apache exploded. A firestorm engulfed the atrium and Shari had to jump back and close the doors to the upper chamber. Thankfully the palace had a fire suppression system and she smiled as water from the overhead nozzles came on automatically and drenched her. The rest of the palace was being soaked as well, and the atrium fire would not spread.

The final guard unit had been obliterated.

63

Calmly returning to the president's office, stepping around the dead body by the door, she apologized to her captive. "When my forces arrive, we'll bandage that hand and you'll be fine. I know you're not comfortable but for the moment it can't be helped. Is there alcohol? I could at least get you a drink."

"Yes, please," said the aging field marshal, clearly in pain from the knife wound. "In that cupboard." He nodded towards the wall. "Anything would help."

Shari found a full bottle of vodka, and also—conveniently—a first aid kit. "I'm going to pour some of this on your hand as disinfectant. It will sting."

"Ahhhh!" he screamed as she splashed vodka on the wound. Shari used a gauze bandage to stop the bleeding and secured it with a metal clasp.

"Use your free hand to hold the bottle itself. Have as much as you like."

Abbas took a long drink. Shari finally had time to focus on herself and—finding a bathroom in the suite—cleaned and bandaged her own wounds. The face staring back from the mirror did look like a demon from the pit. No wonder the field marshal had been so terrified. But after a few minutes with soap, water, and a towel, she looked borderline human again. She walked back to where Abbas was handcuffed to the railing—sipping vodka in misery.

"Distract yourself by considering which country you'd like to be expelled to."

His face brightened with hope. "You'll set me free?"

"As long as you renounce all claims to the presidency and swear to never return to Africa, yes."

"Seriously?"

"I'm not being charitable. It's important every leader knows they'll be treated respectfully if they surrender."

"You're most generous, Empress."

"I can afford to be. By the way, do you have a television here?"

Soon, with the field marshal still handcuffed to the rail, they watched the CNN coverage. Another military expert, Colonel Jill Gonzalez, was being interviewed about the imminent demise of Shariya's empire, and the foolishness of this tribal girl who had no capacity to understand modern warfare.

The anchor interrupted. "I'm sorry, we have a new development," he explained to the audience, adjusting his earpiece. He looked up at the teleprompter and could barely conceal his astonishment at what he was supposed to read.

"I, well, I…it seems we've just learned that the entire Sudanese army, which includes the bulk of the Egyptian military forces, has just—"

He pulled off the earpiece in frustration—despite being live—and shouted to the studio director. "Larry, is this for real? Seriously?"

After receiving urgent assurance, he donned the earpiece again, composed himself, and continued the broadcast. "As I was saying, we've just learned that the combined armies of Egypt and Sudan have surrendered unconditionally to the Army of Death, commanded by the Empress Shariya. I, we, I mean, this was quite the opposite of what was expected. Colonel, what are your thoughts on this new development?"

Forest Creature

The colonel was equally flustered. "Er, your network is reporting that the Sudanese have *surrendered* to Shariya?"

"Yes, it seems so."

"But that's impossible."

"Apparently it's happened."

"I'm sorry. I'm highly skeptical, but if that has really occurred, then Empress Shariya has conquered all of Africa. The hold-out countries were awaiting the outcome of this war, but if Shariya's beaten Sudan, they'll surrender immediately. As will Egypt. That nation threw most of its military forces into this battle and if this report is true, Shariya now owns those forces."

The Angel of Death turned off the TV.

"As the colonel said, with the conquest of the Egyptian and Sudanese armies, the few remaining countries in Africa outside my empire will have no choice but to join."

"Yes, I agree," said the despondent field marshal, who now smelled of both gasoline and vodka.

The empress sat down in one of the conference chairs and decided they might as well chat while waiting for her forces to arrive. "Where do you think I should establish my imperial capital?"

"You're thinking of leaving Bangui?"

"If we're going to rule Africa, I think we need someplace with more infrastructure, better airports, hotels, and so forth."

"You could do worse than right here in Khartoum."

"I was thinking about that. It seems a lovely city, nestled between the two Niles."

"It's a long way from the southern part of the continent, or the western. But Africa is very large and it's not necessarily an advantage to be in the middle of it. Wherever you are, you'll need a plane ride to get somewhere else."

"True. And I like your palace. The damage I caused can be mended. By the way, I think the gasoline has mostly evaporated."

"Thank you for not burning me alive."

"Thank you for surrendering your military forces."

"I've never been to England."

"I have friends there. I'm sure I could arrange a residency permit and funds to make you comfortable in retirement."

"Right now I'm wounded, handcuffed to a banister, and have just suffered one of the most unlikely military defeats in history. I should be consumed with hatred for you but for some reason I'm already looking forward to a permanent European vacation."

Shari smiled beneath her black veil. "I'm so glad we could do business."

64

Two days later, Tai, Eduardo, Doctor Anzio, and General Barasa sat with Shari in the former president's office in the Khartoum Palace. The sounds of repair and rebuilding were nonstop but heavily muffled by the walls.

From the moment Shari declared she was moving her capital to Khartoum, rebuilding became a top priority. The bullet holes from the miniguns were the least of the problems. When the Apache itself exploded, the atrium's roof collapsed, and the fires destroyed everything in this part of the palace. No matter. It was being rebuilt quickly, no expense spared, and the work continued even at night.

The five were clustered around the large TV built into the wall and listening to the latest coverage by CNN. It was a roundtable of experts, still trying to debrief from the Empire of Africa's miraculous victory over the Egyptian and Sudanese forces. It seemed likely the Conquest of Africa, as it was being called, would command the news cycle for days.

One of them was reporting statistics.

"Here are numbers to consider," he said. "Assuming the other countries in Africa join the empire, which we understand is likely to happen soon, Shariya's empire will be eleven point six million square miles, the second largest in history after that of the British, which was thirteen point seven million square miles, and significantly larger than the Mongol Empire at nine point two million.

"However, unlike the Mongols, who required seventy years to reach their peak expansion, or the British, who required several centuries, Shariya's African Empire will have been built in roughly six months."

"It's a feat of territorial conquest unmatched in human history," noted one of the experts. "And here's another statistic. Historians estimate—and it's only a guess—that in building the Mongol Empire, Genghis Khan was responsible for perhaps forty million deaths, which was a significant percentage of the Asian population at the time.

"As far as we can tell, Shariya's forces, in completing the conquest of Africa, killed less than two thousand in actual combat. That's roughly how many murders are committed per year in Chicago."

"Let's return to the Battle of Khartoum, as it's being called," said the host. "Has anyone discovered any clue about what happened? Do we know why the Sudanese and Egyptian forces suddenly surrendered right at the point where they were about to destroy their opponents?"

"No, Jim, we don't. But there's one theory floating around, and frankly, no one has another."

"Let's hear it."

"Well, it's possible that Shariya used her main army as a diversion and somehow managed to send a far lighter force against Khartoum itself, undetected. They might have been able to capture the Palace and perhaps make a prisoner of Field Marshal Abbas, the President of Sudan and the one ultimately in command of the combined army. He may have ordered them to surrender.

"The problem with that theory is why he would have done it? They might have shot him otherwise, but that would not even be a credible threat because a dead president would not stop his army. Also, satellite imagery shows no significant military assets approaching the city, and it would have required at least some to capture the Palace."

"So, bottom line, we just don't know," confirmed the host. "What is the Empire itself saying about how it happened?"

The earlier expert weighed in. "The Shariyan press office has refused any comment, merely reciting the grim facts on what time and date the surrender occurred, and that it was unconditional. Meanwhile Abbas, we are told, is very much alive. Seems he's being held in captivity, but not ill-treated."

"And we also understand," noted another, "that Egyptian president El-Masri accepted the Empire's offer for him to surrender Egypt and depart with his family—much as have so many other African leaders. He's already left the continent."

"It's entirely possible," said a third expert, "that we'll never know how Shariya managed to win this battle. But I think one thing we do know is this. All of us misjudged her. We believed we were dealing with a primitive, inexperienced African girl from out of the jungles, who had no concept of modern war and was going to be taught a very sobering lesson."

The host jumped in. "I guess we still don't know who this mysterious Shariya, this Angel of Death, actually is, but I don't think the world will ever underestimate her again. And on that note, let's take a break for our sponsors."

Shari clicked off the television.

"So, Eduardo, how are negotiations going with the remaining countries?"

"Egypt and Sudan are formally part of the empire, as you just heard. The others have already signed Memos of Understanding, agreeing to be absorbed. We're working out details. The best news is that, while we said we'd worry about South Africa later, their president called this morning and confessed he sees no reason to 'postpone the inevitable' as he put it. He asked to be allowed to stay in office, after pledging loyalty to the empress."

"Your victory's complete, Shari," said Tai. "How do we celebrate?"

She took a moment to consider, and then looked at them, smiling.

"What would you think of an imperial ball? This palace is beautiful, or at least it once was and will be again soon. We need some event to formally acknowledge the move of the capital from Bangui. The grand ballroom here is perfect. Let's say three weeks from this Saturday."

"Fantastic idea!" agreed Tai.

"Eduardo, you figure out the invitation list," she ordered. "But I'd like it to include at least one representative from each country in the Empire, and some from outside Africa as well. Diplomats, UN-types, that kind of thing. You must know scores of them. I'm not looking for world leaders. Just, you know, sort of 'friends of the Empire.'"

"I understand, Shari. But will *you* attend? It's what everyone will ask."

"I will be there incognito, full gown, veil, and gloves. But not my normal attire. Something different, so no one suspects. This is a Muslim country. Arrange to have a few dozen women similarly dressed so I'll fit in."

"So when they ask if you'll be there, the answer's 'no'"?

"Correct."

Shari looked at the large map of Africa which they'd already re-installed from the palace in Bangui. She'd grown fond of it, watching the empire expand across the continent as they'd colored in the different nations.

Astonishingly, now it was all hers. She wondered what she would do *after* the ball.

Forest Creature

65

THEIR MORNING STRATEGY meetings had resumed but were now held on an expansive balcony, almost overhanging the Blue Nile. Across the river was a broad treeless plain, but along the riverbank everything was green. This time it was only her prime minister, as the others were busy with consolidation tasks. She'd finished breakfast and was now enjoying a second cappuccino, having become addicted to them in Paris.

"Shari," said Eduardo, "you'll remember the last time we talked about the Persians, and how we'd need to keep our eye on them?"

"Certainly."

"There's disturbing news. After moving tanks and other military equipment across Iraq—which they now control—and up to the Saudi border, the Saudi royal family reached an accommodation with them. They were allowed to send Shia representatives to all the major mosques in the region."

"Saudi Arabia allowed that?" asked Shari, shocked.

"The royal family has no appetite for actual war. They've not fought one for ages. The Persians requested—politely—that the Shias not be kept from the important mosques, and said that they only wanted to have a presence there.

"What we've learned, thanks to our friends in London, and no doubt through their friends in Israel's Mossad, is that the whole thing was kind of a trick. The Shia 'representatives' immediately contacted the radicalized Madrassa clerics and joined forces. No one thought that possible because of the Shia/Sunni split. But the radicalized clerics are no friends of the ruling family, and they saw the Persian outreach as an opportunity."

"OK, go on."

"So, these Persian representatives or whatever we call them cut a deal with the radicalized Madrassa clerics and agreed to put aside their Sunni/Shia differences in support of a common goal."

"Which was?"

"A coup."

"My God, do we know when this may happen?"

"It happened yesterday," Eduardo announced solemnly. "Yet the world doesn't know it yet. The radicalized clerics are right now being installed as rulers of the Kingdom, sovereign in domestic matters, as long as they submit to the expanding Persian Empire and allow it to use Saudi Arabia as a base for subduing the remaining countries not already under the Empire's control."

"So Saudi Arabia will be turned into a radical theocracy, just like Iran." Shari had started pacing, as she always did at this point in the conversation.

"Yes," agreed her prime minister. "British analysts see this rare Sunni/Shia cooperation as possibly the ending of the schism."

"Which would be very bad," Shari mused.

"A unified Islam, able to put aside doctrinal differences, becomes a far more dangerous threat," Eduardo agreed. "But in any case, Saudi Arabia, our primary bulwark against the Persians, has already fallen. An announcement is likely any day. As Prime Minister, I'll be expected to comment officially."

"If they're in control of Saudi Arabia, they'll easily absorb Kuwait, UAE, Syria, Afghanistan, and maybe Turkey, correct?" Shari was continuing to pace, barely noticing the waters of the Blue Nile running swiftly beneath the balcony.

"Yes, it's likely to happen fast, as with our empire. In a strange way, all this is beginning to look like events leading up to WWI."

"How so?" she asked.

"Well in WWI, sort of without anyone planning it, two empires, or I should say two military alliances came into being. As they became powerful, each country realized it couldn't stand on its own, and must join one or the other."

"Oh, right, you had Germany, Austria/Hungary, and Turkey on one side, with England, France, and Russia on the other, right?"

"Yes, exactly. But that was all a bit far-flung geographically. Here we have the Empire of Africa now encompassing all this continent. And I suspect we're about to have—what we discussed earlier—the Persians controlling the Islamic countries east of Egypt, up to the Pakistan border. This time the two entities are internally contiguous, meaning you can draw a single line around them. You couldn't do that with the alliances in WWI."

"What's the significance of that?"

"Well, it creates an interesting dynamic if you look at a map. These two empires are vast. Ours is bigger, in terms of land area. The two empires come together at a very tiny point, but don't quite touch. Something's in the way."

"Israel."

"Exactly. Israel is understandably terrified of being Ground Zero when the Persians fight the Africans."

"Maybe the Persians won't fight the Africans."

"All intelligence suggests they will. The African Empire was never religion-based. You might say it was superstition-based, at least in the beginning. The Angel of Death and all that. But the Persians are trying to recreate an Islamic *Caliphate*. They're trying to do two things. First, establish hegemony over the Islamic world, and then, presumably, try to expand the Caliphate to the rest of the globe. But their first step is Islamic hegemony."

"Which means they'll try to take over North Africa."

"Precisely. So while we may not be interested in fighting *them*, they'll insist those Islamic countries of North Africa be allowed to join *their* empire. And they'll be aggressive about which countries those are. It won't just be the Mediterranean coast. They'll insist on a lot of sub-Saharan Africa as well. Look how far Islam has spread south. Draw a line across Africa, roughly through Congo, Uganda, and Kenya. They might insist that Islam is everything north of that line, or even include that line."

"Which would reduce our empire by about two-thirds," noted Shari.

"And so weaken us we'd not be able to hold even that territory eventually."

"We have to oppose them," concluded the empress.

"Yes."

"I see why Israel is terrified."

"Precisely."

"Maybe we should take Israel off the chessboard," mused Shari.

"How can we do that?"

"What's our relationship with them, is it cordial?"

"Yes, but minimal, as you've ordered with everyone."

"Could I reach them and make a proposal, diplomatically? Not right now, but in a few months, perhaps?"

"Yes, I'm sure you could."

"Let's propose a land swap."

"Explain."

Shari led him back to the conference room.

"Look at the map. If they give up this thin wedge of southern Israel down to the Gulf of Aqaba, we could give them a large area of the Sinai bordering the Mediterranean, almost up to the Suez Canal."

"They'd lose access to the Indian Ocean."

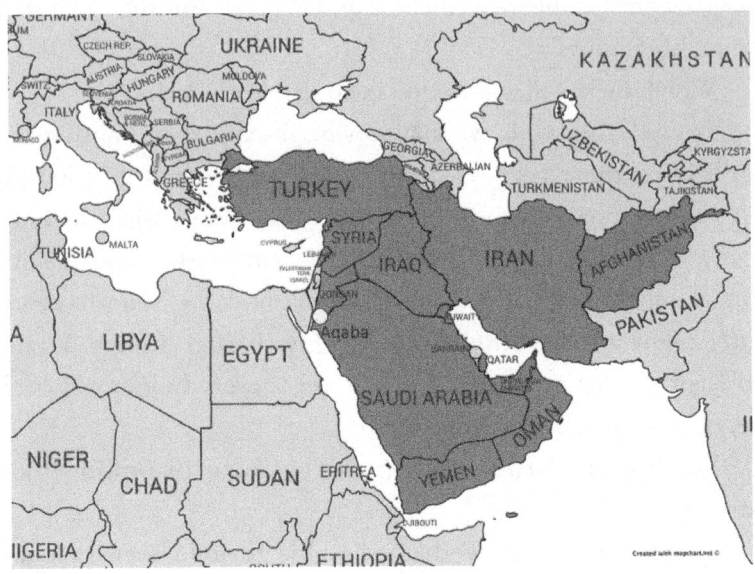

"They're going to lose it anyway when the Persian/Shariyan war breaks out. Whichever of us wins will have plowed through Southern Israel to reach the other. They need to stay out of that fight. Also, we'll make it a good deal for them and make sure they end up with more land than they have today. And it will be coastal land, which has greater value."

Eduardo studied the map closely.

"You want them to give you the city of Eilat, and perhaps fifty kilometers north of there."

"Yes, something like that. Look, Eduardo, there's another point. In addition to going up against the Persian Empire, this is also starting to look like a religious war. I mean, if they're building an Islamic Caliphate, and we oppose it…"

The Prime Minister invited her to take a seat at the conference table, and sat across.

"You don't want this to be a war against Islam. Crusades, 2.0."

"Exactly. It's one of the reasons we've been very explicit about the Empire of Africa embracing freedom of religion."

"I don't think it's a problem, for two reasons."

"Good, let's hear them." Shari relaxed back in her seat.

"First, a vast number of people in your empire are themselves Muslim, not least your Defense Minister and your Prime Minister. Barasa, a Muslim, leads your armies, and is obviously not leading them in opposition to his own religion."

"Valid point," she mused. "And the second?"

"The dream of a global Islamic Caliphate is not exactly top of mind for most Muslims around the world. Like everyone else, they're just facing day to day problems, trying to feed their families, and live peaceful lives. The Caliphate idea is more a rallying point for modern extremists. Sure, the Mullahs in Tehran might like to frame their conflict with Africa in religious terms, but it won't take hold. It's not plausible."

Shari sighed. "OK, good. Then let's ensure we keep that part of our messaging. We stand for free markets and fair, effective government. Persia is about tyranny."

"I'll insist our communication office keeps that in mind," said Eduardo, making notes on a legal pad. "Anyway, back to geography. If your plan with Israel works out, you'll control Eilat, and the battle lines will be clear. When the Persians and the Shariyans meet, it will be at Aqaba."

"Yes."

"Interestingly, that's where Lawrence of Arabia won his great victory against the Turks. It was a pivotal location in WWI."

"Well, it may be again," Shari prophesied.

66

THE DAY OF the Imperial Ball, Eduardo asked Shari to join him for a small ceremony in the conference room, an hour before any guests would arrive.

"Who's attending?" she asked. "Do I need to be veiled?"

"No, it will be just you, me, Tai, the general, and Dr. Anzio."

"Is there a dress code?"

"I know nothing of women's clothing, Shari. But Tai and I will be in suits and ties."

"Tai *owns* a suit? I've only seen him in jeans."

"He bought one yesterday, just for this purpose. He asked me for help with the tie. He's been terrified of Windsor knots since Oxford."

Shari laughed.

The Angel of Death arrived in the deep-indigo, Givenchy masterpiece Francois had given her after the photoshoot.

"They rarely ask for these back since they've now been worn," he'd explained. "So I just hand them out to the models as gifts."

It was a slightly off-shoulder, asymmetrical, flowing gown with a fitted bodice. She'd accessorized with delicate teardrop diamond earrings. After watching a YouTube video, the empress applied the sheerest coat of soft pink lip gloss and added a light touch of mascara. Except at the photoshoot, Shari had never before worn makeup for fashion.

She must have done it right because the four men gasped as she entered. This was the woman featured in Vogue-Paris who'd stunned the haute couture world. Except for Tai, they'd never seen Shari dressed glamorously.

"Well, I'm glad I wore my best suit," said Eduardo, smiling. "You just upped the neighborhood considerably." The empress smiled appreciatively.

"A pity you have to wear the veil so often," said Tai. "If all those national leaders could have seen who they were pledging loyalty to, we'd probably have conquered Africa much sooner."

Barasa, the hardened general, was simply speechless, but the psychiatrist made up for it. "My undergraduate degree was in art history, and I've studied the most famous paintings and sculptures throughout Italy. But it's only today that I've seen a Renaissance painting come to life."

Shari blushed, not yet used to receiving compliments on her physical appearance. "Gentlemen, I ... I don't know what to say."

"It seems our empress is as tongue-tied as I am right now," declared the general, finally discovering his voice.

"Then it's time her Strategic and Economic Affairs minister made a strategic rescue," said Tai. "Let's get this ceremony underway and then we can attack the champagne bar before guests arrive."

"What ceremony *is* this exactly?" asked Shari, smiling, eyes aglow with curiosity.

"If I could ask you to take a seat here, in this chair," directed Eduardo.

Shari noticed it was one of the most elegant chairs in the palace, made more so today by sheets of gold lace draped over the arms and set out from the wall about two meters.

"I'm to sit, while the rest of you stand," she said, self-consciously. "It seems impolite."

"Not in this case," Tai reassured her as she took her place.

"So, if I can say a few words?" Eduardo began.

Shari nodded.

"Well, we've all been a bit informal as we built this empire. We've referred to you first as Shariya, and then as empress. All that was driven by PR factors. We had an empire, so we had to have an empress. It looked good in the press releases. That kind of thing. But, well, Tai suggested, and all four of us agreed, that—"

"Agreed on what?"

"That we should formalize it. If you're going to be an empress, well, you need a—"

"What do I need?"

"Close your eyes, Shari," said Tai, and she did so. "Hands in your lap, palms up."

She felt something placed on them.

"Now open your eyes," said her prime minister.

Shari gasped. On a silver tray covered by blue cloth, was a crown. It was minimalist and made of gold. On the front were—in filigree—four lions, two on each side, facing the center of the crown. And in the center was her diamond. The first one, still uncut, the one the villagers had made into a pendant. She surmised the lions were Emil and the three girls. Yes, one of the four had a mane.

"Who created this?" she asked, astonished.

"We all did, Shari," said Tai. "You forgot to ask for your diamond back, so I kept it, knowing someday what we'd use it for. I contributed the diamond and the idea of a crown."

"I insisted on the lions," explained Eduardo. "They will always be your symbol and Tai tells me they were your first family." He grinned at his subordinate.

"Did I mention I'm an art history major?" asked Dr. Anzio, also grinning. "I sketched out the overall concept and had a distant cousin, a jewelry designer from Vicenza, create it in eighteen karat gold. Italian jewelry, I hope you're aware, is the finest in the world."

Shari said nothing as she held the crown in her hands, staring at it.

"Oh, and my cousin designed it," Anzio continued, "so that if you ever wished to take the diamond and have it faceted, he could make that happen and remount it. The design would serve equally well."

Shari thought a moment. "No, the diamond should stay rough.

It should stay opaque. That's what I was when I found it—opaque. And I still am. We can't see into this diamond, so it represents those memories I can't see into as well. Please leave it as it is."

"Very well."

"Shari," said Tai. "Our general here is too modest to explain what he did, but I said all four of us contributed. There's an engraving in the gold behind the stone."

Shari turned the crown over and—when she saw what was written—suddenly remembered how to cry.

The Angel of Death burst into tears.

Tai grabbed the crown, and the doctor had a tissue ready.

Barasa again found his voice. "I flew to Vicenza with Roberto," he explained. "The jewelry designer showed me how to do it, with an engraving pen. I know my writing is not elegant, but I had to write the letters myself."

Shari forced herself to come under control, knowing how solemn the moment was. She took the crown back and looked at the writing again. There it was, in simple, poorly formed, printed letters. *KATINKA*.

"You said her spirit was leading us," said the general.

"And always will be," agreed Shari. "It's perfect. Again, I don't even know what to say. I'm completely overwhelmed by this."

"Good, because it's not your turn to speak," said Tai with mock seriousness. "Eduardo, it's time."

The prime minister took the crown from her hands and went behind the chair.

"I, Eduardo Danjuma, Prime Minister of the Empire of Africa, with this symbol of sovereignty, and in the presence of your senior ministers, do hereby crown you Shariya, Empress of Africa. Long may you reign."

Then he set the crown softly on her head.

They all clapped, except for Dr. Anzio who was filming the ceremony with his mobile phone.

"My turn to speak yet?" she asked, smiling.

"Nope," said Tai. "Just stay where you are. And let's do the eyes closed, hands up thing again, please."

Shari complied.

"Eduardo, can you do the honors once more?"

Shari felt something new placed in her hands and she opened her eyes.

She was holding the strangest object. About eighteen inches long, it was a metal stick of some kind, with the gold head of a snake at the top. It seemed to be made perhaps of bronze, with gold plating creating the curves of the snake's body, as the stick tapered near the bottom.

"Whoever wields this scepter," explained Eduardo, "henceforth controls the Empire of Africa. We are writing this into our new constitution. It is the ultimate symbol of power on the continent."

"A *scepter?*" exclaimed Shari. "Like for a king? But where did it come from? This is not something recently made in Italy. It looks very old."

"It's three thousand five hundred years old," said Tai. "Have you ever heard of *Pharaoh Hatshepsut?*"

"No, tell me."

"*Hatshepsut* was the second female pharaoh of Egypt. She was victorious in battle during her earlier years and then had one of the longest, most peaceful reigns in Egyptian history. On the wall of her tomb, in the Valley of the Kings, was written…"

Tai consulted his notes.

"'To look upon her was more beautiful than anything; her splendor and form were divine.' This scepter belonged to her."

"How did we acquire such a thing?" asked Shari.

"When Eduardo and I were in Cairo working out the details of Egypt joining the empire, I took half a dozen soldiers and entered the Museum of Cairo. It's filled with antiquities, and this was the very thing I was hoping to find."

"Did you steal it?"

"No. I had a little discussion with the Museum's curator. First, I explained I was a minister with the Empire of Africa and represented Shariya herself."

"Yes?"

"I told him that since the empress had brought all Africa together under a single ruler, it was appropriate that she have a scepter as a royal symbol of power. I explained that of course we could make one, but I suggested that because this scepter had been waiting over three thousand years to be wielded again by someone worthy of it—a woman as powerful as Hatshepsut herself—someone who could carry on the task of ruling over the greatest Empire in Africa, maybe the Museum would like to present it as a gift to the empress.

"I suggested that maybe its time of being a museum oddity, ogled by ignorant tourists, was over and that it should return to its rightful place in the hands of a pharaoh."

"What did he say to that?"

"He considered my words, and then—himself—unlocked the case, bowed before me, and offered it up in both hands."

"This scepter, once owned by Pharoah Hatshepsut, represents the Africa you've conquered," said Eduardo. "You are its ruler, its empress. It's a symbol of the entire continent that you can hold in your hand."

Shari was silent for several moments, and everyone waited respectfully. When she spoke it was to Dr. Anzio directly although she was addressing all of them.

"This represents something else as well. It represents my new life. I've built a new life, haven't I? To replace the one I lost."

"Yes, Shari," acknowledged the psychiatrist. "You have indeed."

Tai broke the awkward silence that followed. "Well, let's not get too solemn and portentous. As Minister of Strategic Affairs, with the powers vested in me, I hereby declare the bar open!"

The others laughed, but Shari could not take her eyes off the ancient scepter.

67

THE PARTY WAS in full swing in the palace's Grand Ballroom with one wall being a vast expanse of windows overlooking the Blue Nile.

Guests were from all over Africa, and from all over the world. There were no foreign heads of state here. Shari didn't want that kind of meeting. But UN dignitaries, NGO officials, ambassadors and consular officers, and at least one representative from each of the many countries now part of the Empire.

It was a diverse group, but the dress was formal. The men were in black tie. Elegant women wafted about in beautiful gowns. Alcohol in all its forms—not just champagne—was flowing from four open bars. Servants plied the crowd, carrying endless trays of exotic hors d'oeuvres, no expense spared. Caviar on toast. Swan pilaf. Tiny shish kebabs of roast eland. Morsels of smoked Nile perch on thin wheat crackers. Even ostrich canapes.

Earlier, when reviewing the menu with Eduardo, Shari had been appalled at the ostentatiousness. Not only did the food seem over the top, but the decorations, the chamber orchestra, the servants in lavish costume—all of it seemed a bit *Marie Antoinette.*

"Only one chance to make a good first impression," Eduardo had explained. "You're not living the high life at the expense of your subjects because it's not a zero sum game. The economy is booming and personal income is soaring. You're making a statement of imperial power and you need to make it. Your empire is new and must be assumed fragile. Flattering your guests by treating them to luxury will be remembered by all of them. It will leave—as they say—a good taste in their mouths and underscore your wealth and power. Believe me, if they saw the opposite, rumors of weakness would begin immediately."

Shari trusted his instincts as a diplomat. Perhaps *ostrich canape* was a necessary chess move.

The fifteen-piece orchestra, set up in one corner of the vast room, was playing softly but giving those couples who wished an opportunity to dance. Several were doing so.

Shari, in full Islamic veil, was a lurker, approaching different groups, catching a sentence here, a conversation there. It gave her a sense of the mood and what topics were of interest to these diplomats and dignitaries.

She'd maneuvered herself within earshot of two middle-aged men standing at one of the cocktail rounds, discussing something in earnest.

Many languages were spoken; French, Arabic, English….But this was…She moved closer to listen. This was…

She froze. This was Russian. This was the language she spoke with…

With her father…

Shari was hit with an adrenaline shock so powerful she nearly lost consciousness as a hundred thousand memories assaulted her brain simultaneously.

Her champagne glass crashed to the floor, startling everyone. Then the empress crumpled and fell.

Lying on her side, she pulled her knees into a fetal position, eyes shut tightly, and began screaming. They were the inhuman screams of madness and terror, as if a demon had pierced her soul.

The band quit playing and everyone froze, horrified at the sounds coming from the veiled woman writhing on the floor.

Eduardo, the Shariyan official closest when she fell, raced to her side. Anzio arrived next, and the two created a barrier, making sure no one other than palace staff would be able to touch the quivering form, or worse—pull back the boshiya mask. Half a dozen security guards pushed through the crowd, surrounded the woman, and awaited orders.

Shari was shaking as if in an epileptic fit.

The doctor checked her vitals and performed several other tests before ordering the largest guard to physically pick her up in his arms.

"Get her to the couch in Eduardo's office," he ordered quietly.

"Do not let anyone remove her veil," the prime minister added urgently.

Anzio stayed with her as the guards carried the still-quivering form out a nearby door. Eduardo turned to the room and spoke soothingly.

"Ladies and gentlemen, I'm most terribly sorry. I've been told this guest has occasional seizures, and we'll get her to a doctor quickly. I'm also told they pass, and there is no long-term significance. Please, everyone, do carry on. I know those screams were a bit unnerving, but—well—remember the bars are open. Please indulge, and I will return as quickly as possible."

Barasa, the Empire's Defense Minister, had moved in quickly. "How can I help?" he whispered urgently. Tai was there as well.

"General, you're in charge 'til I get back, and it might be a while. Make sure the food and drink keep flowing. Let's not worry about the speech I was going to give. Just stay here so someone senior in the government is on-site and can settle everyone."

"I can do that."

If I'm not able to return at all, well—you're in charge. Do as you see fit. Tai, come with me."

As the two officials walked calmly out the same door, people were already converging on the open bars, and the conversation picked up quickly.

"Ah, a medical problem, no long-term issues. That's good to hear."

"But those screams were terrifying, weren't they?"

"Why, yes, they were. And my vodka tonic does need a refresher, actually…"

Eduardo found Shari in his office, half a dozen guards securing the entrance from the outside. Anzio had removed her boshiya veil and the empress was lying on the couch with a small pillow under her head. She sobbed uncontrollably, hands covering her eyes.

The doctor motioned Eduardo over to a corner. Tai knelt down beside Shari and placed a hand on her shoulder.

"Roberto, what the hell? What's happening?" asked the prime minister. "It looked like epilepsy or something."

"I don't know yet, but I think it's psychological, not physical. Her vitals are good, blood pressure up a bit, but of course it would be. Something has disturbed her deeply."

"Disturbed *Shari*? *Nothing* disturbs her. She's the calmest woman I've ever met, except in battle, obviously. Today was the first time I've ever even seen her cry."

"Best if we wait a moment," admonished the doctor. "We don't want her to feel pressure right now. She'll tell us in her own time."

"But—"

Anzio reached out and touched Eduardo's arm. "I think she must have seen or heard something and it startled her. I'm guessing it may have touched on her prior life. Possibly a memory was triggered."

"Good God!" said the prime minister.

The sobs quieted and Anzio took Tai's place, kneeling beside the prostrate form.

"Shari, what is it? What's happening?" asked the doctor. "Tell me what you need, what can I do to help."

The empress kept her eyes shut, but the shivering lessened. Anzio touched her, reassuringly.

"It's me, Shari, Roberto. Can you talk? Can we talk to you? Did a special memory suddenly come back? Was it something out of your past?"

But the troubled form shook her head slightly and refused to talk. At Anzio's suggestion, they just waited.

※

Over an hour later the tears and the shivering finally stopped. Shari opened her eyes and Anzio handed her a tissue. The empress stared at the object, then took it slowly and tried to clean her face.

"Can you help me upright? I don't seem to be in control of myself."

They raised her to a sitting position on the couch. The doctor handed her a glass of water, which she drank eagerly.

"Just give me a moment, please," she said.

"Of course," said the doctor. "Take your time."

Shari drank a second glass, and then covered her face with her hands, trying to process everything.

"Oh my God," she said, staring at the wall.

A few moments later the empress stood up, unsteadily. Then she walked slowly over to the window. The Blue Nile flowed by, endlessly, and the treeless plain was beyond. She stared at the scene, her brain trying to knit together both her worlds—her two sets of memories; the person she once was, and the person here today.

She turned back to the men, utterly calm now, like the Shari they knew.

"They were speaking Russian," she explained. "There were people speaking Russian at the ball."

"Russian? You recognize *Russian*?" asked the doctor.

"They were speaking Russian," she said again.

"There were two diplomats from the Russian embassy on the guest list," noted Eduardo. "It must have been them."

"You recognize *Russian*?" the psychiatrist asked again. "This could be important."

Shari was fully in command of herself now. She sat down on the opposite settee.

"I speak Russian fluently. It's a first language to me. I didn't know I spoke it until I heard it just now."

"OK, this is a clue. This might help us determine something of your background."

Shari shook her head slowly.

"No, Doctor, we don't need to use this as a *clue*."

"What do you mean?"

"Because everything came back."

"*Everything* came back? You mean it was a triggering event?"

"All of it. I know who I am. I know where I came from. I know how I ended up in the middle of Africa. That's why I fell to the floor screaming. It all came back. And it was like being hit by a freight train. I was reliving—those final hours."

"Who are you? Please, tell us quickly in case it fades or somehow is lost again."

"It won't be lost. I know who I am. My memory returned. My name is Sophie Ana Martine. I'm from Les Avants, Switzerland—near Montreux. We lived in a large chalet overlooking Lake Geneva. 125 Chemin de Naye. I could draw you a sketch of the house where I grew up, and every room in it. And the furniture in it. I could show you the path I took when I walked to the train station. And the names of my friends in school. I had a pet turtle named Raphael."

"My God, what else!"

"I'm a ballerina, an extremely good one. Or at least I was. And I competed in Tae Kwon Do and Shinkendo tournaments. That's where the martial arts came from, obviously. My father was an archeologist. The family was in Central African Republic on a dig. I watched as my parents were murdered at our campsite outside of Bangui. The murderers wanted to kill me too, but I escaped. I fled the camp and ran for hours through the jungle. Then in the dark—I must have run into a tree or branch or something. That's where those memories end.

"When I woke up, my present memories began. I remember

waking up. We've been over that so many times. I just didn't know how I came to be there in the first place. But now I know."

"You saw your parents murdered and later ran at full speed into a tree?" asked the psychiatrist.

"Yes."

"Of course. Psychological trauma plus a blow to the head. No wonder your memory was gone."

"But now it's back. This changes everything."

"It does change everything. I'm just thinking…" Doctor Anzio's voice trailed off.

"What?"

"Well, our little ceremony earlier. You saw the scepter not just as a symbol of power in Africa, but as a symbol of your new life. You were acknowledging what your subconscious already knew: that you'd healed emotionally; that you were ready to face the past. I don't think it's a coincidence that your memory returned within a few hours of that moment."

"And that was also the moment I remembered how to cry."

"So, hearing the Russian language being spoken—that was the triggering event."

"Yes."

"Congratulations, Ms. Sophie Martine, on your memory returning," said Eduardo. "But now I must ask, because it affects all of us, what will you do with this knowledge?"

"My parents were murdered as a paid contract hit." She paused, remembering the scene. "The killers said: 'We have to kill the daughter. If we don't kill her too, we won't get paid.' Why would they have said that?"

"Apparently," said Tai, "because whoever ordered the killing of your parents needed to make sure you died too. For some reason, that was important. Can you imagine a reason for any of this?"

"None."

"What orders do you have for us?" asked Eduardo.

Sophie considered the question while the greater part of her brain was still processing the deluge of memories she could now access.

"Doctor, are there any physical or mental symptoms I should be prepared for? I'm asking a medical question. Anything I should know of what might now happen?"

"Your vitals are good. I've never heard of any complications from an amnesiac's memories returning—other than the obvious impact it has on their life. I'm told it's just like a switch is flipped and the memories that were previously gone are now back. Everything's immediately normal. But how do you feel, physically I mean? And, well, mentally too, I guess."

"It's just what you say. Everything feels normal. Sorry about my little meltdown back there. It just happened so fast; it was debilitating."

"No need to apologize. I think you recovered amazingly quickly," said the psychiatrist.

"Hmmm."

"I might prescribe a mild sedative or sleeping pill. Just to help you calm down."

Sophie considered it. No, she didn't want to suppress anything. "Only if you insist. My brain's been through so much this evening, I'd rather not throw chemicals at it. But I'd not like to be alone tonight. Can you find Anka and ask her to stay with me? Maybe find a cot or something and place it next to my bed? And Roberto, could you stay close at hand? Eduardo, please arrange for the spare room in my suite to be turned over to him tonight. Would you mind, Roberto?"

"Not at all. I think it's a good idea, in case, well, who knows what you might need tonight, or if you wake up with a terrible dream or something."

"As for orders beyond that…I can't make any decisions now. I need to rest. Tomorrow we can plan."

They started to leave the room.

"Oh, one more thing, Roberto."

"Yes, Shari."

"The crown all of you gave me earlier today, with the diamond."

"Yes?"

"Please send it back to your cousin in Vicenza. I want the diamond cut and polished after all."

"You want it faceted, fully polished?"

"Yes, everything's changed. My memory's returned. Nothing's opaque anymore. I want that diamond polished. Please polish the hell out of it for me."

68

THAT NIGHT SHE slept deeply. Her dreams were lively even though the next morning—perhaps fortunately—she could remember none of them. Waking early, she tossed on a robe and went down the hall to her office. After ordering coffee, she turned on her computer and clicked the Google search bar.

"Nicholas Martine, Julianne Martine, Sophie Martine, murder, Africa," she typed.

She found the articles. There weren't many. A piece in Lausanne's *Le Matin*, followed by another with a few more details, weeks later. The University of Geneva's newsletter had an obituary for her father and links to the *Le Matin* article. That was it. If any African news source had covered the incident, it hadn't gone on-line.

She read what was available quickly. On May 22nd, roughly eight months ago, local authorities had discovered the remains of Nicholas Martine, his wife Julianne, and a native servant, all three with evidence of gunshot wounds. They were sure it was murder. The remains had been mauled by animals—Sophie paused at that point, forcing down tears—but the identities had been proven in multiple ways. The body of their daughter, Sophie, a seventeen-year-old ballerina, had not been found. But the police believed the smaller body, no doubt murdered as well, had been dragged off by animals and would probably never be discovered. A large quantity of supplies, including cash, was missing from the camp, fueling the belief that it was simply a horrific murder and robbery. Such things were not uncommon in Africa. The authorities expressed sympathy but noted they'd warned the Martines to always have guards. Evidently, they usually did, but the family had stayed at the dig late Friday after everyone else had left.

Sophie remembered it all. She turned away from the screen and this time couldn't stop a tear. She reached for a tissue just as coffee arrived.

The follow-up article provided the information that Julianne Martine's brother, Stefan Arquette (oh my God, Stefan!), had flown to Africa to identify the remains and collect personal items. With his confirmation of identity, the case was closed. Even so, Stefan had stayed on a full month, hiring armed patrols to search the bush and try to find the young girl's body. Eventually he'd given up and returned home, after posting a $5,000 reward for anyone who was able to find her body and assuming dental records could confirm it.

Five thousand dollars, Sophie knew, was a fortune in that part of Africa. She was very close with her uncle and knew he must be devastated. Well, he had a pleasant surprise coming.

Turning back to the computer, she began a different kind of research. After ninety minutes the Empress of Africa had learned a great deal about the forensics of dental records, x-rays, skull reconstructions, and 3-D printing. She took a shower, dressed, and met Eduardo for a private breakfast.

"The thing I can't get out of my mind," Sophie explained, "is that statement: 'We have to find the girl. We won't get paid unless she dies too.'"

"I wonder if they ever got paid," he asked. "Since they'd not have been able to produce a body."

"Before we can even begin to learn why this—assassination team—was sent in, we need to make sure they *do* get paid."

"Excuse me?"

"They need to find a body."

"You lost me."

Sophie stood up and began pacing. "Until whoever hired them knows 'the girl died too,' I'm theoretically still at risk. We don't know who these people are, where they're from, their motives, how powerful they are, anything. This puts us at a huge disadvantage. The only way we gain an advantage is to convince whoever's interested that the girl did in fact die too."

"How do we do that?"

"My uncle, Stefan Arquette, has dental records that can prove if a corpse is the correct one. We need to find a corpse that's similar to me. Then we need to make sure its skull, or what's left of it, has dental markings that will match the x-ray."

"And how do we do *that*?"

"We build one. Take a 3-D x-ray of my skull, including my teeth. Download it to a 3-D printer. Build a replica using skull-like material. They're already doing this in medical schools to recreate skull fractures and so forth for teaching purposes. The technology's well advanced. There's a company in Frankfurt that specializes in it. Send them the x-rays digitally, a week later a skull replica comes back. I've printed out everything you need in this folder."

"But will it fool a coroner in Bangui?"

"Probably not. But it will fool an x-ray machine. And coroners can be bribed."

"Brilliant."

"Eduardo, I'd like you to make all this happen, personally. I don't want anyone else in on our secret. Can you do it?"

"I think so. I'll need to find some place that can create this head x-ray of you and make up some reason why it's needed. Oh, wait, it's easy. We're going to build a bronze statue of the empress—thirty feet high—but we need an accurate representation of her head. The artist has asked for this."

"Perfect. Later we'll find a reason to cancel the project. A thirty-foot high statue, my God, that would be hideous."

"Not of you, Shariya."

"Especially of me, but thanks for the compliment."

Eduardo grinned.

"So," she continued, "once you have the fake skull, find a way to pair it with a corpse—I'll leave that detail to you—swap skulls, and somehow deposit the whole thing in the wilderness. Come up with a cover story. Maybe you're on a safari or something. Have one of your guides discover the body, alert the authorities, and when the coroner inspects the remains, make sure he doesn't inspect too closely. Make sure the skull is x-rayed and a copy sent digitally to Stefan Arquette, who posted the reward money. At his end, they'll compare it to the original dental records, and they'll match. Make sure your guide collects the reward as it would look fishy if he didn't. And when it's done, make sure the news media covers it fully. It needs to go out on the newswires. Tag the release heavily with the names Sophie Martine, Nicholas Martine, and Julianne Martine. Have our national press office in Bangui send it. Whoever hired the murderers will have set a keyword alert, and they'll see the release."

"And once it goes out, someone, somewhere, monitoring any news about Sophie Martine, will pick it up," mused the prime minister.

"And the executioners will finally be paid."

"And you'll be safe."

"And my uncle will at least think closure's been granted."

"You'll tell him the truth, right?"

"Yes. He's the only blood relative I have left. After the dust settles, I'll find a way to bring him here secretly and reveal myself."

"You'll reveal that the niece he thought dead is actually the Empress of Africa. That's going to be an interesting conversation."

"Yes. Best I lead up to it carefully."

69

"Is there anything I can do to change your mind? I'll miss you dreadfully."

Three weeks after the Imperial Ball, Tai and Shariya were in the very secluded courtyard of the palace—a beautiful garden with a flowing artificial stream and even a waterfall fountain. During reconstruction, Eduardo had arranged this area specifically for the empress's privacy. It was nestled into her private wing of the palace—an area off limits to all but confidants. To the east was an open view of the Blue Nile and the grassy plain beyond—restricted only by a vast curtain of sheerest fabric—giving the scene an almost surreal quality while ensuring no one across the river with a telescope could intrude.

Yesterday Tai had resigned his position and announced he was returning to England. They were seated and having tea for their final goodbye. Shari's veil was off.

"I'll miss you equally," he reassured. Then he took a moment to say more. "I've never felt so close to another person."

The empress let the words hang in the air, staring at him meaningfully, both knowing she felt the same way.

"Anyway, the Chief has a new assignment in mind. Hey, before I forget, as we agreed I finally came clean with him about who you are and where you're from. Anyway, with the conquest of Africa complete, there are other priorities. Seems I'm quite in demand, having 'performed a miracle' they're telling me, on this one." Tai chuckled. "But it wasn't me who built the empire."

"In many ways it *was* you," protested Shari. "You were the one who discovered the diamonds. You arranged for the De Beers venture. You had me place the money in bitcoin and declare it our national currency, which made the government wealthy. You changed our revenue system to lottery-based, which freed up the economy and sent revenue soaring. Eduardo tells me we're so awash in cash we're now loaning money to the developed world."

"It worked out quite well, didn't it?"

"And a YouTube-based educational system? My God, that was brilliant. Almost zero cost and the University of Africa is overseeing our entire K-12 program across the continent and making both literacy and higher degrees available to everyone—for free. We've made traditional school systems and classrooms obsolete."

"That *was* a pretty cool idea…"

"Oh, and then saving my butt when the helicopter picture came out by turning me into a fashion model and flooding the Internet with celebrities in front of a helicopter? Tai, you're a genius. And as you know you're also my best friend."

He reached out his hands and she took them eagerly.

"But what you don't know is, I wish we could be more."

There. She'd said it.

He laughed softly. "OK, maybe that's the one thing you could do to change my mind. Click your fingers, make me straight, and then marry me."

She dropped Tai's hands and clicked her fingers hopefully.

"Well," she asked. "Did it work?"

He shook his head. "My eyes find you a work of art. But you deserve more than I could give. If I were that person, I'd be on my knees, with a ring, proposing desperately."

"And I'd be on my knees accepting it, desperately."

He stared at her. "Kidding aside, are you serious? You'd really accept a proposal of marriage from a lowly MI6 agent?"

"Well, you'd need to court me a bit first. But assuming you didn't screw that up too horribly, I expect so."

He turned away, and Shari saw him brush away a tear. She pulled him back and gave him a hug, not sure what else to say.

"Shari, I'll cling to those words," he said, separating again. "Whatever I've done has been repaid—by those words."

Her eyes met his, and this time they were twinkling in amusement. "Not yet it hasn't."

"What do you mean?"

"I have a going-away present, Tai."

"Seriously?"

"This time *you* close your eyes and hold out your hands."

He did so. Shari placed into them ten of the large, rough diamonds from the limestone hole at the Lobaye River.

"OK, eyes open."

He stared at the gems. "Shari! Where did you get these?"

"The same place I got the one you examined back in Bangui. On my first solo flight in the Apache helicopter, I returned to that spot on the river. I had a daypack and located the spring-fed limestone hole where I found the first one. I retrieved all the diamonds and kept them safe ever since."

"You mean, you did this *after* Congo joined the empire, but before you sold the diamond fields to De Beers?"

"Yes. It was on public land in Congo and still is. Public land is owned by the crown." She gave him an impish grin.

Tai nodded. "True. But why did you hoard them secretly? You had the right to, of course, but…"

Shari looked over the garden contemplatively. "Insurance. I had no idea what would happen with Africa and my position as empress. I still don't. I wanted financial security."

"That makes sense."

"Now I want you to have it as well. Tai, this is nothing compared to what you've done for the continent. Africa should give you a thousand of these stones, not just ten."

"But ten of these are worth, what did we say, five million apiece? That's fifty million dollars!"

Shari grinned again. "Whatever you do with MI6, you'll not have to worry about promotions and pay scales. Or even that 'book deal.'"

"Are you sure about this? Shari, I'm speechless. And I'm never speechless."

"Never surer about anything. I'm giving gifts to others as well."

"But you'll keep some for yourself, I hope."

"Oh, just a few," she said, smiling again.

"Well," Tai reasoned, "if you're rich from diamond wealth, among other things that means you're incorruptible—a rare quality for an African leader!"

"Precisely!" she laughed. "That's my story and I'm sticking to it."

Tai turned serious. "Thank you, Empress."

"You're very welcome, Strategic Advisor."

They shared a moment without speaking.

When Tai stood up and turned away, the MI6 agent walked over to the fountain and let his hands enjoy the flowing water. He gazed out over the Blue Nile in the late afternoon sun, as if knowing this magical setting would soon all be in the past.

Finally, drying his hands on his jeans, he returned to where Shari was waiting.

"Speaking of Strategic Advisors, you're about to be without one."

"No thanks to you!"

"I understand you've found a way to clandestinely summon your Uncle Stefan to Khartoum. You'll reveal yourself to him?"

"Yes, tomorrow night. It will be the shock of his life. Hopefully a good shock."

"You've told me a lot about him. He's the one who taught you economics, right? And indoctrinated you with free market concepts?"

"Yep. It all came back when my memory returned. That's who I learned it from."

"Maybe you should make your uncle the new Minister of Strategic Affairs."

Shari stared at him.

"Well, wouldn't that make sense?" he asked.

"Total sense. I should have thought of it myself."

"He'd technically report to Eduardo, just as I have. But it would allow him to stay here and be part of what you've built. I bet he'd love that. I bet you would too."

"I would, absolutely. He runs a chemical business in Geneva, but I'm sure he could hand that off to someone and move here if he wished."

"How are you going to reveal yourself?"

"Tai, I'm so scared. He's the only relative I have left."

"Why scared?"

"What if he disapproves of what I've done?"

"You think that's possible? How could he disapprove?"

"He knew me as a young, precocious ballerina in Montreux. I've become the Angel of Death. I've killed so many people! What if he sees me as a murderer?"

"You're no murderer!"

"Tai, I've killed hundreds…"

"That was warfare."

"I started those wars!"

"You're really worried about this?"

"Beyond terrified. In Switzerland, teenagers are grounded for a month merely for being out past midnight. I conquered Africa—without permission."

"But Stefan's your uncle, not your parent."

"He's next in line and was always kind of a second father."

"So, what will you do, how will you handle it?"

"I have to lead up to it very carefully. I need to find a way to learn what he thinks of Shariya, if he approves or considers her evil."

"Let me guess. You're going to interview him while veiled."

"Yes."

"And then reveal that his niece still exists?"

"I have to lead up to it carefully. I don't want to give him a heart attack. Stefan has some coronary issues."

"Can I give you advice?"

"Please do."

"You're overthinking this. There's no bad news here for Stefan. Find a way to be alone with him, tell him you have some shocking, wonderful news, and then just remove your veil."

"I can't, Tai."

"You're going to tease this out, kind of torture him?"

"If the end game is wonderful news, then it's not torture no matter how I lead up to it. But I need to know what he's going to think of me. I can't just remove my veil."

Tai accepted defeat. "OK, there's not a lot of case studies to work from. I guess just play it as feels right. If I were Stefan, I'd want it quick and simple. But I understand you have issues here."

"A lot. Tai, we'll meet again, won't we?"

"Anytime. My bags are packed and I'm heading for the airport. But anytime you need me, for any reason, anywhere in the world, I'll come."

"Same here," said the empress. "Anytime you need me, for any reason, anywhere in the world, I'll be there."

"Or for no reason at all?" He grinned.

She looked at him meaningfully. "Yes, I'd like that. For no reason at all. I think no reason at all would be the best reason."

They hugged again, and Shari watched as Tai left the garden. Then she turned and stared out over the river. Tomorrow would be the meeting with Stefan.

The Empress of Africa glanced around at the courtyard walls, the garden, and the miniature stream, knowing beyond them was the elegance of the palace itself with all the trappings of imperial power. She tried to see it through her uncle's eyes. What would he think of her, of what she'd done?

How could she possibly explain?

70

Stefan Arquette waited in a windowless conference room inside a government building near the Imperial Palace. Khartoum was always hot but the air conditioning here was efficient. Experience as a businessman had taught him African bureaucrats might be dressed in anything from Western-style suits to shorts, sneakers, and a t-shirt. For this first-time meeting, Arquette was conservative in a gray suit, white shirt, and no tie. While it was always better to overdress, a tie might seem pretentious. He had one in a suit pocket and could perform an emergency upgrade if needed.

Glancing around the room, it was clear he was not being greeted in style. The conference table and chairs seemed old, and there was a faint odor of mildew, common to most third-world countries. A dozen unopened bottles of water were set in the middle of the table, each with a light coating of dust.

This must be one of the lesser meeting rooms, he decided, and the choice likely deliberate. "This discussion is more important to you than to us," might be the message—not a bad tactic for beginning a negotiation.

There was a polite knock on the door, and it opened. Arquette jumped up. A slender middle-aged man entered—casual slacks and a short-sleeved shirt, glasses, jet-black hair, and an overall swarthy appearance. "Good evening," said the bureaucrat as they shook hands and were seated. The two ritually exchanged cards and Stefan studied the one received. "Assistant Director for Procurement, Ministry of the Interior, Empire of Africa." His own said "Managing Director, SCI, Geneva."

The Assistant Director opened the conversation. "Mr. Arquette, first, apologies for this rather modest setting. I was asked to keep your arrival at Imperial Headquarters as low-key as possible, although I'm not sure why it matters. For that purpose this room is ideal."

"The room is fine," replied the businessman politely. "All I care about is the air conditioning, which is magnificent!" he joked, and the bureaucrat chuckled.

"Yes, I agree with your priorities. I see we have water, but may I offer you coffee, tea?"

Arquette knew that ritual would consume another half hour, and declined politely.

"Well, shall we turn to business then?" asked the bureaucrat, equally content—it seemed—to dispense with ceremony.

"Yes, please," replied the Swiss businessman gratefully.

"First, thank you for responding to the RFP for the soap contract and coming here in person to discuss. I've glanced through the document, and it seems reasonable. We may wish to proceed."

Arquette was startled. This was not how business discussions went, especially in this part of the world. He bowed politely, acknowledging the statement.

"If you have any questions, anything I can clarify—?"

It seemed a lame response even to him. At this point in the negotiation dance, the purchasing agent should be pushing back against some of the terms, certainly the price tag.

Two weeks earlier Stefan's sales department had received a strange communication from the Empire of Africa: a Request For Proposal for selling a large quantity of soap. SCI had never sold to any government directly. Their clients were often factories, universities, retail chains and such. Never a government, even though he'd marketed heavily in Africa. But now the Empire of Africa *itself* was reaching out to him? Why?

Nonetheless, his sales team was thrilled at the prospect of a potential five-million-dollar soap contract. They'd dropped everything and put together a proposal, complete with PPT deck, a considerable appendix, and ending with price and payment terms. They'd sent the whole thing off by email a week ago.

And then nothing—until out of the blue the Khartoum purchasing office had asked for—virtually insisted on—an in-person meeting and made clear it must be with the Managing Director himself, and alone. A confirmation number for a business class ticket had been included. They'd also provided a room voucher for the Khartoum Hyatt, which was convenient to government offices. On arrival, a driver with signboard was just off the jetway and whisked the Swiss businessman through immigration.

And now, after being chauffeured to Imperial Office Building 4 for a seven p.m. meeting, when he was ready to go over the proposal in detail, answer their questions, and no doubt haggle on the price, his contact appeared largely uninterested.

It was as if the meeting was a formality, a pretense. Yet for what? Soap was soap.

He could do nothing but play along.

The purchasing agent was staring at the proposal, flipping through pages randomly, pretending to study them. The man glanced at his watch, then back to the document.

Another man entered the room, clothed in an ornate—almost ceremonial—guard's uniform. He nodded to the purchasing agent, who seemed relieved by the interruption, to have perhaps been waiting for it. "You may proceed," said the guard. "They're expecting you."

"There is someone else who needs to review this contract before we can continue," explained the purchasing agent to his guest. "If you will accompany me…"

He stood abruptly and motioned Stefan to follow.

"Is there a problem? Anything I should be prepared for?" asked Stefan, having to turn to his client for advice. This was beyond strange.

"There is no problem. I do not know the purpose of the meeting, only that I was asked to arrange it."

"Whom will I be meeting, if you don't mind my asking?" asked Stefan. It was a reasonable question.

"It is not my place to make introductions. Others will do that."

They walked outside two short blocks to the palace itself, the heat of the day ebbing swiftly in the night-time desert air. At the gate was another man, waiting for them—a guard captain perhaps, as the uniform was more ornate. The purchasing agent turned to Stefan.

"I will leave you now. Perhaps we shall speak again. It has been a pleasure…"

He nodded stiffly and departed quickly back towards the office complex.

The captain bowed courteously to Stefan. "Greetings from the Imperial Court," he said. "I will escort you to the one who wishes to meet you, and it's my duty to prepare you for this meeting."

"I'm sorry. I really have no idea what's going on. Who am I meeting? Is this a supervisor, someone who must approve the soap contract?"

"I do not know the purpose of the meeting, but I doubt it has much to do with soap. Please follow me."

The gate was opened, the guard courteously invited Stefan through first, and then led the way.

"If the meeting has nothing to do with soap, then what is it about—and who am I meeting?" asked Stefan as they walked down a broad, tree-lined walkway towards a side entrance. Tropical birds fluttered about, and one of them cawed angrily as they passed.

"I will be taking you to an interior courtyard in the palace, a very pleasant setting. It's a garden, with trees and flowers, and even a stream flowing through it. Quite lovely."

The man had not answered the question.

"But...*who* am I meeting?"

The guard stopped, and looked at him with an air of seriousness.

"Sir, you are being granted a private audience with Shariya, the Empress of Africa."

Stefan felt his knees go weak, and his stomach churned.

"I...I'm to meet Shariya herself? The one they call..."

The guard chuckled in a kindly fashion, as they continued walking. "Yes, the one they call the Angel of Death. But you do not need to be frightened. The empress herself asked for this meeting. All I know is that she has a matter of confidentiality to discuss with you. I do not know what that matter is, nor do I need to know."

"But I'm completely unprepared for this. I'm really going to be introduced to the Empress of Africa?"

"Yes. You've been granted that honor and it's granted rarely. She sees almost no outsiders. Please follow me."

Stefan wished he'd added the tie but knew it was too late.

Trying to overcome rising anxiety, the Swiss businessman followed the guard captain through a door, past a beautiful atrium, up a flight of stairs, and down a long hallway to what must be the back of the palace. They came to another guard, who opened another door after saluting his captain. Now they were going down a flight of stairs, through an archway and then—outside to an enclosed courtyard that opened onto a breathtaking view of the Blue Nile and beyond.

He took it all in, wondering what explanation there could be for the most mysterious woman in the world to desire a meeting with him. It made no sense. He was a businessman in the field of industrial solvents. He taught economics part-time in Geneva. There could be no explanation.

"Please wait here," directed the guard. "Make yourself at ease."

The palace functionary left quickly.

Stefan stared after him, but then detected an unusual scent of violets. Was it perfume? He turned and she was there, standing a few meters away, adorned head to toe in an embroidered purple abaya gown and matching opaque head covering.

The slender form was both feminine and elegant and seemed to exude an air of sensuality. Sensuality and power. The figure in front of him was like nothing he'd ever experienced. There was an energy, a vitality, beneath the veils. He could sense this yet, even so, was at a disadvantage, with even her eyes covered.

"Monsieur Arquette, n'est-ce pas?"

She spoke perfect French, with a Parisian accent. The voice was silken, confident, yet cleansed of all arrogance or haughtiness. So might an important hostess have welcomed a distinguished guest to her home.

"Your Highness…" he replied, in the same language. He bowed, clumsily, not knowing if it was the proper way to address her. And then saw no reason to pretend otherwise.

"I'm sorry, this meeting has taken me by surprise, and I've not been told even how you are to be addressed. Forgive me."

The figure waved a gloved hand dismissively. "There is nothing to forgive. The meeting was at my request, and I know you're unprepared."

She faced him directly, although he could still see no face. "I wish to put you completely at ease. Please call me Shari. It's a nickname my friends use, and I like it."

"It seems insufficiently honorific, Empress, but I will address you as Shari if that is your command." Stefan could not believe he was having a private conversation with the Empress of Africa.

The woman laughed softly. "Monsieur Arquette, I am not here to *command* anything of you. And there doesn't need to be anything honorific about my name. This is an informal meeting, and you're not one of my subjects. You're a guest. I know you're apprehensive. That's unavoidable. But I need you to relax. We have much to discuss."

She paused, considering. "May I offer you a drink?"

Stefan wanted his wits about him. "No, I'm fine, thank you."

"You're not fine. You're wound tight as a spring. You need a drink." She rang a small bell and a servant appeared. "Anka, please bring the refreshment cart."

"At once, my lady." The servant vanished.

"You see, everyone treats me as royalty. The palace staff calls me 'my lady.' You say 'your highness.' I suppose the title empress is to blame, but we chose that mostly as a PR move to help solidify the idea of an empire."

Stefan's mind was reeling. Not only was the ruler of Africa indulging him with a private audience, she seemed willing to share personal feelings, treating him almost as a friend. This made no sense. The food and drink arrived, and Shariya politely dismissed the servant.

The veiled woman handed Stefan a tall glass of something over ice cubes, already prepared on the cart.

"Monsieur Arquette, I know you're scared to death of offending me and are utterly perplexed about this meeting. I would like to make you a proposal."

"Please do," he replied, not knowing what else to say.

"If you drink this rather large vodka tonic then I promise not to be offended or angered by *anything* you say or do in this meeting. I will personally guarantee your safety. You will be able to relax completely and say anything you want without fear because I always keep my promises."

"And if I don't drink it?" Stefan wasn't sure why he was playing along with the game.

"That's not an option."

"I see."

The woman knew how to both project power and be polite about it. She hadn't threatened him; merely said 'that's not an option,' as if the choices available were outside anyone's control. Despite the fear, he was intrigued. The woman behind the veil was clever, and very diplomatic.

He took a sip. She was right. He was a bundle of nerves and did need the alcohol. Despite the mixer he recognized the vodka as Finlandia, his personal favorite. Was that a coincidence? He looked at her quizzically.

"I know far more about you than you'd expect," she said, reading his thoughts, "including your favorite brand of vodka. Yes, it's Finlandia."

"But, my lady, I mean, I mean, Shari. What possible interest could you have in me at all? Please, what is the purpose of this meeting?"

She was watching him closely from behind her veil. He could almost feel the intensity of the gaze yet could make nothing of it. The mood was one of hospitality, not danger. Shariya was still standing, watching him. She had not responded to his question, and he had to say *something*.

"Finlandia is excellent vodka," he noted at last. "But am I to drink alone? It seems impolite."

"Don't worry about being polite. What's important is that you be relaxed. You are in no danger. Do you trust me when I say that? Given my reputation, I can understand why you might not."

He looked again at the shadowy form behind the veil and wondered if he could trust the person saying those words. His instinct was strong that he could, but the analytical part of his mind was aware he was alone with what was probably the most dangerous human life form on the planet. If the stories were true, this woman was a ruthless killer.

She'd conquered all of Africa in six months—a feat unmatched in human history. Lethally dangerous? Unquestionably. Yet the aura of hospitality was real. The figure behind the veil was emanating warmth and friendship, nothing else. Even so, this woman would see through lies instantly. She was not to be trifled with, falsely flattered, or manipulated with guile. He could see no option but utter honesty, and—again—instinct told him this was the right path.

"I can't give you a simple answer to that question. I'm sorry. My head says you're a dangerous person, and I should feel afraid. But I do not feel afraid. My intuition says I can trust you. And..."

"And what?"

"I think I very much *want* to trust you. If you're casting a spell on me, it's working."

She laughed instantly, and it was a delightful sound, breaking whatever tension might have been building. The ready laughter, much more than the alcohol, did make him feel safe. He took another sip.

"Monsieur Arquette, I apologize again. I can't imagine what you're thinking, about why you're here and why I wished a private audience with you. You'll understand soon enough, but I suppose I'm toying with you right now and that's rude. I should get to the point, but if you'll indulge, I'd rather chat for a bit first. Do you mind?"

"*I* don't mind. It's your time I'm concerned about. I don't recall ever before having a private audience with a head of state. I'd not be surprised to wake up suddenly and find all this an odd dream."

"Odd? Oh, you have no idea how odd this is going to get."

Stefan did not reply.

Shariya went to the serving cart, poured herself a sparkling water on ice, and returned. He noticed she walked with utter grace—the elegant gown contributing to the artistry of her movement.

He could still make nothing of the face. Behind her veil there was only shadow.

"You're correct," she said. "It's not right to ask you to drink alone. I may have something stronger later, but for now this will do. Please sit," she requested, gesturing towards a settee and low table. "Do you mind if I ask some questions?"

"Not at all," he said, placing his drink down.

She paused, perhaps struggling, and then blurted out awkwardly, "I have no idea how to do this."

"What are you trying to do, exactly?" Stefan took another sip, becoming more relaxed.

"I have something hugely important to discuss with you, to reveal to you, but I need to lead up to it slowly. I may do it all wrong, and if so, I apologize again."

"Shari, your Excellency, may I ask if this has anything to do with soap?"

She laughed again as if he'd made a joke. "The Empire may decide to buy soap from SCI," she explained, "but that is not what our conversation is about, and it's not why I needed to bring you to Khartoum."

The businessman was so confused he could only stare back at her.

"Please forgive the subterfuge," she pleaded. "The soap contract is not off the table, but it's not important."

"What *is* important?"

"Your answers to my questions."

"I'm eager to hear them."

There was another long pause, as the empress glanced east to the broad river and the plain beyond, now mostly in darkness.

Then she turned back and looked at him directly. "Mr. Arquette, my first question is this. What do you think of me?"

He could only stare, speechless.

"It's a very simple question. Please, be honest."

"It is the most un-simple question I've ever been asked in my life!" Even as he said the words, he realized the vodka was having an effect. He was speaking more openly and casually than he'd thought possible. Well, that's why she'd served it to him.

"Yes, you're right, I'm nervous even to be here alone in this courtyard with you. How can I answer a question like that? Where would I begin?"

"With economics. What do you think of my economic policies?"

"You wish to talk economics? Here in this garden?"

"If you don't mind."

"Well, I can answer that easily. This is not false flattery. The Shariyan government is following the most enlightened economic policies of any government, anywhere, in the history of human civilization. I teach that subject at university."

"I know. That's why I'm asking."

"How do you know all this?"

"I'll explain later. Please continue."

"Well, you're executing free market principles in an almost textbook-perfect fashion. And it's working. You're transforming the continent. If you stay the course, you'll have one of the most vibrant economies on Earth in less than a decade."

"I know you can't see my face, but I'm smiling beneath my veil. I consider that a high compliment coming from you."

"Your highness, I mean Shari, why am I here? Why do you know that I teach economics? How do you know my favorite brand of vodka? Why do you care about my opinions at all? I'm utterly baffled—"

"I know you are," she said, waving her hand dismissively. "But I already apologized for that, and you granted me leave to question you. Aside from economics, what else do you think of me? As a ruler of my people? As a person?"

Stefan paused, trying to decide what to say. But he knew honesty was the only path.

"Well, you seem to be a fair and benevolent ruler. Your subjects almost worship you. The African Empire is not a democracy, but I suspect if it were you'd be elected in a landslide. You are the closest thing to a benign dictator perhaps the world has ever known."

"You don't think I'm evil?"

"Certainly not, based on what I've seen you accomplish—and how you've done it."

"Yet I'm a killer. Surely you know that. I'm an exceedingly dangerous person. Do you know how many men I've killed, by my own hand?"

"No."

"Hundreds. My armies, the revolutions I triggered, far more. So now what do you think of me? Honest answers only, please."

"The men you killed, was it in open warfare, did you need to kill them? Did they deserve to die?"

"Some did deserve it. In other cases it was mere warfare. Those men did not deserve to die, those who were merely serving evil men. But if those armies were to be defeated, yes, they had to die."

"You seem quite certain of that."

"Believing it is the only thing that keeps me sane."

"Well, you've revolutionized a continent. You've rescued it from corruption and dysfunctionality. You've delivered hope and prosperity. Your conquests had positive outcomes."

"Go on," she urged. The woman in the veil was staring at him intently,

"They call you the Angel of Death, but they might equally call you the Angel of Salvation. I know it would be dangerous to lie right now. Yet I don't need to. In my opinion, you've performed a miracle in Africa. You are to be admired."

"You're not just saying this because you want to sell your soap?"

And now it was Stefan's turn to laugh. "I've already forgotten about the damn soap."

"Then—then I thank you. I can't tell you what your words mean to me. To hear those words—"

The woman turned away and in a delicate gesture moved a hand briefly under her veil. Stefan realized she'd brushed away a tear.

"Shari, I meant those words. But, again, I don't understand why you care about my opinion. I'm just one person—as you say, not even a citizen of your empire."

"Right now I care about your opinion more than anyone else's in the world and before you leave this garden you will understand why. But I need you to be patient."

"Very well."

"Monsieur Arquette, I have good news, but you will find it shocking and I'm going to lead up to it slowly. I'm doing this for your sake, do you understand?"

"Good news is always welcome, however delivered."

"Then—here we go. You had relatives, I understand, who died in Africa."

"You know that story as well."

"I do. It was your sister and brother-in-law who were murdered in CAR. And your niece."

"Yes."

"Do you mind if we talk about it?"

"It's painful, but we can talk about it if you wish."

"I do, but it's going to hurt. I'm going to speak openly of things I'm sure are difficult."

"Please say whatever you wish."

"They found the bodies of your sister and brother-in-law quite soon after the murders. But they found the remains of your niece only a few weeks ago."

"Yes."

"You saw the lab results, the dental records. They were conclusive, beyond doubt?"

"There was no doubt. There'd never really been any from the point they discovered the body."

"I am very sorry for your loss."

"Thank you. Since we are talking about such things, if I can say…"

"Please say whatever you wish."

"Their deaths robbed me of my soul. My heart was ripped out by their loss. I have no children of my own. Sophie was to me a daughter—the child I never had. With her death, I lost my own will to live. I still function. I'm still a businessman. I still sell chemicals—soap and so forth. Yet I no longer care. The beauty of life has vanished for me."

"The *beauty* of life? Is there such a thing?"

"I believe so, yes. I used to possess it, to appreciate it. But not now."

"Those are very strong words."

"True words."

There was another long pause, and Stefan could make nothing of the emotions going on behind the veil.

"I am going to change the subject."

"Yes, please do."

"You have wide experience as a businessman in Africa."

"Indeed, for many years."

"One of Africa's most endemic problems was corruption. Bribery.

Payoffs. That kind of thing. Have you encountered it in your dealings on this continent?"

"Of course."

"Monsieur Arquette, I am not concerned with your past business affairs. This is not a legal inquiry. We are having a private conversation. But is it fair to say that you have had to pay bribery money on occasion to ensure contracts were accepted?"

"It would be foolish to pretend otherwise."

And now Stefan was truly perplexed. Was all this a circuitous dance to entice a bribe? No, screamed his instincts. There was something far more complex at work here. Yet his guard was up. Thoughts of friendship with this woman were set aside.

"I do not know as much about the corruption problems as I should," she continued. "You have firsthand knowledge. Let me ask a question. In a situation like this soap contract that you discussed with our purchasing agent, if this had been a question of needing to pay a bribe to seal the deal, what percent might have been requested?"

"I'm not sure I understand what you're asking, or why you're asking it."

She laughed and waved a hand dismissively. "Don't worry, Monsieur Arquette. I'm not seeking a bribe. Corruption is being stamped out across the continent. I would hardly allow it in the imperial court."

"Forgive me. Old habits die hard. I've been in so many African meetings where…"

"I understand. But I'm asking a *historical* question. How much would you have paid to a purchasing agent in Khartoum to seal a five-million-dollar soap contract? Under the prior rulers?"

"Perhaps as much as ten percent, typically wired into a Swiss account."

"Five hundred thousand dollars?"

"Yes."

"OK, I appreciate your honesty. In Ethiopia, where a license for foreigners to trade was required, how much might you pay for such a license, before that country became part of the Empire?"

"Maybe ten thousand dollars up front, and a few hundred each year."

"Fine. The port of Mombasa, in Kenya, was known for rampant corruption. A ship offloading cargo would pay what bribe to the dock officials to be allowed to do so?"

"It would vary, depending on the cargo. Perhaps as little as one thousand. Perhaps ten times that."

"I see." She paused before her next question, looking at him closely.

"And what would it take, Monsieur Arquette, to bribe a medical examiner in CAR to overlook a fraudulent skull reconstruction of a body found in the wilderness?"

The vodka glass, which was halfway to Stefan's lips, paused. He'd seen the x-ray with his own eyes; compared it to Sophie's old medical records. He'd examined the signature from the coroner. But bribing a coroner would be easy. It would cost almost nothing. Perhaps a hundred euros. Less than that.

And then the implication of her question struck him.

The vodka glass slid out of his hand, fell to the floor, and shattered.

He stared at the mess, unable to think what to do about it.

The servant appeared and with a few swift motions, the debris was removed. A new glass, already filled, was placed in front of Stefan. He stared at it for a moment and then reached out and drank deeply.

"Shari, the dental records prove that was Sophie's body. Why are you suggesting someone would fake a skull reconstruction?"

"Because I know someone did."

"You know…Who! Dammit! Who?"

"Me."

"What!" He jumped to his feet in shock. "What do you mean, *you!*"

"I paid the bribe. I arranged for the fraudulent skull. It was I who convinced you, and everyone else, that it was Sophie Martine's body."

They were both standing now.

"Empress, why did you do this? I don't understand."

"Those who murdered your sister and her husband were executioners, and they were paid to make sure Sophie died also. It was necessary to make them, and everyone else, believe that she *did* die."

Stefan stared at the shadowy, veiled woman. "Are you suggesting Sophie *might still be alive*?"

"Monsieur Arquette, listen to me very carefully because this is so important. She witnessed her parents' murder, saw it all from a place of hiding. It destroyed her. Destroyed her mind. Sophie Martine, the one you knew, the teenager from Switzerland, died that day. But her body did not die. Her body survived, and eventually her mind came back. But not the same. Not the same person. She was essentially reborn as someone completely different."

Stefan no longer feared this woman. His soul was seeing an opportunity to return from the dead. The living held no horror for him at all.

"Shari, I want a simple answer. Is Sophie Martine, my niece, still alive? *Yes or no!*"

The woman stared at him, both knowing the enormity of the crossroads before them. Stefan could not breathe. The empress reached out, touched his arm, and spoke one word.

"Yes."

Stefan gasped and then fell to his knees, covering his face with his hands, unable to stop the tears. He needed time to think, to digest this. No, he didn't. He just needed to find Sophie, if she truly still lived.

He forced himself to stand. "My God. Where is she? Is she safe?"

The veiled woman handed him a tissue. "She's here in Khartoum, healthy, and very safe."

"Khartoum! My little Sophie is alive and living in this very city?"

"Monsieur Arquette, she is not the Sophie you knew. She is a completely different person. More different than you could possibly imagine. The Sophie Martine you knew is dead. Let's be clear on that. But the one who was once your niece is alive. You must trust me. She's been through so much and you must be prepared for what has happened to her, for what she now is. And you must be prepared to be shocked. Totally, utterly shocked."

"Ah, I see," he said, beginning to calm down even while his heart soared. "She's changed and you need me to understand this. OK. But it doesn't matter. She's changed. How could she not have? If she's been through so much, I will devote my life to helping her recover. Can you take me to her? I—. My God, I'm just—" Stefan dabbed his eyes again.

"The girl I can take you to is perhaps as far from your little Sophie as anyone could be. Can you handle that?"

"If she breathes, if she carries my sister's blood in her veins, then nothing else matters. Nothing else matters, do you understand?"

Stefan realized that Shariya, the Empress of Africa, was now the one crying. It registered somewhere intellectually, but he could make nothing of it, so frantic was he to be reunited with the one he thought lost forever.

He was back on his knees now, supplicating himself in front of the empress. "Can you not have me taken to her, right now, I beg it of you. Please, where is my little Sophie?"

"You do not need to be taken to her. She is here in the courtyard. But she has done such terrible things—"

And then Shariya, Empress of Africa, the Angel of Death, ripped off her head covering. Her eyes, face, and hair shone down upon Stefan Arquette.

"Have I changed so much, Uncle, that you do not recognize me?"

Blonde hair cascaded downwards and framed a tear-stained face. It was all there: those flashing blue eyes, the slender nose, and even the pouty lips. It was not the Sophie he remembered. Yet it was Sophie grown up—grown into an astonishingly beautiful young woman.

It was impossible, it could not be possible. Yet it was so. Shariya, the Empress of Africa, was none other than his sister's child. He stood back up clumsily.

"Sophie?" he said with a puzzled expression.

"Uncle?" she replied, her lips forming a smile.

He opened his arms and she rushed into them.

In moments his legs gave out, and—with Sophie's guidance—Stefan fell back onto the settee.

❧

Dr. Anzio appeared and quickly took his pulse and blood pressure.

"Maybe we over-medicated?" suggested the empress, realizing her uncle was asleep.

"Perhaps. But from what I could see from a distance, even with the replacement drink he had less than one full glass, total. And the dose of triazolam in each was tiny. I knew it would knock him out eventually but not quite this fast."

"Well, maybe the timing's perfect. He just learned the Angel of Death is his niece. I can't imagine the shock. A good night's sleep is probably what he needs. "

"I think pre-medication was smart, given his coronary history. Vitals are fine. But how are *you* feeling?"

"Like a huge weight got removed. I can breathe again."

"I'm not surprised. I could hear the conversation, and it sounds like he completely approves of what you've done."

"At least in the abstract. That was before he knew it was *me* doing it."

"I think you're fine. I'll have servants take him to one of the rooms and prepare him for bed. He'll sleep through the night, and I'll stay in the same room on a cot, as we discussed."

"Thank you, Doctor. Now we'll just have to see how my breakfast with him goes in the morning. We'll have plenty to talk about."

"Shari, that last glass of vodka is half full. Why don't you finish it?"

"Doctor's orders?"

He nodded.

She picked up the glass, drank the contents, and glanced at the clock. "I think it's my bedtime too."

71

THE NEXT DAY Shari realized a change had occurred. Revealing herself to Stefan and having her actions validated was the final piece necessary to bring back the girl she once was. Sophie Martine, lithe and innocent ballerina, the one her uncle knew, was now no longer dead. How that could be, after all she'd been through, was a mystery, but she knew it had happened. Sophie had returned—in full. Even so, she was equally Shariya, Angel of Death.

She could float onto a stage and perform as Odette in Swan Lake. She had only to send signals to her body, and it could do this. She could equally hide under a log in the jungle and leap up and massacre a dozen slavers. She possessed both skills. Which was the real her? She could perform either role, yet how could she be both?

The empress was sitting on her balcony, looking over the river, when the sliding door opened and her uncle walked in. They exchanged another long hug, and she gestured to the opposing chair.

"When I woke up," he said, "there was someone sitting in the room and the first words out of his mouth were: 'Sir, it was not a dream. Empress Shariya, your niece, awaits you for breakfast.' Those were the most beautiful words I've ever heard in my life."

"I'm glad," she said, smiling.

"He also explained you were a complete amnesiac until a few weeks ago—that's why you never reached out."

"Yes. And when I did, it had to be done carefully. For lots of reasons."

Her uncle nodded, but Shari noticed he was having trouble making eye contact. She reached over and squeezed his hand.

"Stefan, please look at me."

He did so.

"I'm sure I handled everything yesterday in the most dreadful manner. But I had to lead up to it slowly. Can you forgive me?"

Her uncle sipped coffee while looking out at the water. Then he turned back and spoke with conviction. "Forgive you? Sophie, I'm living a dream here. I am concentrating one hundred percent of my mental energies to *not wake up* from this miracle. I thought you dead! You're alive! How can *anything else* matter?"

"It can matter a lot. Remember what I said. No longer your little Sophie. I'm now Empress of Africa, the Angel of Death—probably the most dangerous person on Earth. Can you love such a person? Can you even *forgive* such a person? I've been so scared of what you would think of me, and of what I've done!"

He paused and again looked out over the balcony rail at the fast-moving waters of the Blue Nile. "We played once. We played on a swing. I pushed you high in the air and you screamed with delight. 'Stop!' you cried. 'Push me higher and I'll never come down!' Do you remember that?" he asked, turning back to her.

Sophie let the images flood into her mind from a distant past; thrilled she was still connected to the person her uncle remembered. "I do remember that. You scared me to death on that swing. Yet I loved it."

"But now look what you've done. You've pushed yourself higher than I ever could have. You've conquered a continent. You're an empress!"

"But being an empress is much like being on that swing. It scares me to death."

"Why?"

"Over a billion people are now my subjects and expect me to run an empire. If that's not cause for fear, what is?"

"You may be the first ruler in history to say so. I think it's healthy."

"Healthy or not, I'm still afraid."

"Then ask yourself who could do a better job. If the answer is no one, then you should feel inspired."

Shari waved her hand in a broad sweep.

"There are many who could do a better job. You know more about economics, for example."

"No doubt. But leadership is different. It's intangible. You seem born to it. Otherwise, you couldn't have accomplished all this—" he nodded towards the palace, but she knew he meant the empire. "How *did* you accomplish it? The last time I saw you, in Milan, the challenge was going to be keeping up with your high school class while on a dig near Bangui. Now you've conquered Africa! Sophie, how in the world…?"

The empress held up both hands and smiled. "Stop. I'll give you the full story some evening over wine. Promise. But right now, I just need your approval—your acceptance. If possible, your love."

His eyes softened. "Oh, Sophie, are you really worried about that?"

"My parents are dead. You're the closest thing to my parent. I feel I should be sent to my room or something. I don't know. Surely you can't approve of everything I've done!"

"Why not?"

She lowered her voice and turned away slightly; eyes downcast. "Because, Stefan, like I said yesterday, I've personally killed hundreds. My armies, even more. And that doesn't count the thousands who died from the civil unrest I inspired. I've conquered Africa. My *sensei* back in Montreux would be furious."

"And you think *I* will be?"

She looked up. "Seventeen-year-old girls are grounded for a month just for being out past midnight."

"Oh, I get it. You're looking for parental supervision. You want me to step in, scold you harshly, send you to your room, and then in the morning it will all be over, and you'll be little Sophie Martine again. Is that it?"

"Something like that."

"Well, I'm not going to send you to your room. I don't even know in this palace where it is. But you don't need that. You need something very different."

"What do I need?"

"Come over here, Sophie."

She did.

"Sit down, here on my lap—I hope that won't seem too improper."

She did that too.

"OK, now bury your face against my chest, and cry your eyes out. Cry for what happened to you, for your loss. For your mom and dad. That you *must* do."

"What are you talking about? I don't need to cry my eyes out. I'm…"

She hesitated and then collapsed against his shoulder. The tears wouldn't stop. The sobs continued for nearly twenty minutes. He held her the whole time, gently drying her eyes with a tissue. And his own as well. Eventually, the Angel of Death looked up, brushed away a final tear, and calmly resumed her place at the table.

"Feel better?" asked Stefan.

"OK, I guess I *did* need to do that."

"We needed to grieve for Nic and Juli. We needed to do it together."

"Thank you."

"You've conquered Africa," said Stefan, taking another sip of coffee. "I look forward to hearing the story of how you did it. But I'm curious about one thing."

"What?" asked Sophie.

"What happens next?"

"Let's talk about that. Do you remember how I used to come

home from school every night, saying I hated what all of you were doing to me?"

"Of course."

"I was just being a rebellious teenager, but I said that because I wanted to be a normal girl, living a normal life, having friends—you know—meeting boys and stuff. That's all I ever wanted—just to be normal. But all my time was spent training. Training with martial arts, training as a ballerina. You and Dad were training me on economics and geo-politics. Now I've conquered Africa and you're asking me what I want to do next."

"Yes."

"When do I get to have a normal life?"

"Do you think you could go back to Switzerland and join your class in school as if none of this happened?"

Shari teared up again and shook her head. "No, I couldn't. And I seem to have a job here, don't I?"

"Yes. But your whole life is in front of you. What are your goals and dreams today?"

"One of them has been fulfilled: meeting you again and being together again. Having you accept me for what I've become."

"Yes. Check that off the list. Yesterday was the happiest day of my life."

"Mine too. When you held me, knowing who I was. That moment—"

"Yes, for me too. OK, so what's next?"

"Stefan, I touched on this yesterday, but maybe you don't remember. My parents were killed by professionals as part of a contract hit. Before I escaped, I heard them say: 'We have to kill the girl too, or we won't get paid.'"

"Yes, I remember you saying that."

Her uncle looked away briefly.

"Stefan, do you know any reason someone would want to kill my parents, and equally important, why they would want to kill me, their daughter?"

"No, I don't. I can't imagine," he said quickly.

Too quickly?

Shari stared at him, but he returned the gaze.

"I faked the dental records so whoever wanted me dead, would now believe I *was* dead, and I'd not be in danger. But, Stefan, I must know. That's what I must now dedicate my life to, this mystery: Finding out who murdered my parents, and why. That's my next chapter, I think."

"But you have nothing to go on, Sophie. Where would you begin?"

"That's the problem."

"No one loved them more than I did. But they're gone. And if you're safe, maybe it makes no sense to devote your life to that. Maybe it's just a mystery that should stay in your past unless some lead comes along."

She stood up from the table and walked over to the rail, watching the Blue Nile on its journey from the highlands of Ethiopia.

"It will haunt me forever, Stefan," she said at last, returning to her chair. "But you're right. I have nowhere to even start. I'll put a team of investigators on it, but I doubt they'll learn anything. I was hoping you might have a clue or something."

"I'm sorry, Sophie."

She looked at him curiously. "It's going to take a while to get used to being called *Sophie*. Everyone in the palace calls me Shari."

"I'll happily call you anything you'd like."

"Sophie's nice. It helps me remember who I used to be."

"And still are. I don't believe what you said yesterday. Sophie's not gone. She's sitting across from me, drinking coffee."

The Angel of Death smiled and looked again at the river. "You may be right. I was thinking that very thing this morning. I believe now—with your acceptance—Sophie really is back. So may I change the subject?"

"Of course."

"Will you join me here? Can you hand off your business to

someone? I just lost an important advisor, our Minister for Strategic and Economic Affairs. The job is mostly about economic policies. If you want the position, it's yours."

He smiled. "I'd love that, if it's what you want. Now that I've found you again, there's no way I'm leaving."

"I'm going to approve the soap contract."

Stefan burst out laughing. "Who cares about the stupid soap contract?"

"I do, and so do you. It's a perfect cover. This soap contract you can spin as the first step in what might be a vast marketing opportunity between SCI and the Empire of Africa. That's why you're moving to Khartoum, to keep the ball rolling, to maintain close relations. Only a few at the top will know you're also serving as strategic advisor to the empress. That can be kept clandestine. Otherwise, it might look odd. We don't want eyebrows raised."

"Yes, that makes sense. I'll promote René, my number two, to Managing Director and I'll continue as Chairman of the Board. That gives me the perfect cover to move to Khartoum and nurture a business relationship with the Empire of Africa."

"I've already cleared it with Eduardo, our prime minister. He sees no reason SCI shouldn't be one of our suppliers given its leadership in the field. He says it's not nepotism if we keep it above board and require competitive bidding and so forth."

"The sales team in Geneva would be surprised otherwise."

"Good, then that's settled," she declared, slipping into her persona as ruler of a continent. "I'm going to introduce you to Eduardo right after breakfast. He's cleared his calendar and I think you and he will—"

There was a knock on the door, and the servant girl entered.

After their victory over Sudan, which Anka made possible, Shari had tried to promote her to higher station but Anka refused. "Any other position will take me away from you," she'd explained. "I will be your assistant, your servant, your helper, whatever you want to call me. Please, just let me stay close to you."

Shari had honored the request while increasing her salary ten-fold. Anka was now her personal servant and Executive Secretary, and the only one with unimpeded access, anytime, night or day. Anka presented Shari with a FedEx envelope on a silver tray. "This just arrived, Empress."

Sophie glanced at her uncle and then opened the package. There was a letter inside which she read quickly.

"What is it?" asked Stefan.

"It's from Lord Winterset, Director of MI6 in London. He helped me several times as we built the empire." Shari paused, remembering the submarine wolf-pack that had stopped an invasion.

"And he sent it by FedEx," her uncle commented thoughtfully.

"Which is silly. He could have texted me."

"It's a trick we use in business. Sending via overnight courier elevates the matter to something more consequential. He needs you to take it very seriously."

"You're probably right. Here, read it yourself." She handed it to him.

My Dearest Shari, Empress of Africa,

Tai urged me to use your nickname but as we've never met or even spoken I at least included your formal title. I hope the combination yields both a warm greeting and a respectful one.

Allow me to jump right to business. I have a favor to ask. It's unrelated to Africa but something I hope you'd consider doing for my organization. It's not trivial, and I'd not ask such a thing except that our mutual friend assures me you feel a sense of obligation regarding an earlier matter.

Best not to discuss remotely. I'd be ever so grateful if you could visit me in London incognito, perhaps as Danielle Crecy. You're invited to a private breakfast at MI6 offices. If convenient, might we say 10am on the 8th of this month?

I confess that London is miserable this time of year. Please bring a decent umbrella and whatever else you need to stay warm. I have a charming gas fireplace in my office. Make it into the building, and you are welcome to stand in front of it for as long as you wish.

I very much look forward to meeting and believe you'll find our visit worthy of your time.

Most truly yours,

Admiral Lord James Winterset, K.B.,

Director

"You owe him a favor?"

"A big one. Now I'm curious."

"Your next chapter may be about to begin."

"I'm never going to have a normal life, am I?"

"Sophie, people who build empires rarely have normal lives."

Shari rose to her feet, restless energy once more driving her to pace back and forth.

Her eyes went automatically to the Blue Nile.

She watched as the river rushed by on its way to rendezvous—less than a kilometer downstream—with the White Nile, and eventually the Mediterranean Sea. This water has no idea what's about to happen to it, she thought, and then realized the same could be said of her.

She, also, was on a long journey and could only guess at its destination. The Empire of Africa was complete. She thought of Emil, of Omylo's village, and of everything that had happened since she awoke on that riverbank. All those battles. But who was she supposed to fight next?

The *Art of War* came down to knowing when, where, and how to fight. Sun Tzu had taught her these concepts, but had never touched on *who*. Or why.

Were these not far more important questions? Looking at the river once more, hoping for wisdom, she saw a log float by and grasped instantly the metaphor. "Rudderless," she whispered out loud, completing the thought verbally. It has no control over where it's going. On the other hand, it doesn't care.

But she cared. What was her next challenge? First, she had a favor to grant to a man in London. Granting that favor, she suspected, might change her life; yet in what way she did not know.

Shari glanced back at the river, noticing the log was already out of sight, around the next bend.

She envied a journey with no decisions to make. But she needed to make some.

It was time for the forest creature to come out of the jungle. It was time to fully resurrect the girl she once was. It was time to update her dreams.

She turned back to her uncle, waiting at the table. "Hey, Stefan, want to help me pack?"

"Sure," he said. "And I'll organize Africa for you, while you're gone."

"Just promise you won't screw it up too badly," she said, laughing, and walked eagerly through the door.

THE END

AUTHOR'S NOTE

Thank you for reading Forest Creature, and I hope you enjoyed it. I'd like to clarify a few details.

1. **Anastasia.** I took the same artistic liberty with Anastasia and her age—at the time of the Russian Revolution—as did the 1997 animated film *Anastasia* which depicts her as a young child of about six. (Historically, she was seventeen.) The *Angel of Death* trilogy was written (first draft) in 2019, and I based the historical timeline loosely off that date. Chapter One opens with the phrase: "Approximately 100 years later," meaning one hundred years after the Russian Revolution, which would be 2017. The Anastasia subplot is explored further in the second and third books of the trilogy, but the overall timeline assumes the opening chapter is somewhere around 2017, or fairly close to that. Confused yet? I certainly was, and finally needed an Excel spreadsheet to organize all the dates and ages—which become relevant later in the trilogy. In general, everything lines up pretty well in terms of blending historical facts with the plot's timeline. Finally, a small technical point. There were two Russian revolutions that same year, 1917: March and October. The tsar was deposed in March, but October

was when the Leninists (Bolsheviks) seized power. In the prologue, Helene refers to the March revolutionaries as Leninists. Some of them certainly were but most were simply "anti-tsarists." We'll just put it down to slight confusion on her part.

2. **Dansa Milano.** There is no such ballet competition, but *Prix de Lausanne* is real. In the novel, Stefan refers to it as "the Swiss competition" and suggests it's beneath Sophie. But in truth *Prix de Lausanne* is a major international ballet event.

3. **Congo.** I used further artistic license to include as a plot element that the two Congos had merged. As of publication date, of course, they haven't and may never. It simplified some details of the plot and geography to show them as merged, but in truth I did it because it's always been my hope that they *would* merge, and thus better organize the world map. Meanwhile, the maps shown in *Forest Creature*, an astute reader will observe, do in fact show Congo as two countries. I ask forgiveness for this slight inconsistency.

4. **Montreux.** I chose Les Avants, a mountain suburb of Montreux, Switzerland, for Sophie's home in part because I used to live in a different mountain suburb of Montreux (Blonay) when I was twelve, and attended the local school. When Sophie mentions "Corrine, that really nice girl…" I borrowed that name from a real-life Corrine that was a friend of the family in Blonay. My descriptions of the area are from personal experience. And the distinction between "Parisian French" and "Swiss French" is very real. I learned French in Montreux, and was told years later that I didn't speak it like an American; I spoke it with a Swiss accent. I took that as a compliment but learned later it was probably not meant as one.

5. **Experience in Africa.** While I've travelled to over half a dozen countries in Africa, ironically I've not visited any of the places featured in *Forest Creature*: CAR, Chad, Congo, Cameroon, or Sudan. Recently, at a business conference in Europe, I had occasion

to meet Queen Diambi of Congo (Google her!) and when she heard I'd written a novel based in that part of Africa, insisted I come visit her in Democratic Republic of Congo. Not only was she eager to show me her own country, she also explained that she knew, personally, all the tribal kings of Cameroon, and would make appropriate introductions there as well. I hope to take her up on this someday, but it was not feasible to postpone publication while the author gained more first-hand experience, although I was tempted. Also, it was in one of the countries I *have* visited, Sierra Leone, that I learned first-hand how endemic superstition and the occult is in West Africa. The rumors about Shari and her magical lions were based on that experience.

6. **Lingala.** The language spoken by the primitive tribe that rescues Shari from the forest, is a real tongue, but most often associated with tribes in the Democratic Republic of Congo. As Shari's tribe is located very close to that country, I chose it as the language they spoke. However, artistic license was used in the creation of the compound word *Shariya*, from "Shari" and "Ya." In truth those words have no actual connection to Lingala.

The story of Sophie Martine continues in *Covert Ballerina*, which takes place mostly in Russia, and further in *Exchange Student*, which takes place mostly at a high school in the American Midwest. The *Angel of Death* trilogy is a single story, and was originally envisioned as a single book. But—realizing how long it was going to be—I found it cleaved easily into three pieces and became far more digestible. I hope you'll read the next two as well, and equally that you'll enjoy them. (Amazon.com)

Warmest regards,

Jacques Voorhees

ACKNOWLEDGEMENTS

My father Koert Voorhees — who worked tirelessly editing, reviewing, and promoting the entire Angel of Death trilogy and gave me a thousand reasons to complete it.

My wife Derry — with whom I consulted frequently and on whose support I could always rely.

My sisters Beth Walter and Casi Biebl — who read over countless drafts and contributed their wisdom to character and plot development.

My son Alex — who advised on everything from sword-fighting to publishing.

My friends Teresa Wyatt, Cathy Craig, Bud Stowe and Kim Burgess Dick — who were patient enough to read and improve the very early, very rough, versions of the manuscript.

My editor Monique Happy — who helped my writing become tighter, cleaner, and more professional. (mohappy@att.net)

ABOUT THE AUTHOR

Driven by business ventures in the diamond industry and a lifelong wanderlust, Jacques Voorhees has embarked on scores of remarkable journeys spanning eighty-two countries and six continents, immersing himself in vibrant cultures, breathtaking landscapes, and unforgettable adventures. Jacques captures the essence of these extraordinary destinations through his travel writing, available at www.jacquesvoorhees.com.

In 2020, Jacques released his first full-length fiction novel, *Chrysalis*, a time-travel story set in eighth-century Ireland. Building on this success, Jacques ventured into the realm of action/ adventure thrillers with *Forest Creature*, the first installment of his *Angel of Death* trilogy, followed by *Covert Ballerina* and *Exchange Student*. (www. amazon.com)

Jacques currently lives in Keystone, Colorado with his wife Derry. They have three children: Erik, Kristen, and Alex.

Bonus excerpt: First four chapters of *Covert*

1

The man with the facial scar tried to ignore the smell of borscht and fried onions while examining his forged documents. Some looked very old, yellow and crinkled. Others were recent photocopies or printouts. There was a small booklet that looked like a passport from another age. Two were birth certificates. He poked through the collection, picking up several for closer examination.

"Quite impressive, Fyodor," he finally allowed. "These look real. You do excellent work."

"Best in the business. That's why you hired me," grumbled the thin, elderly man cooking lunch in his walk-up apartment on the outskirts of Moscow. He added more oil to the onions which noisily flared up in smoke, and stirred the soup. "Where's the cash?" he queried gruffly, looking at his guest seated at the table facing away from him.

"Here in this briefcase," said the man with the scar, placing the documents in a large manila envelope, and standing up. "Take my seat, Fyodor, and count your money. I'll stir your damned borscht," he said, smiling. "You've made me very happy."

The forger sat in the chair, intently tallying up the stacks of crisp euros with a pen and paper while his customer managed the stove. Several minutes went by.

Suddenly a gloved hand reached around and yanked Fyodor's head back, while a blade sliced open his throat. It was done so quickly and expertly there was no time even for a scream. The eyes went lifeless as the blood flowed down the body and onto the floor.

The man with the scar turned off gas burners, reclaimed his briefcase filled with cash, and left the apartment. A private jet awaited at Sheremetyevo Airport, and he would be back in St. Petersburg before sunset. The police would probably find the body in a few days, but he wasn't worried about an investigation. The police reported to him.

2

The young woman, dressed in a dark-gray pant suit and silk blouse under a waterproof trench coat, placed her wet umbrella in a rack and approached the secretary who guarded the office of the MI6 director—head of the British Secret Service.

"I'm Danielle Crecy," said the new arrival. "I have an appointment with Lord Winterset."

"Yes, Ms. Crecy, you're expected. Let me hang that coat up for you."

"Thanks, it's miserable outside."

"It's called *London in winter*," said the secretary, smiling. "That cold drizzle never seems to stop." She deftly hung up the coat, walked a few steps down the hall, and opened a door.

"My lord, Ms. Crecy is here."

Admiral Lord James Winterset emerged quickly from his inner sanctum. Danielle had never met this mysterious man to whom she owed so much, and appraised him quickly. Perhaps mid-sixties. Graying hair, a firm chin, fairly tall, and with piercing green eyes. His suit looked expensive but so did everyone's in London, as she was noticing.

He was evaluating her no less intently. She sensed he wanted to give her a hug, and she'd not have minded at all. Perhaps decorum wouldn't allow that; not in front of a secretary who likely did not know her real identity. Winterset would have told no one that Ms. Crecy was actually the terrible *Angel of Death* who had conquered Africa in six months and was now its Empress; or that her real name was Sophie Martine.

She used an alias because the Director had asked her to come incognito. She'd played Danielle Crecy before, when—as part of a tactical disinformation campaign—Sophie had briefly become a fashion model. Her haunting beauty on the cover of Vogue-Paris had electrified the haute-couture world.

High cheekbones, platinum blonde hair, and astonishingly large blue eyes were among the reasons she'd remained hidden behind a hijab veil while in Africa. Only a handful of people in the world knew what *Shariya*, Angel of Death in a tribal tongue, actually looked like.

So she was here as Ms. Crecy. If someone recognized her as a one-time fashion model, that was fine. But she doubted Winterset had invited her to London for that purpose. He'd requested she come urgently regarding a matter "unrelated to Africa."

The MI6 director had once made possible the sinking of a foreign invasion fleet from Persia that would have destroyed her empire. If he wanted a meeting with her in London, incognito, he'd get one.

Keeping up appearances that there was nothing extraordinary about this encounter; nothing remarkable about the head of Britain's MI6 for the first time meeting the clandestine *Empress of Africa*, they exchanged a light handshake.

"A pleasure to meet you, Ms. Crecy," he observed, neutrally.

"My lord."

"Please come in."

Once inside, and with the door closed, he dropped all pretense.

"I feel I should give you a hug or something," he confessed.

Danielle gave him one.

"Do I get to ask about Tai?" she said, naming the MI6 agent who'd helped her conquer the previously-dark continent.

Winterset gestured to the divan, and took the opposing seat.

"He knows we're meeting, and asked me to send you his love."

"Ah, his love," she replied enigmatically.

"I understand the two of you became quite close."

"I'd have preferred closer. But of course Tai's not the reason I'm here."

The director met her eyes in seriousness. "Your time is valuable, Ms. Crecy, and I won't abuse it."

"Please, it's Danielle, and you're entitled to as much time as you'd like. We both know why."

"I promised breakfast. We have a café on the top floor which I closed to everyone including staff, so we'll be able to talk privately. Let's go there now. We have a lot to discuss."

"You realize I have no idea what we're discussing."

"I suppose that gives me a slight tactical advantage—and I expect I'll need one."

3

COLONEL VICTOR BELINSKY, Deputy Director of the FSB, Russia's successor to the feared KGB of Soviet times, studied the large traffic circle outside his office window in St. Petersburg. He found the rotating cars mesmerizing, like a colony of ants following some herd instinct.

At fifty-five, Belinsky's body was nearly as hard and lean as it had been in his twenties when he'd been a captain leading Spetsnaz troops, Russia's elite special forces. His hair was cut short, like a soldier's, but was now mostly gray. Light brown eyes peered out with intensity, and his tanned face bore a thin scar down the right side—remnant of a knife fight with rebels in Chechnya. His opponent had not survived the encounter, and Belinsky now owned the knife. He kept it mounted on his office wall, along with other grisly souvenirs from his past.

He'd hated the scar until a woman once told him she found it attractive. She'd stroked it softly, after some aggressive lovemaking. Belinsky couldn't remember who she was, but her words had stuck. No longer embarrassed, he now paired the scar with a deep smile and an intense gaze that he'd learned made women melt.

He watched the cars for several minutes before finally turning back to his desk. He was too busy to consider…ants.

With the director himself now in hospital and likely to remain there, Belinsky expected a promotion soon. He was already *acting director* and could have justified relocating to Moscow, but he had bigger plans.

He reached for the folder atop the in-box. Yes, bigger plans indeed. He was grimly satisfied with their progress. The only thing bothering him was that no one had ever recovered Sophie Martine's body. Not that it really mattered.

The leader of the team he'd sent to CAR confirmed she'd been killed along with the parents, and it was hardly surprising that animals had dragged off the body itself. Still, it was a minor loose end, and he didn't like loose ends.

The intercom buzzed.

"Yes?"

"Dimitri would like to see you, sir."

"Send him in."

Belinsky was always happy to see Dimitri Tarasov. Aside from being his number two at the Agency, the man was also an ally in the much larger scheme.

"Good news, Colonel." Tarasov was beaming and held a manila file.

"Always welcome. Pull up a chair. Tea?"

"Champagne or vodka might be more appropriate, considering what I've just found. But I filled up on coffee earlier, so I'll pass."

"Now I'm curious. What do you have, Dimitri?"

"They found Sophie Martine's body."

Belinsky smiled, and reached into a drawer where he always kept a bottle of vodka and glasses.

"If true, this requires a toast, my friend. I insist. I'll pour while you talk."

"I'll start with an apology. One of my subordinates, a clerk, was in charge of the newswire alerts we'd set, and when this came in he put it aside, not realizing the importance."

"We had to make it look routine. I realize that."

"Exactly. Anyway, no harm done. It happened roughly three weeks ago. Some hunters on safari near Bangui came across what appeared to be the corpse of a young woman, mauled beyond recognition by animals. It was half a mile from the excavation site. They alerted local authorities."

"Sounds promising, but do we have confirmation?"

"We do. Her uncle, Stefan Arquette from Switzerland, had posted a reward for anyone who could find the body. The authorities contacted him, and a Bangui medical examiner sent x-rays of the skull and teeth from the corpse. Apparently they matched the records Arquette had on file. He paid the reward, and the remains were shipped back to Switzerland."

"How did we find out all this?"

"News articles. There weren't many. The local Bangui paper—print only—carried a piece, but our web-spiders didn't see it. Fortunately, a couple of news outlets—a university newsletter in Switzerland and a Montreux paper—did publish it online and we caught it. Again, the clerk who was responsible put it in the wrong pile and only discovered his mistake this morning. He was distraught, and couldn't quit apologizing."

"Bah, no matter," growled Belinsky, waving his hand through the air dismissively. "Let's see the file."

Dimitri opened the folder and handed across two sheets of paper. "Here's a printout of the university newsletter, and the Montreux paper is here."

Belinsky read them first quickly, then a second time more carefully.

"Looks rock solid," he said. "Do you agree?"

"Absolutely, sir. You can't fool dental records. I did some checking, used our consulate in Bangui, and they confirmed the facts. The reward was paid to a local hunting guide who's been buying drinks for all his friends ever since."

"Well, speaking of drinks, let's toast."

"With your permission, sir?" asked Dimitri. Belinsky nodded.

"To the House of Romanoff!"

The FSB chief smiled grimly. "To the House of Romanoff indeed!"

The two glasses clinked in mid-air.

4

Danielle and the director filled their plates from buffet tureens and sat at a corner table. Tall windows afforded a view of the London skyline. It was February and the clouds were low.

"I understand you speak Russian," said Winterset, spreading currant jam on a croissant.

"My father spoke only Russian to me as a child when we were alone. His mom was Russian, and he wanted me to learn it."

"Your mother?"

"From Paris. I grew up near Lake Geneva, so we spoke French as a family."

"Where did you learn English?"

"It was taught in school, and my Uncle Stefan—who used to live in London—often spoke it with me, so I'd gain that language as well."

"You speak English with a slight French accent, which is charming."

Danielle smiled, acknowledging the compliment.

"Do you speak any other languages, while we're on the topic?"

"I'm fluent in *Ningala*, which is a tribal tongue from central Africa. In the last few months, I've been studying Arabic—now that our capital's moved to Sudan."

"Yes, of course. Well, I'm not much for small talk. Shall we turn to business?"

"Please do."

The director looked at her closely for a few moments and she returned his gaze.

"Best I just take the plunge. Look, as Shariya, you're the leader of a newly created empire in Africa. What historians will make of you I can't imagine. Perhaps they'll cast you as sort of a female Genghis Khan."

"I'm not sure that's a compliment."

"Genghis Khan, minus the bad parts."

"Better," she said, smiling

The director took a sip of coffee. "Merely consolidating your gains, establishing your rule, addressing all the problems that exist in Africa, all that could take several lifetimes."

"What's your point?"

"Is it really what you want to do?"

Danielle looked at him curiously. "I think there's an expression in English: You break it, you own it. Something like that?"

Winterset smiled. "Well, you certainly own it. Tai shared with me how it all happened. Damndest story I've ever heard."

"Why am I here, my lord? Certainly not to discuss my story."

The director gazed at Danielle piercingly.

"You are here because I believe that—despite your age—you are one of the most talented, resourceful, and capable people on the planet. And I'm very much in need of someone like that right now. Someone who speaks Russian fluently."

Danielle stared at him, confused. And then it came to her.

"You want me to go to Russia and be a spy for MI6."

The director was silent and took another sip of coffee.

"You must be mad," she said, quietly, glancing briefly out the window.

"Not mad. Desperate."

"All out of agents?" asked Danielle, smiling again.

"The job requires someone with unique skills."

"I already have a day job. But now I'm curious. Why do you need me as a spy in Russia?"

"May I ask a few technical questions first?"

"Sure."

"If you wanted to leave Africa, for several months at least, could you?"

"What Africa needs right now is not an empress. We expanded so fast. What we need are ministers, deputy ministers, and so forth. Managers. People who can run things and get results. Eduardo's hiring as fast as he can, but it's not a quick process. There's so much corruption, we're having to fire people almost faster than we're hiring new ones. There just aren't enough qualified applicants available. And the continent is huge."

"What if we could loan you the people needed?"

"Is that possible?"

"I would think so. We have many here with such skills. It wasn't that long ago the British Empire pretty much ran Africa. And we did a not-too-terrible job of it. We could send Eduardo several hundred civil servants, of various experience levels. But if you, personally, weren't there?"

"I don't think I need to be there. Eduardo's highly competent. He just needs good people under him."

"We could fill up much of your civil service. Not just with Brits, but by helping Eduardo find locals. We could turn our embassies and consulates all over Africa into recruiting stations. We'd send down experienced HR staff to supplement the diplomats."

"That would be amazing, my lord."

The MI6 director smiled. "Danielle, my title is for the most formal occasions. You can drop it in our private discussions."

Her eyes twinkled. "OK, but I kind of like saying 'my lord.' Those of us who grew up in boring democracies are always intrigued by Britain and its world of kings and queens. It adds such a fairy-tale element."

He laughed softly. "Well don't forget, as an empress you outrank me considerably."

"Hmmm, I suppose that's true. But for now I'm merely Danielle Crecy, a commoner. And if I slip and add 'my lord,' occasionally, you'll just have to forgive me." Her eyes twinkled at him, teasingly.

Winterset grinned and then waved his hand through the air dismissively. "Back to the subject. Helping you out staffing-wise would support British interests, as it would give us a close working relationship with the Empire of Africa. Good for both governments, I'd think. We'd make sure the trains ran on time. That kind of thing."

Danielle nodded. "It's my greatest fear. I can win battles and take over countries. But Eduardo needs more staff. I guess that's partly why I came. Maybe I'm desperate too."

"We could help each other."

"Can you grant me a moment?"

"Of course."

Danielle excused herself from the table, walked to the other side of the room, and stared out the windows. The view of London was obscured by the ever-present fog and rain. It was so different from the desert outside Khartoum, where the sun was a physical presence, an adversary which slept only at night. Here, there was almost no difference between night and day. The sky was irrelevant. In Africa, the sky was everything.

And that was the point, wasn't it? Africa was not her home. She was a young girl from Switzerland, so ridiculously out of her depth she couldn't let herself think about it, much like a trapeze artist could not afford to look down. She didn't want to return to Les Avant—her geranium-covered village. Someday, perhaps. Yet was Africa where she belonged?

She was good at killing. Good at battle. Very good at inspiring revolution. When those were priorities, she was perfect. But there was something more for her, she suspected.

She used to be someone else entirely—a ballerina. She once floated onto a stage in Milan and left them gasping. She could speak—Russian!

There was someone else, another person, living inside her. Maybe it was time to find out who that person was. To be that person.

Uncle Stefan was right. There was not a single lead for learning who had ordered her parents' murder and hoped to kill her as well.

Now that she'd been declared legally dead, she was safe enough as Danielle Crecy. And rediscovering the other persona in her and visiting Russia—where her father's family came from—would at least help her connect to some roots.

She returned to the table.

"I can answer your question now. The answer is yes. If Britain can help Eduardo ensure the trains run on time, yes, I could leave Africa—almost indefinitely. You want me to go to Russia. I think that's what I want too. There are so many questions I have about that country, and my connection to it. Or at least my father's connection."

"Thank you, Danielle."

"And maybe I need a vacation from the violence of the last year. A place to get away from it all."

"It won't be a holiday. You'll be a deep-cover agent. We'll have to find a role for you in Leningrad, one that would bring you close to those in power."

"St. Petersburg, you mean?"

"Yes, sorry. I'm too young to know it by its original name, and too old for its current one. To me, it will always be Leningrad."

"St. Petersburg is home to the Mariinsky Ballet."

"I've heard of it. Their answer to the Bolshoi, correct?"

"The Mariinsky is as superior to the Bolshoi as an eagle is to a sparrow," hissed Danielle.

"Excuse me?"

"Well, that's how I'm told the Mariinsky ballerinas see it. No doubt those at the Bolshoi believe the opposite. There's quite the rivalry."

"How do you know about this?"

"I've always wanted to perform at the Mariinsky. It's my life's dream."

"Perform? What are you talking about?"

"I'm a ballerina. Before we moved to Africa, I was on track to becoming one of the premier ballerinas in Europe."

"Seriously? You're a ballerina—on top of everything else?"

"Yes, I'm not kidding."

Winterset considered the new information, and then asked: "To be blunt, are you good enough to dance at the Mariinsky?"

"I'd need a private coach, an instructor, for at least a month or so to get back in shape. The hard part would be getting a position there. It's almost impossible."

"We can get you in. We've got the connections. That's not a problem. It's a perfect cover. As a Mariinsky ballerina you might easily come in contact with high government officials."

"You still haven't told me what the mission is, but I guess it doesn't matter. Give me what I need in Africa, and the opportunity to perform on the stage at the Mariinsky, and I'll do anything you want in Russia."

Winterset grinned. "Your negotiating skills are horrid."

"Are they? If you solve my biggest problem and help fulfill my greatest dream, I'm quite satisfied with my negotiating skills. But if I *can* ask for something more…"

"Please do."

"I'd like to be a fighter pilot."

"A fighter pilot? For heaven's sakes, why?"

"I learned how to fly an Apache helicopter and I'm already instrument rated. You know about that, right?"

"Yes, military colleges will be studying your gunship attack on the Khartoum palace for decades."

"I want to fly fighter jets."

"Any particular kind?"

"Whatever can land on carriers."

"We're replacing our Harrier fleet with F-35Bs. That's a vertical-take-off-and-landing fighter."

"Can we make F-35 training part of the agreement?"

"It would delay us a bit, but that's tolerable. Again, why do you want this?"

"A useful skill. My empire needs an air force. Egypt has one, but we need to expand continent-wide. I can oversee that better if I'm a fighter pilot myself. Do we have a deal?"

The director reached out his hand and they shook briefly.

Covert Ballerina is available at Amazon.com

Made in the USA
Monee, IL
20 December 2024

74634744R00215